Jenni has worked in broadcasting as a presenter and producer with BBC Radio Four, and in television as a director for both ITV and the BBC, making award-winning programmes about human relationships, as well as several series on landscape archaeology and history. She lives in the West of England.

CROW STONE

'If I went back to a psychotherapist, I could re-flesh those moments . . . But I'd prefer not to know — I don't want to hear the voice I heard when the roof collapsed in the flint mine . . . The point of coming back is to bury it for good . . . ' Kit Parry is reluctant to take the job shoring up the quarries under her hometown of Bath — a place as riddled with unwanted memories as it is with Roman ruins. But when events at the mine begin spiralling out of control, Kit must face up to the past she's tried so desperately to bury. When she stumbles across evidence of a lost Mithraic temple, the mysteries in Kit's past become entangled with what turns into a dangerous obsession.

JENNI MILLS

CROW STONE

Complete and Unabridged

CHARNWOOD
Leicester

First published in Great Britain in 2007 by
HarperPress
an imprint of
HarperCollins*Publishers*
London

First Charnwood Edition
published 2007
by arrangement with
HarperCollins*Publishers*
London

British Library CIP Data

Mills, Jenni
    Crow stone.—Large print ed.—
    Charnwood library series
    1. Quarries and quarrying—England—Bath—
    Fiction 2. Temples, Roman—England—Bath—
    Fiction 3. Bath (England)—Antiquities, Roman—
    Fiction 4. Suspense fiction 5. Large type books
    I. Title
    823.9′2 [F]

    ISBN 978–1–84782–046–4

Published by
F. A. Thorpe (Publishing)
Anstey, Leicestershire

Set by Words & Graphics Ltd.
Anstey, Leicestershire
Printed and bound in Great Britain by
T. J. International Ltd., Padstow, Cornwall

This book is printed on acid-free paper

For my mother, Sheila Mills

LEVEL ONE

Corax

Corax, the Raven — the messenger of the gods. Just when you think life is on track, along comes a socking great bird, squawking news of a divine quest. My advice is, shoot the bloody thing.

Martin Ekwall, interviewed on
Time Team, Roman Temple Special, Channel 4

1

Look at this. A sea urchin, so close we could snog each other. My eyes are crossing with the excitement of it, let alone the proximity. I feel like calling to Martin to get his fat arse down here, so I'll have someone to share it with. But Martin couldn't care less, and neither could the sea urchin.

I'd guess it's been dead for a hundred million years or so. When it was pottering about, doing whatever sea urchins do in the warm, shallow sea, dinosaurs tramped the shore. It looks like a bun, doughy white, slightly heart-shaped. The stuff of life turned to stone.

I'm lying on my back. Stone is digging painfully into bone; the floor is nodules of chalk and outcrops of flint, none of them dovetailing with the knobbles of my spine. My nose is a couple of inches away from the white ceiling with the sea urchin in it. Until I saw it, I was trying to turn over, so I can wriggle back the way I came in — feet first, because there isn't room to turn round. This is a fairly delicate moment. I don't think the entire lot is going to come crashing down on me, but it's always possible. The tunnel's hardly more than body-width. Even by Neolithic standards, this is poky.

'You OK?'

Martin, in dusty red overalls, is waiting at the end of the passage where it opens into the main gallery: a luxurious four feet high, so he can crouch on hands and knees and turn round, lucky bugger. He's too big to crawl any further so, being the woman, I get all the shit jobs as usual.

'Happy as a sunbeam,' I hiss. We rarely shout underground, unless it's 'Get the fuck out quick.' I've perfected a penetrating whisper that seems to travel

3

down tunnels. Martin's heard me, because he grunts. It's hard to know who are the sparkier conversationalists: archaeologists or mining engineers.

This wouldn't be most people's idea of Saturday-afternoon fun, but I've lost count of how long we've been doing this kind of thing. We even did it right through the years of my marriage. Martin's favourite archaeology happens underground. It's dirty and it's dangerous, and you can't have much more fun than that. We'll probably go on doing it as long as our joints hold out, or the luck.

Luck shouldn't come into it, of course. As the engineer, I'm the guardian of the luck, the one who understands stresses and loads and how water seeps through stone, and can therefore take an educated guess as to whether we're going to die today, entombed in a flint mine.

These galleries were dug out between five and six thousand years ago, by people who had only recently discovered farming. They're amazing: they have proper air shafts, and pillars to support the roof. The light of my head-torch picks out five-thousand-year-old carbon stains on the walls, from the oil lamps the miners worked by. The gallery I'm investigating is a dead end, never properly dug out, a speculative tunnel that either failed to produce any decent flint or perhaps was one of the last to be opened before stone tools were superseded by bronze. *Sorry, mate, no call for flint axeheads any more. Ever thought of reskilling in metalwork?* Poor old flint miners. The thought of a Neolithic Arthur Scargill pops disconcertingly into my head, reminding me of those little yellow 'Coal Not Dole' stickers Martin and I used to wear in our student days. *Flint Not Skint.*

Sea urchin apart, though, I don't like this place. There's something claustrophobic about it, even for someone who makes a living out of going underground.

4

The side galleries nip and pinch spitefully as you crawl down them. I keep thinking I should have brought a ball of string to make sure we find the way out again.

We'll look bloody silly if we can't. Particularly as no one knows we're in here.

The point is, if Martin's right and he can raise the money for a proper dig with the university's blessing, I might get paid for this afternoon's spur-of-the-moment expedition. That would be useful, because if I turn down the Bath job there may be lean times before I get a better offer.

And I will turn down the Bath job. No doubt about that.

I say goodbye to the sea urchin, and finally succeed in wriggling on to my stomach so I can start shuffling backwards down the tunnel. It seems much further when you can't see where you're going, and it's with enormous relief that I feel Martin grasp my ankles to let me know I've made it out to the main gallery.

'Whew. Don't ask me to do that again in a hurry.' I flip over on to my bottom, and bang my hard-hat on the tunnel roof. 'Next time it's your turn to slither up the miners' back passages.'

Martin giggles, easing back on to his haunches. He may be six foot four and built like a bear, but he's as camp as a Boy Scout jamboree. He's had my arse in his face more times than I care to count, crawling through underground tunnels, and never shown the slightest interest in it, which suits me fine.

'So, what do you think?' he asks, offering me a swig of water. It tastes of chalk dust.

'Well, it's going to be expensive to dig. You'll need to prop it to make it safe.' I look around, my head-torch casting wild, wobbling shadows over the walls. 'And I think you should steer clear of the side galleries altogether.'

'Which are, of course, the most interesting from an

5

archaeological point of view. Most of the main shafts were worked over thoroughly in the nineteenth century. Damn . . . ' Martin is chewing it over. I can see his heavy jaw grinding away as he nibbles the inside of his cheek. ' . . . and blast. And fuck. If I had the money to employ diggers who knew what they were doing, I might risk it, but I'm going to have to take on students and anoraks. 'Ooh, durr, Dr Ekwall, I seem to have brought down the ceiling with one blow of my mighty trowel.' '

'Don't joke. It's that delicate.'

Martin frowns. 'I suppose the insurance will be prohibitive.'

'And there's one tiny technicality,' I remind him.

'Ah. Yes.'

We don't have permission to be here. Martin picked the padlock on the shaft cover. We broke in and we're trespassing. Legally we don't have a leg to stand on, even if we could stand up. An unofficial recce saves paperwork, but the drawback is that if anything happens to us down here we'll be waiting a hell of a long time for the rescue party.

'Quarter to four,' he says. 'Better get a move on, or it'll be dark before we're back at the jeep.'

We crawl back towards the central shaft, the one we climbed down earlier, my knees giving me hell in spite of the borrowed pads. I didn't come prepared this weekend for going underground, and all Martin's gear is miles too big. I have a prickling feeling between my shoulder-blades, and fight the temptation to keep twisting round to look behind. For God's sake, what am I expecting to see? A flare of light far away down the passage?

It's bliss to stand up again under the shaft. The light above is fading fast, and I can just make out an early star in the violet sky as I set foot on the iron ladder back to ground level.

By the time we reach the top my arms are killing me. I could swear my belly's on fire too. While Martin's on his way up, I unzip my fleece to take a look. I was in such a hurry to get out of the passage that my sweater must have ridden up as I inched over the chalk floor, and there are ugly red grazes across my abdomen. Should have worn overalls. An icy wind flicks across the hollow in the hillside, and I zip up again.

Martin swings the trap-door shut over the shaft, and crouches to padlock it. The sun is almost touching the metal rim of the sea, and there's a tiny sliver of moon in the sky, no more than a nail paring. Back in the Neolithic, the hillside was probably cleared right up to the entrance to the flint mine. Those old miners liked a spectacular view when they came up from below. Martin's theory is that flint mines were as much sacred sites as industrial estates, the underworld being the realm of the ancestors.

'You didn't like it much in there, did you?' he asks. He has the unnerving habit of reading my thoughts.

'No.'

'It's funny, I don't like this one either,' he says. 'Some of those side galleries feel . . . spooky.'

'I just got a bit claustrophobic. It was very tight.'

'Sorry. Get fatter. Then I wouldn't send you in.'

'You'd still send me in and I'd get stuck, like a chimney sweep's boy.'

'If only you were.' Martin sighs, and starts to undo the chinstrap on his helmet.

My nose is beginning to run in the freezing air so I reach into my pocket for my tissues. 'Ah, shit.'

There's nothing in my pocket. My tissues have gone. My stomach does a flip, and I go cold all over, then hot. My fingers are scrabbling down to the very bottom of the pocket, but all they find is fluff and an old sweet wrapper.

Martin looks up, his face ghostly with chalk dust. 'What's the matter?'

'We've got to go back. My . . . ' I have to improvise, or no way will he let me go back in. 'My car keys have fallen out of my pocket.'

He rolls his eyes. Yeah, well, I don't feel like it either. But I have to go. I feel sick with panic.

'The spares are three hundred miles away in Cornwall,' I remind him.

'Have you got the slightest idea where they fell out?' The patient tone of someone really, really pissed off, but too nice to say so.

'That last tunnel. I'm sure. I blew my nose just before I went into it — can't have zipped up the pocket properly afterwards, and I turned over at least twice in there.'

'You twit. Be quick. I want to be gone before dark. If the landowner sees a light, we're stuffed.'

Something coughs behind me, and I swivel in sudden panic, just in time to see a huge black bird flap out of the beech trees and swoop across the clearing.

'Jesus!' There's always something numinous about places like this, entrances to the underworld. 'That must be the biggest bloody crow I saw in my life.'

'Not a crow,' says Martin, uncoupling the padlock. 'Raven.'

'Raven? Here? Come on.'

'Definitely. Right size, right croak.' Martin is the kind of bloke who knows these things.

'I thought they hung around mountains and wild Welsh cliffs.'

'Not exclusively.' Martin peers towards the frost-tipped clump of bramble where the bird landed. 'Unusual, I admit. Might have been a pet.' The raven is hopping about by a tree stump, getting excited about the smell of rotting rabbit or something equally whiffy. Doesn't look much of a pet to me.

'Perhaps it's the shade of a flint miner, come back to moan about us disturbing his nap.'

Martin throws back the cover with a crash loud enough to wake the dead. I sit on the edge of the shaft, feet dangling.

'Get on with it,' he says.

'I'm just thinking maybe I should ring the AA instead.' But of course I'm not thinking that, because it wasn't car keys I lost. I'm thinking of the number of times I've tested my luck underground, daring myself to do what always scares me, and every single time, as I wait to go down, fingering the thing I always carry with me, not much bigger than a fifty-pence piece, rough on one side, smooth on the other. The thing I can't stroke for comfort this time because that's what fell out of my pocket, as if it had decided of its own accord to leave me. Martin would never understand why I have to go back for it; he thinks I'm enough of an idiot as it is.

'Are you woman or are you wimp?'

'Wimp.' I stretch out one leg, feeling for the rungs of the ladder. Coal miners sometimes spat for luck before they got into the cage that took them underground. Gods live in the tunnels, and they can turn on you just like that. But there's instinct too, a sense that some miners develop for where the danger lies, a feel for the state of the rock. As I start to climb down I try spitting, but it's pathetic, just a *pht* of moisture off the end of my tongue, not a good rounded gob.

'Hi-ho,' says Martin, from the top of the shaft. 'Hi-bloody-ho.'

★ ★ ★

There are good holes in the ground and there are bad holes in the ground. As I come off the ladder on to the chalk floor of the flint mine, this has turned into one of the bad sort. I know it from the way the shadows bounce and weave round the light of my head-torch; I smell it in the musty dead scent of the air.

Martin jumps down beside me.

'You didn't have to come,' I tell him.

'Don't be daft.'

'No point in us both getting killed.'

'Ha-bloody-ha.'

I can tell he's feeling it too. The place wasn't exactly welcoming the first time, but now it's positively chilly. That's not physically possible, of course, because underground is warmer in winter than up top. We're a couple of uninvited guests, tolerated out of politeness when we first came to call, now unmistakably given the cold shoulder when we presume to pop back for a second visit.

'I don't want to sound stupid, but which gallery was it we went down?'

'That one.'

It would be. The smallest and darkest out of a set of very small, very dark openings.

This time the gallery seems interminable. My knees have stiffened; they hurt, hurt, hurt, but I have to go on putting them down over and over again on the hard, knobbled floor. There's still a hell of a lot of razor-sharp flint in this mine.

How could I have been so stupid as to leave my pocket unzipped? I can hear Martin behind me muttering, 'Fuck,' softly with every breath, a mantra to get us through this ordeal. 'Fuck, fuck, fuck.' It bounces off my bum, matching the rhythm of the pain in my knees.

Chalk is made up of masses and masses of tiny, hard shells. When I was a student we had to take a piece of it and rub it with a nail-brush — abrade it, my geology textbook said, the same thing the chalk is now doing in revenge to my knees — then look at it under the microscope. The surface twinkled with minute shells

10

belonging to foraminiferans, single-celled creatures that drifted aimlessly in their billions through sunlit Cretacean seas.

The Cretaceous follows the Jurassic, and is followed in its turn by . . .

The entrance to the side-passage. I stop. Martin's helmet butts my bottom.

'Do you want *me* to go in?' he asks. Generous, but —

'My keys, my problem.' I take a deep, wavering breath. 'Right. Ready or not . . . '

I wriggle in on my stomach. As Martin's breathing fades behind me, I can hear the hush, hush, hush of my Gore-Tex trousers against the rock. I start counting the movements of my elbows against the sides of the tunnel. It probably fell out where the sea urchin floated above me, when I rolled over to examine the ceiling. Maybe, after all these years, it was seeking the company of its own kind. With every shuffle, my fingers reach blindly forward, patting the tunnel floor.

'Found them?' Martin's voice sounds hollow, distorted by echoes in the passage. Of course I bloody haven't. My car keys are where I always leave them when I go off potholing with him, sitting safely and sensibly with my handbag and credit cards in the hallway of his cottage.

'No, but I just met Fungus the Bogeyman.'

Martin laughs. The echoes turn it into a creak that sets my teeth on edge.

Now, where is that blessed sea urchin? I roll over on to my back, feeling my hip bones scrape the tunnel walls. The head-torch shows a featureless stretch of chalk ceiling. I turn back on to my stomach and start pulling myself along again slowly, fingers still groping every inch of the tunnel floor. For some unknown reason Martin is laughing again — I can hear the creak of it coming down the tunnel, just as my fingers close

11

on a small hard disc, polished and smooth on one side, rough on the other.

A creak, the same jarring note as fingernails on a blackboard. Suddenly it's not Martin laughing, and it's not funny.

Ah, shit.

The sensible thing is to stay on my stomach, shoulders hunched to make as big a breathing space as possible, but something has gone wrong in my head and instead I'm trying to turn over, as if I could push my face up through the chalk and out into the open air, while the creak turns into a crack and then a rushing, pattering sound . . . Arms and legs are flailing, or would be if there was space to flail; instead, I'm battering weakly at the sides of the tunnel. I have to see. I can't bear to be trapped like a blind mole in the darkness. Just as my head-torch flicks on to the solid bun of the sea urchin, chalky rubble and stones rain down over my legs. The ceiling's going, somewhere down the tunnel, and once one bit collapses there's nothing to hold the rest up.

My fingers clamp down hard on what's in my hand, branding it into my palm. Madness to have come back for it, but I couldn't have left it here . . . There's a swirl of dust fogging the head-torch, making me cough. As it darkens I picture the thousands of tons of earth and rock that lie between me and the sky, and brace myself for the crushing weight of it all on my chest.

2

The night I found the tunnel there was a big white moon as bright and hard as chalk. It was a few days before my fourteenth birthday. The air was warm, but there were goosebumps on my arms; the moon's light was chilling. I was cold with sitting still, cold with waiting. When I started the climb up the quarry face, I didn't care whether I lived or died.

The entrance to the tunnel was a patch of shadow on the rock, covered with long creepers and dreadlocks of ivy. There was a ledge in front, a platform just big enough to park a bum on, or I would have missed it altogether. The sweat was running off me by then, and for all my misery I was scared half to death.

The moon had climbed the sky as I went up the quarry face. It shone down like a searchlight, but missed me on the ledge. I sat there in the darkness, breathing in great gasps. I couldn't go back down. I didn't think I had the strength left to go up.

I leaned back, expecting to find rock, but the ivy parted, and there was the adit, the tunnel leading into the mine. It must have been part of the earlier workings, forgotten when they moved on to quarry a better seam of stone. I ducked through the leaves and crawled in.

There were legends about those tunnels. About ten or fifteen years before, three schoolboys had made their way in, as schoolboys often did back then, and hadn't come out again. They got lost in the maze of passages that wove through the hillside like tangled ropes. When they didn't come home, the police were called. They went in after them with torches and tracker dogs, and they got lost too.

We knew really that they came out, all of them, safe

13

and sound, but we liked to scare ourselves with the idea that they hadn't and were still there, doomed to wander through the veins of the rock for ever. Maybe one day we would hear their ghostly singing beneath our feet. *Hi-ho*.

The year after the boys got lost the entrances to the tunnels had all been blocked up. Sometimes a hole would appear mysteriously in someone's garden, or a pet dog would vanish and people would say they heard subterranean barks and yelps, but those were the only reminders that the underground world of my imagination existed.

I believed in it, even if I couldn't see it, and I wasn't afraid of starving terriers or schoolboys' ghosts. Then, I was never afraid of anything underground. Caves fascinated me; in one, I was sure, I might one day find the First Englishman.

I got to my feet and took a blind step into the real darkness, fingers brushing the rough-hewn tunnel wall to keep me straight. I won't go far, I told myself. Just a few steps. Just far enough. Then I'll find somewhere to curl up against the wall and wait until sunlight fingers between the strands of ivy. I walked forward, testing each step on the uneven floor with my toes.

I turned round to look back. I couldn't see the entrance.

In my panic my fingers lost contact with the tunnel wall, and I snagged my foot on a rock. I stumbled forward, lost my balance, and ended up on hands and knees. When I managed to get to my feet again, the tunnel wall had vanished too.

I could hear my breathing in my ears, tight and harsh. The sound of it had changed, and the sound of the silence around me was different too. It seemed hollow, vast, empty. I knew I must be in some large space; perhaps a huge cavern the quarrymen had cut out of the rock.

I reached out with my hand, groping empty air. I could see nothing, feel nothing. The darkness was smothering. It wrapped itself more tightly round me the more I struggled. I told myself the wall of the tunnel had been only inches away when I fell. I just had to go back a pace or two, and I would be able to reach out and touch it. I turned, took one tentative step, terrified I would stumble again. Then I took another, my hands waving uncertainly in front of me, blind-man's buff. Still nothing. And nothing. And nothing. And nothing again. Then I understood I could no longer be sure which way I was facing.

Oh God oh God oh God. There was nothing to tell me which way I had come or which way to go, and the darkness wound so tightly round me it was crushing the air out of my body. *Please, God, let me find a way back. A safe way.*

But that was Crow Stone, when I was another person.

Please, God, help me to find a way back out now.

The sea urchin floats above me, set for ever in its chalky ocean. It couldn't be more indifferent.

3

I can still see the sea urchin so I know I'm not dead. It sits in a circle of light that's ominously yellow. My head-torch battery must be failing.

That's not a pleasant thought. Even if I'm not dead I might as well be, once the torch goes. It's just about possible to be ironic while I can still see, but in the darkness I suspect I'm going to cry. I don't want to do that if I can help it. I don't want to die feeling sorry for myself, though I suppose it's the one time you're justified in feeling that way.

I don't want to die

How long have I been here? It's so quiet. Not even the creak of settling rock.

'Martin!'

Pathetic. Hardly a bat-squeak. Throat too dry, tongue too big for my mouth. The air's full of dust — but at least there's still air. For the moment.

'Maar-tin!'

My ears feel wrong. They're ringing, maybe something to do with the air pressure. I can hardly hear myself.

'Maaar-TIN!'

Don't want to bring the rest of the roof down, shouting. Come on, Martin, answer, you bugger.

Fuck.

Dust and chalk fragments on my upper body, one hand's free and I can feel that, even reach up to touch my face, but from the pelvis down I'm pinned. My legs seem to be under a lot of rubble. I *can* feel them, though, and I think I'm wiggling my toes — I *think* — so the weight hasn't broken my back. I suppose I should count myself lucky.

On second thoughts, lucky isn't quite the word.

It reminds me of the games we used to play as children: *which would you rather? Be crushed to death by an enormous weight? Slowly suffocated? Starve? Die screaming voicelessly, tormented by thirst?*

None of the above, thank you. I think I will just have that little cry, after all.

But I'm not crying. I'm shaking.

Jesus

Stop it. I'm shaking hard enough to bring the rest of the ceiling down over my face.

My body won't pay any attention to what I tell it. It goes on shaking. Big, shuddering tremors start in my legs, travel up to my shoulders and into my head. Is this what soldiers get the night before battle: a mad uncontrollable jerking dance of fear?

Judging by the silence, Martin's in more trouble than I am. He must be under the main fall. Between me and the way out.

'MAAAR-TIN!'

Got to stop this shaking.

Breathe.

Think about anything other than dying.

Chalk is fossil heaven. Even the dust is a universe, composed almost entirely of tiny shells, minute cartwheels and rings and florets, the remains of plankton, which can only be seen under the electron microscope. Coccoliths, the smallest fossils on earth.

Easier, now.

Unlike angels, they actually know how many coccoliths you can get on to a single pinhead — upwards of a hundred.

I suppose my lungs are full of the bloody things.

How long does it take to die underground?

The human body can survive weeks or months without food, but only days without water. *Days like this* — I'll never stand it. My tongue's like sandpaper.

17

No, it's already died in my mouth and is slowly setting, like cement.

'Mmmm-MAA — '

Everything tightens, my lungs shut down. *I can't breathe.*

I'm starting to shake again and that isn't a good sign.

And now the bloody torch is flickering and — *blink* — it's going to go and — *blink* — it's back no it's not *blink* it's gone it's dark I'm stuck here in the bloody dark I'd rather die just get it over with

The Camera Man watching with his single bloodshot eye his long pale fingers reaching for me the darkness

HOLY *Mary Mother of*

It's *back*. Thank God. The light's on again. Shaking so much I hit my head on the ceiling and the damn thing came back on.

Breathe, Kit, take it slow and steady. I have to get myself under control, make the most of the light while it's still on, start trying to dig myself out instead of lying here like I'm already fossilized.

Which would you rather? Suffocate, or bleed to death, wearing your fingertips down to raw stumps as you feebly try to claw your way out?

There's something scrabbling around my feet.

Or be eaten from the toes up by rats? Slowly gnawed and nibbled, inch by bone-crunching inch?

Ha-bloody-ha.

A waft of fresh but sweat-scented air reaches my nose.

'Martin, you fucker, you took your time.'

⋆ ⋆ ⋆

Above ground, the air has never smelt so good, even though it's laced with rotting rabbit. It strikes me, sitting on the grass by the mine-shaft, that I can't remember anything about the last fifteen minutes or so since Martin hauled me out by my ankles, spluttering chalk dust.

I've almost stopped shaking. That's a plus.

'Got a cigarette? I need a bloody cigarette.'

'Kit, I don't smoke. Never have, as you well know. Where are yours?'

'Fuck knows. Under half a ton of chalk, probably.'

God knows how long Martin must have spent shifting rubble patiently out of the tunnel before he could get to me. I hope I was helpful, on the way out. I probably wasn't.

'So, nothing came down where you were?'

'Not a sausage. Fortunately it was a fairly small collapse as roof falls go. *Pitifully* small, I'd say.' He tries to smile. His face is pale, though, and it isn't just chalk dust.

'Yeah, well,' I say. 'You weren't under it, Nancy Boy. I'm counting that as a near-death experience.'

I dust myself off a bit, and look at the sliver of moon. She's on the turn. Funny thing, all these years of looking at moons, I'm still not sure which way round is the crescent and which is waning to dark. I promise myself I'll find out now, for sure, and never forget.

Martin squats down beside me, and puts his arm round my shoulders in a big, rough, rushed hug. It's so rare that we touch, I find my eyes filling with tears.

'You OK? Really?' he asks.

'Really. I think. I'll tell you after a hot bath.'

'Didn't you hear me calling? I could hear you.'

'Struck deaf by terror, I guess, as well as dumb.' My ears still feel funny. Like I was in an explosion.

'I thought for a moment I'd lost you.' His eyes look shiny in what's left of the light.

'You came and found me, though.'

'If I hadn't you'd have dug yourself out and come after me.' He shudders. 'I felt like a cork in a bottle after squashing my shoulders into that passageway. Anyway, if you can make it, we ought to start down before it gets too dark to find the track.'

'Yeah, I'm fine.' I shove him away, and try to get up. There doesn't seem to be any strength in me, and I can't push myself off the ground. He puts his arm under mine and hauls me to my feet. 'I can walk.'

'Like a geriatric.'

Did I get up the ladder on my own? He surely couldn't have carried me. I have a dim memory of trying to cling to the rungs with no strength in my arms, Martin pushing from below. Right now, I'd love him to give me a piggyback, but I shake him off all the same.

We set off slowly through the beech trees. The ground drops away sharply in front of us. Through the last crisp copper leaves, lights glimmer on the farmland below. In the distance there is a smudge of orange that must be Worthing. I'm listening out for the raven's cough, but there's nothing except the crunch of our feet on the beech mast. My feet feel like lead.

★ ★ ★

One late winter afternoon when we were students, at the end of a long day walking in the Peak District, Martin and I came over a bluff with the wind in our faces. There were about two miles of darkening moorland between us and our tea, and not a glimmer of light below us, just a dipping, rolling plateau of green and brown tussocks, broken only by scattered clumps of rocks and trees.

We set off down the hillside, too cold, tired and hungry to talk. And then the wind brought us, from nowhere, the sound of singing. It was the eeriest thing I've ever heard, voices out of a wild twilight emptiness. I could have sworn the sound came from beneath our feet, and for one primordially terrified moment I was on the point of legging it. But then I looked at Martin.

There was a wistful expression on his face. 'Hi-ho,' he said.

Amid a cluster of broken rocks away to our left, I saw the first bobbing light. And then another. Then a third. An orderly file of cavers in their helmets, schoolkids probably, judging by their size, came tramping out of the hidden entrance to the pothole like the Seven Dwarfs.

The next weekend I hid my fear and went caving for the first time with him.

★ ★ ★

'You're not thinking of driving back to Cornwall tonight?' asks Martin, as we reach the gate to the bridleway where his battered red jeep is parked. My car is at his cottage, twenty miles away.

'Without car keys?' I may be emotionally screwed but I never forget a cover story. Though God knows how I'll deal with explaining — *Ooh look, my keys are in my handbag after all* — when we get back.

'Curses, knew we forgot something.' Martin tries unsuccessfully to get his own keys into the lock of the jeep, gives up and peels back the canvas roof flap so he can get his hand in to open the door from inside. 'You could always nip back.'

'Fuck off and drive me to the nearest quadruple Scotch.'

He holds open the door for me: the driver's door. The passenger side hasn't opened within living memory. He claims he likes the jeep because it's got a sense of humour, which is something you definitely can't say about a Range Rover.

'Seriously,' he says. 'Alcohol. Food. Early bed.'

'Provided you've got some sheets on the spare bed.' I agree. He isn't looking at me, pretending to fumble with the keys. 'Clean ones,' I add. Martin's all-male potholing weekends are legendary. In case you hadn't noticed, there aren't any proper potholes in Sussex.

'I'll change them.'

'You'd better.'

'And I'll cook you crab cakes, if we stop at Waitrose on the way back.'

'Maybe it's worth almost dying.'

'God, Kit, you're really going to milk this, aren't you?'

He starts the jeep, which pretends for one heart-plummeting moment that the battery is flat. 'Like I always say,' remarks Martin, as the engine finally catches, 'a vehicle with a highly developed sense of fun.'

We lurch down the bridleway, whose ruts have ruts. Branches snatch at the windscreen, squeaking on the glass like fingers on a blackboard. I keep hearing that creak again, and feeling the hail of earth and stones on my legs. I try not to imagine what it would have been like with the weight of the roof fall on my chest.

I couldn't have dug myself out. I was pinned like a butterfly. Whatever he pretends, Martin saved my life. The jeep's motion throws me towards him. He turns and grins. I haven't even thanked him, but where do you find the words? We're not going to talk about what happened this afternoon. It's not what we do. Emotions R Not Us. We'll eat crab cakes sitting in front of the fire and pour Californian chardonnay down our throats, but there are places Martin and I never go.

'Well, I suppose that knocks my idea of excavating a flint mine next season firmly on the head,' he says, as we pull on to the road at the bottom of the hill. 'Back to the drawing board. Or, rather, back to the book on mystery cults. I'd much rather be digging. Which reminds me — how's your job search?'

I look at him, in the green glow of the dashboard light. I hadn't thought until now that I'd be saying this. 'Found one,' I say. 'I'll tell you over supper. Filling in a bloody big hole in the ground, basically. You'd hate the job. Burying something for ever.'

★ ★ ★

Three hours later, I'm sharing the hearthrug with a pile of dirty plates. Darkness is a thick, velvety blanket round Martin's cottage, and the chardonnay is doing much the same job to the inside of my head.

'Have another slurp,' says Martin, pouring. 'It's terrible stuff, but it reminds me of San Francisco.' A wistful look comes into his eyes, then he smiles wickedly. 'Only a few weeks, and I'll be able to fill the cellar again.'

Poor old Martin. The public face of archaeology is still relentlessly heterosexual, although it's attracted quite a few old queens I could name. And, apart from Martin, I've never met a real caver who cares to admit he's gay. He gets by, but he looks forward to his Christmas trips to California. I think he lives in hope of finding himself at a party singing 'Auld Lang Syne' next to Armistead Maupin.

We got friendly the first week at university because we didn't find each other threatening. Going drinking with him is the nearest I get to a night out with the girls. He wasn't out then, even to himself, and certainly not to his father who was a vicar, but I guessed he was gay the night we met. I chatted him up because he was studying archaeology; still sometimes wish I'd chosen that instead of geology and engineering. When I turn my hand to re-erecting Bronze Age stone circles for him, or rebuilding Roman siege engines, I can kid myself I've got some level of archaeological knowledge, but he just uses me for the practical stuff: he's the big thinker. He jokes about not enjoying writing his book, but he adores it, really, teasing out all the esoteric stuff about Roman religion.

Firelight glints, red, gold, on my glass, brimming with pale yellow wine. I raise it to him. 'Here's to lots of busy little Californian Christmas elves. On rollerskates.'

'Mmm.' Martin drinks deeply. 'Though naturally I would hope Santa decides to explore your chimney too.'

I cough as my wine goes down the wrong way. 'I can't keep up.'

'That's what Santa says, too.'

'Stop it, Martin. It gets tedious.'

'You're just jealous. When was the last time you got laid?'

'None of your business.'

Martin looks like a puppy that can't understand why no one finds scratchmarks on the furniture appealing. He's happier if he can come up with a reason for my lack of interest in sexual banter.

'Have you been getting calls again from Nick?'

'No, thank God. Splitting the money from the London house seems to have shut him up for a bit. And I changed my mobile number.'

'You should have divorced him as soon as you broke up. I resent him getting half of what that house is worth now when he pissed off to Wales nearly ten years ago.'

'More than half. It's only fair — I'm keeping the place in Cornwall, don't forget.' I shouldn't feel I have to justify myself to Martin, but I always do where Nick's concerned.

'You're too soft on him.' Martin's frowning. He once threatened to punch the lights out of Nick on my behalf, even though I can't imagine he has ever punched the lights out of anyone. 'He's always taken advantage of you.'

'Pity you didn't tell me that before we got married.'

'I thought it.'

'I'm not psychic. Next time say it aloud.'

We lapse into silence. It occurs to me that if I hadn't come back from the flint mine this afternoon, Nick

24

would have had the lot. I haven't got round to changing my will.

Martin settles back in his leather chair with the scuffed arms. I get out my cigarettes, glancing over to check he isn't in one of his anti-smoking moods, gearing up for California. He frowns, but doesn't stop me lighting up.

'So what's this new job, then?' he asks. 'I thought you were looking for something abroad. What changed your mind?'

The trouble with sitting on the hearthrug in a four-hundred-year-old cottage is that you freeze on one side from the draughts and roast on the other. The left half of me's sweating like a side of pork, but my right side keeps shivering.

'It's Bath,' I say, sitting on my right hand to stop it shaking. 'Green Down.'

'The stone mines? I didn't think they'd got the funding yet.'

'They haven't, but they've already started emergency work. The consultants reckon the whole lot could come down at any time.'

'What you'd call a big headache.'

'And technically they're quarries, not mines, even though they're underground. Stone is quarried, not mined.'

'They're going to fill them all?'

'That's the plan.'

Martin spits a fragment of cork from his wine into the fire. 'Criminal. Burying three hundred years' worth of industrial archaeology.'

'What about all the people living on top?'

'I don't suppose they'd fancy moving? . . . No, I guess not.' He sighs heavily. 'Not really my period, but fascinating stuff. You know they were dug out in the eighteenth century by Ralph Allan? He and his pet architect, John Wood — mad bastard with a penchant

25

for freemasonry — were effectively responsible for developing Georgian Bath.'

'And Wood's son. John Wood the Younger.'

Martin nearly kicks over the pile of plates in his surprise. 'Blimey, Kit, you've been doing your homework.'

I don't tell him that I did the homework a long time ago, that I was at school in Bath and we used to go on educational walks round the Circus and the Royal Crescent and all the other famous buildings that the John Woods, Elder and Younger, designed between them. Martin thinks I was brought up in Bournemouth. But there's quite a lot I haven't told him.

'You know,' he says, leaning forward to poke the fire into a roaring blaze, 'I reckon there's something deeply perverse in your nature, Kit. This afternoon you nearly get yourself killed in a roof fall, and now you're about to take a job where it's possible an entire suburb will land on your bonce.'

I stare into the fire. 'Glutton for punishment, I suppose.'

'Anyway,' Martin continues cheerfully, 'we'll call the AA out first thing in the morning so they can come with their lock-picking gear and get you on the road.'

Lying always gets me into this kind of mess.

★　★　★

And knocking back too much wine always stops me sleeping.

Martin's snores echo down the stairwell while I prowl the kitchen in search of tea. Proper tea, that is, the sort that comes in bags, not the poncy caddy full of Earl Grey leaves Martin insists on.

'You get bored in the night, flower, read this,' he said, thrusting into my arms a hot-water bottle and a pile of manuscript. 'Tell me if you think it's too racy for

26

Oxford University Press.'

How did he know I'd be awake at two in the morning?

Maybe it's the wine. Maybe it's what happened this afternoon. Every time I turn on to my back I think of my chalk coffin, the suffocating air full of coccoliths and the light from my head-torch getting dimmer and dimmer.

The teabags are in the canister marked *Flour*. Last time I stayed they were in the biscuit tin.

Mug of tea at my elbow, I settle down at the kitchen table with the latest chapter in Martin's book. 'My very favourite mystery cult. You'll like it,' he said. 'Big butch soldiers. Lots of gender-bending. And ravens.'

'I can do without ravens.'

'No decent mystery cult that doesn't have a raven or two.'

> In Persia, where Mithraism originated, ravens were associated with death because it was customary to expose corpses for excarnation — known as 'sky burial' in other cultures — leaving the flesh to be stripped away by birds and other scavengers. Symbolically, the neophyte has to die and be reborn before he can be admitted to the mysteries of the cult.

'I love this kind of stuff,' he said to me earlier, when we stopped discussing my next job and turned to what he's researching. 'Weird as hell, nothing written down, so everything has to be pieced together from the archaeo-logical evidence. Our best guesses come from wall paintings and mosaics in Italy, but there are temples up by Hadri-an's Wall, and one was excavated in London too. Seven stages of initiation. Ordeals at every stage. Men only but, of course, the big laugh is that most of it's nicked from an even older eastern mystery religion, the cult of

27

the Great *Mother*, of all things, popular in Rome at the same time. Don't you just adore it?'

Firelight and enthusiasm sparkled in his eyes.

'And then the real symbolic giveaway is that they build their temples underground, or at least tart them up to look like caves. You couldn't get much more Freudian than that, could you? Wait till you hear what they got up to during the initiation ceremonies — typical bloody soldiers, the slightest excuse to dress up as women . . . '

In the Mithraic myth, the raven takes the place of the Roman god Mercury, and bears his magical staff, the caduceus. He brings a message from the sun god, ordering first the hunting then the slaying, in the cave, of the bull — a sacrifice we can be almost certain was borrowed from the cult of Magna Mater. From the animal's blood and semen gushing on to the ground, plants grow, generating new life.

Blood and semen. The dark heart of all male-centred cults. I look up from the manuscript, and outside everything is blackness, no light visible for miles from Martin's cottage tucked under the lip of the Sussex chalk escarpment. It feels a long, long way from Green Down, and everything that waits for me there. Another sentence from the manuscript catches my eye, a translation of some priestly invocation.

I am a star that goes with you, and shines out of the depths.

It makes me shiver. Suddenly I'm tired, after all, and my feet are cold, and I remember that hot-water bottle still holding a ghost of its warmth between the not-very-clean sheets upstairs.

★　　★　　★

The same words are still reverberating in my head a couple of weeks later. I'm sitting in my silver Audi outside the semi-detached house on the outskirts of Bath, thinking about the circular motion that has brought me back here. There's a big crack in its honey-stone facing. Underneath, hundreds of years ago, men tunnelled into the stone and drew out the bones of which Bath is built — oolitic limestone, carrying the imprint of millions of sea creatures, ammonites with their perfectly coiled shells, like snakes with their tails in their mouths.

My fascination with the bones of things, stone and fossils and the darkness underground where they lie, has never gone away, in spite of what happened that summer. I grew up here, and lived in this ugly yellow house until I was fourteen. I had no plan then to become a mining engineer. I wanted to track the origins of the human race. I saw my future in some heat-blasted gully in Africa or the Middle East, pacing the scree and looking for patterns. Turning over stones and occasionally recognizing the shape of a knucklebone, a fragment of tibia maybe or, if I was very lucky, a whole transfiguring skull.

Instead here I am, completing the circle, back where I started before I was fourteen and the big black car took me away.

Streaks of rain are beginning to dry unevenly on the honey-stone walls. I start the engine, put the car into gear and drive away up the hill, heading for the site.

On the day the black car took me away — big-bodied and lumbering, it was, a dinosaur with headlamp eyes and a radiator grille like long, shiny teeth — we drove this way. I can't remember what I was thinking. I probably thought I was going to be famous. Time fossilizes, strips away thought and emotion, so all I have left is the bone of memory — the sight of a neat row of quarrymen's cottages, the smell of the car's leather upholstery.

If I went back to a psychotherapist, I could probably reflesh those moments. Remember the exact point I realized I wasn't ever going back to the yellow house. Trace how I had succeeded in destroying everything. Understand I would never again see Poppy or Mrs Owen or Gary. It didn't upset me then. Everything was unreal, just as it feels unreal now: a past fossilized and forgotten.

But a therapist would pick away at my memories, scraping a little fragment of dried-up flesh off the bone, culturing it and growing it and proving to me that I *was* hurt, I *did* cry, that I screamed, in fact, as they were dragging me out of the doorway and down the steep path to the waiting car.

I'd prefer not to know. I've put a lot of effort into not knowing. I don't want to hear the voice I heard when the roof collapsed in the flint mine. The point of coming back is to bury it for good.

★   ★   ★

The entrance to the underground quarry is in the middle of a recreation ground, not far from Green Down's high street. The site offices are metal-sided cabins, painted blue, green and yellow, jumbled like Lego bricks over a carpet of hardcore. Outside the high, solid fence some little kids in Manchester United strip are kicking a football in a bored sort of way. A security guard lifts the barrier to let me in. The boys stare at my car as I drive past and I wave, but they don't wave back. I remember leaning on the wall years ago, watching another group of boys playing football. Just as in that long-ago summer there's a cloudless sky, but today's is cold and brittle blue, like ice on puddles.

30

I park the car in the only space, next to a stack of pallets. A knot of men in hard-hats are gathered some way off by a cabin. One breaks away from the others and walks towards me, but I need to get into the right clobber, and I'm hopping about on the cold ground, rummaging behind the passenger seat to find my work boots, trying to make myself look half-way professional before he catches me in my socks . . .

I've still got my back to him when he reaches me.

'Mrs Parry?' he says. He's wrong, of course. *Ms.* I'm not married any more, though I've kept Nick's name. 'You've timed it well. I'm the site foreman, by the way — Gary Bennett.'

And I'm back in the summer I turned fourteen.

LEVEL TWO

Nymphus

For such a very macho creed as Roman Mithraism, it seems unusual, to say the least, that initiates at this stage were required to play a woman's role. Etymologically, *nymphus* is an interesting term. It means 'male bride', but no such word exists in everyday Latin. It is derived from *nympha*, a bride, or young woman, but as we know, women were rigorously excluded from the cult. In murals the Nymphus is shown wearing a bridal veil, and is considered to be under the protection of the planet Venus. He is joined in mystical union with the god by the Father: an adept who has attained the seventh and final level of enlightenment. The clasping of the right hand, the *iunctio dextrarum*, was an important part of the initiation ceremony, to pledge fidelity. This may be the origin of the modern-day custom of shaking hands on a contract. (It is also one of the many reasons why modern conspiracy theorists have sought to trace the origins of freemasonry back to Mithraism.) At a given moment in the ceremony the veil would be pulled away and the male bride revealed in all his masculine glory.

From *The Mithras Enigma*, Dr Martin Ekwall, OUP

4

Digging: that was me, the summer I turned fourteen, always digging. Whenever I lifted my hand to my face I could smell moist earth on my fingers. Even when we were just hanging out, Poppy, Trish and I, my hands scrabbled obsessively at the soil, the way other people pick at the skin round their thumb or fiddle with their hair.

'Your nails are disgusting,' said Trish. She was right. They were always black-edged. Trish's were filed into neat ovals, and she pushed the cuticles back every night with an orange stick so we could admire the half-moons. Right now she was painting them silvery-pink, her dark hair falling across her face. She looked up suddenly, and her hair flopped back to reveal the eyes that fascinated me, the way they changed with the light like the sea does. 'Don't you think this colour's cool?'

Silvery-pink was cool but I wasn't. A teenage girl who was obsessed with the bones of things was never going to be cool.

We were sprawled beside a big old oak, heads in the shade but skirts hitched up our thighs to let the sun get at our legs. Freckles had already erupted like sprinkles of cinnamon on Poppy's knees. The field was laid to pasture, and some tired cows were grazing at the other end. Occasionally one moved a few slow steps, as if it could hardly be bothered to go to a juicier patch. Here, under the tree, the grass grew more sparsely, and my fingers were idly picking at bare soil, feeling for stones.

Green Down, where we lived, was a suburb that was almost a village, built on one of the hills that surround Bath, and it didn't take long to reach open countryside.

35

Heavy lorries rumbled up the lane to the quarries scooped out of the slope, but the fields in the valley bottom were peaceful. If I dug here I would find something, I knew it. The fields and hills held secrets: hidden valleys, mysterious embankments and ridges marking where Roman villas had once stood, or where the Saxon Wansdyke marched across the fields.

None of this interested Poppy and Trish. But I was always hopeful.

'There are ammonites in this field,' I said.

Poppy was gazing at the sky and chewing strands of her bobbed reddish hair. When they dried, her split ends would fan out like fuse wire.

'No, really,' I said, as if someone had bothered to reply. 'If I borrowed your nail file, Trish, I bet I'd dig one up in a jiff.'

They didn't have to ask me what ammonites were. I'd told them, plenty of times. 'They had shells like big coiled-up snakes,' I explained, at every possible opportunity. 'They lived at the bottom of the ocean millions of years ago.'

If anyone was so daft as to enquire, 'What are they doing here, then?' I would go on to enthuse about how the hills round Bath were once the bed of a shallow sea, where dead creatures fell and fossilized. My friends' eyes glazed over, as unresponsive as the ammonites.

'Look,' I went on, trying to get my fingers under a big lump of stone embedded in the soil. 'I bet there's a fossil in this.'

Trish began to paint Poppy's toenails with the silvery-pink varnish.

Sometimes I couldn't believe how little they noticed. Trish lived in an old Georgian rectory in Midcombe, where there was an ammonite built into the garden wall. It was enormous, more than a foot across, with deep corrugated ridges on its coils. You couldn't miss it. But they did. 'Oh, is that one?' Trish asked, when I pointed it out to her. She couldn't have cared less. I'd have given my left arm to bag a fossil that big. You could find little ones easily, right on the surface, early in the year when the fields were freshly ploughed. Sometimes there was only the imprint in rock, but often the ammonites themselves seemed to have crawled up from the sticky earth, fragments broken by the plough, occasionally nearly whole stone spirals. I had quite a collection in my bedroom. They looked like catherine wheels. My father said they reminded him of very stale Danish pastries. I thought they were beautiful.

I watched Trish. Her long dark hair, enviably straight, hung across her face as she bent over Poppy's leg, curtaining them in a private tent. She never offered to paint my toenails.

Trish had been my friend first. We got to know each other by accident, rather than choice: we were the only two in our class who hadn't been at the school right through from juniors. All the rest had known each other since they were seven. They didn't like Trish because she was called Klein, and they didn't like me because I was a scholarship girl. None of them realized that the most Jewish thing about Trish was her surname, and the only clever thing about me was my scholarship. For nearly three years, we had been best friends by default.

But late last year, things began to change. Trish suddenly got tall, and I stayed short. Trish — ugly old Trish, with her big nose and wide mouth, just as awkward as me, I'd always thought — started to get looks from boys. Trish had a starter bra and sanitary towels. And Trish had discovered Poppy.

Poppy had arrived in Green Down just after Christmas. Her father worked for the Ministry of Defence and had been posted from Plymouth to Bath. She immediately latched on to Trish and me. I didn't mind at first. It made me feel like I had a wide circle of friends. Now I wasn't so sure.

37

Trish straightened up, popped the brush back into the bottle and screwed down the top. Poppy wiggled her freckled toes, admiring the silvery-pink. 'Do Katie's,' she said to Trish.

'I'm not going to *waste* it,' said Trish.

'I don't want mine done,' I said quickly. Trish was right. I wouldn't be careful: it would get chipped, and I didn't have any nail-varnish remover to take it off properly. Still, I'd have liked her to paint my nails silvery-pink.

'So,' said Poppy, 'what are we going to do now?'

They both looked at me. They wanted me to invite them back to my house. But I wanted to stay in the field, with the worn-out cows and the ammonites.

'Let's do biology,' I said, to buy time. Trish looked pleased; this game starred her. She fished in her satchel.

There was no hurry. No one was waiting for us. My dad wouldn't be back from rewiring someone's house until half past six. Poppy's parents were in Scotland that week, where her grandmother was taking her time over dying, so Poppy was staying with Trish. Trish's mum was always relaxed about the time they came home after school.

My dad had not yet plucked up the courage to tell me the facts of life. He left that to the school, which had been slow getting round to it too. But this term we'd been thrilled to find our new biology text-book was rather more forthcoming on the subject than our teacher.

Trish pushed her hair into a tight little bun on the top of her head, and flared her nostrils in imitation of Miss Millichip. 'Turn now to page one-nine-four, girls,' she trilled. Poppy and I, playing dutiful pupils, opened our books. We stared at mysterious illustrations that reminded me of the plumbing schemes and wiring diagrams my father worked on at the kitchen table.

'Today we are going to study reproduction,'

continued Trish. We'd had a real lesson on it this afternoon, but Miss Millichip had revealed nothing more exciting than the gestation period of a rabbit. 'What kind of reproduction, Poppy McClaren?'

Poppy giggled. '*Human* reproduction, miss.'

The diagrams bore no resemblance to any human body I'd seen. Were those coils of pipework really tucked away inside me? On the opposite page there was a diagram of the male reproductive system. Staring at it, I felt an odd sensation. It was grounded somewhere not far from the pipework, but it seemed to swell up through the whole central stem of my body, so even my lips and tongue felt thick and hot and clumsy.

Trish's mother, more advanced than the average Green Down parent, had explained matters to her daughter more than a year ago, so Trish considered herself an expert. 'A woman,' she intoned, 'has an opening called the *regina*.'

'Are you sure?' asked Poppy. 'It says here it's called the *vagina*.'

'Of course I'm sure,' said Trish, loftily. 'It's Latin for 'queen'. It must be a misprint in the book.'

Poppy looked sceptical, but neither of us felt brave enough to contradict Trish. Her mother had come from London, and worked as a photographer's model before marrying Trish's dad.

'And the man,' Trish continued, 'has an appendage called a *penis*.' That did it. We were all off on a fit of giggles.

'Have you ever seen one?' asked Poppy, a little later when we had recovered.

'Of course I have,' said Trish. 'I used to have baths with Stephen.'

'That doesn't count,' said Poppy. 'Your brother's *ten*. I meant a grown-up one.'

I could see Trish weighing up whether to lie or not. In spite of her mother's racy career, her home was probably as modest as the rest of suburban Bath in the 1970s. Fathers and brothers did not wander around naked.

'No,' she finally admitted. 'But I have seen my mother's fanny. It's all hairy.'

I decided it was time to make my own contribution to the debate. 'I have,' I said.

They looked at me, astonished.

'Really?' said Poppy, at the same moment as Trish said, 'I don't believe you.'

'Really I have,' I said. 'It was horrible.'

'Was it a flasher?' asked Poppy.

'No, it was my dad's,' I said. 'I was on the toilet, and hadn't locked the door, and he came in not knowing I was there. It was sticking out of the gap in his pyjama bottoms. It looked like a boiled beef sausage, red and a bit shiny. Except it was more wrinkled, and had this kind of eye-thing at the end, looking at me.'

'What did you do?' asked Trish. 'I would have screamed. I'd have called for my mum.'

She didn't mean to be unkind — at least, I don't think she did — but it stung all the same. Poppy saw my face, and jumped in quickly. 'What did *he* do?'

'He went out again,' I said. 'Then afterwards, at breakfast, he shouted at me for not locking the bathroom door.'

'Was it — you know, up?' asked Trish.

'I'm not sure,' I said. 'It all happened quite quickly, and what I mostly remember was the eye-thing.'

'It must have been up if you saw the eye,' said Trish. 'Because if it had been down, it would have been pointing to the floor, instead of looking at you.'

'But if it had been up, it would have been pointing at the ceiling,' argued Poppy. 'So it can't have been up. Anyway, why would it have been up? He can't have been having sex.'

'It goes up when a man just *thinks* about sex,' said

Trish. 'I expect he must still think about sex, your dad. Maybe it was half-way, on its way up or its way down.'

'I don't know,' I said. My hand slid off the book and came to rest on the comforting earth. I wanted to stop this conversation. I felt embarrassed, as if I'd taken a picture of my dad's penis and shown it to them.

'You know, men are supposed to think about sex almost every two minutes,' said Poppy. 'There was something about it in the *Daily Express*. Some survey scientists did in America. So I don't think it has to go up when men just think about sex.'

Trish looked belligerent. 'My mother said it does. But you might not be able to tell, if they're wearing trousers.'

'I think you *would* be able to tell,' insisted Poppy. 'I mean, it gets bigger, doesn't it? So they'd get a big bump in the front of their trousers.' That set us off giggling again.

'In that case Gary Bennett's jeans might *split*,' said Trish. There was a reverent silence, as we all contemplated this shockingly delicious idea.

★   ★   ★

Gary Bennett was the reason Trish and Poppy were so keen to come round to my house whenever they could. He was only two or three years older than us, but he had already left school and was working as a decorator's apprentice. He had dishwater-blond hair in tangled curls, blue eyes and a mouth like a Roman statue's, and we all three dreamed of that curvy mouth clamped on our own. Mrs Owen, from three doors further down the street, who sometimes brought round casseroles because she refused to believe my dad could cook, was best friends with Gary's mum, a widow who worked at the Co-op. It was only a couple of months since mother and son had moved in across the road, and Trish had noticed him first.

'You've got a *boy* living opposite you,' she told me.

I wasn't much interested. Then the decorator's firm Gary worked for was hired to repaint Poppy's house. Every afternoon for the whole two weeks he worked there she and Trish rushed home from school together to get a glimpse of him.

'Why don't we go to your house and wait for Gary to get home?' asked Poppy.

I looked at my hands. They were scrabbling almost manically in the soil now.

'Come on,' said Trish. I knew her eyes would have gone sea-dark, fixed on my face, willing me to look up so she could stare me into surrender.

My fingers touched something slimy: a big fat worm. I pulled them away quickly. 'My dad . . . '

'He won't be home for ages. And Poppy's got binoculars.' They'd planned this together, I could tell.

★   ★   ★

Early that year, when Trish and I were only just getting to know Poppy, I'd caught a mysterious virus, like flu but longer-lasting. My father had asked Mrs Owen to look after me. She didn't need much persuading, her grey curls bouncing cheerfully as she trotted up and down the stairs with bowls of soup. I got better gradually, but my muscles stayed weak, and the doctor said I needed more time to recover. I would have quite enjoyed being off school if I hadn't been worrying that Poppy would usurp me in Trish's affections.

My father fetched me books from the library, but I soon got bored. Mrs Owen tried to keep me in bed, but I would sneak out and sit in our spare bedroom at the front of the house to watch the street.

This had once been my parents' room, and although

it had not been occupied for more than ten years it was fascinating to me because it still contained traces of my mother. Her old cosmetics were in the dressing-table: worn-down lipsticks in unfashionable shades, creamy green and blue eye-shadows, dried-up mascara. I rummaged through the drawers, slipping costume jewellery on to my wrists and fingers, wrapping silky scarves round my head: first Grace Kelly, then a Woodstock hippie. There were clothes in the wardrobe too, duster coats and full-skirted dresses that would have been already old-fashioned by the time she was gone, but they scared me too much to touch.

Mrs Owen had gone out to do her weekly shop, and I was curled on the window-seat, keeping an eye open for her. It was late afternoon. The streetlamps had not yet come on when I noticed a light in the front bedroom of the house across the street: Gary Bennett's house.

I suppose it never occurred to Gary to draw the curtains when he went upstairs to change out of his work clothes. That afternoon he flicked on the light and came into the room, pulling his sweater and T-shirt over his head, then disappeared into the corner to wash. After a while there was another tantalizing glimpse of bare chest as he came back to the wardrobe and took out a shirt. I watched him button it from top to bottom. Then he turned his back as he tucked it into clean jeans, hunching his shoulders to do up the zip.

I remember those flashes of nakedness, like a set of Polaroid snaps — the skinny white shoulders in the nicotine-yellow light of the overhead bulb, the surprisingly solid arms, the flat slabs of pectoral muscle that were just beginning to develop as his boy's body toned to do a man's job. I would have watched longer, but I heard Mrs Owen's key in the lock and scampered back to bed in my own room before she caught me.

I could hardly wait to tell the others what I'd seen. After my first day back at school, Trish and Poppy came

43

home with me, and we settled to wait in the front bedroom. Shortly after five thirty, the light across the road snapped on and Gary crossed the bay window hauling his jumper over his head. He towelled himself dry staring out of the bedroom window, blissfully unconscious of the three admirers ducking below sill level every time he looked towards our house.

Afterwards hardly a week went by without us making at least one attempt to watch him undress. We weren't always lucky. Some nights he conducted the entire ritual out of sight in the corner of the room. Or he didn't get back until too late; I had to make sure Trish and Poppy left before Dad got home. Once his mother came into his room in the middle, and — perhaps telling him off for making such an exhibition of himself — crossed to the window and pulled the curtains shut.

By spring Gary's chest was harder and broader, and his hair had grown longer. The lighter evenings frustrated us. He no longer needed to turn on the light, and the reflection of the sky on the window made it impossible to see much inside. But that didn't stop us hoping. Perhaps warmer weather would help. Lately he had begun to fling open the windows, and once even leaned bare-chested over the sill for a full two minutes, staring into the street. Trish had timed it.

If Gary noticed our bobbing heads, he showed no sign. But two or three times lately I had passed him in the street on my way to school, and instead of ignoring me he had given me a wink or a wave. I would go hot and red. I was beginning to wonder how much longer we could get away with spying on him.

But that wasn't why I was reluctant today. My dad didn't like my friends coming round; he never said as much, but somehow he made it clear. I knew our time on our own together was important to him. He felt bad about being out at work when I got home, and bad about there not being a mother to get my tea. He didn't get back till six at the earliest, but it was hard to persuade Trish and Poppy that they should leave.

'Oh, come on, Katie,' said Poppy. 'I told Daddy you were a keen birdwatcher, so he'd lend me the binoculars. We've got to try them out.'

'We'll be able to see Gary in *close-up*,' Trish added persuasively.

But what if he saw us? Still, I couldn't help being excited. This might be the way to see more. Poppy swore she'd once spotted a flash of white Y-fronts when he reached up to take his shirt from the hanger, and we wanted to believe her, but Trish and I had never seen anything to confirm it.

Trish knew I was wavering. She pulled herself to her feet.

'It's that or we go to the tennis club,' she said. '*Without you.*'

Her father was an architect. My dad was a handyman. He couldn't afford membership of the club where Poppy and Trish had lessons every Saturday.

'OK,' I said, reluctantly freeing my restless fingers from the earth. 'Come on, then.'

★ ★ ★

The Bath I knew was very different from the one the tourists see: Georgian crescents, terraces of tall honey-stone houses, elegant squares. Where I lived, on the city side of the hill below Green Down, there were circles and crescents, but of modern, semi-detached houses, squat and yellow, faced with cheap, reconstituted stone. The inhabitants made up for the ugliness by going to town on their front gardens. There were sundials and birdbaths, pink paving and bright green gravel, armies of regimented scarlet salvias.

'All it needs is a weeping Jesus,' said Trish scornfully, as we passed one particularly elaborate example. A

45

fishing gnome hunched hopefully over a wishing-well, a nymph spilled water from a conch, and red snapdragons, yellow pansies and violet lobelia tumbled out of a stone wheelbarrow.

'I think it's pretty,' I said nervously. There was a weeping Jesus on our living room wall, and I couldn't quite see how he fitted into a garden. Our Jesus had big, sad eyes and in the picture he was knocking on someone's door. He reminded me of a Kleeneze brush salesman at the end of a long hard day. When I was younger I thought he was weeping because he knew he wouldn't find my mother at home.

Trish's wave took in the dribbling nymph, the constipated gnome and the oversexed snapdragons. 'It's *naff*,' she said. I still didn't get the connection with Jesus.

Our house was silent and smelt of wet washing. It always did, regardless of the weather. Every time I let my friends in through the green front door, with its lozenge of cloudy glass, I was conscious of how cramped it was. Trish's home in Midcombe was especially lovely, an old Georgian rectory looking out on to roses and open countryside. Poppy's big modern house on the other side of Green Down was architect-designed, and sat in nearly an acre of immaculate lawns and terraces, kept private by tall pines.

My dad had concreted most of our tiny garden and drawn wavy lines on it before it set, to make it look like crazy paving.

My mother's room was airless, warm and musty. I thought I could catch a whiff of perfume, as if she had spilt some on her way out ten years ago.

'Put the binoculars here,' said Trish, marching over to the window and taking charge as usual.

'He'll see them,' protested Poppy.

'Not if you draw the curtain a bit and poke them

46

underneath.' Trish was about to station herself behind the binoculars but Poppy shoved her out of the way.

'They're Daddy's. I get first go.' She knelt on the floor. 'He's not back yet. But I can see a Led Zeppelin poster on the wall.' A strand of red hair had found its way into her mouth again, and she was chewing it rhythmically. 'And there's a guitar in the corner.'

'Hold on,' said Trish. 'He's coming down the street now.'

I could see his boss's van pulling away at the top of the road. He walked easily, nonchalantly. I wondered if he was planning the evening ahead — a pub, with his mates, perhaps meeting a girl. We had never seen Gary with a girlfriend, but that didn't mean there wasn't one.

He swung in through the front gate. Five long minutes crawled by. Perhaps his mum was making him a cup of tea, asking about his day.

'Get on with it,' muttered Poppy, through clenched teeth. Then, a moment later, she breathed, 'Yes . . . ' Trish and I, huddled on the floor below the level of the window waiting our turn, wriggled in anticipation.

'He's in the room,' reported Poppy. 'I can see . . . he's taking his T-shirt off.' Silence. 'Aaahh . . . '

'*What* can you see?' asked Trish.

'His glorious chest,' said Poppy. 'His lovely, lovely chest. Oh!'

'Yes?' we said in unison.

'He's got a little hairy triangle just at the top,' said Poppy, sounding disappointed. 'I've never noticed that before.' We didn't rate chest hair. 'He's gone now to get washed.'

'Give someone else a chance,' said Trish. 'You've had your turn.'

'Katie next,' said Poppy. 'My binoculars, her house.'

I slithered into place. Being shorter, I had to get up on the window-seat instead of kneeling, and then the angle of the binoculars seemed wrong. I was just

47

moving them to get a better view when Gary returned to the window, towelling under his arms. Something seemed to catch his eye, and he opened the window wider. I focused the binoculars on his chest as best I could — it wasn't *very* hairy — and then realized as I lifted them that he seemed to be staring straight at me. I gave a little squeak, and fell off the window-seat.

'What? What did you see?' hissed Trish.

'His Y-fronts?' speculated Poppy, dreamily.

But I didn't have time to reply, because suddenly I could hear feet on the stairs. The bedroom door swung open, and there was my father.

I saw him take in the scene — three teenage girls, giggling and sprawled on the floor, in the bedroom he had once shared with his wife. There was a terrible silence that seemed to go on and on.

'What are you doing in here?' he said eventually, in a mild, calm voice. 'Katie, you know I don't like you coming in here.'

Trish and Poppy heard nothing in my father's voice except quiet disappointment, but I heard something far more dangerous. They didn't know my father as I did.

'I'm sorry, Mr Carter,' said Trish. 'We . . . we were just messing about.'

My father appeared to take this in peacefully, as if resigned to the whims of teenage girls.

'Well, you'd better let me run you home,' he said. 'And, Katie, you'd better go to your room and start your homework.' So softly, so reasonably, that no one but I would have understood.

'He whistled while he was driving us home,' Trish told me, the following day. 'He seemed . . . well, a bit remote, he didn't speak to us or anything. But he didn't seem angry.' She didn't know that whistling, through clenched teeth, was how my father signalled extreme fury. 'I can't believe . . . well, he didn't act cross at all.'

When my father returned, he came straight upstairs

48

to my room. I was sitting on the bed, trying to take in a chapter of my history textbook on the Corn Laws, though all the time I could think only of what my father's feet would sound like on the stairs.

He was even faster than usual; I had no chance. He crossed to the bed, and dealt me one hard heavy blow to the side of my head. I was knocked backwards, shooting an arm out to save myself and making the briefest of contacts with his merciless right hand. I crashed against the framed photo of my mother on the bedside table. It fell to the floor, and the frame and glass shattered.

All my father said was 'Pick that up.' He was trembling. Then he left the room.

My head sang with pain. I lay back on the bed, breathing hard, feeling no surprise, only the usual hollowness. I waited till I felt less dizzy, then picked up the photo of my mother, shaking the smashed glass into the waste-paper bin and reminding myself not to walk barefoot until I had had a chance to Hoover properly. I placed the broken frame and the photo back on the bedside table, propping it against the lamp.

Some of the hollowness was hunger, but I didn't dare go downstairs. My heart was still thudding, but I made myself finish the chapter of history and trace a map of the Somerset coalfield for geography homework before I got into bed. It was still light outside, and for a while I lay awake, listening to the sound of the hi-fi downstairs playing Bobby Darin and Roy Orbison. It was my fault, of course. I shouldn't have let Trish and Poppy come back.

But I also kept remembering Gary Bennett's face. I thought his eyes had met mine, through the binoculars. I was sure he had winked.

5

When Gary Bennett comes over to me, the first thing he sees is my arse. I'm bending over lacing my boots. First impressions count. Now he'll probably always file me under 'buttocks'.

As I straighten up, trying not to show how shaken I am by hearing his name, he's taking off his hard-hat as if he were doffing it to a lady. I recognize him immediately. He must be in his forties now, but he still has the same Roman-statue face, firm jaw and carved mouth, a bump in the middle of his nose and the same half-humorous expression that tells you he doesn't take the world too seriously. There are deep lines etched into his cheeks either side of that mouth, and the hair is different, clipped very short and silver-grey. It suits him, though I miss those lovely dark-blond curls.

He doesn't recognize me, thank God. Why should he, anyway? The name's different and so am I. In those days I wore long hair in a curtain round my face, and rarely had the nerve to meet anyone's eyes. Besides, I doubt he ever looked as hard at me as I did at him, across the street when he didn't know I was watching. I could have mapped those features as accurately as I had traced the Somerset coalfield from my geography textbook. I knew the contours of his bare chest even better.

It looks as if he's filled out a bit since then, though it's hard to tell under the big yellow jacket. His legs are sturdy, in mud-spattered jeans, and I can't help noticing he's shrunk. No: I reckon I've grown. I thought of him as tall and long-limbed, but he was actually no more than average height. There's a small pimple on one side of his chin, pushing through the late-afternoon bristles.

He holds out his hand to shake mine. 'Come on over to the meeting room,' he says. 'Kettle's on.'

No, not a glimmer of recognition in those weathered blue eyes. If you'd been where you were supposed to be, all those years ago, everything would have been different.

'Good journey? Come far?' he goes on, waiting politely for me to finish lacing the second boot. When I straighten up, he's gazing at me with just the faintest shadow of worry in his face. 'I'll take you underground on Monday. We won't rush you. There's a lot to get through this afternoon — nearly the full team will be at the meeting. It won't be too technical.'

Is he patronizing me? Surely he realizes I understand technical, maybe even better than he does — that's my job. But there's no point in making an issue of it and seeming arrogant on my first day, even if I don't want Gary Bennett to treat me like some token bimbo. I'm already alarmed by the way he doffed his hard-hat. To make a point, I reach back into the car and pull out my own, setting it firmly on my head before we set out for the site office.

He leads the way across the hardcore, past piles of wooden pallets, steel and timber struts, to the nearest and biggest of the metal-sided cabins. In spite of all the gear, not much is happening. The project is still waiting for the official nod from the government that will release the funding. Until then all that can happen is emergency work, to shore up the most immediately dangerous places underground.

Narrow steps rise to an open door. There's a kitchenette at one end of the cabin, and a man in a grey sweater is topping up his mug from a big urn of hot water. He turns and gives me a thin smile. 'Coffee or tea?'

'Rupert,' says Gary, 'this is Mrs Parry, our new mining engineer. Rupert's our bat man.'

His hair is the same shade of grey as his sweater, and dishevelled above a long face. He looks as if he doesn't see enough sunshine, and his hand when he extends it is dry and papery. I almost expect him to rustle.

'You're up and about a bit early,' I say. Oops, misjudged that one. Along with my coffee he gives me a frosty look. 'Sorry,' I add. 'I expect the last mining engineer made the same remark. The profession's noted for its sparkling humour.'

'I respect the work you've come to do, Mrs Parry,' he says. He has a high, penetrating, plummy voice that makes everyone look round. 'Just remember that the law requires you to respect the bat colonies.'

The mines are home to several species of bat, all protected, some extremely rare, and at this time of year, all tucked up and hibernating. Rupert must take his job seriously indeed if he turns up for midwinter planning meetings. Gary takes my elbow and steers me firmly past into the main conference room. 'Don't worry,' he murmurs. 'He's obsessive. Treats us all like that.'

Just as firmly, I dislodge Gary's hand from my elbow by the simple expedient of handing him my coffee so I can take off my jacket. As I do so, on the opposite side of the table, a guy with long stringy hair and a nose like a camel's looks up. His eyes get stuck somewhere around chest level.

The meeting room is more luxurious than I'd expected. A space heater blows out warm air, display boards show maps and photographs of the work in progress, and even the chairs and table aren't tattooed with as many coffee-rings as usual. There's a white projection screen on one wall. About fifteen people are milling around, hanging fleeces and high-vis jackets on the back of chairs. The bloke in the corner unfolding the laptop could be the hydro-geologist, getting ready to show off his charts and diagrams of how water flows through the caverns — one of several specialist consultants. Long Stringy Hair is probably the archaeologist; archaeologists usually look a mess. Everyone in the room is male, which is hardly a surprise.

I have never got used to first days, trying to work out who might be on your side, and who thinks you have no place in the team. When I did my postgrad training at the Camborne School of Mines, I was the only woman in my class. You don't get many girls saying, 'I want to be a miner when I grow up'. Nor so many boys, now we hardly have a national mining industry. Most of the British jobs are like this one, making safe long-disused workings; the real career opportunities lie abroad. My predecessor in this job got a much more glamorous offer, and swanned off to Congo last week, at twice the money I'll be getting.

Usually I know at least one person on the team when I start a new job, but that isn't so today — unless you count Gary Bennett, and he doesn't know I know him. So what are they all thinking? *Just our luck to get a bloody woman?* Or *God, she must be tough?* I'd prefer something along the lines of *She looks like she knows her job,* because the truth is I do. Today I just have to keep reminding myself of that.

A big, heavy man comes over as I'm pulling out a chair. He's got a moustache that looks like someone slapped it on his face at a seventies fancy-dress party and he forgot to take it off. My head just about reaches the RockDek logo on his navy fleece jacket.

'Brendan,' he says, with a slight Scottish accent. 'McGill.' He separates the names as if I should know who he is. 'Mine manager,' he supplies helpfully, when I fail to react.

I have to get a grip. Finding Gary here has thrown me. I'm behaving like the kind of fluffhead who polishes her hard-hat every night, instead of a woman with more than ten years' experience in propping up big holes in the ground.

'Gary looking after you?' asks Brendan.

'Er — yes. Fine.'

'Don't know what we'd do without him.' Brendan gives Gary a friendly, masculine biff on the shoulder. 'He's the only one of us who comes from these parts, and worked in the quarries over Corsham way. Mind, I like to think I know a thing or two about limestone myself . . . '

'Of course,' I say, brain at last heaving back into action. 'Didn't you work on the Gilmerton collapse?'

He looks relieved. The woman isn't a fluffhead, after all. 'With Roy Bailey. He speaks very highly of you.'

He wouldn't if he could see the way I'm behaving this afternoon.

'I heard it was Roy who worked out the collapse wasn't going to stop at Ferniehill.'

'Let's just hope nothing like that happens here,' says Brendan. He has soft toffee-coloured eyes that are good at looking concerned. 'There are six hundred homes on top of this lot.'

Gilmerton's notorious. It was an old limestone mine like this one, under some sixties-built housing estates to the south of Edinburgh. One chilly November morning the residents of Ferniehill began to notice cracks in their cosy little bungalows. Within a few days it became apparent that the whole street was sinking slowly into the ground. The council had to evacuate about five hundred people, and knock down a load of houses and flats.

'Scary,' I say.

'Especially if you're underground when it happens.'

'Nobody was, though, at Gilmerton?'

'Only one fatality. A goldfish that one of the evacuating families left outside in a bucket of water. Froze solid.'

Gary and I both laugh. But I can't help feeling sorry for the poor old goldfish.

'Anyway,' says Brendan smugly, 'we should be safe as houses with my hi-tech canaries.'

One of the purposes of this meeting is to assess how the new type of underground alarm system Brendan's installing here is working out. A network of ground-movement monitors is supposed to send back messages based on microseismic analysis, the tiniest movements in the rock that can warn of an imminent collapse. Gary hasn't so much as frowned but I can tell by his suddenly bland, polite expression that he isn't entirely convinced.

'Roy said when he first phoned you about this job you weren't very keen on taking it,' says Brendan, soft toffee eyes suddenly not so soft and boring into me like drill bits. 'What changed your mind?'

'The money, of course.'

Brendan grins. 'I like a woman with a sense of humour. And not superstitious, I see.'

'Superstitious?'

'Starting a job on a Friday. Maybe that only means something north of the border. Miners in Lanarkshire where I grew up would never start a new stope on a Friday.'

The raven swoops across the clearing and lands in a clatter of wings. Miners won't go underground if they see a bird at the entrance of the mine: it heralds a collapse.

'I'm not superstitious,' I say. As if to prove me wrong, there's a flash of colour at the corner of my eye, making me jump. On the other side of the room, someone has just Power-Pointed a map of the workings on to the screen. It looks as complicated as the London tube map, in nearly as many colours; the tunnels go on and on, riddling the whole hillside. Brendan catches my shock, and misinterprets it.

'And these are just the ones we know about,' he says. 'Could be lots more. This area's been quarried since Roman times.'

The consultant is checking that the mouse works; the pointer spirals indecisively then begins to creep across the map from north-west to south-east. My heart has started to race and my chest feels tight. *Crow Stone . . .*

'And we're going to fill the lot?' I say, desperate to say anything, needing to distract myself, just as everybody else stops talking. It's come out all wrong: ditzy, as if I haven't done my homework.

Everybody laughs. As we all sit down and Brendan begins the introductions, I can still see amusement in their eyes. I want to believe it was a kind laugh, but maybe it wasn't, because I should know as well as they do that ahead of us are years of constructing steel frames and pumping concrete, until the underground voids are solid and stable.

Bury them and all the secrets they hold, for ever, ever, ever . . .

One of the consultants — I missed his name, worrying about what a tit I'm making of myself — has launched into the main business of the afternoon. The project is a collaboration between a number of different partners. This guy's from Garamond, the engineering firm who devised the overall strategy; Brendan's site team, including me, work for RockDek, a mining company sub-contracted to carry out the stabilization. The wall-screen now shows a street plan of Green Down superimposed on the underground map.

'Weight restrictions on the main road and into Stonefield Avenue?' says Brendan. The seventies moustache droops with disapproval. 'That's going to mean diverting the bus route. We've got another public meeting in a couple of weeks' time, and nobody's going to be happy when we tell them they're going to have to walk an extra half a mile to the bus stop. Or they can't have their new cooker delivered because we won't allow big lorries down the high street. Are you saying the risk of the quarries collapsing is greater than you previously thought?'

Brendan and Gary, I've noticed, are the only ones to refer punctiliously to the underground workings as quarries. Everyone else calls them mines, though technically, they're not. From what I remember hearing of Brendan that would be typical: he has the reputation of being a manager who thinks detail is important. That's why people employ him. He has one of the best safety records in the business, even when he worked abroad, where sometimes hazard assessment is not so much relaxed as non-existent.

'The load limit's just a precaution,' says the consultant. 'Factoring in new thinking about possible frost damage. Anyway, I heard you had a bit of a panic last week when some of the alarms registered movement in the rock.'

'We're getting a lot of false positives on the geophones,' says Gary. 'The alarms would be going off all the time if we didn't set the threshold artificially high.'

'Then what's the point of the system?' asks the consultant.

'Trouble is, we're so close to the surface that every time a woman with a pram walks over the top, it trips the sensors. I'm exaggerating but . . . '

'You're exaggerating,' says Brendan, with the calm but slightly desperate tone of one who knows he is right and everyone else is wrong. 'We'll see the benefits when the full network's in place. Of course there are teething troubles before we calibrate the system.'

'Mrs Parry?' says the consultant. 'You've worked with these alarm systems before?'

'They're not very common in this country,' I say, with the unnerving sense that this is another test I'm going to fail. 'This one's from Australia, isn't it?'

'Where it goes off every time a fucking kangaroo hops along,' mutters someone else. Brendan shoots Gary a look.

'Brendan's right,' Gary says, Mr Loyalty. 'Teething troubles, that's all. It could save lives in the long run, and that's got to be worth it.'

Rupert pipes up irrelevantly, in his high, sharp voice, complaining about the possibility of constant alarms disturbing the bats while they hibernate. The warm room is making me dozy, and my eyes drift towards the darkening window overlooking the recreation ground. The little footballers must be having trouble seeing the ball by now. Their running feet thump on a thin crust of soil, beneath which is a honeycomb of galleries and pillars, muddy underground trackways the quarrymen call roads, heaps of waste stone, mile after mile . . .

Someone's watching me.

Out of the corner of my eye I can see the stringy-haired archaeologist staring, his mouth set in a hard line. He's in his early thirties, I'd guess, younger than me, with cavernous red-rimmed nostrils and a face on the slide, like an unstable slope. He looks down at his papers quickly when he realizes I've caught his gaze. My eyes shift focus and, over his shoulder, catch a shadowy, slight, dark-haired woman in a red fleece staring back at me from the glass of the window. From this distance she might be in her early thirties too, though close up that pale skin will betray her. Her eyes are secretive and sad. I rub a hand across my face and she does the same, brushing a spiky-cut fringe back from a high forehead. It looks like she's waving, and I wonder if *she* knows what I'm doing here. *Katie, Katie . . .*

I have to wrench my concentration back to the room. But even while I'm trying to fix in my head the names of the different areas of the workings they're discussing

— Stonefield, Mare's Hill, Paradise Woods, Chog Lane — I keep catching my reflection's reproachful gaze. *What's wrong with you? You've done a dozen jobs like this, Kit, you should know what you're doing by now.*

★ ★ ★

The meeting breaks up an hour later. Gary escorts me back to my car, in case I'm too dim to find it myself. He's probably right. It wouldn't surprise me this afternoon if I managed to fall down the hole in the middle of the site: a vertical shaft, our main access to the quarry workings. Fortunately they've planned for idiots and floodlit the area. In spite of the lights, darkness seems to well up from the shaft entrance.

'Where are you staying?' Gary asks, polite as ever. I can't see his eyes, deep in shadow under the brim of his hard-hat.

'Bathford, for the moment. A hotel I found on the Internet.' I may not be making Africa money, but I don't do so badly that I have to stay in B-and-Bs. 'I'm going house-hunting this weekend. The estate agents told me there's plenty of properties to rent.'

'Do you have any plans for dinner tonight?'

Uh-oh.

'I've got the OK to take you out on expenses,' he goes on, quickly.

I'm instantly embarrassed. Why should I assume he fancies me? He must have read my wary expression, and decided to make clear that this is an official duty, not a come-on. Still . . . a leisurely bath and a quiet evening by myself was what I'd had in mind for tonight.

But quiet evenings leave too much time for introspection. And although this is Gary Bennett, a part of my past though he doesn't know it, surely I can encase him safely in ice, like Gilmerton's goldfish. We're colleagues. We're going to have to work together for

59

months, maybe years, and I may as well get used to it. So I make myself smile. 'That would be very pleasant.' Behind him I can see a sleek black car bumping over the hardcore towards us. 'I'd better go and check in at the hotel first, though. I've got some calls to make.' If he wants to think they're to a husband and family, that's fine by me.

Gary grabs my arm, just a moment too late. I'm drenched as the black car hits a puddle beside me. 'Wally,' I snarl. The bastard could easily have avoided it. 'Who was that?'

'Dickon,' says Gary. 'The archaeologist.'

'Pity he can't drive.' I pluck at my sopping trouser leg.

'I'll pick you up about seven thirty, then?' Gary asks. 'Is it the hotel by the weir?'

'Yes.' Frankly, I've no idea, but it's called the Weir House, which suggests it almost certainly is. I give him my mobile number, in case I'm wrong.

As I drive across the site, I see him in my rear-view mirror, looking after me. Then he turns and heads towards a 4×4, so mud-covered it looks like it climbed out of the ground. I indicate left out of the site entrance and hope to hell that's the right direction for the hotel. The way I've been behaving all afternoon, I doubt it.

6

When I woke up the morning after my father hit me, the side of my head was throbbing, and I could see purplish-brown bruising seeping out from my hairline when I pulled my hair back from my face. It was too sore to run the brush through; I gathered it gently into a ponytail, wrapped a ribbon round it, and let the shorter bits at the sides fall forward. Messy, but normal.

By the time I got downstairs he had already gone to work. I poured cereal and milk into a bowl, but when I picked up the spoon I didn't want to eat. I scraped it into the bin instead.

There was something glinting at the bottom under the soggy cornflakes: smashed glass. The photograph of my mother in its broken frame had gone from my bedside table. My father must have come into my room while I was asleep. I imagined him scooping up the glass quietly so as not to disturb me, listening to my breathing and tenderly slotting back together the splintered pieces of the frame.

Leaving the house, I saw Gary across the road, coming out of the Bennetts' garden gate. He didn't close it behind him; he was still trying to get one arm into his denim jacket. Perhaps he'd overslept. For a moment, our eyes met. He gave a brief, embarrassed nod, then set off briskly up the road.

Had he seen me the night before? I remembered his eyes locking on to mine through the binoculars. Maybe the lenses had caught the light and given me away. I followed him along the road. At the end, he turned left towards the bus stop, and I went right, uphill, towards Green Down and school.

In summer I liked to walk, thinking about ammonites

61

to help me up the steep bit. I knew they would be buried deep in the soil under the pavement. Sometimes I wished I could curl up like them and lie hidden for millions of years.

Trish would be toiling up the other side of the hill, from the south. If I'd timed it right we'd see each other at the top and walk through the village together. I was later than usual. I didn't think she'd wait. Often I'd spot her striding ahead, and have to run to catch up.

There were a dozen or so green blazers coming up the hill, and a few more straggling along the main road towards school, but no sign of Trish with her thick plait of dark hair. As I got closer to St Anne's, there were more and more green uniforms. It was like looking for graptolites in rock; at first you can't see any, then you get your eye in and there are zillions of tiny fossilized creatures winking back.

I went through the school gates and tried to look like everyone else.

★　★　★

'O rose, thou art sick,' said Mrs Ruthven, the English teacher, her eyes fixed on the beech trees through the classroom window. Out of the corner of my eye I saw Trish jabbing a finger towards her mouth to mime puking. Poppy, all long legs and freckled arms, hunched her shoulders, hiding giggles. Mrs Ruthven shifted her weight — she had one leg shorter than the other, and wore a special shoe with a built-up sole — and continued, oblivious:

> 'The invisible *worm*
> That flies in the night,
> In the howling *storm* . . . '

We were doing the Romantic poets this term, and I

thought Wordsworth was dull, sometimes too difficult to understand but mostly just plain wet. But Blake's short lines stuck inside your head, and throbbed there, even if you weren't always sure what they meant.

> ' . . . has found out thy bed
> Of crimson *joy*,
> And his dark secret love
> Does thy life *destroy*.'

Mrs Ruthven swivelled back to the class, pivoting on her platform shoe. 'What's this about, Trish Klein?'

She *had* seen, after all.

'Sex, Mrs Ruthven.' Trish was wearing her most innocent expression.

Mrs Ruthven sighed. She was one of the younger teachers, which meant none of us was yet scared of her. She was our form teacher as well, and she was learning fast that it was a mistake to be too pally.

'Earthly love, yes, but what else?'

Silence. Everybody looked down at their book in case she picked on them.

'What were we talking about last week?' She surveyed the rows of blank faces. We were still at the age where we thought poetry was something to learn by heart, not something to discuss. 'Didn't I say you couldn't separate the Romantics from the political and industrial upheavals that were going on around them? You could see the rose as literally sick, poisoned by the industrial revolution. It's a metaphor that works on many levels. How else do we know Blake was interested in the industrial revolution?'

No one else was going to answer, so I stuck my hand up. ' 'Dark satanic mills'?'

'Very good, Katie. The poem we looked at last week, the one you know as a hymn. 'Jerusalem'. 'And did those feet in ancient time . . . ' Blake is harking back to an earlier, more innocent age, before man scarred the landscape. He called his poems 'Songs of Innocence and Experience', didn't he?'

Poppy and Trish were passing notes to each other now under their desks. Poppy's parents had got back last night from Scotland: they'd promised Poppy she could ask some friends round at the weekend. Of course Poppy had invited me; but I wasn't the one she consulted over the rest of the guest list.

'Blake lived in London, but what would he have found if he had come to Green Down? Because we live, remember, on top of one of the first great industrial landscapes of the eighteenth century.' Mrs Ruthven was struggling. The mascara had run under her eyes. Her sentences kept going up at the end, as if she was afraid we would argue with her. 'The underground quarries, remember?'

The bell went, stranding her in mid-sentence. There was the usual banging of desk lids as everyone scrambled to get out of the classroom and down to lunch to bag the best tables.

'Katie,' said Mrs Ruthven, as I got to my feet. 'A word.'

I could see Poppy and Trish already among the crowd at the doorway, pushing and shoving. They didn't even glance back to check where I was.

'Yes, Mrs Ruthven?'

She looked out of the window again, waiting until the last straggler made it through the door and we were alone. The platform shoe tapped sternly on the parquet.

'Things aren't going too well this term, are they, Katie?'

I felt heat flame my neck and cheeks. 'Mrs Ruthven?'

'Don't pretend you don't know what I mean. You're one of the best pupils in the year, but no one would know that from your marks lately.'

'Sorry, Mrs Ruthven.'

64

'As your form teacher, I'm concerned when other teachers start talking about you as a pupil who's — well, not *failing*, but failing to live up to her promise. Maths in particular, and you'll need that if you want to study sciences ... Are you finding it harder? Is there something you don't understand?'

'No.' I wouldn't have dared confess even if there had been. 'Really. I understand it all.'

'So what's your explanation? Have you found it hard to catch up after being ill last term?'

I looked at my feet. 'I don't know.'

'Is everything all right at home?'

'Fine.' I glanced desperately towards the door, trying to think of something else to say. 'Really, everything's fine.'

'Well, I expect better. Maybe I should have a word with your father.'

'No,' I said. 'I'll try harder. Really.'

Mrs Ruthven set her lips like the line under a sum, and looked sorrowfully at me. I thought she was going to say something else, but instead she picked up her briefcase and limped out of the door.

I hadn't lied. I did understand the maths. And things were as they always had been at home. But there didn't seem to be much time for homework, these lighter evenings. Trish and Poppy were in no hurry to get home after school. But Trish always sailed through everything, and if she didn't, no one seemed to be bothered, the way my dad would be.

The wood-panelled dining-hall, with its reproductions of Pre-Raphaelite paintings, was as noisy as an aviary. Girls perched on every bench, giggling, shrieking and clattering cutlery. There were no spaces left at the table where Trish and Poppy were sitting.

'Couldn't you have saved me a place?'

'Sorry,' said Poppy. 'Pauline Jagger made us move up when her friends got here.'

65

I could see a space on a table at the other end of the room, under Rossetti's *The Beloved*. It was full of girls from the year above, none of whom I knew. I squeezed on to the end of the bench, feeling miserable. Resentfully the older girls shuffled along to make room. Across the hall, Poppy and Trish were laughing about something, their heads together.

I bent my head to my plate.

★   ★   ★

At break-times we were allowed on to the sports field, if we kept to the edge and didn't scar the turf. I caught up with Trish and Poppy on their way there. We usually made for a spot near the tennis courts where there was a grassy bank under the trees. We'd come to think of it as ours.

'Piss off,' said Trish, to a group of nine-year-olds, who were playing some sort of Queen of the Castle game. They scattered, trying to pretend that that was the next stage of the game anyway.

It was a hot, heavy afternoon, threatening rain. The horse-chestnuts round the sports field were in flower, and their white candles glowed against the dark grey sky. There was a distant buzz, the saws at the stone quarry down the hill.

Trish was picking daisies. She started to lace them into Poppy's hair. Poppy sighed a little, and pretended to collapse back into Trish's lap. A worm of envy turned in my gut.

'I found a copy of *Lady Chatterley* in the back of my mother's knitting cupboard,' said Trish to Poppy, 'and you'll never guess where the gamekeeper put the daisies.'

My heart was in my throat. It pushed the words out from where they usually hid. 'My dad hit me last night.'

There. Now I had their attention.

66

For the rest of the day, Trish couldn't leave the subject alone. 'How often does he hit you?'

'Not often.'

We were on our way to the science labs for double biology. Rumour had it the rabbit's reproductive system was the only spark of sauciness we were going to get this term; we would now move on to the sheep's lung. Poppy had talked to one of the girls in the year above, who warned her that the specimen was none too well preserved.

'Exactly how many times not often?' Trish persisted. Our shoes squeaked on the polished floor as we turned the corner towards the stairs. Two pairs of shoes: the third pair, Poppy's, was a way down the corridor, trying to catch up.

'Maybe . . . once every three or four weeks.'

'The last time Dad hit me I was seven and I'd stolen from Mummy's purse. He spanked my hand with a ruler.'

'Daddy's never hit me,' chirped Poppy, breathlessly, from behind, having run most of the way down the corridor, at risk of detention. Trish ignored her.

'I mean, it's not like you'd done anything wrong.'

'It's when something happens to upset him,' I explained. 'He just gets mad and flips. Then it's OK again. He doesn't really mean it.'

Trish chewed her lip. 'But *how* did we upset him? We weren't doing anything.'

No, unless you counted spying on the house across the road through binoculars in the hope of seeing Gary Bennett's willy.

'He doesn't like anyone going into that room.'

'But it's your spare room. It's not like he sleeps in there.'

'No.' I couldn't explain. Trish's family was easy and

friendly. They were in and out of each other's rooms whenever they felt like it.

We started climbing the stairs, Poppy panting behind us. She stumbled as we went round the turn and dropped her books, but Trish didn't stop to help her pick them up.

'It's an awful bruise.'

'It's not much.' My legs ached with going so fast up the stairs. I regretted telling them now.

'He could have fractured your skull.'

'It wasn't *that* hard.'

We reached the biology lab. I sighed with relief.

★   ★   ★

Half-way through biology, Miss Millichip divided us into pairs to do an experiment on breathing. The sheep's lung had yet to make an appearance, although there was a whiff of something clinging to Miss Millichip's lab coat that suggested it wasn't far away. I hated doing experiments in pairs, because there was always a chance Poppy would beat me to it and team up with Trish, and I would be left on my own. But I needn't have worried. Trish swiftly claimed me.

'So what's the worst thing he did to you?'

'Really, not much more than the odd bruise. Honestly. Blow into this.'

Trish blew a long puff of air into the bell jar. 'What are we supposed to do with this now? Hasn't he ever hit you where it shows?'

'We have to measure how far the water level's dropped. Once he did knock my shoulder out. But he did medical training in his national service and he knew how to put it back into its socket.'

'One point four inches. Did it hurt?'

I winced. 'Like . . . hell.' The words felt strange in my mouth. I couldn't really remember how it had felt.

'You ought to tell someone.'

'No.'

Trish shrugged. 'Well, it's your fault, then, if it keeps on happening. Your turn to blow.'

I blew into the flask as hard as if I wanted to burst it.

* * *

Miss Millichip wore a gold cross round her neck, and what Mrs Owen would have called 'sensible' skirts with concertina pleats. You could see them peeping out under her white lab coat. When we had finished the breathing experiment, she called us to gather round the big desk at the front.

Trish elbowed her way into the front row. I followed, then wished I hadn't. On the desk lay something pinkish-grey, wrinkled like hands that have been in water too long, a pouch with a macaroni tube poking out of one end. It smelt foul, coppery, sickly. No, more than sickly — dead, and for a long time too.

Miss Millichip pointed to the diagram behind her on the blackboard. She could draw beautifully, and she'd chalked a picture of the lungs in three different colours, labelled with neat capitals.

'As you can see, this is one of a pair. The tube at the top — what's it called, Trish Klein?'

Trish squinted at the blackboard. 'The bronch . . . bronchius?'

'Hard *ch*. Like a *k*. Bron-kus. No *i*. The bronchus here . . . ' Miss Millichip poked the floppy macaroni with a blunt, unvarnished fingernail ' . . . is one of a pair of tubes leading from the windpipe into the top of the lungs. When the diaphragm — where's your diaphragm, Pauline Jagger?' Pauline pointed vaguely to her abdomen. 'Not bad, but up a bit. Here . . . ' Miss Millichip poked Pauline with the same finger she'd used on the macaroni tube. 'When the diaphragm flattens out, it creates a space for the lungs to expand and air is pulled down the bronchus, inflating the lungs — so . . . ' She inserted a bright yellow drinking straw into the macaroni tube, then bent forward and blew hard down it. The wrinkled grey pouch filled like a sad old balloon. A fetid smell, ammoniac and somehow familiar, wafted across the desk. It suddenly seemed very warm in the room. There were beads of sweat behind my ears.

'The oxygen molecules pass through the walls of the tiny tubes inside the lungs — the what, Katie Carter?'

'Bronchioles, Miss Millichip.' My voice seemed to be coming from somewhere far outside me.

' — and into the bloodstream, where they are exchanged for carbon dioxide, which passes back through into the bronchioles. The abdominal muscles contract to push the diaphragm back into a dome shape, the intercostal muscles collapse the ribcage, and the air is pushed out of the lungs — so!' She pressed down with the heel of her hand on the horrid smelly thing and a puff of foul air shot out of the macaroni tube straight into my nostrils. Sweat burst out of every pore and someone sprinkled black confetti in front of my eyes.

I came to on the floor. Miss Millichip was fanning my face with a set of notes about the eyeball — I could see something like a small fat pink squid flashing backwards and forwards — while the rest of the class clustered behind her, staring at me open-mouthed. They all looked disappointed that I'd regained consciousness.

'Groo,' I said, or something like it. My tongue seemed to have got stuck to my bottom teeth.

Miss Millichip's face was very red, and radiating alarm. 'Bryony, would you go and fetch the nurse? How are you feeling, dear?'

'Unk. Ouughar. Arghright.' I tried to sit up.

'Lie back, dear. The nurse is coming. You fainted.

Best be still for a bit.' She drew a hand tenderly across my forehead. My hair flopped back off the side of my face. 'That's a nasty bruise. How on earth did you get it?'

★ ★ ★

The nurse was concerned about the bruise too. She thought it might have had some connection with me fainting.

'No. I must have done it when I went down. Hit my head on something, I expect.'

'Don't be silly. A bruise doesn't come out that quickly.'

'Well, maybe it happened when I bumped my head in the bath last night. I was rinsing my hair underwater and when I came up I banged against the hot tap. I didn't know it had bruised, though. Is it really bad?' I opened my eyes as wide as I could. 'Have you got a mirror? Can I look?'

She was almost convinced. 'I think we should get you X-rayed.'

'Oh, no. Feel. It's fine. No hole in the head.'

'You might have concussion.'

'Honestly. I'd know. I'm fine.'

'Have you got a headache? Did you have one last night or earlier today?'

'Absolutely nothing. But . . . ' I allowed myself to look guilty ' . . . I didn't have any lunch today. It was stew, and I hate that. And I've got my period.'

'Ah.' The nurse thought for a bit. I could tell she didn't much want to take me down to the hospital on the other side of town. She stared hard into my eyes. I stared back, praying they weren't crossing.

'OK, then. But I'm going to drive you home, and have a word with your mum. If you feel dizzy again she's to take you straight to Casualty.'

'There's just my dad. He wouldn't want you to worry. I can walk home on my own, really.'

But I wasn't going to get away with that. The nurse bundled me into her Morris Minor and drove me down the hill. Of course my father wasn't going to be in. He wouldn't be back for ages, but I didn't tell her that. I said I'd go straight round to Mrs Owen's as soon as I'd unloaded my books and made myself a jam sandwich, and I promised faithfully I'd pass on the message to my dad about taking me to Casualty if I had another dizzy turn.

She drove away up the hill, probably glad to get the weekend started early. I watched her go, then went into the house. Jesus looked down at me with his big, sad eyes from the living room wall. Now he was unhappy I was such a good liar. I hadn't even started my periods yet.

When my father came home at six o'clock, he brought with him a big brick of Wall's ice-cream: coffee, my favourite. He pushed it tentatively across the table towards me. Our eyes met.

7

How much a girl's taste in men changes over the years. When I was at university, we liked wispy, fairy-looking men. Not men like Martin — Martin was never wispy. He could never have fitted the bill, being gay and built like a prop forward. The men who were popular had no chests to speak of, were practically concave, with narrow little shoulders and bony wrists. They looked like stick men, malnourished, but we thought they were sensitive, intellectual types. Ha.

I married one. Stupid. Martin told me not to.

Then, later on, all the nice girls liked a stockbroker. Well, perhaps not literally. Most of them were wankers. But somehow the fashion changed to big butch shoulders, solid jaws, smooth well-cut suits, even a bit of a comforting tummy. Lots of business lunches; it told you he'd be a good provider.

I missed out on that phase. I was still stuck with Mr Sensitive. Only by then that wasn't the best description of Nick. We were still supposed to be living together, in the Chiswick house we could only afford with my money. But increasingly I was spending time in Cornwall, at the weekend cottage bought out of my overtime when I was on the oil-rigs. I hated Nick's clever media friends, I hated my job with Shell. So, suddenly it was a weekday cottage, and I was learning how mines work.

By the middle nineties, *rough* was in. Horny-handed artisans. Muscles, cropped heads, even the odd tattoo. It wasn't a bad time to be in the digging business. Lots of opportunities. Martin took most of them, but I had my moments. Mr *Insensitive*, as we should call my ex-husband, had now left for the west coast to write his

73

media novel, witty and ironic, never completed. He thought of himself as living life in the fast lane, but it was only Aberystwyth.

I'm thinking all this, sitting opposite Gary Bennett in the restaurant he's chosen. This afternoon Gary had looked like Rufty-tufty Millennium Man in his hard-hat and faded navy sweatshirt, but tonight he's staggered me by turning up in a suit, charcoal wool, well cut, well pressed. By comparison I feel scruffy, even if these are my best trousers, with a black cashmere jumper. It's a relief to discover that he hasn't bothered to clean the mud off the 4×4.

His taste in restaurants doesn't fit either. It's not exactly my sort of place. Rather too much dark red velvet and wood panelling. We've been tucked into a cosy corner, so the waiter doesn't have to pay us too much attention. The food's OK, classic French, a bit heavy on the sauces, but what's underneath tastes fresh.

Gary's chewing his way enthusiastically through steak *au poivre*, which is exactly what I would have expected him to pick off the menu. I'm toying with duck, and a very big glass of red wine. His hands have long, sensitive-looking fingers and he keeps his nails neat and clean. I can't remember when I last filed mine: the usual mixture of lengths and serrated edges. I lay my fork on the plate and tuck my hands under the table.

In a moment I'm going to have to say something, but I can't think what. The conversation hasn't been too agonizingly stilted so far — his time in Northern Ireland, with the Army, my two years in Canada — but it's not exactly flowing. I'd better have some more wine.

His head comes up from his steak just in time to see me reaching for the bottle. He halts his fork before it gets to his mouth, balances it carefully with its morsel of bloody meat on the side of his plate, and says: 'Let me.'

Glug glug glug. A lovely smell of blackcurrants comes out of the bottle. But I have a horrible feeling I'm not going to find it such a lovely smell in retrospect. It tastes like Ribena tonight, but it will be battery acid in my gut tomorrow morning. I try to put my hand over the glass, but Gary is intent on filling it to the top. 'Whoa. You'll get me drunk.'

'You're not driving. Someone's got to finish the bottle.'

'Let the waiter have it.'

Gary looks outraged. I can't think why: he told me the company's buying this meal. Or do they have one of those miserly policies where employees have to pay for alcoholic drinks themselves?

'It's Gevrey-Chambertin.'

'The waiter'll probably appreciate it a lot more than I do.'

'Don't you like it?'

I feel guilty. 'Sorry, I didn't mean it to sound like that. It's lovely wine. It's just that I don't like getting drunk.'

'On less than a bottle?'

'My ex-husband was an alcoholic. Is an alcoholic, I mean. Leaving me didn't cure him.'

'Oh. Right.' Gary ponders this, masticating the last mouthful of steak. He lays down his cutlery. 'I'm divorced too.'

Oh, no. I've let myself in for an evening of post-marital angst. The polite thing would be to ask him about it, but I can't bear the thought of hearing how someone else screwed up. Luckily at this moment the waiter pays us his hourly visit. He has that obsequious look on his face that tells you he's about to ask how we have enjoyed our meal.

He doesn't know what he's got coming.

'Waiter!' I say, quite loudly, with as much outrage as I can muster at short notice.

His head snaps up. His hand hovers uncertainly near my plate. 'Madame?'

I can't stand pseudo-French waiters. Especially those who spend most of the evening ignoring you, then expect a giant tip because they remembered to ask you if everything was all right.

'This wine's terrible. It's corked.'

The waiter stares. He can't believe I've just said that. The bottle is more than three-quarters empty. I watch confusion and suspicion dance backwards and forwards across his face. He's wondering if he dares contradict me.

'But, Madame, the bottle — '

'My husband drank most of it. He's got a palate slightly less sensitive than pre-cast concrete.'

You can almost see Gary's palate, his jaw has dropped so much.

'I took my first mouthful just now,' I go on, 'and I can tell you this wine is definitely corked.'

The waiter looks at my almost full glass. He's certain I'm lying, but the restaurant's dark, and he hasn't been near enough to see me drinking. He looks at me. I see him weighing it up: *Tip, no tip?* It's a dodgy moment. If he says he'll get the manager, I'm stuffed. I try to hold his eyes, not my breath. 'Would Madame like another bottle?'

Phew.

'No, thank you. I just expect not to be charged for this one.'

'Of course, Madame.' He picks up the bottle as gingerly as if it held liquid gelignite. As he walks away, I see him sniff it suspiciously.

Gary almost has control over his jaw again. 'What the fuck was that all about?' He's trying not to laugh, in case the waiter hears us, but I know it's all right, he doesn't mind me making him look like an idiot.

'It's a trick I learned from my ex-husband. How to drink in posh restaurants for free. It only works in the really snobby ones, where the customer is always right,

76

and a fuss embarrasses them. Of course, Nick would have had the second bottle.'

Gary is laughing openly now. 'I really buggered things up, didn't I? You didn't like the wine and you don't like the restaurant.'

'I did like the wine. And the restaurant's OK . . . '

'Just pretentious?'

'Yeah. Well. Sorry — is it your favourite?'

'I've never been here in my life before. I usually stick to Pizza Express.'

'You could have taken me there, you know.'

'On company money?'

'You're right, we should sting the bastards. Anyway, we've saved them the price of a bottle of wine.'

'Saved *me* the price. They're Welsh Methodists — they have a policy you can't claim expenses for alcoholic drinks.'

'Thought so. You were taking it way too personally when I suggested letting the waiter finish it.' I lean back in triumph. 'Anyway, we'd better get the bill and go before he's brave enough to get stuck into the remains of that bottle.'

Gary leaves a generous tip, I notice. As he helps me into my coat, those long, sensitive fingers brush my shoulder then jump nervously away — a bit like this evening's conversation. It hadn't occurred to me before: why is the site foreman taking me out for dinner, and not the mine manager?

★   ★   ★

He's still laughing when he orders drinks at the hotel bar. 'You're not going to play the same trick here, are you? I don't think my blood pressure can take it twice in one evening.'

'Nick's rule was never do it anywhere you wanted to go back to.'

'He sounds like quite a character, your ex.'

'Take it from me, he wasn't.'

Gary carries the drinks over to a table on the veranda, overlooking the weir. At least, I assume it overlooks the weir, because we can hear it, white noise in the background. The view must be lovely on summer evenings, but all that's visible tonight is our own reflection in the window glass, Gary with his square, solid face, as full of dents and clefts in the lamplight as limestone, me with choppy hair that will never sit smooth however well it's been cut, and a heart-shaped face too sharp to be pretty. I look a bit less sad tonight, but still tired and secretive. We could be a couple who have known each other so long we've run out of conversation, or two strangers too shy to know what to say to each other.

'So what does he do, your ex?'

'He was a journalist, of sorts. He could have been quite good, but he spent too much time in the bar.'

'I thought that's what journalists do — and still manage to write.'

'Slurring doesn't show up on a page. Nick was a broadcaster.'

'Ah.'

'He still does some freelancing, but mostly he sits in the pub he bought with the proceeds of selling my house, and drinks away the profits. Aberystwyth doesn't have a lot of hard news.'

Gary's on fizzy water, I notice. He follows my eyes to the bottle, and shrugs. I'm on decaff. Nick would have been laying out the lines of cocaine by now. I live dangerously, and pop into my mouth the chocolate mint that comes with the coffee.

'Do you have kids?' asks Gary.

'No, thank God. I'd probably not have had the nerve to throw Nick out if I had.'

'I can't believe that. You don't exactly strike me as submissive.'

'It's different when you have children to think about. I couldn't have done this job, for instance. We'd have been dependent on Nick. You got kids?'

Something unreadable crosses Gary's face. It might be indigestion, revenge of the steak *au poivre*, but I don't think so.

'One. Living with my ex-wife.'

'You get access, though?'

'No.'

I wait, but he doesn't elaborate. Asking outright seems rude, but I ask anyway.

'It's complicated. She's with a South African driving instructor, who keeps an Alsatian dog he calls Ripper. Jeff claims he taught it to tear the balls off black men. I keep away, just in case. It looks colour-blind to me.' He swallows a big mouthful of fizz, and his eyes crinkle, in the way they seem to do when he's searching for the proper way of putting things. 'But that's enough about me. Do you mind if I smoke?'

'Only if you don't give me one.'

He pulls a pack of Extra Mild out of his jacket pocket and proffers it.

'I'm supposed to be giving up,' I say, bending towards his lighter. 'I always try at the start of a new job. Never succeed.'

He snatches the lighter away. 'Then don't let me encourage you.'

'Fuck off.' We're already sparring, like I do with Martin. I grab his hand and pull it back. He clicks the wheel and I light the cigarette, fingers still curled round his hand, protecting the flame. Why am I doing that? I don't like touching people. I let go, and take a long pull on the filter.

He lights one for himself.

He's looking at me. 'Why did you pull that trick in

the restaurant tonight?'

I don't know.

'I told you, I get pissed off with pretentious.'

I wanted you to notice me.

'Doesn't anyone ever call your bluff, Kit?'

'Sometimes. That's what makes it exciting.'

He taps ash off the end of his cigarette, very carefully, on to the edge of the ashtray. 'I just hope you don't behave like that underground.'

'It's because I *don't* behave like that underground that I need to play games in posh restaurants.'

'I see.'

He doesn't. He's looking at me very intently now, as if he's trying to get inside my mind, and although I'm trying to hold his gaze, all my instincts tell me to pull the shutters down and look away.

'Bloody hell, Gary, these cigarettes taste of nothing.' I have to keep talking; there was almost a moment there. That couple I can see in the window looked very serious. 'If you're going to kill yourself, you might as well do it on something you know you've smoked. I need a refill of coffee to get some sort of buzz going.'

He gets up, putting his cigarette carefully on the side of the ashtray. 'Are you sure you don't want something a bit stronger with it? A brandy? Whisky, maybe?'

'Oh, go on, then. Laphroaig, if they've got it.' My weak spot, rough and smoky. '*And* another chocolate,' I add.

'Please.'

'*Please.*'

I watch him going to the bar to fetch the coffee. Not many men would jump to it like that. He has nice shoulders in the charcoal jacket, a comfortable walk. There are muscles shifting under the material. But he probably loathes me by now for being such a madam. The cigarette he left in the ashtray twists a long spiralling thread of smoke into the air, then stutters a set of little puffs, like an SOS.

It feels too hot in here. My jumper's damp from perspiration, sticking to my back.

— *walking slowly down the steps towards him, my eyes fixed on that deep pale V of his chest, his long hair curling on to his collar-bones. He would smell my sweat as I held out my hand, just like I smelt his —*

For a moment I almost forgot I'd known him before, in another life.

It couldn't be clearer that he's forgotten me. If he remembered, there's no way he'd have invited me to dinner tonight or any other.

What the fuck am I doing? I must have been mad to come back to Green Down. Suddenly I'm tired, too tired to understand why I took this job against my better judgement.

I know, I know, it's Friday night, not yet gone eleven, Saturday tomorrow. I don't have to be at work, I can stay up late and then lie in. But I'm knackered. I'm going to drink the Laphroaig he's bringing back to me, smoke another of his tasteless cigarettes, say, 'Thank you for a lovely evening,' and head for bed.

8

Our kitchen smelled even damper than usual: soapsuds and wet wool. Mrs Owen knelt like a woman at prayer, a mat of newspaper spread beneath the open oven door to catch the orange-brown drips as she tackled two months' worth of baked-on grease. Her formidable hindquarters moved rhythmically up and down as she rubbed. I was at the sink, scouring the metal racks. My hands were raw pink from the hot water, my fingertips grooved with wrinkles like raisins. My father was out at work: I never saw him on Saturday mornings.

'Water!' came a muffled roar from inside the oven. I scrambled to obey. My other task was to keep the plastic washing-up bowl full of fresh water so Mrs Owen could rinse her cloth. 'I think your father imagines it's the fairies do this.' Her head was still inside the oven. 'This bit's a tough ol' bugger. Is that water clean?' I squatted beside her, the water slopping over the sides of the bowl. The strong, sharp smell of oven-cleaner made my eyes water. Mrs Owen shuffled backwards on her knees and her stiff grey curls emerged from the oven. She looked like a human Brillo pad.

'You ought to be out with your friends, petal,' she grumbled, plunging her cloth vigorously into my bowl. More water slopped out on to the newspaper. 'Bleedin' Jesus, now look at my dress.' She laughed, a big child cheerfully splashing in puddles. 'One more go.' Her wire-wool head disappeared again.

I settled back on my haunches and sat cross-legged on the floor, balancing the bowl on my lap, always the handmaiden to Mrs Owen's domestic priestess. My dad didn't think it was the fairies who cleaned and dusted and washed the sheets; he thought it was me.

The radio was on in the front room, and I could hear crackles of laughter and applause. We always turned it on when Mrs Owen came round because the clock in the kitchen didn't work, and I had to keep listening out for the pips at the beginning of the lunch-time news, because then it was time for Mrs Owen to wash her hands, shake her soggy dress and vanish as utterly as an elf before my father came home.

With a final grunt, she emerged, holding aloft her greasy cloth. I proffered the bowl. She plunged and wrung. I put the bowl down and we both plucked at our sopping chests.

'I don't know what your dad cooks in there but it's always filthy.'

Mrs Owen didn't believe my father *could* cook, so she supplemented our diet with homemade casseroles and slightly leaden Victoria sponges. She blamed my lack of height on poor nutrition, which was not true. My mother was petite. There was a photograph of her on honeymoon in Cromer. My dad, arm round her shoulders to protect her from the cold Norfolk winds, towered above her, though he was not especially tall.

Mrs Owen crumpled the newspaper and tossed it into the bin. She peeled off her rubber gloves, and fumbled in her pocket for cigarettes. She wouldn't smoke one: she just liked to remind herself they were there. 'You've made a good job of those,' she said, eyeing the racks. They gleamed. 'Stick 'em back in the oven, and we'll have a nice cup of coffee.'

A drink and a chat were Mrs Owen's only reward for her labours, and I never had the heart to refuse. I filled the kettle.

'Not too strong, petal,' Mrs Owen warned. 'Gives me palpitations.' She settled herself at the table. I knew she would have liked that cigarette, but my father didn't smoke, and the scent of tobacco mixed with the cleaning smells would get us both into trouble.

The kitchen in our house was small, and hadn't been altered since my father and mother had moved in after I was born in 1962. There was just room for the red Formica-topped table and two red plastic chairs. The cream paint on the units was chipped, and the plywood cupboards on the walls had sliding doors that had warped and sometimes got stuck half open. I hadn't been able to close the one from which I'd taken the coffee jar, and I saw Mrs Owen staring thoughtfully at it. 'Time your dad redecorated,' she said, as I put the coffee in front of her.

I imagined the smouldering Gary Bennett, on a ladder slapping paint on the ceiling while I watched his overalls tightening over his muscular bum every time he lifted his arm. I knew it wouldn't happen. My dad wouldn't pay someone else to decorate; he'd be up the ladder himself. Or, more likely, he wouldn't do it at all.

'He always says he's too busy,' I said, hoping this would prompt Mrs Owen to talk about Gary, who had recently done her kitchen. But she wasn't so easily led.

'And them cupboards ought to go,' she said. 'Don't cost much to buy a whole new kitchen from MFI. Wouldn't take a practical man like him long.'

Poppy's mother had ordered a German-made kitchen that had cost more than a thousand pounds. It had little violet and green sprigs of flowers on the doors, and a lovely marbled worktop. But Poppy's kitchen was three times the size of ours, and there was a swimming-pool in their garden. Her dad drove a big grey Daimler, and her mum had a sky-blue estate as a runaround.

'You *are* quiet,' said Mrs Owen. 'What's the matter? Cat got your tongue?'

'Sorry,' I said. 'Tired. Didn't sleep too good.'

'Your father should never have sent you to that school.' Mrs Owen's brow corrugated like her curls. 'It's wicked how hard they work you. And you always with your nose in a book. I don't know, mine were never like

84

you.' Mrs Owen's two daughters had both married sensible milkmen. They'd met them together at a dance in the church hall, and had moved into neighbouring streets to raise fat, milky babies. Their idea of serious reading was the knitting pattern in *Woman's Weekly*. 'What I say is, what's the point of teaching girls about science?'

My fingers traced an ammonite's spiral on the tabletop. I was keeping an ear open for the pips.

Mrs Owen took the hint and lumbered to her feet, her coffee only half finished.

'Better be off. Keith'll be on his way.' She always pretended she was going because her husband would be home soon, rather than my father. 'My goodness, it's gone black over Bill's mother's.' She peered out of the kitchen window at the gathering rainclouds. 'Switch the light on, Katie, let the dog see the rabbit.'

She was always coming out with these weird phrases, invocations to appease the everyday gods of women's things and weather. I peeled myself from the plastic chair and got up to find a clean tea-towel while she rinsed the mugs.

'Your dad'll be soaked. Give him my best, won't you?' She knew full well I never told him she'd been there.

As she put the mugs away, I had a sudden urge to give her a hug, yearning for the feeling of her big soggy bosom against my cheek. But that wasn't something I ever did. She ruffled the top of my head when she went past me on her way to the door, and like a cat I pushed up against her hand. That was the closest we came to physical affection. When I heard the front door close behind her, I sat down again at the table and thought about my mother.

★ ★ ★

My last memory of my mother isn't even a memory. It's more a feeling of being warm and enclosed, the details so sharp yet at the same time insubstantial that I may have made the whole thing up. It's Christmas, or near it, I think — there are lots of glittery things around, and I can see firelight on shining spheres. A rack of clothes is drying in front of the fire, wet mittens, socks and my little blue coat, giving off a damp woollen smell. I've been playing out in the snow, but now it's dark and time for bed, and I've eaten a bowlful of something sloppy and sweet and comforting that's a bright orange-yellow. I'm wearing my pyjamas, and I'm sleepy, curled up on the wing backed sofa, and my mother is reading to me, a story about Wynken, Blynken and Nod, three fishermen who are being rocked to sleep in the arms of a crescent moon sailing through the sky like a boat. Or was it a wooden shoe? I am drifting too, wrapped in the wet, warm smell of the steaming clothes.

Whether that was the last time I had seen my mother I wasn't sure, but it was what I remembered as the last. Before the New Year she was gone. Every December after that my father brought out the packets of tinsel, the lantern-shaped Christmas-tree lights that always seemed to fuse and that he patiently fixed, year after year. But it was never the same. The unearthly boat in which Wynken, Blynken and Nod sailed the skies had taken away my mother too.

⋆ ⋆ ⋆

My father never talked about how she had left, or why.

'She's gone away,' he said vaguely, if I cried for her when I was small. 'Sssh now. Be good, or she might hear you and never come back.'

But she never did come back, however good I tried to be.

Nobody ever explained. What I knew, I overheard. One day, in the school holidays — I must have been eight or nine by then, but I still hid under the dining-table, playing house by myself — Mrs Owen was babysitting, while my dad was out at work. She had invited two of her friends round. They sat in the back room, with the french windows open to waft out the smell of their cigarettes. They didn't know I was there.

Mrs Pegg must have spotted the photo of my mother on the mantelpiece. 'Imagine that,' she said, exhaling a whispery stream of smoke, 'going off and leaving your kiddie.'

I sat Beau Bunny against the table leg, and lifted the edge of the cloth to hear better.

'No grandparents?' asked Mrs Joad.

'All dead,' confirmed Mrs Owen.

'Poor lamb,' said Mrs Joad.

'Poor little petal,' Mrs Owen agreed. That was what told me they were talking about me. She always called me her little petal.

'Don't she even write? Send birthday cards?'

'She went off just like that. Wouldn't think a mother could, would you? Cut off completely.'

'Heartless.'

'Cut his balls off, I'd say.' Mrs Pegg sniggered. 'You'd think a man'd go after her.'

I heard a rustle as Mrs Owen leaned forward on the settee. There was the smack of her lips on the cigarette. She lowered her voice. 'She was in the family way when she went.'

'Not his?'

'Someone else's, is my bet. She was seeing another man.' She whispered something that sounded like 'sojer'.

I wanted to hear more but must somehow have given myself away. The tablecloth whipped to one side. Three faces peered in at me, breathing tobacco breath, wondering how much I'd understood.

'Poor man,' I heard Mrs Joad say, as she pulled on her plastic mac on the doorstep. 'Left to bring up a kiddie by hisself. Manages well, though, dunnee?'

Something inaudible from Mrs Owen — probably 'Thanks to me.' Her back was towards me so I sidled into the hallway.

'Of course,' Mrs Pegg said, bending her poisonous yellow curls towards Mrs Owen's grey ones, 'there's always two sides, in't there? Perhaps he *druv* her away.'

'Oh, no,' said Mrs Owen. 'He's a lovely man. Polite always. Ever so nice.'

Her loyalty was misplaced. Not long after that, my father decided he didn't like Mrs Owen being in our house all the time. He told me she was nosy, and maybe he told her too, because she seemed rather pink about the eyes when she took me up the hill at the end of the holidays and said that this term I was big enough to walk by myself to and from school. A lesser woman would have taken umbrage, but it says a lot for her that she kept nipping up the road with casseroles.

'I saw this recipe in my magazine,' she'd say to my father, 'and Keith won't eat fancy food so I thought of you.'

The casseroles were delicious, but if my father came home from work angry, they went into the bin. Once, she gave me a Christmas present, a hairbrush set in blue marbled plastic that I thought was lovely, but my father marched down to her house on Christmas morning and made her take it back.

On my eleventh birthday, I was brave enough to raise the subject of my missing mother. 'Do you think Mum'll send a card, now I'm almost a teenager?'

'No,' my father said curtly, and I knew never to mention it again.

Suddenly he was there in the kitchen doorway, watching me. His short curly hair was dark and shiny with rain, and it made him look younger than he usually seemed, though his face was tired and there were lines beside his eyes. The shoulders of his jacket were covered with raindrops that sparkled under the kitchen light. He wore overalls to work but always put a sports jacket over the top to travel there and back.

I felt myself go red, and tensed, knowing I had been watched and not knowing for how long.

'Sorry, Dad. I haven't done anything about lunch.'

'Don't fuss.' He waved me to sit down again. 'I'll make us a sandwich. There'll be some of that ham.'

That was all right, then. It was a good day.

I sat back at the table as he opened the refrigerator door to get out the ham and tomatoes. There were silvery sprinkles in his black hair. It struck me that I didn't even know what age my dad was. Maybe thirty-four or -five? Quite old when you thought about it. But I didn't think about it. He was just my dad.

I wondered how it would have been if my mother had stayed. Would he have been less angry, more fun? I tried to imagine a Saturday when I would help my mother clean the oven and make us a cake for tea. She and I might go shopping in the afternoon, while my father watched *Grandstand*. But then, maybe, I wouldn't get to do the things he and I did together now at weekends, like looking for ammonites, or going to the climbing wall in Bristol where he showed me how the quarrymen would go up the rockface. *Three points of contact, Katie, that's what keeps you steady . . .*

'Look in the hall,' said my father, his back to me, slicing a loaf. His movements were always careful and exact, like the wiring diagrams he drew, or his plumbing schemes. He used to work as an electrician in the

89

quarries, but he got nervous exhaustion and had to resign and go self-employed. He could do plumbing as well as electrics. He was clever at anything practical.

I went out into our hallway. The light through the lozenge in the front door fell on a pile of books on the table. Dad had stopped off at the library on his way back. He knew the kind of thing I liked. There was a John Wyndham, *The Chrysalids*, and a book called *The Story of Britain*, an old hardback in a polythene jacket to protect it, though it didn't look as if too many people had taken this one out. 'From the geological shaping of the land to the development of civilization,' the cover said.

It had glossy black-and-white pictures. As I flipped through, there was something that looked like a fossilized tulip — a sea lily, according to the caption. I saw a trilobite like a huge stone woodlouse, and a whole page of ammonite marble, dozens of spirals in a sheet of polished black rock. There was a chapter devoted to the first humans in Britain. *Homo erectus*, *Homo heidelbergensis*, Neanderthal man, *Homo sapiens*. I muttered the names to myself like a rosary, tracing the row of skulls on the page.

'What are you doing?' called my father.

'Looking at the book. The one with the ammonites.'

'Not the book, nitwit. The bag.'

There was a brown-paper bag next to the books, so small I had overlooked it, folded in a neat square over something wrapped in cotton wool. I unwrapped it. 'Brilliant,' I said, walking back into the kitchen. 'How did you find that?'

It was an ammonite, the size of an old penny. It had been split in half, so that one side was still rough brown stone, but the flat top surface had been polished to a gloss, tan and gold and grey, revealing the ammonite's secret spiral chambers.

'The book or the ammonite?' He was smiling broadly.

A *very* good day, then.

'Both.'

'I saw the ammonite in a shop window as I was walking down Walcot Street,' said my father. 'And the book was thanks to your favourite librarian.' He put a plate with a doorstop sandwich in front of me. 'Mayonnaise, no mustard, as the lady likes it.'

'Which one's that?' I wasn't sure I had a favourite librarian.

'The young one.'

'There aren't any young ones.'

My father picked up his own doorstop — heavy on the mustard, it would be — and sat down opposite me. 'Hair in a bun. Miss Legge.'

'Is that her name? She's ancient.'

'Rubbish. She's a lot younger than me. I asked her if she had anything on ammonites. We looked in the index, and bingo.'

I took a bite of my sandwich. 'It looks great,' I said, through a mouthful of ham and salad. I opened the book and showed him the ammonite marble. He raised his eyebrows.

'I like yours better, eh? It's in colour. What are you up to this afternoon?'

'Poppy's having a pool party. Could you drive me up there? It starts at three.'

'It's *raining*,' said my dad.

'So we'll get wet. That's what happens when you swim.'

★ ★ ★

I sat in my room, in front of the dressing-table, fingers rubbing the cool polished surface of the ammonite. I imagined the shrieks and the splashes, feet skidding on rain-slippery tiles by the side of the swimming-pool. I saw myself sitting ignored on the edge, kicking my toes

91

in the water, pretending I was having a good time, watching a scum of wet leaves and dead insects rocking on the surface. I didn't want to go to Poppy's party after all.

I felt like the girl in my Edward Dulac poster on the wall next to my bed, a waif-like creature kneeling in a huge dark pinewood, hiding her face in her hands. *Some are born to sweet delight, some are born to endless night.*

'Katie?' My father's voice came up the stairs. 'Time to go.'

I heard his feet on the stairs. The door opened.

'Come on, you'll be late.'

I could see him in the dressing-table mirror. There he was, by the door, hovering awkwardly behind the hideous pink lump in the foreground that was me.

'What's the matter?'

My eyes filled with tears again. I put my face into my hands like the girl in the poster. He came over and I felt his arm round my shoulders. 'Come on, sweetheart, nothing's that bad, surely.'

'I look like a freak.'

He peeled my hands away from my eyes. I could see him in the mirror, kneeling beside me, his concerned freckled face next to my shiny red one. 'You look nothing of the sort. You look lovely.'

'No, I don't. I look like an ugly blancmange.' I was wearing a pink blouse he had bought me from the market. It wasn't my colour.

'Mmm.' He looked carefully at my reflection in the mirror. 'I admit it clashes with your nose. Put something else on, then.'

'Everything else is dirty,' I moaned, 'or horrible. I haven't got the right kind of clothes. Trish and Poppy . . .'

Trish and Poppy had pocket money. They went into town to buy clothes at Miss Selfridge and Top Shop.

They were going to be in bikinis this afternoon, and all I had was my black school swimming-costume with its high front and crossover straps.

My father's lips made a hard straight line in his face. 'Trish Klein looks like a little . . . madam, sometimes. You don't want to grow up too soon, Katie.'

'But they're growing up and leaving me behind.'

My father looked at me in the mirror. He took in my long dark brown hair, straight like my mother's, not curly like his, my blotchy reddened skin, my narrow shoulders hunched in misery. The blouse was awful, the colour of internal organs. It reminded me somehow of a dog's tongue. It was made of cheap nylon, and my father always bought things a size too big so I could grow into them. He sighed. 'Perhaps I should ask Mrs Owen to buy more of your clothes.'

'No-oo!' I wailed. I was wearing one of the sensible A-line skirts she'd bought me; it skimmed my knees, neither short nor fashionably long. I plucked fretfully at the blouse, just above where my breasts had recently started to sprout, two hard little apples in their first A-cup bra, almost lost under shapeless shiny pink.

'They'll just laugh at me.'

My father closed his eyes as if praying for a miracle. He didn't say anything for a moment, but I felt his arm tighten across my shoulders.

'Look,' he said eventually. 'Look in the mirror.'

I looked. No magic transformation. Pink face, pink swollen eyes, pink dog-tongue blouse.

'You're pretty,' he said. 'I know your old dad's bound to think that, but you are. You've got lovely hair.' He twisted his fingers clumsily in the shining strands. 'Go and splash your face with cold water. And if you don't want to go to the party, I'll take you to the climbing wall again. Or the cinema. I'd be proud to be seen with you.'

I didn't go to the party. We went to see *Rocky* at the Odeon instead. Afterwards, walking back up Milsom

Street to where we'd left the car, I tried not to look in the shop windows.

We were passing Jolly's, the big department store, when my father spoke: 'I think you're old enough to shop for your own clothes now. I'll give you an allowance.'

My eyes slid away to the shop window. There was a mannequin in kick-flares and a top that knotted under the breasts, leaving the midriff bare.

'But not,' my father added quickly, 'anything too extreme.'

'The clothes or the allowance?'

'Both. I'm not made of money.' He was smiling at me, but I could tell he felt out of his depth.

I felt a huge bubble of happiness push its way up from my stomach, so forcefully I thought I'd have to belch with joy. Milsom Street looked wonderful, its pavements still shiny from rain, the summer evening sky washed blue and yellow above the rooftops. The air was fresh and smelt of wet leaves. I wondered if Poppy and Trish had noticed I wasn't at the party. I hoped they'd missed me. But I didn't care.

'Hey,' said my father. 'There's your nice librarian over there.'

LEVEL THREE

The Soldier

You can see why Mithraism was so attractive to the Roman army. Its appeal lay in its simple code of duty and honour. The god's followers are his soldiers, who take a binding oath to serve him. *Miles*, the Soldier, represents the third grade of initiation. His symbols are his lance and helmet; his element the solid, reliable earth. His loyalty must be tested, and his courage proved. This is where the ordeals begin.

From *The Mithras Enigma*,
Dr Martin Ekwall, OUP

9

The sky is a receding blue circle. It's bitterly cold. My breath hangs as mist in the shaft while I go down the ladder, slippery with frost.

Gary Bennett's just above me. Looking up in the dim light, I can see his heavy steel-toecap boots on the rungs. As Martin would say, send the woman down first so you've got a nice soft landing. In fact, this couldn't be more different from unofficial visits to flint mines; there's a platform half-way down, to catch us if we slip. Nowadays this is probably the most regulated, safety-conscious industry in Britain. A bit late, really, for all those earlier miners who died of black lung or in coal-gas explosions.

Above Gary is the archaeologist, the one with the red runny nose and stringy hair, whose eyes keep swivelling to my breasts. I can hear him sneezing. His name's Dickon, very emphatic on the last syllable. I wish he'd learn to wipe his nose. I'm sure any second it's going to drip on me. Not, perhaps, a good idea to look up, after all, even though I'm curious to see more of Gary from this angle.

God, I had a hangover on Saturday morning. I woke in a panic about five a.m., certain I was going to find Gary's head on the pillow next to mine. Luckily, no. I seemed to have made it to bed on my own.

Do I mean luckily?

I'm only joking. I do remember most of Friday night. I behaved with commendable control, given that the first Laphroaig was followed by several more. Nick would have been proud of me. If you're going to drink, he'd say, learn to hold it, like I do. Then he'd fall over.

I don't think I said anything too embarrassing. I

remember talking very intensely about mining, and about how going underground is always about daring yourself, but making sure you have the best possible odds of coming out again alive. And Gary nodding, and looking at me with those weathered blue eyes, and lighting another of his tasteless cigarettes for me. He's a good listener, I'll give him that.

My foot touches mud: the bottom of the shaft. It's already warmer, though distinctly damp: the temperature in the stone mines is a constant fifteen degrees or so, summer and winter. Gary jumps down the last couple of rungs to land beside me, and heads for the switchboard on the wall. The daylight doesn't illuminate much, so I can hear rather than see Dickon reaching the end of the ladder . . .

And *feel* it. Bloody hell. That was deliberate, I'm sure. The bastard meant to brush an arm across my breast.

I'm vibrating with anger and ready to confront him, when Gary flicks the switches and everything suddenly goes bright.

God, it's beautiful.

The light shows us huge spaces like the undercroft of a cathedral, a rocky ceiling supported by pillars that taper towards the bottom. The stone is every shade of creamy yellow you can imagine. It's like butter, like honey, like toffee. When you get it above ground, limestone weathers and turns greyish. But down here it's juicy, running with sap, soft, delicious and golden.

'You been into an underground quarry before, Kit?' says Gary.

'I've never worked in limestone. Most of the stabilization I've done has been in Cornwall — old copper and tin mines.'

The stone's soft because it's full of water. In the ground, limestone soaks up moisture: quarry sap, it's called. Above ground the sap will evaporate, and the rock will harden and cure. But before that it is easily worked, sliced out of the earth like cheese. It's a freestone, and the men who shaped it into blocks were called freemasons. You can cut it in any direction, saw it like timber, carve it as easily as wood. It carves *more* easily, because there's no grain to consider.

The stones that built Bath's Pump Room might have been lifted from right where I'm standing. It's a pity they can't run coach tours through here: the American and Japanese tourists would love it, camera flashes bouncing off the ceiling like underground lightning.

The archaeologist blows his nose and it feels like somebody farted in church.

Gary sees my expression, and smiles. He has a lovely smile. It's like the rock: sunny and solid and reassuring. For a moment I could almost forget that this glorious cathedral has to be filled with concrete.

I look around again, this time using my professional eye. Jesus Christ. I've been in some wobbly places, but this beats the lot.

The big caverns like this one are called voids. Artificial metal and wood tunnels run through them. They look like long cages with great spidery steel or timber struts for walls, and solid reinforced roofs. We have to stay inside them because it's too dangerous to walk outside. For the past year, since the construction phase of the project began, teams of miners have been building these roadways to take us metre by metre through the quarries, and they're nowhere near finished yet. After concrete has been pumped into the voids and the job is finished, far in the future, the steel roads will still be here, wormholes through the fill, so bats can fly in and out.

'You ready for this, Kit?' says Gary. He strikes me as a bit over-protective, but that's not uncommon among the men I've worked with. He pats the self-rescuer on his belt, and for about the fourth time glances to check we haven't lost ours. Just in case the roof falls in. If it

99

does, and buries us, we've got about an hour of breathable oxygen in these little bottles.

Fu-u-uck.

Weirdly, though, the main thing I feel is relief. The electric light, the glinting steel roadways running through the voids have chased away the ghosts. It's nothing like I remember it in that long-ago dry summer. But the smell is the same, that sharp, damp, limey scent you can almost taste.

'The miners use the vertical shaft because it's the quickest way into the areas we need to stabilize,' says Gary, as we start to walk through the metal-sided tunnel, boots skidding on the muddy ground. 'But we bring the heavy plant in through the Stonefield entrance, a couple of streets away. A lot of the entrances to the workings are level access, adits into the hillside. They're almost all blocked off now, and have been since the 1960s.' He glances at me. 'But I expect you know that.'

'Don't assume anything,' I say. 'This is nothing like my last job. Christ, look at some of these pillars. That one looks about as load-bearing as a Twiglet.'

'This is one of the oldest parts of the mine,' Dickon chips in. 'Worked out in the early eighteenth century. Very typical, tapering shape to the pillars, partly because they've been robbed for stone over and over again by later generations, but also to support the roof. They're made as wide as possible at the top, to form a series of near-arches. Keeps the ceiling up.'

'No, it doesn't,' I find myself saying, before I can stop myself.

'Pardon?' Dickon swivels his head sharply and for once looks at my face.

'The old quarrymen might have thought that, but they would have been wrong. It's true that an arch is more stable than a flat ceiling, but these pillars are far too widely spaced to form proper arches. That's partly

100

why there's a problem.'

Dickon's jaw drops, though I can't think why. He must know that a mining engineer understands basic structures; and so should an archaeologist. The look he shoots me is distinctly poisonous. Well, I don't like your dripping nose, sunshine. Or your wandering hands. I'm going to make damn sure you know you were out of order touching me. Perhaps he's not used to being shown up by a woman because he strides off at a lick, shaking his head.

Gary raises an eyebrow at me, with an amused grin. 'You've made a pal there.'

'Sorry. Maybe I was a bit brusque. But he was explaining it like I was a schoolgirl. And wrong, too.'

'This is the first underground job he's had.' Dickon has already disappeared round the corner into the next void; Gary dawdles and keeps his voice low. 'We had a brilliant bloke before him, retired now, knew everything there was to know about mining and quarrying. Dickon comes at it from a different direction — his speciality is railways and tramlines, industrial transport. If we come across a set of wheel ruts or a metal rail, which we do quite often, he's your man. As for the rest, he's picking it up as he goes. He's keen, I'll give him that.'

The metal roadway is solid and comforting, insulating us from the vast uneasy darkness beyond. We could be astronauts, looking at the void from the safety of a space station. There are cables running above our heads, carrying power for the lighting, and the messages from Brendan's hi-tech canaries. I can see why he's so concerned with the ground-movement monitors: some of the pillars are badly faulted. It's a relief when we follow the roadway round the corner into what is clearly a more recent section of the quarry; the pillars are broader and solid, and the voids are smaller chambers.

Dickon must be getting over his fit of pique because he's waiting for us, pointing to a pillar with a dark, wedge-shaped shadow at its foot.

'Wheelbarrow.' His eyes slide back to my chest. 'Abandoned here when the mine closed a hundred years ago. The wood eventually rotted away and left a black mark, exactly the shape of the barrow.'

The thought makes me shiver. Mine aren't the only ghosts.

'I still can't hear anything,' I say. 'How far away are we from where they're working?'

'About three-quarters of a mile from the crew in the northern sector,' says Gary. 'And that's as the crow flies. There's another team building roads southwards. But it feels spooky, when you've spent your life in working mines and quarries. It's so quiet. Where are my ear-protectors?' He clamps his hands to his head in mock panic. 'You must be used to this, though, if you've done a lot of work in old mines.'

I never get used to it. These places still fill me with awe and wonder. How did people — *men* — have the nerve to do this with no more than picks and candles to tunnel into these hidden places and risk flood, firedamp, being blown apart or buried alive? My feet slither and splash in creamy puddles. There's water trickling down the walls in places, gleaming in the light.

'Does anybody ever get lost?' I ask.

'Impossible,' says Gary. 'Nobody, but nobody, infringes the safety regulations. I make bloody sure of that. Everyone stays inside the roadways, even when we're constructing a new one. You don't f — muck around, this place is too dangerous. If Dickon here wants us to take a closer look at a particular feature, we build over to it. No short-cuts for anybody.'

The underground road takes another turn to the left, past a floor-to-ceiling dry-stone buttress built of the discards the quarrymen call gobs. I feel less tense now that I know we're heading northwards. Every so often, another wood or metal tunnel branches off, leading to another part of the mine. We seem to have been walking for ages. The dampness of the air mists the light; bright as it is, it can't penetrate far beyond the walkway.

Dickon starts a little whistle, an irritating tuneless hiss through his teeth, as another cathedral undercroft opens up around us, an uneven landscape piled with humps of discard stone. I glance nervously at Gary. Which of us is going to say something?

'We're under the main part of the village, where the shops are,' says Gary. 'Stop that, Dickon. The miners will go mad if they hear you. At least try to respect the superstitions. Especially here.' He indicates a couple of the pillars, wearing white shrouds of reinforcing concrete. 'We call this Co-op Cavern. Had a bit of a roof fall here a few months ago, nothing too serious, but it meant the poor old Co-op up above had to ask the deliverymen to park their lorries five hundred yards down the road and carry the stock in on foot until we got the pillars supported.'

'How far's the Co-op above our heads?'

'About two metres, that's all.'

'*Christ.*' How do people live with that kind of uncertainty?

'Found anywhere to live yet?' asks Gary.

'Well, nowhere in Green Down,' I say quickly. Both men laugh.

'Trouble is, wherever you go in this area there are underground workings,' says Dickon. I can tell he's the sort who enjoys being the bearer of glad tidings. He blows his nose with a horrible liquid trumpeting sound. 'Actually . . . ' sniff, sniff, it's *still* dripping, would you believe, and he's left a bogey on the end ' . . . where you're living, Gary, that's got quarrying underneath. I was looking at an old survey map in the council archives last week.'

'Well, thanks, *Dick*,' says Gary. He's striding on at a pace that suggests he'd like to leave Dickon behind. But you don't get rid of him that easily.

'Seriously, Gary, you should get a survey done or you might find your insurance is invalidated.'

'It'll be invalidated for bloody sure if I get a survey that proves I'm living on top of disaster.'

'Sell it,' I butt in. 'Let some other bugger find out.'

Gary shoots me a hard look to check I'm joking.

Dickon takes me seriously. 'That would be immoral.'

'Listen,' I say, as we round a corner into another set of pillared chambers, 'sometimes it's immoral to tell people things they don't need to know.'

He's still trying to work that one out when I hear muffled thuds and crashes. I look at Gary and raise my eyebrows.

'That's the works,' he confirms.

⋆ ⋆ ⋆

We can see the occasional white flash of light ahead, at the end of a long chamber with pillars that taper like Superman's torso. Beyond that the workings recede into darkness. I glance at the plan. We're almost at the north-eastern extreme, under an area called Mare's Hill.

The fizzing light of welding equipment reveals sharp fragments of activity, the creation of a new section of steel walkway. I can make out ten or so hard-hatted figures. Their high-visibility waistcoats turn them into bright silver scribbles against the darkness.

'Most of this team are free miners from the Forest of Dean,' says Gary. 'Bit of rivalry between them and the Welsh miners on the other team, but they're a great bunch. Tough as hell, good workers. It's a hereditary thing, going back to the Middle Ages. They're the only people allowed to dig the coal there, but I don't think many can make a living from it now.'

I imagine them out there among the trees, dark, silent

men with muscles like knotted rope, the sound of solitary picks echoing through mossy branches. Tock, tock, tock, like woodpeckers.

We're almost at the end of the walkway now, and the miners have noticed us. One by one they put down their tools, and stand there, waiting, arms folded, in the last pool of electric light. Behind them the darkness is intense.

'Hi, guys,' says Gary. 'Hi, Ted. Just showing the new engineer the workings.'

Ted, the one nearest me, is a big bloke with tattoos snaking up his corded arms. He pushes up the peak of his hard-hat to get a better look. His eyes are flinty, his mouth set like concrete.

Even Dickhead Dickon can tell something's wrong. I can hear him shifting uneasily from foot to foot in the thunderous silence that's fallen.

I guess no one thought to tell them that the new engineer is a woman.

10

It was the sound of a hammer that woke me, penetrating my sleep like someone knocking on the inside of my head. *Tap tap tap.* Very quiet taps. As if someone was trying not to be heard. I looked at the bedside clock, expecting to find it was the small hours of the morning, but it wasn't yet midnight. *Tap tap tap.*

I knew immediately it was a hammer and not anything else because all my life I'd known the different sounds hammers could make. I could tell this was a small hammer, hitting the head of a small nail, hardly more than a pin, driving it gently into wood. The sound pattered through my bedroom window, opened wide to let in a breath of humid summer air. It came from my father's workshop in the garage.

I pushed back the sheet and swung my feet on to the floor. An orange glow filtered through the curtains from the streetlamps on the hill above our house. Beau Bunny, the toy rabbit I'd had since I was tiny, and a committee of my old teddy bears sat on a wicker chair next to the window. Their beady eyes watched me disapprovingly. I saw myself as a ghostly white shape in the dressing-table mirror. It struck me that I often felt like a ghost in the house.

I crept out of the room and down the stairs — *tap tap tap* — through the narrow hallway that tonight smelled of fried fish — *tap, tap tap* — into the kitchen where the washing-up from supper was still piled in the sink. The back door stood open and I slipped through it. The concrete yard was gritty but blessedly cool on the soles of my bare feet. The orange streetlamp made everything unnatural, harder, lurid, shadowed, like frames in a comic strip.

The garage was set well back from the road, separate from the house, at a lower level because the street dropped away downhill. My father had made an entrance in the side, with three steps leading down into the garage. Light sliced out through the half-open door.

As far back as I remembered, it had been my father's workshop. I loved creeping in to watch him. He had set up a heavy workbench with a vice, and built metal shelves against the back wall with hooks to hang his tools and dozens of compartments for nails and screws and nuts and bolts. He would let me sit on the top step — 'No nearer, mind, while I'm working' — and I used to stay there for hours on end, as he measured and sawed, planed and trimmed, nailed and glued. Most of the time I had no idea what he was doing. Because I was so quiet he used to forget I was there and never bother to explain. Now I edged round the door so I could peer down at him as he worked, too absorbed as usual to notice me.

On the bench lay the photograph of my mother in its damaged gilt frame, the sidepiece twisted and splintered like a broken limb. It was a studio portrait, carefully posed. The photographer had sat her sideways, and she was turning her head to look over her shoulder at the camera with the half-smile of a cut-price Mona Lisa. She wore her dark hair in a short, urchin style like Audrey Hepburn, feathered on to her cheeks. From where I stood it looked as if her eyes were on my father as he worked to repair what he had broken.

I guessed he had tried to fix the old frame and given up. He was making a new one out of pale, sanded pine, measuring the final piece against the half-assembled frame to be sure it fitted. His back was half turned to me, his concentration intense, his fingers careful and precise. Satisfied, he picked up a spatula, dipped it into the pot of glue, coated the mitred corners and slotted the piece into place. He searched along the shelves and selected a couple of tiny nails, holding them against the wood to check the length. Then he used a lightweight hammer to drive them in and secure the joints. *Tap tap tap.* A nail hit by my father always drove straight into the wood. He fitted picture clamps to the corners, checking the angles with a carpenter's try square, screwing each clamp nut the exact same number of turns to hold the joint under pressure while the glue set.

My father had not taught me woodwork, but I had learned the principles by watching him. There was no way those joints would come apart.

He picked up the photo in its old frame. The hardboard backing was still in place, and he began to pull out the tacks that held it to the frame. He caught his finger on one, and put the picture down quickly, sucking the torn skin. A droplet of blood had fallen on to my mother's face, and he took out his hanky to wipe it carefully away. I felt my eyes sting, and slipped away across the yard before he saw me. It was starting to rain, big fat drops that pressed like thumbs through my nightdress to my skin.

I lay awake in bed for a long time, listening to the downpour and the dark mutters of thunder. I wondered where my mother was now, and whether she knew how much my father still loved her.

★ ★ ★

I saw Trish as I came up the hill on Monday morning. She was just ahead of me, lolloping along with her satchel slung over her shoulder like an afterthought, books tripping over each other to escape.

'You're going to lose your *Aere Perennius*,' I said, puffing a bit with the effort of catching up. Trish whirled round, startled, and the Latin book fell out on to the road. A passing cyclist swerved and shouted.

I stepped into the road and picked it up. 'You'll have to dry it out.'

'Who cares?'

I wiped it on my sleeve. The pages were already crinkling. 'How was Poppy's party?'

'Gross. Helen Mansell was sick in the pool. We had to get out.' Trish shoved the book into her satchel and started walking again. 'Where were you, anyway?'

At least they'd noticed I wasn't there.

'My gran was ill,' I lied. My gran was more than ill; she'd been dead twenty years.

'I thought she lived in Blackpool?'

'Oh, yes,' I said. My fingers nibbled at a seam of fluff in the bottom of my pocket. 'We had to drive up there. Didn't get back until four in the morning.'

'Is she very ill?'

'Pneumonia.'

'Oh, Katie, that's awful. Is she — you know?'

'Dying? No, I don't think so. Dad said the crisis was over, and she'll probably pull through.'

I'd never known her, or any of my grandparents. My father's mother was not even sixty when a heart-attack had taken her, still mourning a husband who died in a Japanese prisoner-of-war camp. Like him, my mother's parents had been killed in the war, in one of the bombing raids on Bristol, and my mother had been brought up by my great-grandmother.

I hated people being sorry for me. When I first got to know Trish, I couldn't bear the look of pity on her face when she realized my mother had left. So I gave myself a living granny, conveniently located at the other end of the country so there would never be any danger of having to produce her.

'She must have weak lungs, your gran — didn't she have pneumonia last year as well?'

My fingernail popped right through the lining of my pocket. 'Dad always says she should stop smoking.'

109

'Anyway,' said Trish, 'you didn't miss much. I don't blame Helen for honking. Rather too much showing off — 'How do you like our pool? Don't drop ice-cream on our lovely, lovely patio furniture.' Poppy's parents are a bit — you know. *Nouveau.*'

'New?'

'*Nouveau.* As in gold-plated bath-taps.'

'Oh.' As so often with Trish, I wasn't quite sure I followed, but it seemed easiest to pretend I did. Anyway, I didn't much like Poppy's mother myself. She always looked sideways at me when I went round there for tea as if she expected me to eat with my fingers.

We were coming up to the Ministry of Defence offices now, where Poppy's father worked, with the rolls of barbed wire topping the fences and the sentries in their dark uniforms and white spats at the gate. A car was just drawing up to the barrier, a big grey one. A sentry strolled over to check the driver's pass. Trish started waving. The passenger door opened and Poppy got out as we drew level.

'*Great* party,' said Trish. 'I was just telling Katie. Really great.'

'Shame you weren't there,' said Poppy, blowing a kiss to her dad and slamming the car door. 'We missed you.' I looked at her closely. She really did seem to mean it.

★ ★ ★

During Latin, Poppy passed me a note.

We're going shopping in town after school. Want to come?

Yes, I wrote underneath, and passed the note back, wondering when they'd planned this.

'*Nonne*,' said Mr Clayton, the Latin master, pointing with the chalk to the two words he'd written on the board. 'And *num*. Two different ways of introducing a question. Can anyone remember what they mean?'

110

There was a silence. No one raised a hand.

'Surely,' said Mr Clayton, '*surely* someone wants to take a guess?' Surely, no one did.

'*Nonne* means 'surely' ', he said, strolling between the rows of desks, holding his hands in a steeple as he always did to indicate deep thought. 'In other words, it's a question expecting the answer yes. So *num* . . . ' He stopped and looked expectantly round the class, his hands still a steeple, waggling his little fingers at us. But none of us was very interested in Latin. '*Num* introduces a question expecting the answer no. Trish, what on earth happened to your textbook? It looks as if you took it swimming with you.'

While everyone laughed, I found myself wondering whether Poppy would have prefaced the question in her note with *nonne* or *num*. She couldn't have known that my dad had promised me a clothes allowance. She must have been expecting me to say I wouldn't go.

Well, too bad. I didn't have the money yet, but I could choose what I'd buy. I looked at Poppy, with her fuse-wire plaits, her neat, freckled face. She gave me a quick grin and a thumbs-up. I wasn't fooled.

★　★　★

I had been in Top Shop before, by myself, but it was different today, knowing I would soon have money to spend. I took my time. Disco Tex and the Sex-O-Lettes thudded in the background. There was so much: rail after rail. I let my hand stroke the slipperiness of a satin halter-neck top. I had to have a pair of those wide trousers with turnups. And I'd surely look good in one of those peasant blouses? *Nonne*?

Somehow I had accumulated a pile so huge I kept tripping over the trailing skirts as I made for the changing rooms.

'No more than five,' said the assistant. She had big

panda eyes circled with glittery black shadow, and was chewing gum. I began to untangle my armful of clothes, trying to decide which ones to take in, which ones to leave outside.

The curtain of the communal changing area whipped back. Poppy and Trish came out. Trish thrust her bundle of clothes, all inside out and crumpled, at the assistant. 'Naff,' she said. 'Cheap and nasty, the lot. C'mon, let's try and find somewhere they sell better stuff.'

I gave my armful to the assistant, trying to convey that I, too, had suddenly noticed the shoddiness of the material and the crooked stitching. It must be very sad, I thought, having to work in a shop where the clothes were so poorly made, and as I handed them over I mouthed, 'Sorry.'

She ignored me, chewing her gum and staring straight over the top of my head. I hurried after Trish and Poppy.

★ ★ ★

'Tell you what,' said Trish, when we were out in the street again, 'let's go and try on bras. I need a new one.'

'Marks & Spencer's is at the other end of town,' Poppy objected.

Trish gave her a withering look. 'You don't buy your bras at Marks, do you? Mum takes me to Jolly's.'

'Well, so-rree,' said Poppy. 'Pardon me for naffness.'

'There's a much bigger range,' said Trish, reddening.

'And much bigger prices.

'Your mum can afford it, can't she?'

Poppy shot a glance at me. 'M & S is better value,' she insisted. 'They've got some really pretty ones too.'

'Jolly's is nearer.'

Poppy gave in, flicking another glance at me.

★ ★ ★

I was about to set foot on the white and gilt staircase in Jolly's that led to the upper floor when Trish caught my arm. 'Not that way. Lingerie's on the ground floor.'

Lingerie. I had never felt the word in my mouth, languid and foreign and erotic. I said it quietly to myself, under my breath, elongating the *jjjhhh* sound as I followed Trish and Poppy through the department store. I wore pants — that was what my dad called them, his voice pushing out the word so briskly and dismissively I knew he was embarrassed by it. *The airing cupboard's full of your pants, Katie, can't you put them away?* Or drawers, that was what Mrs Owen said. *Get them drawers hung out on the line, Katie, to let a bit of fresh air into them.* But here they were 'briefs.' It said so on the price tags. A simple, discreet, elegant word. Something slipped on by lady lawyers with long shapely legs in sheer black stockings. Or loose and silky, like 1930s film stars wore, when they were called 'French knickers'.

What would it feel like to wear those? I imagined they would be cool and slithery. You would feel deliciously naked as their wide legs wafted fresh air towards your secret bits. I wouldn't dare go out in them, I thought. It would be like going out with no pants at all.

Trish and Poppy were by the bras. Poppy was looning about putting one of the bigger sizes on her head like a cap. The sales assistant, formidably bosomed herself, shot us a disapproving look, and Poppy hastily put the bra back.

'What've you got?' asked Trish, not looking up. The bras rattled on their plastic hangers as she riffled through them.

'Nothing yet,' I said. 'I can't see anything in my size.'

'What size are you looking for?' asked Poppy, waving a froth of coffee-coloured lace at me. 'This one's really pretty.'

'I usually get thirty-two A.' Usually? I had one bra,

and I only wore it on special occasions. It was plain white cotton and it had come from the starter-bra section at Marks & Spencer.

'Poppy,' said Trish, from behind another rack, 'can you see anything decent in a thirty-four C?'

C? Trish was a C-cup? I tried to get a glimpse of her chest through the rows of bras. She couldn't have grown that much, could she, in the week since we'd last crowded into the changing rooms at school to strip off for a swimming lesson? Surely — *num* — she wasn't that much bigger than me?

Trish emerged from behind the rail, holding three or four black ones, and a really racy plunge bra in scarlet. 'Come on. They're going to close in ten minutes.' She disappeared into the fitting room, closely followed by Poppy carrying the coffee-coloured lace and another in pink.

I snatched off the rail the first two bras that came to hand, and dashed after them to the fitting room. But this wasn't like the communal changing rooms in Miss Selfridge and Top Shop. There was a row of slatted wooden doors, like in a Western. I could see Poppy and Trish's legs beneath one, and started to push my way in.

'Hey,' said Trish. I caught a glimpse of her breast, a luminous white arc tipped with pink. 'No room. We can't all three get in. Find your own.'

'Trish's tits are taking up all the space,' said Poppy.

I shoved my way into the next cubicle. The doors clattered behind me like those of a Western saloon after the town drunk gets kicked out.

'I think that one's a bit tarty,' came Poppy's voice from next door. 'But a good fit. Gives you an enormous cleavage.'

I hauled off my school dress. Reflected in the mirrors on two sides I watched my own bare chest revealed. My breasts looked to me like a story I'd made up. They were hardly more than pimples.

114

'I'm going on a diet,' I heard Trish say. 'There's a grapefruit-and-egg diet Mum used to do when she had to slim down to model underwear.'

'Your mum modelled underwear?' said Poppy.

I resolved to go on a diet too. Maybe if my waist got smaller, my breasts would look bigger.

'No, not the pink,' said Trish, behind the wall. 'Clashes with your hair. But the coffee one's good.'

'Shame it has to go under clothes,' said Poppy.

They sniggered.

I put my arms through the shoulder straps of the first bra. It was a horrible fleshy shade, the colour of old ladies' surgical stockings. Even on the tightest hook, it was miles too big. The cups sagged like wrinkled balloons.

'How're you getting on?' called Poppy.

'Fine,' I said. 'Good fit. Fine.'

One of them must have lost their balance because there was a great thump on the fitting-room wall, then a gust of shrieks and giggles.

'Get off,' said Poppy.

'Get off? It's you fondling my tits.' More laughter.

I undid the bra, picking it off my chest like a scab.

'Hey, Katie,' said Trish, between snorts of laughter, 'Poppy had a really brilliant idea on Saturday.'

'What?' I had a headache coming. My stomach hurt too.

'She said . . . '

'It was your idea, Trish, I just thought of what we could say.'

'She said we should write a letter to Gary Bennett.'

'A letter?' I hooked the bra back on to its hanger. Was there really any point in trying on the other?

'A letter saying one of us is his mystery admirer, and offering to meet him. An *assignation*.'

'That's a stupid idea,' I said. 'What's he going to do, invite us all out on a date?'

115

'We pick straws, silly. The one with the long straw gets to go on the *assignation*. Go with him to Crow Stone for a snog in the bushes.'

I levered my breasts into the cups of the second bra. It was the same hot-pink style Poppy had picked up, low-cut and padded, with a contrasting trim of black ribbon round the top of each cup.

'It's a one-in-three chance,' said Trish.

I stared at myself in the mirror. The bra was a perfect fit. It plumped up my little breasts into firm globes, filled them out so that for the first time I saw myself with the body of a woman. I turned to look in the second mirror for the side view. I had an outline, a proper shape. I felt a silly grin start at the corners of my mouth.

'So what d'you think?' said Poppy.

'It's great,' I said. 'Terrific. Count me in.'

I pulled my dress on over my head, and looked at the new shape the bra underneath it gave me. I put my hands on my hips, I sucked in a big breath, and watched my bosom rise with my ribcage. I could knock somebody's eye out with boobs like these.

'You found anything you like?' asked Poppy, from next door. 'I'm going to get the lacy one, and Trish can't make up her mind.'

'No,' I said. 'No, I can't be bothered. It wasn't that nice.' I looked at myself in the mirror again. I stood on tiptoe, stuck out my chest and pretended to be the girl on the cover of the Roxy Music album.

I heard the door of the next-door cubicle swing open.

'Ready?' called Trish.

'Ready,' I said, reaching up and taking down the other bra from the peg. I picked up my school satchel and pushed out through the doors.

Trish glanced with a sneer at the surgical-stocking bra in my hand. 'You're not thinking of buying that?'

'Course not,' I said, as scornfully as I could manage.

'I was just trying it on for the size.' I walked out of the changing rooms, and hung the bra back on the rail. 'I've got loads of bras at home. You made up your mind?'

'I'm going to wait till Saturday and I'll get Mum to come in and help me choose,' said Trish. I glanced down at the bras she was putting back. They weren't C-cups at all, they were Bs. And no wonder she wasn't going to buy them right now. They cost more than a couple of dresses would at Top Shop.

Poppy had finished paying for her bra and was putting her purse away. The middle-aged saleslady with the enormous bosom like a bolster started to rearrange the bras on the rail, clattering the hangers to show her disapproval of the way we had left it. Instinctively I rounded my shoulders and tried to look as concave as possible. But I could feel the new bra hugging me, two secret strong hands cupping my breasts.

★ ★ ★

It was only when we got outside that I started to feel anxious.

'Right,' said Trish, standing on the pavement. 'What are we going to do now?'

I could feel the elegant dummies in the shop window staring accusingly at me. I expected the heavy doors of the store to swing open, and a posse of sales assistants, led by Bolster Bosom, to pour out waving and shouting, *That's her! That's the thieving little bitch who stole a pair of new breasts.*

'Let's *go*,' I said, my shoulders prickling, expecting a heavy hand to close on my arm at any moment. 'I really should get home.'

That didn't suit Poppy and Trish at all. They wanted to see *Rocky*.

'There's a showing in a quarter of an hour,' said Trish, looking at her watch. 'Just right.'

117

'Better get a move on, then,' I said, 'or you'll miss it.'

'Don't be ridiculous,' said Poppy. 'The cinema's about three minutes away. Anyway, aren't you coming?'

I'd seen it on Saturday, of course, with Dad, but I couldn't tell them that. 'I've got to get home,' I insisted. 'Look, I'm going to head for the bus stop. Don't want to miss one and have to hang around.'

'You're antsy,' said Trish.

'My dad,' I said, inspired. 'You know. I don't want to upset him.'

'Oh. Sorry. I forgot.' Trish pursed her lips, looking concerned. 'Are you all right, Katie? We were worried on Saturday when you didn't show. I mean, we didn't know about your gran, we thought — '

'I'm fine,' I said, casting another despairing look at Jolly's doors. 'No problem. Just . . . got to get home. In case.' I backed away. I didn't want to turn sideways on to them in case they noticed my new silhouette.

'Katie?' said Poppy. 'You can always tell us, you know.'

I put the biggest smile I could manage on to my face and shook my head to indicate there was nothing to tell. As I turned the corner, I saw that Poppy was still gazing after me, but Trish had turned away to look at the clothes on the snooty dummies.

* * *

I had just missed a bus. I could still see it in the distance, chugging along the road, and I thought of running to catch up but I wasn't sure what that would do to my new breasts. I was sure the bra was making them grow. I worried they might spill over the top, like dough left in a warm place to rise.

There was a bench near the bus stop, and I sat on one end of it, leaning my head on the sooty wall behind. The pavement smelled of traffic and stale pee. My feet kicked at discarded beer cans, a leaf fall of cigarette butts. From here I had a good view back along the road towards the city-centre shops, and I'd have plenty of warning if Bolster Bosom and her posse of enraged store detectives came steaming towards me. I'd run then, all right.

Thinking of what I had done, I felt my breasts shrivel back to normal size. Smaller, even. The secret strong hands of the bra were cupping empty air. I'd never stolen anything in my life before. I stared at the cars crawling past, feeling sick. I had taken something I hadn't paid for. Weren't you supposed to get some sort of thrill out of stealing? I wasn't excited any more; I just had a big solid lump of undigested fear sitting at the top of my stomach.

'Katie,' said a woman's voice I didn't recognize. I nearly shot off up the road. 'Katie Carter. Isn't it?'

An unfamiliar woman was standing at the other end of the bench, looking at me. But I knew I'd seen her before. She had short dark hair flicking on to her cheeks like feathers and she wasn't very tall.

I felt the bra-hands on my chest clench into my body and squeeze my stomach shut. For a moment I couldn't breathe. I stared at her, aching with hope. I wasn't sure if I was going to cry.

'I'm Janey Legge. From the library, remember?'

The hands let my stomach go and all the hope dropped out of me on to the dirty pavement under the bench. There was nothing left inside but disappointment.

'I'm sorry,' she said. 'I didn't mean to startle you. You've gone a funny colour — are you all right?'

'I'm fine,' I said. I hoped she couldn't hear the wobble in my voice.

She sat down on the bench next to me, looking worried. Now she was close to me, I could see how stupid I'd been. She was years younger than my mother would be. Her hair wasn't short at all, it was long, caught up into a bun at the back of her head, with short feathery bits pulled out to curl on to her creamy cheeks. It had a reddish tint that didn't look natural. Her face was thinner than my mother's too, with a pointy ski-jump nose, and high cheekbones.

'Are you sure you're all right?' she said.

She wasn't my mother. How dare she worry about me? How dare she make me think —

'I've seen you lots of times at the library,' she went on, 'and your father was telling me all about you on Saturday. He's ever so proud of you, you know.' She smiled at me. There was a fleck of dark plummy lipstick on one of her front teeth.

'I don't remember *you*,' I said. I did, though. I'd just never taken much notice of her before.

A pulse jumped under one of her eyes. 'Well, I know you,' she said. 'Always getting out books on archaeology. We notice things like that, the other librarians and I. We call you the Little Digger.'

She was wearing a fluffy lilac wraparound cardigan instead of a coat, over a dress that tried to be the same shade but just missed. There was a thin gold cross on a chain round her neck. I couldn't think what to say to her.

'So, Digger,' she said, 'what a surprise bumping into you at my bus stop, eh? But your dad said you lived up on Green Down. Maybe we'll keep bumping into each other, now we've done it once.' She unzipped a big tapestry shoulder-bag. 'Banana? I always get peckish on my way home.'

'No, thanks,' I said coldly. 'I'm dieting.'

She raised her eyebrows. Her cheekbones were sharp, with little dabs of red blusher under them. 'Exercise,' she said. 'Exercise is better than dieting. Do you dance, Katie?'

A bus was coming along the road. I squinted at it over

120

Janey Legge's fluffy shoulder. Not my bus. I wondered whether to get on it anyway, to escape from her. The bus drew to a stop beside us, and the noise of its engine drowned out whatever Janey was saying. She looked round at its number. 'Well, this is mine. Been lovely talking. And you will, won't you?'

'Will what?'

'Remember me to your father. What a lovely man. You can tell him I said that.' She stood up, adjusting her bag on her shoulder. 'See you soon.'

Over my dead body. I stared after the bus as it pulled away towards the bridge, trying telepathy to make it explode. But there was no fireball, no mushroom cloud. It carried Janey Legge and the rest of its passengers safely across the river.

11

Back at the hotel I'm folding clothes when the telephone rings. It's Gary. 'Sorry,' he says. 'That didn't go very well, did it?'

'You can say that again.'

'Right.' He pauses uncertainly. 'What are you doing? You keep fading away on the phone.'

'I'm packing.'

'*Packing?* Just because a few miners were unfriendly?'

I stop trying to squash a red mohair jumper into my case, and tuck the phone more firmly under my chin. 'Of course not. I found a place to rent. I'm moving out of the hotel tomorrow or the day after.'

'That was quick.'

'I spent the weekend going round the letting agencies. Got a cottage in Turleigh.'

'There's smart.' His voice carries a note of envy. 'Places don't come up there very often.'

'I was lucky. It's somebody's weekend retreat from London, but they've been posted to Minnesota, poor sods.'

I'm *really* lucky. It's about ten times as nice as my Cornwall cottage, fond though I am of that. Cornish cottages are generally made of damp granite and poison you with radon, but Turleigh is cosy limestone. It has two en-suite power-showers, solid marble worktops in the kitchen, and a remote-controlled garage door.

'There must be a snag,' says Gary. 'Maybe it's haunted.'

'I can live with that.'

'Anyway. I just wanted to make sure you weren't upset.'

'Upset? What about?'

'Well. You know. The miners.' He sounds uncomfortable, and so he should.

'You get used to it. Just like they're going to have to get used to me.'

'OK,' says Gary. He sounds doubtful, though. 'Well. I guess so.'

'I've got to go,' I say. 'I'm expecting a call.' After I've put the phone down I think, Yeah, right. A call from Granny.

I pull open the top drawer in the chest under the window, and pull out handfuls of underwear to cram into my case. All black or nude colours, plain, strong and practical. One falls on to the floor and I bend to pick it up, admiring its smooth curves that fit my smooth curves exactly. Its shape reminds me of a suspension bridge: perfect engineering. Was it Howard Hughes who designed a bra for Jane Russell on the cantilever principle?

Bollocks, Kit, says Martin's voice in my head. *Go and buy a bra in shocking pink.*

★   ★   ★

In the night, I'm suddenly awake, staring into darkness. The room is pitch black, except for the red light on the television and a yellow line under the door. The only sound is the hiss of the weir water outside.

It's nearly six weeks since the roof fall in the flint mine.

I'm here under false pretences. By rights I should be dead.

I turn over, then over again. I keep seeing the face I haven't seen since I was fourteen. And fingers. Long, sensitive fingers. Fingers like white stalks, groping towards me in the dark . . . No. The room is too hot. I want to sleep, but know I won't. I'm afraid to sleep, in case Death realizes he missed me and I don't wake up

123

again. I can taste garlic from dinner, and wakefulness, metallic and dry, on the back of my tongue.

Can't someone turn the weir off?

White noise. White night.

★   ★   ★

I'm at my computer the next morning on site when the summons comes. It's like the blast of icy air that comes into the Portakabin with Rosie, the admin assistant with whom I'm sharing an office. The purdah principle: lodge the women together so you can keep an eye on them. To do that, we've been given our own office eunuch, thankfully absent at the moment.

'Brendan wants to see you,' says Rosie. She's balancing two brimming cups of coffee and trying to close the door with her bottom. 'We have to get a new kettle.'

Our eyes swivel automatically towards the third desk. It carries a computer, its screen plastered with yellow Post-it notes, a pharmacopoeia of vitamin pills and antihistamines, and one of those really naff figurines of Priapus they sell in gift shops in Greek tourist resorts. A trowel, an archaeologist's third hand, is propped in the crook made by its disproportionately huge member. Dickhead's not here at the moment, praise the Lord and pass the ammunition, preferably a fragmentation grenade I can pop under the cushion of his special posture stool. It's the sort that's supposed to straighten your spine, but Dickon still manages to look like a long curved streak of piss when he sits at it.

Rosie and I especially loathe Dickhead today, because last night he left late and locked up forgetting he'd left the kettle on. It didn't cut off automatically when it boiled, and the element has burned out. So every time we want a cuppa we have to totter over the frozen puddles to the big cabin where the kitchenette is. For

Rosie and me that's about every half-hour, and we're already fed up.

'I don't suppose it's the kettle Brendan wants to see me about?'

Rosie makes a face. ''Fraid not.'

'Well?'

'He should tell you.' She puts down the coffees, one on her neat desk, one on mine, which is already building up sedimentary layers of crumpled paper. She sticks one finger up in the direction of Dickon's posture stool.

Rosie and I have only known each other for a day and a bit, but I can see we're going to get along. I give her about forty seconds before she cracks and tells me the bad news. It's bound to be bad news: I've felt it coming since yesterday, underground, a minor quake to be sure, but destructive nonetheless.

She sits down at her desk, framed by a gallery of happy bouncing brothers and sisters and friends, all doing impossibly athletic things on ski slopes or rockfaces or amid raging torrents. Rosie's in her late twenties, when the joints are still elastic, and I bet her lithe, slender body is bouncing there alongside her chums, behind the camera snapping photos. Perhaps her boyfriend figures in some of them. He's one of the miners working on site: Huw, Welsh, from the Valleys, not one of Ted's crew.

'So?' I say.

She twists her jaw-length blonde hair into a corkscrew and secures it on top of her head with a bulldog clip. She's not finding it easy to meet my eye.

'Well . . . ' She faces me, and looks angry, helpless. 'Oh, rats, this is awful.'

'Cough it up.'

'Ted's crew have complained. Say they don't want a woman working underground.'

'Thought so. I could see it in their faces yesterday.'

'But they can't stop you, can they? It's sex discrimination, surely.'

My fingers find a dried-up wad of gum on the underside of my desk, and pick away at it. 'Well, technically it is. But . . . ' I don't know why I'm so calm.

The door opens, letting in more needles of freezing air. It's Gary. He's furious. 'I've just heard.'

He can't stand still. He's striding up and down our tiny seraglio, which gives him about one and a half steps before he bangs into Dickhead's stool. In the end he gives up and sits down on it abruptly.

'Heard?' I say.

'You must know. Fuck, I can't believe it. The free miners say it's bad luck to have a woman underground.'

'Yep. Brendan wants to see me.'

'I don't know what the hell he thinks he can do about it. They're threatening to quit. I've just had three in my office, claiming the last time a woman went into the workings there was a collapse the following day. That was you, by the way, Rosie. I can't believe — ' He slaps his hand on Dickon's desk. A nasal spray teeters on the edge, and falls to the floor. He looks at me properly for the first time since he came in. 'Why aren't you more upset?'

I glance down at my ragged fingernails. 'I am upset.'

'You don't bloody show it. I suppose you're used to it . . . '

'Actually, no, I'm not.' Suddenly I am angry, after all, really angry. I can feel tears pricking at the corners of my eyes, and a terrible wobbly feeling round my jaw, but I'm buggered if I'll give in to it. 'I've been all over the fucking world and nobody's ever refused to work with me before. And now a bunch of superstitious, pig-thick . . . '

The door bangs open again. It's Dickon. He's trying to hide how pleased he is behind a big stitched-on look of concern. 'Kit, my God. I've just heard. It's awful.'

126

No, you greasestain, it's a sodding disaster. I really must not cry in front of him. Fuck, fuck, fuck, just think of granite, serpentine, basalt, hard, obdurate rocks under lashing storms, the Cairngorms, Dartmoor tors . . . Do not be nice, Gary. Do not be kind. If you say something kind, I'm lost.

'Kit,' says Rosie, briskly, 'Brendan said *right away.*'

★ ★ ★

After the walk across the sub-zero hardcore to the mine manager's office, filling my lungs with cold air that tingles, I'm back in control, thanks to Rosie the rescuer. I get through the meeting with Brendan by imagining I'm watching from the ceiling. I see myself being tough, practical, not a single self-pitying wobble in the lower lip.

'Of course we're not going to give way to them,' he says. I nod.

'Of course it might be an idea not to go below ground for a day or two,' he muses, chewing his bottom lip to filter the words carefully through his tawny moustache. I look thoughtful.

'Of course you don't *really* have to go underground much at all, do you?' he ponders. I look mutinous. The moustache flattens out in a wide, placatory grin and he hastily backtracks. 'Of course, what I meant was yours is primarily a design and monitoring role, so it's not like you'll be underground every day, is it? I mean, most of your work is done at the computer. There isn't any necessity for you to be a presence at the workface . . . '

You always know you're in trouble when they retreat into manager-speak.

'Brendan,' I say, 'I am going down that shaft again. Maybe not today but some time.'

'Right. Yes. *Of course.*'

127

'The thing about the free miners,' says Dickon, smug that he can reveal his immense intellectual prowess to us, 'is that, seemingly, they're the direct descendants of the Celtic ironmasters in the Forest of Dean.'

'And that makes it OK, does it?' says Rosie sharply.

'No, no. What I meant was, iron working was an almost magical, priestly calling. Think of it — burrowing into the earth, forging the hard metal.'

'Yeah, right, very Freudian.'

'No, no, *no*. It's the danger I'm getting at. Mortality. Life is fragile underground. You could die any time — earth falls, flooding, firedamp, *buried alive.* You have to propitiate the gods. That's why there are so many superstitions attached to mining, same as fishermen and sailors.'

'You get women at sea,' says Rosie. 'I've sailed.'

'Know a lot of female trawler hands, do you?'

'Dickon's got a point,' says Gary, who's been leaning against the wall, saying nothing. He's been looking at me, though. Every time he catches my eye I have to glance away. 'What do you think, Kit?'

'I think, why women?'

'What do you mean?' says Dickon. He's genuinely interested, I'll give him that.

'Why not the colour green or sneezing underground? Why does it have to be women who bring bad luck? It's like we're always demon temptresses who seduce men, then accuse them of rape.'

And then, to my surprise, I see something shut down in Gary's face. What did I say?

*   *   *

'You're not superstitious about women, are you?' I say, at lunch-time in the pub across the road from the site.

Rosie's up at the cigarette-scarred bar ordering the sandwiches; she's forgotten to take the bulldog clip out of her hair. Gary and I are sitting at a table near the fake log fire. The place smells of flat lager and stale tobacco and occasionally you feel your feet sticking to the floor, but we don't have to change out of our boots to come in here.

'Of course not.'

'Only . . . ' I'm fiddling with a packet of sugar the previous occupants left on the table. It's one of those long, sausage-shaped ones and the sugar's gone rock hard. I get satisfaction from rolling it between finger and thumb until it goes soft and squidgy. 'Only I get the feeling it's not only the free miners who'd be more comfortable with me off the site.'

'Bollocks. You're paranoid.'

'Well, Dickon doesn't like me much.'

'Isn't it the other way round?'

'Pardon?'

'What have you got against Dickon?'

Rosie's mouthing something at us, but somebody's put the Happy Mondays on the jukebox and I can't hear what she's saying. I cup my hand to my ear.

'No cheese toasties,' says Gary. 'Bastards. They never have toasties when it's cold.' He puts his hands on his shoulders and flaps his elbows, mouthing, 'Chicken.'

'I'm going down the shaft when I want to.' I find another sugar tube tucked behind the ketchup. 'I'm not going to be intimidated.'

'I never thought you would be.'

'You're sure you don't have a problem with women on the site?'

Gary gives me the full benefit of those clear blue eyes. 'Kit, the best engineer I ever worked with was a woman. In Kazakhstan. She was the mine manager and she really knew what she was doing. Their industry isn't as regulated as ours, but her casualty record was spotless.'

He smiles fondly, and something wrings out my insides. 'Tough little bitch, mind.'

'Little?'

'Don't believe that old crap about Soviet women being built like shot-putters. She could have been a ballet dancer.'

The packet of sugar splits under my fingers and spills crystals over the tabletop. Fortunately Gary doesn't notice.

He's still good-looking. With his fleece off, in an old faded blue sweatshirt, you can see that his muscles are strongly defined for a man in his forties. Swimmer's shoulders, no hint of a gut yet.

— *pulled me against his chest. He smelt of soap and tobacco. His breath on my hair —*

But the main thing is, he isn't Nick.

Rosie arrives balancing drinks, strands of blonde hair escaping from the bulldog clip and falling into her eyes. There's a coke, a St Clement's, and a Becks. The Becks is mine. Gary looks disapproving as I pour the beer into the glass. 'You don't go down the shaft after drinking that stuff.'

'I'm not going down the shaft,' I say. 'Remember? Nobody wants a woman down there.'

* * *

It's not my day. As we're walking back to the site, my mobile rings.

'I'm sorry, Mrs Parry, we've got a problem with the cottage.'

For a moment I can't think what he's talking about. Or who he is. Then I remember. It's the estate agent. I'm supposed to be moving in this evening. My bags are in the car. I was going to drive there straight after work.

'It's the hot water. When the cleaner went in this morning, she noticed there was a problem. It looks like

130

the central-heating pump has packed up.'

'When will it be fixed?'

'Well, we hope to get someone out there tomorrow. But you never know. Best say Thursday?'

'Listen,' I say. 'There aren't any mines under the cottage, are there?'

'Mines?' The agent sounds genuinely shocked.

'Never mind,' I say. 'Ignore my paranoia.'

★   ★   ★

It's after five o'clock, a dirty, grimy afternoon, a thin, spiteful drizzle dampening the outside walls of the offices. The little boys are kicking a football again on the field beyond the gate. They seem to like playing in the dark. Every so often they shriek when two of them cannon into each other, and I don't think it's always an intentional tackle.

The lighted window of our office looks almost homelike, beaming out of the gloom. I'm carrying another cup of steaming coffee over the hardcore. Rosie's left early to buy us another kettle on her way home, but I need to stay on to get my head round the dimensions of the work. There are some load simulations I ought to do on the computer. A mining engineer who doesn't go underground: entirely possible, these days, I suppose, with the technology.

And, hey, what's there to go home to? A charming but utterly bland hotel room; the white noise of the weir. I suppose I should be grateful I have a bed.

In the car park, an engine turns over and over, reluctant to start in the cold. The miners finished their shift not long ago; they'll all be away home now. The motor finally catches and revs, and a set of headlights bounces across the site towards the security hut and the gate.

I need to get my head round the CAD software too.

Brendan's using a package that's different from the one I'm used to . . .

Bugger it. I'm going underground while no one's about.

I take two quick gulps of coffee, tip the rest on to the hardcore then run up the steps and grab my gear from the deserted office before I can change my mind.

* * *

I was half expecting to be thwarted. The shaft is usually locked after the miners come out; no one wants the kids to go looking for their ball down there. But the cover is open, the top of the ladder just visible in a yawning darkness that seems colder and darker even than when I first saw it last Friday. Strictly speaking, going down alone is stupid, illegal too: the company rules say you shouldn't go underground without letting someone know about it. But I don't want to give myself time to think. Screw the rules — I want to get straight down there.

On the other hand, I'd look pretty silly if someone came along and locked me in. In my pocket, stapled to the underground plan that Brendan updates every week, there's a copy of the site regulations. I tear it off and scribble a quick note on the back, leaving the white sheet of paper on top of the shaft cover where it can't be missed, luminous in the dusk, weighted down with a lump of limestone.

My fingers creep for comfort to the map pocket in my waterproof to touch what's inside. Smooth one side, rough the other. Then I start down the ladder, just a bit out of breath.

* * *

Face your demons. She said that to me, over and over again, when I messed up exams and had to resit, when I refused to go to parties or came home white-faced from the new school where I couldn't settle.

Face your demons. It's easier to wall them up. Maybe I should keep them that way. It's not fear; at least, I don't think it is. The things that scare you most, those are the things you have to do over and over again, and I do. It's just . . .

My feet land in the squelchy patch at the bottom of the ladder. The lights are on already — I hadn't expected that. Someone must have forgotten to turn them off. There's a misty halo round each bare bulb, struggling against the huge darkness beyond the steel walkway.

Some are born to sweet delight, and some are born to endless night . . . Fragments of verse out of nowhere, repeating over and over with the same beat as my boots striking the uneven ground. Where am I going? No idea. Haven't really decided; I just need to be down here, alone. The darkness goes on and on. My torchbeam picks out piles of rubble, lopsided pillars and buttresses. The air is full of that sharp, wet-cement smell. A deep sadness catches the back of my throat. Endless night, endless night . . .

Suddenly, uneven rows of pillars are stretching away into the distance, some with white shrouds — the place Gary called Co-op Cavern. I've come at least half a mile, with no idea how I got here. It is Co-op Cavern, isn't it? The plan's hard to read: my hand's shaking. There are underground roads heading off all over the place that I never noticed when I was down here yesterday.

I shouldn't have come alone. Too easy to get lost.

Time keeps jumping in a disconcerting way. Now I'm back in one of the narrow, low-roofed tunnels. My mind keeps switching off, blanking out, like a computer caught up in some mysterious internal processing and refusing to respond when you click the mouse. Hit any key . . .

A dark figure comes striding out of a side tunnel ahead of me, either failing to see me or ignoring me, hurrying ahead like Alice's White Rabbit. I almost drop the torch, my heart bashing at my ribcage. The figure blows its nose loudly.

'Dickon!' I say, before I can stop myself.

Dickon, in an old waxed jacket, yelps and swivels round, as startled as I was to discover someone else underground. Like every archaeologist I've ever met, he seems to have an aversion to wearing high-visibility gear. Anyone less self-absorbed might have asked me what I was doing, but fortunately it doesn't occur to him. 'Bloody hell, Kit. You nearly gave me a coronary, creeping around like that.'

'I thought I was on my own down here.'

'Ditto. Give me a mo to get my breath back.' He sinks down on to a block of stone, patting his chest, his hanky still in his hand. We're both breathless with shock. If I'd had my wits about me, I would have kept quiet and let him go before he spotted me, but now I'm stuck with him. The way he's panting is making me twitchy.

'Sorry,' I say. 'I was just on my way out.' I try to sidle past him.

'That's the wrong way.'

He's right. I'm totally disoriented. His bloody fault — I was fine till I bumped into him.

'You'd better stick with me. I've only got one more thing to photograph.'

Of course. That's why I'm twitchy. Instead of being round his neck, the camera is in his jacket pocket, pushing it out of shape; it's visible as he leans forward and the pocket gapes open. I must have caught a glimpse of it as he sat down. I make a big effort to slow my breathing. It's OK, I can cope. It's just a bloody

134

camera to photograph the archaeology, that's all. Dickon's job is to catalogue what's down here before it's sealed for ever. I'm not afraid of cameras now. I'm not. I use them all the bloody time when I'm with Martin.

'What have they come across today?' I ask, wheezing a bit still, like an asthmatic suddenly aware of an unseen animal. Dickon wipes his nose again and stuffs his handkerchief into his pocket on top of the camera, which makes me feel slightly better.

'There's an old crane I ought to take a look at, apparently, just beyond where we were yesterday. The miners have built a new stretch of walkway to it.' He gets to his feet. 'I usually come down after the shift has ended so I don't get in their way. My wife would murder me if she knew. She reckons I work too many hours as it is. But she's back home in London so she isn't to know what I get up to.'

His laugh is far too suggestive. I hadn't pictured Dickhead married; there's the puzzling question of what woman would be attracted to him. I try to keep as far away from him as I can in the narrow walkway, kicking myself for letting him know I was there, and conscious that I shouldn't be underground anyway. Brendan made it clear I should stay out of the workings, at least until the fuss had settled down. And I had a drink at lunchtime. Only a half of lager, but I could lose my job for being underground with alcohol in my system. Still, Dickon isn't to know — he wasn't in the pub.

'Good job I bumped into you,' says Dickon, as if he's reading my thoughts. 'You could have got yourself lost, you know. You shouldn't come down here alone until you're more familiar with the place.'

'I brought the map,' I say defensively.

'The plan of the workings?' He laughs. 'Fat lot of good that would do you.'

'It's accurate, isn't it?'

135

'Oh, exact. As far as it goes. The workings have never been definitively mapped. The plan's based on above-ground survey techniques, and we've already come across half a dozen passages and voids that theoretically shouldn't be there, according to the map. You only have to get a bit confused,' something in his voice suggests he thinks that's bound to happen: even right-on blokes, and of course he's one of those, know that women are challenged in the spatial-awareness department, 'and you could be up Shit Creek without knowing it.'

As if to prove his point, another passageway opens up on the left. Dickon shines his torchbeam on the quarry face beside it. 'Look. Quarrymen's graffiti. Not a very interesting example. Relatively modern.'

It says: 'Any man farting in this breakfast hole during meal times will be fined 6d.'

'There was nothing to suggest *that* passage existed until we got here.' Dickon dismissively flicks the beam away from the graffiti and probes the blackness with his torch. The light only reaches a few metres before it's swallowed. 'Dead end. Dark, isn't it? Know what we found down there? Bones of a cat.'

'Not very nice,' I say, keeping my voice as controlled as I can.

'Might have been somebody's pet that got lost. Might have been killed by the quarrymen.' He seems to relish the idea. 'Maybe that's the other reason they don't like you, Kit. Your name. Cats are supposed to be bad luck in mines too, aren't they?'

He's so obvious I feel like laughing. What I want to say is: First, Dickon, I've been working underground so long I don't easily scare. Second, being scared doesn't turn me on, OK? Nothing about you turns me on. And third, don't try copping another feel.

So why don't I?

Because it feels like the darkness is whispering round me.

You little tart.

Long white fingers reaching for me . . .

Through the steel struts of the walkway, the pillars seem to go on and on, losing themselves eventually in darkness. For a moment I can believe I've lost myself among them, and Dickon is walking on alone, a tiny figure receding in the distance, talking to himself. But, no, I'm still in the walkway and he's striding along next to me, uncomfortably close. I force myself to sound as natural as possible. 'So you're saying there could be whole areas of quarrying no one knows about? Ones we might miss altogether, unless we go outside the walkways?'

'Kit, we don't go outside the walkways.' Dickon gives me a withering look. He doesn't understand why I'm pressing the point. 'You heard Gary yesterday, didn't you? Any work we do has to be carried out in complete safety.'

The works area looks forlorn without the bustle of hard-hats and yellow jackets. Steel poles and welding gear are piled up near the end of the walkway. To my eye there's been little progress since yesterday, but Dickhead's beside himself with excitement. He grabs my shoulder, and I can't stop myself tensing, but he doesn't notice. His big nostrils flare with enthusiasm; they are as moist and slimy as a cow's. 'Look at that,' he says. 'Early nineteenth century, got to be.'

At first I think he's talking about the buttress — another dry-stone wall put up by the quarrymen to support the ceiling. The workmanship is remarkable, every stone fitting neatly against the next, not a scrap of mortar in sight. But he's pointing his torch into the chamber beside it.

I've never really understood men's enthusiasm for old

machinery. The crane is so black with rust I almost missed it in the darkness, a tall, corroded column fixed to both floor and ceiling.

Dickon starts measuring and photographing, explaining about chog holes and Lewis bolts and stuff I can't be bothered to listen to. The flashes pulse against the cavern walls and give me a headache. Coming down here was futile. If I wanted to make a point, there's no one to bear witness, only Dickhead. I sit down on an upturned bucket, and close my eyes. I wish Martin was there.

'Don't you ever want to go beyond the walkways?' I find myself saying.

Dickon's voice is positively pious. 'It's far too dangerous.'

'Come on, Dick, I bet you do when no one else is here.'

I open my eyes, and there's been another of those disconcerting jumps in time. Somehow I've arrived on the other side of the steel struts. Space and darkness swell round me. I turn slowly, three hundred and sixty degrees, flicking my torch on and watching the circle of light run over the ceiling, the walls, the pillars, like a small bright insect.

'Kit?' comes Dickon's voice. 'Kit, where . . . Oh, bloody hell.'

'Don't tell me you've never done this.'

'Kit, you really should . . . '

But my bright insect has stopped, puzzled. Is that just a flaw in the stone or . . .

'Dick,' I say. 'Come and take a look at this.'

'Kit, there really is a risk. We'll get to it, whatever it is, when they've built the walkway a bit further.'

'Give me your camera.'

'Don't be daft.'

Inside the circle of the torchbeam there is a carving, I think, something scratched on to the rock.

It's impossible to tell much about it from here: I'll have to get closer for a proper look.

'What the hell do you think you're doing?' comes Gary's voice. 'You fucking idiot, Kit. You do *not* go outside the walkways.'

12

'You silly bitch,' says Gary Bennett. He's so angry he's shaking. The veins stand out on his neck, but his voice is icy, contemptuously calm. 'Get back in the walkway right away. That roof could come down *any moment*.'

I don't move, frozen by his voice. *He's going to hit me if I get close enough to let him*. I don't mean Gary. There's someone else here with me in the dark.

'Kit . . . ' says Dickon, weakly. 'He's right. This is a high-hazard area — as soon as they've got the walkway in they have to start filling.'

His words pull me back to the present. This shouldn't be destroyed. I have to stop them pumping concrete into this part of the mine.

The mark on the pillar is a small, gawky carving, scratched into the rock as if someone did it in a hurry.

. . . brings a message from the sun god, ordering first the hunting, then the slaying, in the cave, of the bull . . .

My fingers hover just above the surface. I daren't touch it.

From the animal's blood and semen gushing on to the ground, plants grow . . .

What's it doing here? If I'm right, it makes no bloody sense.

'Toss me the camera, Dickon,' I say, careful to give him both syllables. 'I'll come back once I've got a picture of this.'

'If you don't get your arse in here right away I'm coming to get you,' says Gary. I can't bear the contempt in his voice. My foot twitches. Perhaps he's right. I shouldn't be here. I'm endangering all of us.

Dickon casts a quick, embarrassed glance at Gary. But he's an archaeologist. Even when the roof's about to cave in on their heads, archaeologists just have to know. He throws me the camera. It lands in my fingers like a grenade; I have to ignore the cold, slithery feel of the plastic casing as I start to line up the viewfinder.

'Can you shine your torches over here?'

'You stupid cow, you won't be told,' says Gary, but he shines his torch on the pillar.

Three circles of light, coming together. And in their meeting, a bird, the messenger of the sun . . .

The camera flashes. I hold it steady . . . It flashes again. And again.

I fiddle with the buttons, review the pictures. 'Got it.' And I walk back across the chamber and climb through the struts to safety. I'm shaking, but I did it. If I'm right, it was worth it.

If I'm wrong . . .

I can't go there.

★   ★   ★

I can't settle. The hotel room seems to have shrunk by several feet in every direction. I'm up, down, sitting on the corner of the bed, up again. Then down, at the dressing-table where I've plugged in the laptop, with the pictures downloaded from Dickon's camera on to the screen. One, two, three. I slide-show them over and over again. Up. Pace to the window; look out over the waterside gardens. Frost glitters on the lawn, turned orange by lights in the flowerbeds.

Dickon thought I'd gone mental when we looked at the pictures in the Portakabin.

'Graffiti. Eighteenth century at the very oldest. Interesting, yes, but not . . .'

He's wrong. I know he's wrong. He doesn't know what he's talking about.

And why should you know any more than he?

He's a pompous git. An arsehole.

141

He's an *archaeologist*. You're not.

He's not a specialist, though. Not in this kind of thing. He's an industrial archaeologist who knows rusty old cranes and rotted wheel-barrows, that's all. Why trust what he says?

He's been working in the quarries for the last six months. That makes him a specialist here, doesn't it?

Yes, but he's not a specialist in this kind of . . .

I pick up the phone. I know someone who is.

* * *

'Martin, you old pillock. I've got something I'd like you to come and take a look at. I'll email a photo, but you've got to see it *in situ*.'

'Well, you don't exactly go in for foreplay, do you, Kit? I can't.'

'What do you mean, you can't?'

'California, remember? I'm going next week.'

I stare for a moment through the window at nothing but my own frowning reflection, the mobile squashed between my jaw and my shoulder. The night porter has turned out the lights in the flowerbeds, and the hotel gardens have vanished into darkness. Somewhere out there is the weir: its faint static is in one ear, in the other the hiss of the phone signal on its long journey to the satellite and back.

'Cancel it.'

'What?'

'There'll be terrorists. I heard it on the news. I had a dream. They'll hijack the plane and crash it into the Golden Gate Bridge. Come and see this instead.'

'Kit, I can't . . . '

I kick the dressing-table. The laptop trembles. Earthquake. San Andreas fault.

'Come at the weekend, then. If you don't, this could be buried under foam concrete by the time you get back.'

*   *   *

I flip my phone shut, and perch on the end of the bed again. When I look down, my right leg is trembling. I pick up the glass of wine from the dressing-table: there are concentric rings of ripples on the surface.

Gary said nothing the whole way back to the shaft entrance. Under the walkway lights I could see his jaw moving; it looked as if he was grinding his teeth to stop himself saying something. Even Dickon was lost for words. The walk seemed to go on for ever, but not long enough. I was breathless with what I thought I'd seen; I was scared of what Gary would say when he eventually spoke. I didn't want to face his contempt, but I knew I had to be right this time. There really is something there, and I caught it on the camera: something everyone else has missed, something really old . . .

My head aches with the effort of ignoring the insistent, sceptical voice in my head, asking: What? What did you actually see?

What did you find?

Dickon went up the ladder first. As I put my foot on the bottom rung, Gary said, 'We'll discuss this in my office.' He turned away, and started switching off lights on the board at the bottom of the shaft.

I have to be right this time. No room for doubt, no wishful thinking.

I swallow a mouthful of wine, and light another cigarette. I'm in a non-smoking room tonight, so I tap my ash into my cup, where it floats on half an inch of cold coffee.

143

★　★　★

'Doesn't it ever make you tired, Kit?' said Gary, once we were on our own.

'Tired?'

'Breaking rules. It must get exhausting.'

He's right. I'm knackered. Sometimes it's so much effort. But I can't stop it now. It's habit.

'I don't understand how you've lasted so long in the industry, if this is the way you behave.'

His voice is so clear in my head he could be in the room now. He was sitting behind his desk: nothing friendly about this little chat.

'Tell me one good reason why I shouldn't report this.'

Pitch dark outside, the floodlights on, but all the other offices shut and locked. Apart from the security guard in his hut by the gate, no one on site but us. Gary's office, with its own separate entrance, is at the other end of the big cabin where we had the site meeting on the first day. I couldn't take my eyes off the door to the meeting room behind his desk: shut, but somehow implying that a committee of staff from Head Office was assembled behind it, waiting to sack me.

'I don't usually behave like this, as you put it.'

'So what's got into you? First, you drink at lunchtime before going underground. You know bloody well that alone is enough to get you fired. Next, you go outside the walkways. Kit, this project is so tightly regulated no one can fart underground without asking permission from the Inspector of Mines . . . '

Any man farting in this breakfast hole during meal times . . .

' . . . and we have to be seen to be doing it right so we can get government funding. Without that, there is no project. No project, no work. You're putting all our jobs in jeopardy.'

. . . will be fined 6d.

144

'I know. I'm sorry.'

'How can I be sure you aren't going to do it again?'

Gary's desk was painfully neat. Laptop: closed. Grey plastic in-tray, containing one piece of paper. Red plastic pencil-tidy, with a RockDec biro, a highlighter pen and two pencils, sharpened. Not a photo, not a postcard, not a biscuit crumb. The only thing out of place was the paperclip in Gary's strong fingers, twisting, bending into one shape after another, a shepherd's crook, a light sabre, a one-armed one-legged pipe-cleaner man.

'Gary, I . . . ' The words were getting stuck somewhere between brain and mouth. 'I was really upset by what happened this morning. The miners . . . '

Gary looked at me as if I was a piece of grit in the tread of his boot. 'Kit, it's not pleasant right now, but you know as well as I do that whole stupid business is going to blow over. The miners can't get you kicked off the job. They have to work with whoever the company appoints.'

'It's never happened to me before.'

'Really?' He didn't buy that for a moment, and quite right too. There's plenty of sexism in the industry. Women who work in mining learn to handle it by being as professional as they can.

And never letting themselves flirt on the job . . .

'I mean I've never experienced anything as bare-faced. Nothing so direct as men refusing to work with me.'

'That's hardly an excuse for behaving the way you did. Now you've given them every reason to refuse to work with you.'

'No. It isn't an excuse. I know. But it threw me off balance.'

The paperclip, twisted out of all recognition, snapped. Gary dropped the pieces into the bin under the desk. Then he looked at the ceiling. He opened his

145

mouth, and closed it again. I waited. 'I can see it's not been the best of starts,' he said eventually.

I knew then I was going to be okay. He'd decided to accept the lame excuse.

He should have sacked me on the spot. Except, of course, nobody gets sacked on the spot nowadays. There have to be proper procedures, formal warnings, the whole weary business in case the sackee turns round and sues for unfair dismissal. He must have been weighing it up, calculating how thrilled the company would be to have to go through all that and meanwhile recruit yet another mining engineer at short notice.

'OK,' he went on. 'I should report it, but I won't.'

There was a faint, hesitant knock at the door. Before Gary could say anything, it opened, and Rupert, the bat expert, stuck his head in.

'Sorry to interrupt, Gary. Just wanted to let you know I'm away in London until Saturday, but I've lent my keys to a student.'

'She could have had my spare.'

'You weren't around to ask and I didn't like to take it. The new incubators have been delivered, by the way.'

'Wonderful,' said Gary. 'I'd love to hear about them, Rupert, but Kit and I have some stuff to sort out . . . '

'Oh. Sorry. I see.' Rupert backed through the door apologetically. Gary waited long enough for him to get out of earshot before continuing.

'But even though I won't report it, I'll be watching you. One chance only, Kit. Two strikes and you're out.'

'Thanks.'

'And there are conditions. One, you do not go into the mines outside working hours without telling me. Two, you promise me not to go outside the walkways again. *Whatever* you think you've seen.'

'Right.' My eyes got tangled up with his, and for a long moment neither of us could get loose, but to my relief he dropped his gaze and started looking for

another paperclip. He seemed as embarrassed as I felt.
'Leave the archaeology to the archaeologist, OK?'

★   ★   ★

In my hotel room, I take another big, reflective swallow of wine. I haven't worked out yet how I'm going to get myself underground again, let alone Martin, without Gary finding out. We need to be really close up to examine that marking on the wall. But I'll think about that in the morning. I get up and open the window to let out the smell of fags, shuddering at the wintry blast it lets in.

★   ★   ★

It was the sound of a hammer that woke me. *Tap tap tap*: someone trying not to be heard.

I pushed back the sheet and swung my feet on to the floor. My legs looked sickly and wasted in the orange glow through the curtains. I crept out of the room and down the stairs — *tap tap tap* — through the narrow hallway that tonight smelled of stale cigarettes — *tap tap tap* — into the kitchen. The back door stood open and I slipped through it. The orange streetlamp made everything unnatural, harder, lurid, shadowed, like frames in a comic strip. Bucket, broom, coiled hose: the shapes took on an extraordinary significance against the brickwork.

I edged round the open garage door to look down at my father as he worked.

On the bench lay the photograph of my mother in its damaged gilt frame.

My father was pounding and pounding at it with the hammer.

★   ★   ★

And now I *am* awake, listening to the sound of the weir. I feel as if I've been lying in an ashtray. The room stinks, my mouth is dry, my nose is blocked, sleep and cold have curled my body like a pretzel and I have a headache. A sickly yellow haze seeps under the door: they keep the lights on all night in the hotel corridor.

It always happens like this: something catches me off guard in the night, and I wake up to stop myself dreaming. I roll over on to my back and lean across to check my watch. It's five in the morning; I have to get back to sleep or I'll feel like shit at work. I reach for an imaginary stone, and place it carefully on another, as in one of the dry-stone walls underground. Just to be sure, I also imagine a big bucket of mortar, so I can plaster up the cracks. I take another stone, exactly the right shape to fit. There's an ammonite in it, and I run my fingers over the ridges, then lay the stone carefully on my wall. A trowelful of mortar on top, then another stone.

This one has a carving on it, like the one I saw on the pillar.

What if I'm *not* right? But I am, I have to be.

★ ★ ★

I've emailed the photos to Martin at the university. He claims his computer at home is too old and knackered to download big files. At work, I get a hasty, excited email back.

> i think you're rihgt. Have to see close to be sure thouhg.

I glare at the long curve of Dickon's back, balanced on his posture stool, which forces him to tuck his feet under him, soles up. He hasn't taken the price label off one shoe. It's filthy and scuffed but I can just make out

148

the red disc that says *Sale*.

He seems absorbed in something on the computer screen. I think he's playing Battleships.

Arivnig Fday by train 1515, meet me. Looknig forwd to staynig at Chateau Parry.

I decide to miss lunch in the pub. There are some load calculations I'm having trouble with. I want to check why the last engineer, the one who got the job in Congo, thought it was so essential right away to fill that big cavern where they're working, the void where I saw the carving. The main road passes close by, but the void isn't directly beneath. I've been trying to do some virtual mapping of the area, plotting in the pillars supporting the roof, trying to work out what would happen if one collapsed — would the whole lot go like dominoes? The computer keeps crashing, though, as if it really doesn't want to think about the possibility.

Besides, I don't want to see Gary if I can help it.

But, of course, I do want to see him. I keep remembering the way his eyes tangled with mine yesterday, the feeling of getting snagged on them.

Suddenly it's a hot summer night, and I'm running across Poppy's hallway, scared of my platform heels skidding on the parquet. I'm pulling open the front door and there are Gary and his friends on the doorstep.

Yeah, right. Look where that got you.

Don't even go there.

I pull open my desk drawer to look for some chocolate to keep me going instead of lunch. The door opens and Dickon comes in.

'Thought you'd gone to the pub with the others,' I say.

'Just went to get myself a sandwich. I thought *you'd* be in the pub.'

He's sitting down at his desk, setting down a

cardboard beaker that smells of really good coffee, pulling the plastic off a triangular sandwich box.

'Where'd you get that?' I ask. The chocolate has lost its appeal; I can feel the sugar turning to yeast in my gut.

'Haven't you found the deli yet?'

'Nobody told me there was one.'

He sinks his teeth into the sandwich and bits of creamy mayonnaise squidge out along the seam. 'You still working on those load calculations for Mare's Hill?'

'Almost finished.'

'There's no point, you know. Dan's figures were checked and double-checked. That area's got to be filled as a priority.'

'I don't see why. It's not under the main road, there can't be any significant traffic . . . '

'Take a look at what's on top.'

He's sitting there with a smirk on his face, as if he knows he's got me. I can't see why he should be so pleased with himself. Doesn't he want to save what's underground? I click to open a new window on the screen, pull up the big scale Ordnance Survey map, superimpose it on the plan of the workings . . .

'There's just office buildings . . . Oh.' I've worked it out. I can't bloody believe it. No wonder we're being told to get a move on and fill the area. It's only the sodding Ministry of Defence on top.

'See?' says Dickon. 'Seriously, Kit, I don't like it any more than you do. But I've worked in rescue archaeology for a long time now, and I know when there isn't a cat in hell's chance of saving what might be there, because of who owns the site. Be realistic, girl. The minute the funding comes through — and this is what makes it likely it will come through, sooner rather than later — the foam concrete gets pumped in to prop up Our Brave Boys.'

***

I nip off to the ladies', and when I come back, I find Brendan sitting in my chair. His RockDek sweatshirt is stretched across his big chest, his tawny hair's gone curly in the damp and his droopy moustache makes him look more than ever like a cowboy cop who's arrived to clean up New York. My heart sinks. Forget eyes tangling and hormonal breathlessness. Gary, the bastard, has shopped me after all.

'Kit.' He tries to make it seem he's surprised to see me, even though he's plonked himself at my desk. 'I see you've been running the load figures through for Mare's Hill.'

Why doesn't he snoop about on Dickon's computer? It's probably oozing with kiddie-porn.

'I wasn't convinced it's necessary to prioritize it,' I say, and hold my breath.

'Ach, there's no doubt about that,' says Brendan. The moustache is up and he's showing all his tombstone teeth, which suggests to me he's lying through them. 'I went over those figures several times with Dan, to be certain.'

'But the cavern ceiling is solid,' I point out. 'The bore holes show the quarrying didn't take the stone right up to the subsoil. You've got at least six metres there, which is more than there is over the high street section, and we're not prioritizing *that*.'

'Look at the pillars,' says Brendan. 'They were robbed for stone in the nineteenth century. That crane we found proves the area's been quarried twice.'

'I still reckon — '

'Gilmerton,' says Brendan, playing his trump, to show that this cowboy from Hicksville ain't gonna be taken by the big-city card-sharps. 'That's what they said about the Gilmerton quarries. But it only takes one pillar to go . . . ' The moustache comes down, to remind me of

151

how serious that was. There were fatalities. Goldfish lives could have been saved, if not for dangerous optimists like me. 'Domino effect. The lot could come crashing down.'

We're arguing about load figures. Nobody's said anything about going underground after a beer, or leaving the walkways. And Brendan's just doing his big friendly brother act — *Sorry, sis, you'd know about these things if you weren't handicapped by an undeveloped sense of spatial awareness, but I'm here to save you making too much of a tit of yourself* — instead of lapsing into management-speak again and handing me my cards. It looks like maybe Gary didn't shop me, after all.

I want to tell Brendan we shouldn't fill the Mare's Hill void until we've investigated the mark on the pillar. But he'd say, What mark on the pillar? Which pillar, exactly? How the fuck did you see that, lassie, when the walkway's more than fifteen fucking metres away?

I look helplessly towards Dickon, who knows about the mark but refuses to recognize its significance. He's got his back to me and won't turn round.

'Anyway,' says Brendan, 'I didn't drop in to argue about load calcs. I came to give you some good news. We've sorted the problem with the miners.'

For a second I can't work out what he means, and then I see Ted with the tattoos glowering at me on Monday afternoon. 'Sorted it?'

'Had a word with the union rep. He agreed it was outrageous.'

He would. The free miners don't belong to any union. He doesn't have to back them.

'So, how does that help us?'

'We had a meeting and reminded them there were a lot of Polish miners with EU citizenship who'd be only too happy to work with a woman.'

A horrible suspicion starts wriggling in the part of my

mind where I stow my paranoia. Hasn't this happened unusually fast? Were Brendan and the union rep *disappointed* that the free miners caved in? Did the company maybe appoint a woman specifically because it would get up the free miners' noses?

No, they couldn't be that devious. I spent too many years married to a conspiracy theorist. Poor old Nick saw corporate plots wherever he turned his journalistic eye. And he wasn't averse to a spot of emotional conspiracy, if he thought he could outmanoeuvre me. Brendan and his moustache haven't the subtlety for that.

'Well,' I say, 'that is good news.'

'I don't say they'll be eating out of your hand like sweet little puppies,' says Brendan, 'but you're a big strong girl, aren't you?'

★   ★   ★

I go for a walk to clear my head. I have a computer headache, one of those grinding, queasy niggles that lurks behind your eyes after a morning in front of the screen, not quite bad enough for painkillers but you don't exactly feel like tap-dancing.

The Ministry of Defence compound lies just off the main road: a department that now has something to do with supply ships. From outside it has a sad, derelict air: square, flat-roofed sixties-style office blocks behind a high chain-link fence topped with rolls of barbed wire. Curtainless, smeary windows reflect a leaden sky. I remember it in my childhood, when Poppy's dad worked there: bustle, big sleek cars and snapping salutes. Now there's just one military sentry at the barrier, stamping his feet and glancing longingly at the warm gatehouse. Nobody's going in or out. They moved most of the Admiralty from Bath to Bristol years ago.

The sentry spots a black car coming up the road,

grows two inches and sticks his chest out in case it's a bigwig. But it carries on past. He stays at attention because there are two young women walking along the pavement pushing buggies. They have long dark hair and tight jeans, not even wearing coats, though I'm bundled up like Nanook of the North against the cold. They're pretending to ignore the soldier, but you can tell they're aware of him by the way they walk, leaning towards each other, laughing, moving their heads to shake their long hair back over their shoulders. Just as they pass him, one of the women stops and leans forward to tuck her child's teddy more securely down the side of the buggy.

She must be about the same age as my mother was.

On the other side of the road I'm walking briskly, speeding up my pace to knock that headache out of my skull, and I don't look back to see if he reacts to her flashing her cleavage.

13

Suddenly it was half-term. My father, as usual, was at a loss. Every term, he seemed to forget the holiday was going to happen, and when I reminded him that Friday night there was no school the following week, he looked confused. 'A whole week?'

'Yes.' I tried not to look too smug.

'This is a bit unexpected.' He glanced helplessly at the kitchen drawers, as if he hoped one would spring open and throw out a letter from the school to contradict me. 'When I was a boy, half-term was a *day*.'

I'd heard this before. It went with stories about how hard my father worked at school, rulers thwacked on open palms, and a kindly science teacher who'd almost persuaded him to stay on at the grammar school and try for university. But my father had had his mother to support, a widow who stared out of the window all day, pining for my granddad buried somewhere along the Burma railway. There was no choice. My dad left school and became apprenticed at one of the quarries.

'Your exams are coming up anyway. I suppose it's a good opportunity to do some revision.'

No, it's not, I wanted to say. *It's a good opportunity to loll in fields frothing with cow parsley, and pretend we're going to write a letter to Gary that we'll never post. Or hang out round Poppy's pool. Or go shopping.* I had worn the stolen bra all week in the hope of bumping into Gary on the way to school. It was only with the greatest reluctance I took it off at night before bed.

I didn't say any of this. My father's helpless expression could shift to furious as fast as cloud shadows race on a blustery day.

155

'I wish I could take time off,' he continued, 'but . . .'
He stared out of the window. 'Big job. You know.' He'd
just started work with a team of builders renovating one
of the posh houses on the hill behind the Royal
Crescent.

'That's OK,' I said, relieved.

'Tell you what. Come up and meet me in my
lunch-hour one day,' he said, brightening. 'We can sit in
Victoria Park and have sandwiches. A picnic.'

Did he talk about me to his workmates? I could
imagine how he'd introduce me: *This is my clever
daughter, Katie.* There was pride on his face when he
came to parents' evenings at the school. Wouldn't the
other workmen think it odd, him going off for lunch
with a thirteen-year old girl instead of joining them at
the pub? But maybe he didn't go to the pub with them
anyway. I wondered what they made of him. Did he joke
with them? Or keep himself to himself? And did they
ever see the side of him that frightened me?

'I'd love that, Dad,' I said.

★   ★   ★

On Monday morning I walked over to Trish's house.
Midcombe was in the valley on the other side of the hill,
a village attached to Bath by a steep, umbilical lane.
Coming down it, I could see cottage gardens splashed
like careless paint between low stone walls. Trish's
mother was in theirs, snipping half-heartedly at a
rosebush.

The Kleins' house was beautiful. Unlike most of the
cottages, which were faced with Bath stone, it was
painted white. The windows were arched like those of a
church, graceful and serene.

I paused to stroke the big ammonite in the garden
wall, running my fingers over its ridges. Then I opened
the gate and went in.

156

'Katie,' called Trish's mother, putting down her secateurs with what looked like relief. I swerved off the path leading to the front door under its wrought-iron trellised porch and went towards her. I had always liked Mrs Klein. She didn't look down on me, the way Poppy's mother did. I always had the feeling that if ever Trish and Poppy decided to drop me, Mrs Klein would make them pick me up again.

She was wearing a reddish linen dress, plain but elegant. Her long honey-coloured hair was swept back by a scarf. Her arms were smooth and tanned, and there was no sag under her chin, though I knew she was only a few years younger than Mrs Owen. I hardly reached her shoulder and was half her weight, but I still felt like a lump beside her.

'Hello,' she said, smiling, as if I had made her morning by turning up. I loved her voice too. So clear and crisp. *Hello*. Not *hallo*, or *'ullo*, or *'lo*, the way other people said it.

'I've come to see Trish,' I said. Of course I'd come to see Trish, but Mrs Klein had the gift of making you believe that you might have come just to see her.

'She isn't here.' She tucked a strand of hair back under the scarf. She always looked ready for a fashion shoot, like the ones Trish had said made her famous in the early sixties. Today her lips were painted red-brown to match the dress.

'Robert took her to London for a few days,' she went on. 'They're staying with her grandmother in Twickenham.' She saw my face fall. 'She probably didn't have time to tell you. It was only fixed at the weekend.'

'Oh. Right.' I looked desperately round the garden for something else to say. 'Your roses are lovely.'

She glanced at the old-fashioned pergola. Trailing stems flopped over it like fainting divas, coppery buds almost the colour of her lips. ' 'Albertine'. I ought to have cut it back harder last year. Why don't you come in anyway and have a coffee?'

And manage a whole conversation? But the road back up the hill was steep, and I was hot.

'Thank you,' I said. 'I'd love that.'

She laughed. 'Katie, you're always so polite.' Was that a compliment or a criticism?

The kitchen was vast, and greenly dim because of the wisteria round the window. Trish's mother sat me at the stripped pine table and set a coffee-pot to warm. In spite of the heat outside, an elderly tortoiseshell cat had draped itself over the hot-plate cover on the Aga. It hopped arthritically to the floor as Mrs Klein put the kettle on.

I was amazed: she even ground fresh coffee beans. She measured them in handfuls into the grinder. Some clattered off the tiled worktop on to the floor, and she didn't bother to pick them up. I bent down to help.

'Oh, leave them, Katie, the daily comes in and does the floor tomorrow,' she said. *Tomorrow?* In our kitchen they'd have to be swept up immediately. Not that we had fresh coffee beans, let alone a daily.

Stephen, Trish's younger brother, wandered into the kitchen. He shot me a quick glance of loathing. I sent one back, but he had already turned away and was lolling against the dresser, making me worried for Mrs Klein's collection of blue and white china. She must have had more than a hundred pieces, a patchwork collection of jugs and stray cups and saucers, all bought in junk shops, according to Trish. I wondered if she felt about them the way I did about ammonites.

'Mum, I'm bored.'

'Why don't you go and finish the pruning for me?'

'Don't want to. Can't you . . . '

Trish's mother switched on the grinder and the noise drowned whatever he was saying. He made a face at her. She made a face back, and turned off the grinder. 'If I give you a pound will you finish it?'

'Deal.' He held out his hand. Mrs Klein dug into the squashy leather shoulder-bag hanging on the back of one of the chairs, and laid a pound note on Stephen's outstretched palm. He jammed his hand quickly into his trouser pocket before she could change her mind. She crinkled her eyes in amusement as she watched him slip out of the door, followed more slowly by the old cat, its hindquarters stiff and dragging.

'That boy will buy and sell us all one day.' She poured boiling water over the coffee and brought the pot to the table. I slipped a mat under it for her. 'Don't worry, he's at that age where he's horrible to everyone. I can't wait for him to take common entrance so I can pack him off to Malvern.'

'Why do you send the boys to boarding-school, but not Trish?' I asked.

Mrs Klein sat down on the chair opposite me. 'What a bloody good question. Because their father went.'

'And you didn't?'

'Katie, if I had my way I'd keep them all at home. They're my lovelies, and I miss them every moment they're gone. But it's what Robert's family do.' She stood up again. 'Mug or cup?'

'Cup, please, Mrs Klein.' I'd never manage a whole mug of proper coffee. I might have palpitations, like Mrs Owen. Whatever they were.

She poured coffee for us both, and offered me milk out of a blue and white jug shaped like a cow.

'Do you miss your mum, Katie?'

Shock took the breath out of me. Nobody grown-up ever talked to me about my mother. 'I don't know,' I said. 'I never really knew her.'

'I bet she misses you.'

I looked down at my coffee. Little black specks spun in lazy circles on the surface.

159

'Do you ever think of looking for her?' asked Mrs Klein.

I didn't know what to say. My mother was such an absence in my life she was a presence. There was a hole in me I knew wouldn't ever be filled without her. But I couldn't say that to anyone, let alone Trish's mother. She was trying to make me look at her, staring at me in the hope I'd lift my eyes to hers. I could feel them boring into the top of my head. But I didn't dare look up in case I cried.

'She doesn't want me to find her,' I said, to the black specks on the coffee.

'Rubbish,' said Trish's mother. 'Whatever makes you think that?'

'She never . . . ' It was too painful to say more. I dug my fingernails into a groove on the worn pine tabletop. There was a crease of sticky dirt caught in it, too deep for a duster to reach, but I tried to pick it out with my little finger.

'I don't write to the boys,' said Mrs Klein. 'I always think they'll be embarrassed. I tell myself they're growing up and they don't want their mother slobbering over them. Has it ever occurred to you that your mother might be afraid to get in touch?'

'Afraid?'

'Afraid you'll hate her for going away.'

'Oh.' I scraped out a crumb of dirt with my fingernail, and rolled it into a ball on the tabletop. 'But I'm the reason she went away.'

'*What*?'

'That's what my dad thinks.' The silence from the other side of the table was so thunderous I had to look up. Mrs Klein was staring at me with an expression of horror on her face. Oh, God, she'd never let me come here again, now she knew I was the cause of my mother leaving.

'Your father didn't tell you that, did he?'

'He . . . ' I couldn't remember him actually saying it. I just knew. 'He thinks it.'

'But how could you be the reason your mother went? You were what? Two? Three?'

'She didn't want a child.'

'How on earth could you know that?'

'I . . . ' How did I know that? I wasn't sure. I tried to work it out. 'Maybe I heard her say it?'

'Katie, I'm not a particularly clever woman but I don't believe for a moment your mother would have thought that about you, let alone said it. You've got it all wrong. I expect you and your father never talk about it, am I right?' Mrs Klein fixed her eyes on me again. In the dim green of the kitchen, I noticed they were like Trish's: changing colour, depending where she looked.

I nodded.

'Take it from me,' said Mrs Klein, 'your mother thinks about you. Not a day goes by without her thinking of you.' To my surprise, I could see a fat tear in the corner of one of her sea-green eyes and her nose was turning red. She rummaged behind her in the leather bag, and brought out a tissue, but instead of using it she held on to it and made a little rip in the corner. Now she wouldn't look at me.

'Are you all right, Mrs Klein?'

'Fine,' said Mrs Klein, through lips that had suddenly gone tight. Her lipstick had come off on her coffee cup, and I could see a black crescent of mascara smudged underneath one eye. She finished tearing one thin strip off the tissue and started on another. I didn't know what to do.

'Only . . . ' I was desperate to leave. But I couldn't come up with an excuse to go. I hadn't even touched my coffee.

Mrs Klein cut across me before I could think of how to end the sentence. 'If you want to look for your mother, I could help you. I know how to go about it. If you're interested, that is.'

There was such naked hope in her face it seemed rude to refuse. 'I'll think about it,' I said. 'I . . . I'm not sure how I feel about the idea just yet.'

She got up from the table and took away my coffee cup. I still hadn't touched it, but she didn't seem to have noticed. She put the cups into the sink and stood there for a while, her back to me, gazing out at the garden through the blue tails of wisteria. It was so rampant it had begun to push through the slats of the ventilator over the sink. I could hear the *snip snip snip* of Stephen with the secateurs, earning his pound.

On the table curled in a little pile lay the remains of the tissue. Mrs Klein had reduced it to tiny fragile ribbons. Fairy bandages, for invisible wounds.

The noise of water whooshing out of the taps made me jump. Mrs Klein squirted washing-up liquid over the blue-and-white crockery. 'I hate it when my babies go,' she said, to the window and the wisteria. 'Hate it. Thank God for Trish.'

I stood up. 'When did you say she'll be back?'

Mrs Klein swung round. I think she had forgotten I was there. 'What? Not till Saturday. I'll tell her you came.'

★　★　★

As I reached the top of the hill on the way home, Mrs Owen was puffing up the slope on the other side, bow-legged like an ape and swinging her arms to help propel her hindquarters up the hill. She saw me and straightened up, wheezing. 'Whoof. Kills me every time, that hill.'

'You should take the bus.'

'Petal, this is the only exercise I get. People pays a fortune going to keep fit classes to get this breathless.' She had turned an alarming red. 'Oof. Just let me find me wind.' She flapped her hands as if she hoped they would stir enough breeze to reinflate her lungs. Her chest heaved like an earthquake. 'What are you up to?'

'Nothing much.'

'Come to the Co-op with me and I'll buy you a lolly.'

'I'm not eating lollies. I'm dieting.'

'Dieting?' said Mrs Owen, in the same tone she would have used for 'Picking your nose?' She pinched my upper arm. 'Go away with you. Not enough meat on you as it is. Come on, me belly's sticking to me backbone. We'll have a cuppa and a bun in the caff. My treat.'

That was the end of my diet.

⋆　⋆　⋆

'Mrs Owen?' I asked, wiping fragments of icing off my chin. My eyes stung from the haze of cigarette smoke.

The café walls were painted creamy yellow to hide the runnels of nicotine. All the women in Green Down who pretended to their husbands they'd given up smoking congregated here. They said even the cockroaches in the kitchens were culled by cancer.

'Mmm?' Mrs Owen was happy, on her third cigarette. Two squashy butts tagged with her orange lipstick nestled in the tinfoil ashtray, on top of half a dozen others stamped with different shades. There was a bubble of phlegmy chatter round us, and a cassette deck was belting out the Carpenters.

'What was my mum's name?'

I almost expected the hubbub round us to fade into stunned silence, now I'd said it. But Karen Carpenter launched note-perfect into 'Only Yesterday', and Mrs Owen looked puzzled rather than alarmed. 'Don't you know, petal?'

'No. Nobody's ever told me.'

'It was Kitty.'

'Kitty.' It tasted odd on my tongue, too sweet like the iced bun. 'And she called me Katie? Kitty and Katie?'

'Your father thought it sounded pretty.'

I didn't like to imagine what Trish would think about it, if she ever found out. 'What was her second name? I mean, before she got married.'

'What, her maiden name? Can't think. Something to do with cards.'

'Cards? Like what? Cardew? Christmas?'

'Sorry, petunia. It's popped out of my head. It'll come to me in the middle of the night.' Mrs Owen took a last hopeful puff at her cigarette. There was only a tiny rim of white left above the brown filter. 'She came from Brissle, see.'

Bristol was only twelve miles away. Had she gone back there after leaving us? Surely she'd have gone further. And the man? Was she still with him?

'Who was the man?'

'What man?'

'The one she went away with.'

'How do you know about him?'

'I heard you talking about him once, years ago.'

'Ah.' Mrs Owen squashed her cigarette butt down firmly on top of the others. 'Well. There was talk it was someone at the MoD. One of the men on the gate. She was seen with a man in uniform. She used to go for walks up by there, anyway, where the rec ground is.'

'What about me?' I was outraged. She'd left me at home while she was out with her lover? I'd only been a toddler.

'Oh, petal, you'd've been with her. In the pushchair. She never left you behind.'

'So I saw him,' I said. 'I was with them.'

'You must've been.' Mrs Owen poked at the pile of cigarette ends with her finger. The top one fell off and rolled over the table edge. 'But then he got posted. And that was that. She went with him.'

I don't want a child. Was that when I heard it? In my pushchair? Who said it, him or her?

'What's started all this off anyway?' said Mrs Owen. 'You listen to me, Katie Carter. Some things is best left alone. I don't often agree with your dad, but I reckon he's right not to talk about it. It was a bad, bad time.' She lumbered to her feet, and two more cigarette stubs fell off the ashtray and on to the floor. 'No point digging into what's gone.'

'I just want to know,' I said. 'Just . . . know a bit more.'

'Well, you watch your dad doesn't catch you at it. Eyes like a stinking eel, he's got. And he 'as his pride.' She picked up her shopping and waded through the yellow haze to the till to pay.

14

Walking down the road after seeing Mrs Owen in the village, I could hear music coming from Gary's house. His bedroom window was open; he must have had the day off work. As I got nearer, the track changed and someone turned up the volume. It sounded like helicopters in a desert wind; then drums and guitars kicked in, and a distant, wailing voice. I sat on the garden wall to listen. Something about it made me smile because even I could tell it was magnificently excessive: the electronic wind howled, and the vocals had so much echo they could have been recorded in an enormous cavern. So that was Gary's kind of music, was it? As I went up the steps to our house, the same track started again.

I let myself in and, in the dim light of the hallway, saw a letter on the mat. There was no stamp: it must have been delivered by hand. It was addressed to my father, and the writing slanted to the right, bold violet loops that wanted to be noticed. I hoped it was a cheque from a customer: I might get my clothes allowance at last. Dad was supposed to be working full-time for the renovators at the moment, but I had a feeling he was moonlighting on another job. A couple of evenings last week he'd come home far later than usual.

I took it through to the kitchen and left it on the table for him.

Without Trish, I wasn't sure what to do with myself. I went upstairs and flung myself on to my bed. The white candlewick cover was grubby. I ought to wash it. Suppose I lived in a house like Trish's where I never had to worry about such things because someone else did them? In the sunlight, the glass over my framed poster, the girl lost in the wild wood, was smeared and dirty. It had never occurred to me that picture glass needed a wipe now and then. Was there never an end to cleaning?

I should go downstairs and get a damp cloth and vinegar. That was what Mrs Owen would have said. *Work of a moment, Katie. Do it when you see it.* Instead I picked up the book on fossils my dad had brought me from the library.

So far I'd found it hard going. The language seemed old-fashioned, written for grown-ups. It was like difficult poetry. All I could scoop out of it were slithery half-ideas that fell through my fingers as fast as seawater. But it did explain about limestone.

Where I lay now there had once been ocean. Time moved in a different way, in head-hurting aeons and epochs. It had taken millions and millions of years of particles filtering down through blue water to make the stone Green Down was built of, whole continents drifting like abandoned ships, the slow grinding of rock on rock. The only way to make sense of it was to speed it up like film. Then the violence smashed through like a tidal wave: storms, thunder, lightning, lashing rain, banshee wind, as the earth had some sort of bilious fit and heaved up lumpy hills and jagged mountains. And me? I was just one of those particles, spiralling down through a vast sea, gone in the blink of an eye.

My dad had told me about the fossils that fell out of the rock as the quarrymen worked it. He used to have a job in one of the open quarries. He brought home ammonites, and once a long bone. It had fallen out of the roof of an underground tunnel. We took it to the museum and the man there said it belonged to a bison. He explained there was a time when the climate was much hotter. There were hippopotamus in English rivers, and some of the earliest evidence of humans in the British Isles had been found not far away, in another quarry less than twenty miles from here in the Mendips.

The quarrymen had uncovered stone tools nearly half a million years old. *And did those feet, in ancient times . . .* The first Englishmen, loping across hills I could see from Green Down. English was the wrong word, of course, but that was how I thought of them.

The book talked about Early Man. Far more important, of course, than Early Woman. I pictured him chasing the retreating glaciers northwards after each Ice Age; she tagged along behind, pointing out it was bound to get nippy again one day. Then the cold did come back and sent them south, the ice snapping at their heels. Backwards and forwards, leaving a trace every time in caves and river valleys, a set of stone tools, sometimes a jawbone or a piece of skull.

Homo heidelbergensis, Neanderthals, Swanscombe Man: they were always called after the place they were found. Perhaps, if you dug deep enough here, around the Avon river valley, you'd find Bathampton Man, or Midcombe Man, or Green Down Man.

The sound of the telephone downstairs sliced into my thoughts. I jumped off the bed and ran to answer, feeling half asleep and dizzy.

'Katie,' came Poppy's voice, 'what are you doing?'

'Nothing. Reading.'

'*Reading?* Look at the weather. Do you fancy coming over? Trish has swanned off to London.'

I was second choice, of course. She'd only phoned because Trish wasn't available.

'Well . . .'

'Oh, go on.'

Through the cloudy glass lozenge in the front door I could see how bright the world was outside. I thought of the swimming-pool in Poppy's garden, mosaic-tiled, cool blue. It was the perfect day to swim.

'OK. I'll be over in half an hour.'

★　★　★

Poppy and I stood by the swimming-pool. I couldn't stop my disappointment showing. 'What do you mean, it leaked?'

She pointed to the crack zigzagging across the middle of the pool floor, a lightning strike across a blue sky. The mosaic tiles round it looked like jigsaw pieces tumbled in the bottom of a box. At the far end there was a reservoir of water about a foot deep. A scummy layer of pine needles from the conifers that surrounded the garden floated on it. Otherwise the pool was empty.

'Daddy's furious. He only filled it just before the party.'

'It drained away?' I couldn't work out where it had all gone. Through the crack, yes, but where to?

'The whole lot disappeared overnight. Like someone *stole* it. There's a man coming to look at it this afternoon. Mummy says it's a mystery.' Her platform mules clacked on the poolside as she turned away and walked into the shade. They made her legs, in a pair of blue gingham hotpants that were last year's fashion, look like long, pale, freckled stalks, things that had grown suddenly in the dark.

The house was built on the hillside looking south-west towards the Mendips, and the garden was a series of terraces cut into the slope. The pool was on the terrace by the house, sheltered on one side by a trellis through which a vine curled heart-shaped leaves, motionless in the heat. We sat on sun-loungers, and I kicked off my canvas daps, so flat and childish next to Poppy's platforms. Under my sundress my bare thighs stung where they touched the hot plastic. With the pines surrounding the garden, we might have been in Italy.

The house seemed all windows. The floor-to-ceiling glass reflected blue sky and a yellow-white fizzle of sun. There was no one to look in: each of the architect-designed houses on the estate was well away from the next, hidden by clever landscaping.

Poppy's mother came out wearing an orange halter-neck bikini and big Jackie O sunglasses, her glossy dark hair set in big curls sprayed as rigid as a helmet. She was carrying a magazine and a packet of cigarettes and, like Poppy's, her high heels tapped on the tiles round the pool. I sensed her annoyance when she saw we'd occupied the sun-loungers; she didn't even say hello, but went on down the steps to the lower terrace, where there was a patio with a table and chairs.

The heat made me irritable. Poppy was inspecting her toenails, which she had painted pink again. She looked up and caught me watching. 'Want me to do yours?'

'No, thanks.'

Her eyes flinched away. I hadn't meant to sound so sharp.

'It's too hot out here,' I said.

'We could go up to my room.'

My bare feet were slippery on the polished wooden stairs. Following Poppy, I could see the corrugations the plastic sun-lounger had left on her thighs. I felt the back of my legs under the hem of my dress. They were ridged too.

I had never been into Poppy's bedroom. The house was mostly one big ground floor; the upper level seemed piled on as an afterthought, and was all Poppy's now her grown-up half-sister had gone to live abroad. Almost the whole of one wall in the L-shaped room was window, sliding glass doors opening on to a flat roof-terrace that overlooked the pool. They were half open and as we came in, the voile curtains stirred briefly then hung limp again. The sun was just coming round the corner of the house and its light lay in a golden bar on the floor. At one end of the room there were shelves, on which sat more Barbie dolls than I had ever seen in one place.

Poppy was already pink from the sun, but when she saw me looking at the Barbies she went pinker. 'I don't play with them any more,' she said defensively. 'Some of them were my sister's.'

No wonder she had never invited Trish and me into her room. Trish wouldn't have let her forget the Barbies, ever. There was worse, though. A poster of Donny and Marie Osmond. They were cuddling a puppy.

'Poppy . . . ' I said. I didn't know what to do about the panic in her eyes. 'It's OK,' I finished, aware it sounded lame.

She sat down on the end of the bed. I could almost smell her relief. I went over to look at the Barbies, and saw her eyes following me like an anxious kitten's.

I picked one up, dressed for the weather in a green bikini. I had heard people talk about hourglass figures, but she reminded me not so much of an hourglass as a wineglass: legs right up to her armpits, as Mrs Owen would have said. As I put her back on the shelf, propping her among the rest, I suddenly remembered laying a fat, rosy-cheeked doll carefully to sleep in a nest of blankets under the table in our living room, smoothing her stiff bright nylon hair, tucking the covers under her chin as I imagined a mother would. It was the only doll I could recall playing with. I couldn't remember her name. I had no idea what had happened to her, or who had given her to me.

'They're like tarts, aren't they?' Poppy's voice broke in, and in an instant the remembered doll's face disintegrated into shards of flying plastic.

'Tarts?' Jam? Lemon curd? I couldn't make the connection.

'You know. Prostitutes. Waiting for business.'

'Oh.' She was right. They leaned against the back wall of the shelf like lazy good-time girls in a film. The only exception was Wedding Barbie, in her long white dress and veil, who tried to clutch Boyfriend Ken's little plastic hand as they stared fixedly into their future together. She looked terrified.

171

'I sometimes imagine them having conversations in the night,' said Poppy. 'They're telling each other stories about how it will be when they find rich boyfriends.'

'Meanwhile they have to share Ken.' We both laughed. Poppy got off the bed and pushed the patio doors wider, flapping the curtain like a fan to try to stir the air. I wandered over to the wall cupboards with their louvre-doors and opened them, using them like a fan too.

'Hey,' I said. 'Lovely skirt.' It was cream, peasant-style and flounced in three tiers, false-petticoat lace showing at the hem.

'D'you like it?' said Poppy. 'Have it.'

'No.' I stared at her. She looked like she meant it. 'You serious?'

'Try it on. My sister gave it to me. She bought it on the King's Road in London. It doesn't suit me.'

I took off my dress and pulled the skirt up over my hips. I had forgotten I was wearing the stolen bra, but luckily Poppy didn't recognize it.

'What do you think?'

'It needs something round the waist. Hang on.' She opened another of the louvre-doors to reveal a rail hung with belts. I didn't even possess *one*, I thought jealously. Poppy picked out a belt made of woven strips of multi-coloured leather. She arranged it over my hips and looped the tassels in a loose knot. Her hands smoothed down the skirt, brushing my hipbones, and my skin tingled.

'There.' She swivelled me towards the full-length mirror. 'Wear it with that peasant blouse of yours, the one with the drawstring neck. You look really sexy.'

'Didn't you?'

'My hips are bigger. I looked like a wedding cake.' I had a feeling she wasn't telling the truth, but the skirt did suit me. I began to take it off, self-conscious now even though we saw each other's bodies every week when we changed for swimming. She was watching me with an odd expression on her face. 'Do you really think it's a good idea to write to Gary?' she asked, wafting the curtain again.

'What? I thought it was *your* idea.' I pulled my dress back on, and laid the skirt on the bed.

'No, honestly,' said Poppy. 'Trish thought of it. She said we could tell him we were three lonely virgins, who worshipped his body from afar. He could take his pick, like Paris choosing Helen of Troy. But I'm not sure we should.'

I sat down on the floor by the patio doors to catch the breeze Poppy was creating. 'Well, what harm could it do?'

'What if he took us up on it?'

'He's not going to be interested in us. He's seventeen.' But as I said it, I was disappointed. I knew we wouldn't go through with it, but I wanted to keep up the pretence we would.

'Well.' She pulled back the curtain irritably, clattering the brass hooks on the metal track. 'Trish is always having these big ideas and dragging us into them.'

From below came the chime of the doorbell. I looked at Poppy to see if she would answer it. But she was staring out of the window. The bar of sunlight on the floor had turned into a flood, and was already lapping the edge of the bed. There seemed no refuge from brightness in this house.

'Let's see what Trish says when she gets back,' I suggested.

'I know what she'll say. She'll make us do it.'

The doorbell chimed again. I heard Mrs McClaren's heels rapping on the parquet floor in the hallway.

'It's the pool man,' said Poppy. 'Let's go and look.'

We went on to the roof terrace, and lay down on the hot asphalt roofing to peer over the edge. There was a railing to stop anyone falling off, but we could get our heads under it to stare down at the pool area like a couple of gargoyles. Chips of gravel pricked my legs. Below us, Mrs McClaren came out from the house. Her scalp was pale where the hair parted, and the roots had grown through a duller faded brown. She had pulled on a man's shirt over her bikini, but she still showed a lot of leg. The man following her was keeping a good two yards between them.

'It vanished overnight,' I heard her say.

'Yeah, well, it would.' He jumped down into the shallow end of the pool and peered at the crack in the tiling. He was careful not to go too close to it. 'See, there's your trouble.'

'I can see that,' said Mrs McClaren. Her tone was icy. I looked at the remaining water in the pool but, disappointingly, it remained unfrozen.

'See, that's typical round here,' said the man. 'How long's the pool been in?'

'It was here when we bought the house. We only moved in just after Christmas, so this is the first time we'd filled it.'

'And did you get a survey?'

'My husband thought there was no need. The house is only about ten years old.'

'You should've had a survey. This area's riddled with mines.' He pulled himself out of the pool in one neat movement, sitting on the edge with his feet dangling. 'You got subsidence, see.'

'Of course we had a *search*,' said Mrs McClaren. 'Our solicitor checked for mining activity.'

'See, a lot of mining round here don't show up in the records,' said the man. 'But if you'd asked me . . . I'd've told you there's no point putting a pool in.' He got to his feet, dusting off his trousers.

'So what are you going to do about it?' asked Mrs McClaren.

'Do?' He shook his head. 'We can concrete over the

crack if you want. But put it this way, you'll be pouring money away with the water. Straight into them tunnels. No guarantee it won't happen again. Earth's always shifting, see.'

'You mean our pool is built over a coal mine?' asked Mrs McClaren. Her face was rigid with disbelief.

'*Stone* mine,' said the man. 'Prob'ly.' He looked up, saw us and waved, laughing. 'Two little garden gnomes you got up there.'

Mrs McClaren ignored us. 'You mean it's not *safe?*'

'Ooh, safe as houses, prob'ly.' The pool man picked up his clipboard. 'Not that anyone knows how safe the houses are. But, put it this way, we haven't had a big collapse long as I remember.'

He took out his pen and held out the clipboard to her. 'Sign, please. Did you want the crack repaired?'

'I'll have to consult my husband.' Mrs McClaren stabbed the pen at the docket. 'He may want to talk to our solicitor. Or get a second opinion.'

'No skin off my nose,' said the man, cheerfully.

'What's he mean, tunnels?' whispered Poppy.

I flopped over on to my back and gazed up at the cloudless sky. 'They used to dig stone out from underground. Bath stone, for the houses. He's right. There's loads of tunnels under here. Everybody knows.'

'Seriously?' Poppy sat up gingerly, as if she thought the house might collapse beneath her weight. 'Isn't it dangerous?'

'Don't think so. People used to be able to get into them and everything.'

'Like secret passages? *Brilliant.*'

'They're all shut up now, though. People's dogs kept getting lost in them.'

'You mean they're full of dead dogs? Yuk.' Poppy chewed a strand of her hair. '*Wet* dead dogs now.'

'Doing the doggy paddle.' We flopped about like fish, laughing.

'So where was the entrance?' asked Poppy.

'There was more than one. In the cellars of the pub on the main road — all cemented up now. There's one off Stonefield Lane — that's got a grille on it so bats can get in and out.'

'Bats? Double yuk.'

I thought bats were sweet. Our old cat had caught one once, then didn't know what to do with it. It lay like a crumpled leaf on the hall carpet. I turned it over to see its mouse body, a tiny panting thing, terrified. There was a big tear in its wing, where the cat's claw had caught it. It reminded me of a little broken black umbrella. My father took it away into the garden, said he'd set it free. But I didn't think it would be able to fly.

'Girls?' Mrs McClaren's voice came floating up from below. 'I don't want you on the edge of the roof like that. It's not safe.'

'Oh, *Mum*.' Poppy wriggled to the edge again and peered down. I wriggled after her. The pool man had gone, and Mrs McClaren stood beneath us, hands on hips, Jackie O sunglasses angled up towards us like headlamps, sending out black beams of wrath.

'I mean it, Poppy. Don't upset me. I can already feel a migraine coming on.'

She put a hand to her forehead and massaged her temple with her thumb. The headlamps sent one last dark flash in my direction. It was my fault we were there, they semaphored.

'Come on,' said Poppy, wriggling back from the edge. 'Better do as she says.'

I watched Mrs McClaren make her way round the pool, heels clacking, to pick up her magazine and cigarettes. Then I shuffled backwards slowly after Poppy.

★ ★ ★

On the way home I made a detour along Stonefield Lane. It was hours too early for bats, of course. I'd seen them once, in late summer at dusk. They looked like smoke pouring out of the gap in the rockface.

I wondered if that was the way the Camera Man used to sneak in and out of the tunnels. Really he was an old tramp. There was a story — Mrs Owen had told me — that he'd been a perfectly ordinary man with a perfectly respectable job, but he was spurned by the woman he loved, so he went mad and took himself off to live in a tent in the woods. When it got cold in winter, he moved into the underground quarries.

He was called the Camera Man because he had a thing about cameras. He kept breaking into camera shops and stealing armfuls of Nikons, Canons, Brownies, Instamatics: anything with a lens. He was hypnotized by that single winking eye. He would take his booty back to the tunnels and store the cameras in the quarrymen's breakfast holes until they grew a grey-green film of mildew. He never took photographs, just hid them away. Perhaps he was afraid of them, and that was how he made them safe.

Mrs Owen had told me about the Camera Man, but it was my dad who told me about the dogs getting lost in the tunnels. He said he remembered when three boys got lost too, the year before they blocked up the tunnels for good.

I looked at the narrow gap out of which the bats would come. What happened to the Camera Man when they blocked up the tunnels? Did he freeze to death in his camp in the woods? Or did he still manage to get in and out somehow, wriggling like a mouse through the crack they left for the bats?

The sun was dropping towards the trees, and there were goose pimples on my bare arms. I shivered and walked on quickly towards home.

15

When I go underground on Thursday, I keep remembering the Camera Man. The thought of him still makes me shudder. I imagine long, pale fingers, sweating like the sap in the stone, turning his mildewed trophies this way and that, lifting the viewfinder to a pale, lashless eye.

Coming down the ladder I tell myself something's only worth doing if it scares you.

★   ★   ★

The miner with the tattoos is Ted. John has thin, ropy hair, escaping in dreadlocks under his hard-hat; Pat is the one with blond hair and white eyebrows . . . I'm never going to remember all the free miners' names. But I've got to. I've got to knock spots off any other engineer they've ever worked with.

And afterwards, in the pub, they'll still make jokes about the size of my tits or the shape of my bum coming down the ladder. Doesn't matter, though, because I mustn't mind it, mustn't think about it, mustn't let it get to me . . . For a moment the enormity of it all floors me, dealing with the men let alone stabilizing the mine, as it does every time. Until I remind myself that if I do the bloody job I'm paid to do, and do it the best I can, that's all I need to do. Concentrate on getting it right. Respect comes from that.

Ted's looking at me, waiting for instructions. It's an expression I've seen a million times before. Come on, it says, show us what you think you can do. We know you're going to land in the shit, but we're going to do what you tell us and wait until you're right in it before we haul you out by the scruff of your sorry little neck.

'We've got an area of weakness in the ceiling between those two pillars,' I tell them. 'It's underneath the road going down to the primary school.' Where every morning and every afternoon, several dozen mums in off-roaders and people-carriers rumble down the hill to pick up their little darlings. There's a weight restriction on the road, but that only stops heavy lorries. We've got to get some emergency fill into this void, or one of these days a big hole's going to appear in the middle of Grove Road — hopefully not while a minibus full of schoolkids is trundling over the top.

'Yup,' says Ted, chewing something. 'We seen the map.'

Now, or later? Now.

'Look, Ted,' I say, 'I get your point. I'll try not to patronize you, if you try not to patronize me, OK?'

'Don't know what she's on about,' says Ted to the other miners.

★   ★   ★

Settling in, at last, to the cottage in Turleigh. It's a relief to get away from the noise of the weir at the hotel and unload stuff into a place I can be myself. It's a good kitchen, this, big and low-ceilinged, pale wood and stainless steel, biscuit-coloured tiles. Quality stuff, chosen with care and taste. The dishwasher's broken, but who cares? I've got my very own Aga. That would make Susie Klein smile.

Suddenly my eyes start to leak. I hate those fucking miners. Bastards. Bastards. I don't know how to deal with them any more.

'What's up?' says Martin, from the phone tucked under my ear. 'You've kicked miners' arses before.'

'These are bigger arses.'

'Bollocks. You need me to come and feed you up. It'll

179

look different after a couple of bottles of plonk. You come across any more of those marks underground?'

'I've been looking out. I'd ask the miners, but I don't think they'd tell me.'

'If my theory's right, there'll be more.'

'What theory?'

'Tell you when I see you. You still on to pick me up from the station?'

'I'll be there.'

I put down the phone and pad across the tiled floor. Limestone, *not* local: probably French. With one of those under-floor heating systems so the cold doesn't strike up through your tootsies in the early morning. Maybe I should do something like this in my Cornwall cottage. If I don't sell it.

Everywhere feels temporary. That's why I never get round to home improvements.

Patio doors to the garden; I step outside into the darkness, smelling frost and woodsmoke. Up three shallow steps on to the grass, turning to take in the glow of other cottage windows and black looming trees, then spinning right round to see the spill of light from the kitchen below and my footprints meandering away from it across the glistening lawn. My looping snail-track, my mazy motion. Always going away, never towards.

⋆　⋆　⋆

Friday afternoon, bunking off work, having lied to Brendan that I have to meet a gas-fitter to fix the boiler at the cottage. I had forgotten how lovely Bath is, even in the rain. I cross at the lights and on to Pulteney Bridge with its tiny shops perched over the weir. Rain patters on my umbrella, my high-heeled boots skid on wet pavement. Why did I bother dressing up? It's only Martin. But he likes it, I know, when I make an effort,

French pleat my hair, stick on the slap, pull on a suede skirt and knee boots.

On impulse, I duck into the map shop on the bridge. There's a rather fine antique Speed in the window, the county map of Somerset, but you'd have to be a serious collector to fork out for that. I know it will be pricey without having to ask. Nick used to collect old maps. He always moaned he'd come to it just too late, when prices had already started to rise, that back in the seventies you'd have picked up a map like that for less than fifty quid. It'd be worth eight hundred, maybe a thousand today. He took his collection with him when he moved to Wales, but he's probably poured it down his throat by now. He had some pretty maps, delicately coloured, finely engraved.

The shop is tiny; a stride takes you across it. It's full of light from the windows overlooking the river, and full of maps, hanging on every available inch of wall, or filed in boxes under county names. It makes me nostalgic for the Chiswick house, where Nick hung his collection down the stairwell and along the hall. He loved those maps. It's the only time I remember seeing him with Windolene in his hand; he wouldn't lift a finger to any other housework but he was always happy to polish the glass over his framed maps. He found a chart table in an antiques shop, one with big shallow drawers, and kept the unframed ones in there. He'd spend whole Sunday afternoons taking them out and looking at them, planning journeys in his head. Journeys on roads built for carriages and stagecoaches, through villages that are now towns, and countryside that is now suburbia; journeys that, being Nick, he never took.

Nostalgia. Is that all I can find to say about what I felt? But the marriage was my mistake. Even when I caught them in bed together, I was more angry with her than with him.

'Looking for anything in particular?'

The owner is at my elbow.

'Not really. Unless you've got any maps of the underground quarries.'

He shakes his head. 'Never seen anything like that. I'm not sure anyone got round to mapping them. Lots of little quarrying companies, over the centuries, dig a bit here, break through old workings there. Like the Minotaur's maze. Even that lot working up at Green Down now don't have any clear idea how it all joins up.'

★ ★ ★

'You jammy, jammy tart,' says Martin, as we drive through Bath, which is already filling with Friday-afternoon traffic. 'You lucky, lucky cow. It's so lovely.'

'I guess.'

'Do me a detour. Do me the Royal Crescent. Do me the Circus.'

'It's the wrong direction.'

'Where's the poetry in your soul? The Royal Crescent was John Wood's crowning achievement. He died before he could finish it. His son had to complete his vision. And you can't be bothered to take a teeny-weeny little wiggle off route so we can pay *hommage*.'

We do the Royal Crescent.

'Wood was a fucking genius,' says Martin, as I teeter in my stupid high heels over the drying cobbles. 'Played fast and loose with history to suit his own weird ideas.'

The Royal Crescent sweeps away to our right, a smooth parabola in pale stone, like one perfect arc of the pencil. It makes me want to be able to draw. There are wide, worn butter-stone pavements, front doors painted in clean bright colours. I expect them to fly open and disgorge fifty maids from *Oliver!* singing and dancing fit to bust.

'Believed he could trace classical architecture via the Temple of Solomon and the monuments of the ancient

Britons.' Martin's enjoying himself, in full lecture mode.

I know all this. Wood thought there were lost temples to the sun and moon on Lansdown, and the Circus and the Crescent were his attempt to re-create them. The diameter of the Circus is based on the dimensions of Stonehenge and the megalithic circles at Stanton Drew. Geometry. Freemasonry. Snakes with their tails in their mouths.

'Actually,' I say, 'I did all that at school. We used to come up here for picnics.'

Martin stops flouncing across the cobbles, pretending to be David Starkey, and stares at me. Over his shoulder a big lurid sun is dipping towards Midcombe. 'Well, that was a long way to walk from Bournemouth,' he says.

I feel a fleeting envy for John Wood. He was so much better at playing fast and loose with history than I am. 'On the coach, you pillock,' I add hastily. 'And it was only once or twice.'

★ ★ ★

Martin's great to have as a weekend guest because he adores everything, apart from my driving, which he has always moaned about. He adores the Royal Crescent; he adores the steep roads that take us up out of Bath to the top of Green Down, then plunge us into the valley where we cross the river and climb up again to Turleigh. 'It's like the Dordogne,' he says.

'You can be so eighties.'

'Have you got any Eurythmics? I feel like hearing some Annie Lennox.'

'Not in the car, Martin. Modern people don't listen to the Eurythmics in the car.'

'We'll have her on when we get home. Brake. Jesus, *brake*. Did you have to take that bend quite so fast? My knuckles are so white you could use them in a Daz advert. Oh, God, is this it? I'm going to die of terminal tweeness. It's lovely. Loads nicer than your horrible damp Cornish hovel.'

I press the remote control for the garage door and he nearly has an orgasm. He's less thrilled, though, when he discovers the garage is so narrow he's got to shuffle across the driver's seat to get out. I point out this offers further opportunities for ecstasy involving the gearstick, but playing camp is getting boring now and Martin wants to get settled with a glass of chilled white wine.

He sniffs when I offer him a choice of frozen Marks & Spencer. As I knew he would, he rummages around in the fridge until he's assembled what he considers to be the makings of a decent supper, moans that I don't have an apron and sets to work cooking.

'I should have married you, not Nick,' I say, watching with a glass of wine in my hand.

'Would have saved you a lot of trouble,' says Martin, frying onions. 'But frankly, blossom, you're the worst home-maker I ever met. Don't tell me these tinned olives are all you've got?'

$$\star \quad \star \quad \star$$

After supper we settle down in the open-plan sitting room next to the kitchen, with the fridge only a short stagger away for more wine.

'So, what's the plan?' asks Martin. 'How are you going to smuggle me underground?'

'Don't you worry your pretty little head. I have a scheme.'

'What? Roll me up in a carpet like an Arabian princess?'

'Better. Make sure the security guards are looking the other way.'

'How?'

'We go in a different entrance.'

Even at the weekend, there is a security patrol at the site, to make sure no one nicks the plant or the tools. By myself, I could get into the mines via the main shaft without any difficulty, though there'd always be the risk that the guard would mention it to Gary. But bringing Martin on to the site would be impossible. Visitors are discouraged, and no one apart from us workers is allowed underground because of the insurance.

But there is another way that hasn't been completely sealed off.

'Voilà,' I say, as we turn the corner into Stonefield Lane.

'Voilà? A row of six suburban villas and an undertaker's?'

'We nip down the alley round the side of the undertaker's.' I turn into a track between the buildings. Someone has spray-painted 'Bath rocks' on the wall. Iced-over puddles crackle under our boots. 'Eh, voilà. The Bat Cave.'

Behind the undertaker's the ground dips in a shallow depression, a long-disused open quarry. The undertaker uses it now to park the hearse and a couple of vans. At the far end is a shallow rockface, less than four metres high, and here is the bats' front door, an adit that leads underground. It used to be blocked off apart from a gap for the bats to fly in and out, but it has been opened up again because it offers the widest level access to the workings. We can get heavy plant in through here, though Rupert gets fussy about us disturbing the roosting sites, especially in winter when the bats are hibernating.

The company has sectioned off the area surrounding the adit with a high chain-link fence. There's a padlocked gate. Rupert has the key, of course, so he can come down here of an evening and peacefully count his blessed bats, but two spares are kept in the site offices, one with the security guard, the other in Gary's office. I'm going to steal it.

I've decided not to tell Martin. Not that he'd throw a hissy fit: he may moan about my driving but any entrance to the underworld is fair game as far as he's concerned. He taught me how to pick the padlocks on closed potholes when we were students. No, it's for his own protection. If we get caught, the only one who's broken a law should be me. Of course we shouldn't be in there, and he knows that, but I don't want him an accessory to the theft of company property.

'Right,' I say. 'My keys are on site. I have to go and get them. Meanwhile, you have an important secret mission.'

'I am yours to command, Ô mon capitaine.'

'Just up the road there's a really good deli. Go and buy us some decent olives. Meet you back at the car in ten.'

The site's only a couple of streets away and I stroll up to the security guard's hut by the gate as if I'm the kind of keenie who just can't bear to be away from the office, even at weekends. He's watching reruns of *Buffy the Vampire Slayer* on a little portable television; with any luck he won't be scrutinizing the CCTV screens to check I go where I say I'm going. As I come past the window I see myself on the monitors, caught by the overhead camera at the gate. The angle is less than flattering; I look short and squat, tired and middle-aged in my work clothes. Getting a bit old to pull off this kind of trick. I rearrange my face into girlie mode. Forgotten to transfer some files I needed over the weekend to my laptop, I tell him. And, bother and tush, now I've only gone and forgotten my own key to the Portakabin. What a ditz I am. His face says, *What else do you expect from a woman?*

'No need to come along to unlock the office for me,'

I add. 'I'll just take the master keys and get what I want, only be a couple of ticks.'

'You sure you'll be all right?'

Well, golly, I might trip over my high heels and go head first down the shaft, but I'll try not to. And if those nasty old vampires come lurching up from the Hell Mouth, I'll scream. 'I'll be fine.'

He turns back to the screen, where Giles is ticking off Buffy for not doing enough karate practice. I like that girl. I saunter out of the hut, and head towards the Portakabins, trying to look as if I'm still not quite sure where I'm going. If he comes steaming round the corner shouting at me for unlocking the wrong office I'll smile sweetly and say, *Wrong office? Ooh, silly me. Only been here a week, can't tell one Portakabin from another.*

But he doesn't, and I let myself into Gary's office.

★ ★ ★

Gary's office without Gary positively echoes, it's so empty. His desk is a reproach after the cheerful clutter of Rosie's photos, my piles of paper and Dickon's vitamins. There's a filing cabinet with a printer on top, a spare chair, a shelf that holds a dictionary and nothing else. It's an office that's camped in, by a man who doesn't do office life. Where are the pictures of his wife and kids? Ah, no wife, of course, her picture's in the South African driving instructor's wallet. But what about his son? Maybe Gary doesn't do family either.

Time to remind myself that I'm not here to discover Gary's secret self. I've come to nick the key to the Bat Cave so the Caped Crusaders can explore the secrets of the stone mines. Raiders of the Lost Mark. Indiana Parry and the Temple of Doom. And I know where he keeps the key. Top right-hand drawer of the desk.

But it's fucking *locked*. Shit. Mr Orderly. Locks his

desk at the end of the day and locks the office door behind him. Which suggests the key to the desk is probably on his key ring. Sometimes, Kit Parry, you frighten me with your amazing powers of deduction.

So what do we do now, Indiana? Force the lock, so he can smile fondly on Monday morning contemplating the splintered wood and think, *How that woman lusts after me — she even breaks into my office over the weekend?* No, no, no. Anyway, why should the desk be locked? Men don't lock their desks. Women lock their desks because they share offices and keep Tampax in the drawers and dried-up roses their last lover sent them on Valentine's Day and articles they've torn out of *Marie Claire* on how to have an orgasm even though your boyfriend doesn't know which button to press. Unless Gary has a truly embarrassing secret, like *Randy Rudolph's Rubber Rainwear* catalogue, there's no reason for him to lock that drawer.

The second drawer down slides open easily. It holds a pot of paper-clips, half a dozen biros and a plastic ruler. I take hold of the handle to the top drawer and pull again. It gives a millimetre, just enough to get the plastic ruler into the gap and wiggle it about. Ha! The drawer isn't locked at all. It's stuck on something.

And then, rolling my eyes upwards while I fiddle about with the ruler to sense the obstacle like a blind man casting about with his white stick, my heart hits my larynx and I nearly squeak because there's Gary, going past the window.

Shee-yit. There's nowhere to go except through the other door and into the big meeting room, clutching the ruler and praying to God he won't hear the door close as he pauses to get his keys out.

My heart's beating so strongly it's knocking on the partition wall — *Here I am, Gary, come and get me* — where I'm pressed against it.

I hear his key in the lock of the outer door. Except, of

course — you idiot, Kit — it *isn't* locked. I imagine him trying to turn the key, and looking at it, surprised, because it won't turn. Will he realize somebody's been in, or will he think he didn't lock it when he left last night? I hear some rattling — then the click of the handle. His footsteps cross the floor. The boards vibrate under my feet. I hold my breath. Is he going to try the door into the meeting room? I look around, wondering if there's anywhere I can hide. Not an inch of cover. The only thing I can do is press myself against the wall behind the door. If there was time, I'd head across the room to the kitchenette and get out that way. It'll be locked but I can let myself out with the master keys . . .

Shit.

I try to remember where I put them down. On the filing cabinet as I came in the door? On the floor when I knelt down to try to force the drawer open?

Stuffed, shafted and buggered. I left them on the desk. I can see them now, right in the middle of that big, empty expanse, flashing silver and doing a little jangly key dance to attract Gary's attention.

And anyway, if by some utter miracle he doesn't notice them, any second now Brian the Buffy Fan will be along to discover why 'back in two ticks' has turned into half a bloody hour. I brace myself for discovery. Even the lies seem to have left my brain in an orderly queue, evacuating the doomed building.

But the door hasn't opened.

There's a creak. Gary sitting down at his desk? Staring at the keys? Working it slowly out? God, I wish I could see. If I were Buffy, there'd be a weensy little crack in the partition wall I could jam my eye to . . . but, of course, there isn't.

'Are you there?' Gary's voice. *Fuck*. I freeze. Perhaps he's going to shoot me through the wall. Chop through it with an axe, to show who's boss. *Here's . . . Gary*.

'I know you're there.'

189

I would reply, except I can't work out what to say. I could hit him with the ruler, which I'm still stupidly clutching. Everything I can think of seems . . . stupid. I feel stupid. I feel like a stupid little girl who's been playing Buffy, and now a grown-up is going to look at me witheringly and explain, very slowly, there are no such things as vampires.

'Fuck it, Tessa, pick up.'

I'm so limp with relief I nearly fall down.

'I know you're there because I just drove past and saw your car in the drive,' says Gary.

Who's *Tessa*? (The bitch.)

'We've got to talk. You're being completely unreasonable. We can't do this through solicitors. Ring me, OK? This is the third message I've left. Is that bastard Jeff wiping them? I'm on to you, Jeff. Get Tess to ring me.'

The phone goes down with a crash.

I'm hardly breathing, waiting for Gary to notice the keys sitting on his desk. I can't hear anything. I imagine him staring into space, musing over whatever the faithless Tessa has done. It must be the wife. Ex-wife. Keep staring, Gary. Don't focus. Get up and go, cursing the hussy so hard you simply don't see what's right under your nose.

What the hell's he doing coming into the office on a Saturday, anyway? That's *sad*. Really sad. I wish I could see . . .

The unmistakable tinkle of Windows opening up on his laptop. Shit. I could be stuck here all morning. Martin will be leaning on the bonnet of the car, wondering where on earth I've got to . . .

No. Please no. Don't phone me, Martin.

I glance desperately at my watch. At least fifteen minutes has elapsed since I left Martin, and I said I'd meet him in ten. He's not the most patient of men. The phone's in my pocket, on, of course, because I clearly have no aptitude for burglary and it never occurred to me to turn it off. I slide a hand into my pocket, and grasp the phone, but there really isn't anything I can do about it because it's a dinky little clamshell that makes a *whoosh!* noise every time you open or close it, and there's no way of turning the damn thing off without opening it. My hand clenches over it. I'd quite like to suffocate the fucking thing.

Across the room, the door to the kitchen beckons seductively. If I could get across there, at least the phone wouldn't go off like a bomb. What did I program it with? Can't remember. Probably Beethoven's fucking Fifth. But when Gary walked across the floor of his office, I felt every footstep under the soles of my own feet. The floor must be one big bouncy sheet of plywood — he'll know someone's moving about in here.

There's sweat dripping out of my armpits, swilling under my bra, waterfalling down my back. Jesus, there's probably a big wet patch slowly spreading through the sodding partition wall. *Funny*, thinks Gary, *damp on an internal wall? Kit-shaped damp?* Like this is the Turin Shroud of Portakabin walls.

Next to my ear the printer leaps to life on the other side of the wall, nearly giving me a heart-attack. *Zip zip, zip zip . . .* Please, God, let printing mean he's finished whatever he came in to do. I feel the vibrations again as Gary gets up and walks over to the printer. He's literally inches away from me. I can almost feel him breathing. I ease myself as far away as I can from the wall without actually moving my feet or toppling over, in case he hears my smoker's wheeze through the partition.

Jesus, how long does it take? It would be just my luck to have him printing out an entire novel that he secretly works on in the small hours of the night.

Zip. The printer finally comes to rest. *Tinkle.* There goes the laptop, shutting down. Bye-bye, Gary. Saving your settings. Bye-bye. Please go.

Everything is still again, but I know he hasn't gone. I

haven't heard the door close. I see him in my mind's eye, staring at those keys. Thinking, How the fuck did those get there? Master keys on a socking great ring with a green plastic tag saying *Security*.

The laptop clicks as the lid is shut; the floor bounces again, the outside door opens and closes. Gary has gone.

Instinctively I slide down the wall, in case he glances in through the window of the meeting room as he comes past. Not that it would help. I see his profile clearly going by, but he doesn't look in. His face is set, preoccupied, frowning.

Before he can decide to turn round and come back (*What were those keys doing on my desk?*) I'm through the door and hurtling back into his office.

The desk top is empty.

Empty?

I stare, bemused. Fuck, he must have picked them up and walked out with them. Taking them back to Security? *Brian, you left your master keys on my desk. Now* (knowing, man-to-man laugh) *I don't know exactly what you were up to in there, but put it this way, I won't tell on you if you don't mention my* Randy Rudolph *catalogue.* Brian looks at him puzzled. *Catalogue? Keys? I lent them to Kit.*

I can't quite see how I'm going to bluff it out when they come back, any second now, but it won't help that I'm still holding the incriminating tool of my burglar trade, the ruler. I whip open the second drawer to put it back as fast as possible, like it's red hot and smoking.

The master keys are lying in there.

Well, now I think about it and my heart's stopped hammering, *of course* I didn't leave them on top of the desk. I remember dropping them into the open second drawer to have both hands free while I tried to jemmy the top one. And having the presence of mind to close the drawer quietly before I beat it into the meeting

192

room. Or, at least, I don't actually remember any of this, but it makes a sort of instinctive sense. I sit down on the floor suddenly, my legs folding under me as they've wanted to do for the last ten minutes. God. I was so nearly caught.

The phone explodes in my pocket, with the opening bars of 'There Must Be An Angel Playing With My Heart' by the Eurythmics. Martin, the sod, must have reprogrammed the ring tone last night. Naturally it's him calling.

'Where the hell are you?'

'I got waylaid. Sorry. Be with you in a tick. Just got to . . . ' I'm working the ruler in the tiny gap between the top drawer and the desk ' . . . pick up one last thing.'

'I got the olives.' Don't chat, Martin. Shut the fuck up while I . . . 'What on earth are you doing, Kit? It sounds as if you're trying to raid some poor child's piggybank.'

'Just trying to open a drawer that's stuck. I won't be long.' I cut him off before he has a chance to say more, and turn my full attention to the drawer. The ruler finally slides over whatever the obstruction is. Got it . . . I manage to push it down just enough to free the drawer, tug hard on the handle, and the whole thing comes shooting open.

The key to the Bat Cave, neatly labelled 'Stonefield Entrance', is lying at the front. The rest of the space is taken up by books that have jammed themselves against the top lip of the drawer. There's an Open University prospectus, a fat tome called *Film Theory and Criticism*, and a catalogue from the Early Learning Centre. None of them adds up to my picture of Gary. Does he sit here reading essays on Eisenstein and the semiotics of cinema while the rest of us are playing Free Cell on our computers?

It's tempting to sit cross-legged on the floor and trawl

through Gary's life as revealed by what he keeps in his office drawer. But I don't want to know — not yet, anyway. I'm afraid of dispelling the mystery. I'm nervous of discovering not necessarily rubberware catalogues but mountain-biking magazines that suggest Gary's preferred leisurewear is tight black Lycra cycling shorts, or treasured copies of *Pigeon Fanciers Monthly* and *What Steam Engine?* I'm nervous I'll find a candid holiday snap of him in socks and sandals, or a night out with the gang in which he's sporting a pair of white loafers with a little gold chain across the front. Know the casual footwear, know the man.

I don't think any of these is Gary, either. But let's not risk it. I'd still prefer an intact dream to the real man. I grab the key and go.

What would he have done to me if he'd caught me?

* * *

Martin's leaning against the car, reading the *Guardian*, a couple of carrier-bags at his feet.

'What have you been buying?'

'Never you mind. Hurry up and get the car open. I'm freezing my bollocks off out here.'

'We don't have time to thaw you out. Chuck the bags into the boot and let's get underground.' I reach in to grab the hard-hats.

'I'm not wearing that,' says Martin, as I haul out a high-vis jacket for him.

'We have to look like we belong.'

'I'll look like a half-peeled banana. It's nowhere near big enough.'

Cutting my losses with the jackets, I hustle him round the corner into Stonefield Road and down the alley by the side of the undertaker's. At least the hats make us seem reasonably official, should anyone see us. I unlock the chain-link gate, and we're in.

'I hope you know where we're going,' says Martin, as we scurry down the narrow adit that leads into the underground workings.

'Know the place like the back of my hand,' I reassure him.

'How long have you been working here?'

'Sod off.'

The Bat Cave is also the emergency exit. If there was a bad collapse, cutting the miners off from the main shaft, they could get out this way. Somewhere on the wall near the entrance there's got to be a junction box so you can switch on power for the lighting. The trouble is, I've never been this way before, and I haven't a clue where it is. I keep running my torch anxiously over the walls, hoping it will be obvious.

'Bugger.' The tunnel's opened up into a wide void, bisected by the usual steel walkway. I must have missed the junction box. Martin's dawdling a way back, like a tourist. The circle of his torchlight is flickering over the ceiling.

'How far did you say between us and ground level?' he asks, as I walk back towards him.

'Don't worry, the roof's quite solid here. They didn't take much out of this quarry — inferior stone.'

'Oh.' Martin sounds disappointed. He probably thinks a little risk adds spice to the expedition. 'Do all the individual quarries join up underground?'

'Not necessarily. But a lot do. Each individual quarrying company kept pushing further to get all the stone they could. There was no one to regulate them but themselves. When they broke through into the next quarry, that was when they stopped. And built a wall. Or sometimes didn't, if they thought they could get away with it.'

'So that's why it's so unstable?'

'You just better hope it isn't today it decides to come down.' As I say this, I feel a tickle of fear, remembering

195

the flint-mine collapse.

Somehow Martin senses my uneasiness. 'You really happy to do this?'

'Hey, I asked you. I'm fine.'

'Good, because I'm not. I'm shitting myself.'

I don't believe him — Martin was born without the ability to contemplate his own death — but it's comforting to pretend I'm not the only one who's nervous. As he swings his torch round again, I spot the junction box, liberally spattered with bat droppings as camouflage.

The big cavern leaps into golden life when I flip the switch.

'Ah, God,' says Martin. He's as bowled over as I was when I first came down. 'Wow. It's like church.'

'Just don't launch into a chorus of 'O God Our Help In Ages Past'.'

'Dad would have loved it.' Martin's father, the potholing vicar, died of cancer five years ago.

A single bat, disturbed by the light or our voices, skims across the roof of the cavern.

'Come on,' I say. 'We don't want to wake up the colony.'

But Martin seems reluctant to move on to the walkway. 'You know what Dad used to say when he took me underground — practically every time, it was like his mantra. I used to groan every time he said it if I was with any of my friends. He'd wait till we got into a big cavern like this and he'd peel off his gloves and say, 'You know, son, there are some who worship sky gods, and some who worship earth gods. I find my God in the dark places.' '

'He didn't make you pray, did he, right there, in front of your friends?'

'He wasn't *that* insensitive. We'd all look very solemn, then take the piss out of him when we were on our own.'

I can imagine. I can also imagine what that must have done to Martin, growing up secretly gay among muscular Christianity and teenage cavers, sniggering over precisely which dark places the reverend was referring to. He's never told me that little pearl before.

'Did you mind?'

'Mind what?'

'Other people making fun of your dad?'

Martin sighs. 'Maybe I did. All I can remember is a general sense of crippling embarrassment. But I think about him saying that every time I go underground. Perhaps he was right.'

'You don't believe in God.'

'No.' Martin pulls down his hard-hat, sticks his thumbs in the straps of his backpack in his best Village People imitation. 'Lead on, Lara Croft. Let's make our reputations.'

Because it's the emergency exit, the connection from the Bat Cave through to the part of the mine that's being worked on at the moment is quite straightforward. A couple of branch tunnels have been driven off, but there's no mistaking the main walkway, and with your feet on that it's impossible to get lost.

'I miss him terribly, you know,' says Martin, as we plod along towards the cavern where I found the carving. 'You know what he said to me in the hospital? He asked when was I going to get round to marrying you.'

Martin's mum always cherished secret hopes that I would succeed in making her son see the error of his sexual ways, but I'd thought his father was more realistic. 'Was it the morphine talking?'

'No, he really thought that was what was going to happen. I never managed to get around to telling him I was gay.'

★ ★ ★

197

'Mmm,' says Martin. 'Mmm. Interesting.'

We're standing beyond the branch walkway built for Dickon to inspect the old crane; it looms like a dark, crippled bird beside us. This is almost as far north as the miners have penetrated, pushing beneath the Ministry of Defence compound. Martin's powerful torch is trained on the pillar with the carving.

I hadn't realized I was holding my breath until it all came out in a whoosh.

'Only interesting? Not 'Wow, Kit, our reputations are made'?'

'Well, I hate to disappoint, but I think your Dickon bloke's right,' says Martin. 'It's eighteenth century at the earliest. Maybe much more recent than that. This carving wasn't done by Romans.'

'How do you know?'

'They'd have done it better, frankly. And those marks lower down the pillar are from jadding irons, which quarrymen used to crowbar stone out in the eighteenth century. I've been reading up on it. *Ergo*, the pillar's eighteenth century, *ergo* the carving has to have been done then or later. You should get a photo of those marks, by the way.'

'Shit.' I unshoulder my backpack to get out the camera.

'But . . . ' he circles the bird carving lightly with his fingertip, not actually touching the rock surface. ' . . . I think it's still interesting. It *is* what you say it is: a Mithraic symbol. A raven. First stage in the initiation process to the cult. Because that's unmistakably a caduceus next to it.' He points to the other part of the carving, a thin line with a couple of circles and a cross. 'Mercury's magic staff. Shows the raven is the sun god's messenger.'

On the Sunday night after my weekend at Martin's, the weekend I almost died in the flint mine, I'd seen a picture of the raven and the caduceus almost identical to this one. I was back in Cornwall, but I couldn't sleep again. I was afraid I might never wake up if I did. Rolling over restlessly on to my back, I felt as if I was still in the flint mine, under a mountain of chalk, hallucinating that I had been rescued and dreaming I was in my own bed.

I had to get up. I had to be vertical. When I lay on my back I could feel the weight of it all on my chest. I put my feet out of bed and went downstairs. I sat at the kitchen table, my lovely old junkshop table with its legs clawed by generations of cats, and tried not to think about the flint mine. But what kept coming back was the image of that bloody big bird, like an omen of doom, flapping grotesquely across the clearing and into the trees.

The chapter I had seen of Martin's book was still in my head. I wished I had brought it home with me. There was a word. I couldn't remember it. Psycho . . . psychopomp? The guide that leads you into the netherworld. I went into the study and booted up the computer, called up Google. Ravens . . . *and* myth. Martin was right. Ravens and mystery cults went together like bread and honey. In Celtic mythology, ravens popped up all over the place. There were raven goddesses, raven gods, and it seemed you could trace ravens right back to the Bronze Age as solar birds, associated with sun and light — only later were they seen as birds of evil omen. And in Roman times . . .

I am a star that goes with you, and shines out of the depths

The bird came to be associated with the first level of initiation in a mystery cult the Romans brought back from Persia. The cult of Mithras, the bull-slayer, god of the airy light between heaven and earth.

'You said you thought the carving could be Roman,' I find myself saying to Martin. 'You came all this way — you must have thought there was something in it.' I can hear an unattractively petulant note in my voice.

'You can only tell when you see it in context,' says Martin. He sketches the pillar with his hands. 'Your email photo wasn't clear enough to date the marks on the stone pillar. But you were dead right about the iconography. A raven's just a raven, or possibly only a big black bird, but the caduceus with it means it's almost certainly linked with Mithraism. This carving is similar to a set of icons found in Ostia, Rome's ancient port.'

That was what I'd found on the Internet. I'd seen the raven with Mercury's magic staff, just like the carving on the pillar, on a website devoted to temple mosaics.

'Mithraism was a Roman cult,' I say, determined not to give up. 'It died with the Roman Empire. If it's not a Roman carving, why would anyone else carve a Mithraic symbol?'

'Well, exactly.' Martin stares at the carving a moment longer, then sets off into the darkness beyond the pillar.

'Whoa. Hang on.' I keep expecting Gary to pop out from behind a pillar again and start shouting, and it's making me nervous. 'Don't go off. We could get lost in here.'

'I just want to see if there's another way out of this cavern.'

'Void. You call them voids. There's almost certainly another way out, but it's not safe to keep wandering round where we haven't yet built the walkways. Remember what I said about all the workings joining up? Seriously, Martin, I don't have a map. Nobody has the full map. I don't think we should risk getting lost, not here.'

'What? You mean not only will we die, you'll lose your job into the bargain?'

'Shut up. I'm staying here. One of us has got to stay where we can see the light and the walkway.'

'Unusually sensible of you,' says Martin, already

some way off. 'But don't fret. You can see those lights for miles, probably . . . oh. See what you mean.' His torchlight has disappeared, not even a glow. 'It's not one straightforward space, is it? There are rock walls and chambers all over the bloody shop.'

'Martin!' I don't care if he hears the note of panic in my voice.

'OK, blossom, I'm coming back.' His torch reappears, bobbing some distance away in the darkness. But instead of making straight towards me, it veers off, catching what might be the cobbled mass of a dry-stone wall reaching from floor to ceiling. The torchlight picks its way over it and comes to rest on something on the ground. Suddenly I'm icy cold, desperate to get out into the light.

'Martin. We should go.'

'Well I never.'

'Never what?'

'There's another one.'

'Another raven?'

'No, much more interesting. This might be Mithras himself. He's got the right kind of hat. Come and take a look.'

I cast a quick, nervous glance at the walkway, then follow the direction of his torchbeam, trying to persuade myself it's not so far, really. Not dangerously far. Not even so far I have to switch on my own torch. But I do. The safety of the illuminated walkway recedes further and further. By the time I get to where Martin is standing, it's just a far-off glow between two pillars.

The dry-stone wall is one of those the quarrymen put up to support the ceiling. Dickon has told me you can tell the later ones because they use mortar, but the earlier walls are true dry-stone construction, built by men who knew how to choose exactly the right stone to fit perfectly against its fellows. There's been some sort of collapse in this wall, though, or perhaps it was never completely finished, because a pile of stones is spilling out from the bottom. Martin's kneeling down, playing his torch over one. Our beams intersect: it is sculpted into a bas-relief, incomplete because the stone's been broken in half. What is left shows a man kneeling astride some sort of animal.

'It's *Noddy*,' I say. It is too — he has a pointed cap, curling over at the top, with what looks like a bell in it.

'Don't be so ignorant, woman. That's a Phrygian cap, as modelled by the Persian god of light, Mithras. Actually, I might be wrong, there's also a mysterious Persian who turns up in the initiation ordeals, but since Noddy here looks like he's humping a bull, my guess is that it's the Big Man himself.'

'Why's he humping a bull?'

'He's not humping it, he's killing it. I thought you knew all this stuff. The primal Mithraic legend.'

'Actually, I only paid attention to the raven. The rest of it sort of washed over me.'

Martin sighs. *Bad* pupil. The good doctor will have to instruct.

'Right. Potted version. Mithras, Persian divinity of light, born from the living rock, is told by the sun god he must hunt the sacred bull. He corners it in a cave and kills it, releasing the divine blood that is the life force. For this reason, all Mithraic temples — Mithraea, to give them the proper Latin term — are built underground, or with sunken naves, to remind worshippers of the sacred cave.'

'I knew they were underground. That's why I thought . . . '

'Well, it's just about possible. And this . . . ' he waves his torch at the carving ' . . . this makes it more likely. I think this is a fragment of a tauroctony — the icon showing Mithras slaying the bull, which would have had pride of place in every Mithraeum. Somebody's found it lying around, thought it was just the right shape slab for his wall, and brought it along here.'

'So where's the rest of it?'

'Search me. Could be in another bit of the wall . . . ' his torch plays over a depressingly vast expanse of walling ' . . . or it might be still in the Mithraeum, wherever that is. Or it might be in that one, over there.' The beam picks out another huge dry-stone edifice, between two walls of rock further on. 'Only thing to do is take a look. You carry on with this end, I'll have a go at that one.' He strides off purposefully, backpack bouncing jauntily against his shoulders.

I turn back to the heap of rubble and I'm just wondering where to start when the lights go out.

★   ★   ★

What comes into my head is another fragment of Martin's manuscript, describing the ordeals the initiate had to face. He was made to kneel, naked and blindfolded, in the cave. His hands were bound with chicken guts. He might be tossed, helpless and hog-tied, across deep pits of water or fire — he'd know, from previous visits to the shrine, what the ordeal pits contained. One slip, one fumbled catch . . . Finally, his 'liberator' would approach, offering him a crown or laurel wreath on the point of a sword to celebrate his courage in standing up to the tests so far. But this is a false offer, a temptation, and the Soldier recognizes it. Uttering the words, 'Only Mithras is my crown,' he rejects it.

They leave him utterly helpless, alone, in the dark.

16

The morning my father had suggested for our picnic was overcast and muggy. The night before, he had fussed about the kitchen preparing fillings for our sandwiches. When I got up, he had already gone to work, but there was a note in the kitchen.

HAM IN FRIG. ALSO HARD BOLED EGGS, LETTICE, TUNA MAYONAISE! ROLLS IN BREADBIN. DO NOT FORGET TOMATOS!!!! YOGS!!!!

There was enough to feed a party, let alone the two of us. I found eight rolls in the breadbin, two of them fat stodgy brown things. What had my dad been thinking of? We always ate crusty white bread. And no way would we eat four each. I decided to leave the heavy brown lumps behind. Tuna mayonnaise was a new departure too. Renovating posh houses must have had an effect on my dad's tastes.

I filled the six white rolls. There were also some yoghurts in the fridge that I supposed he meant me to bring too. I liked strawberry and he liked black cherry, bubblegum pink and deep purple, in plastic pots with pictures on. But these were in plain white containers, and when I lifted the lids their contents were pale, unconvincing and rather lumpy. 'Jennets Farm Organic Live Bioculture', said the badly printed labels; it sounded like something out of a science-fiction story rather than pudding. I looked at them dubiously, but put two in the bag with the rolls, the tomatoes and a couple of bags of crisps I found in the cupboard. My dad had gone to a lot of trouble, I could tell, so I went back upstairs to change into the layered skirt Poppy had given me, and slung the tasselled woven belt round my hips. I looked like a gipsy, I thought. A wild and dangerous woman.

Victoria Park was already filling with office-workers looking for lunch-time sunshine, although there wasn't any. The men sat on benches with their sandwiches, the girls lolled on the grass and showed their legs. None of them looked at me, trailing along with my carrier-bag, except one creepy man on a bench by himself under some fir trees. His eyes followed me as I came up the path. I didn't dare turn round to see if he was staring at my bottom after I passed.

My dad was already there when I got to the stretch of lawn below the Royal Crescent. He'd brought a rug, a tartan one I'd never seen before, and spread it on the grass. I felt absurdly pleased. The rug made it an occasion, a Picnic, not just meeting my dad for lunch. He had a carrier-bag too. The dark green neck of a wine bottle poked up from it. We had never drunk wine together before. He sometimes went to the pub on his way home from work, and on his birthday he opened a can of lager with great ceremony and had it with his tea, but I didn't think there had ever been a bottle of wine in the house.

I sat down on the rug and began to take the rolls out of my bag, each one neatly wrapped in kitchen foil. I couldn't stop myself glancing at the wine, feeling pride and excitement. My dad thought I was grown-up enough to drink wine at a picnic. Trish's parents let her drink wine on special occasions. Poppy's father insisted she had a glass whenever they went out for a meal in a restaurant, because he said it hardened her head. Wine was about growing up, learning to drink sensibly.

But my dad didn't open it.

He beamed at me, leaned across the rug and ruffled my hair. 'Isn't this great? I told them at work, 'I'm meeting my daughter for lunch. She'll have made us a picnic.' Proper jealous, they were.'

He had taken off his work overalls. He was wearing his usual faded sweatshirt, but as I looked at him, he smiled again and pulled it over his head. He had a blue short-sleeved shirt underneath. 'Muggy, isn't it?'

Last night I had seen him ironing that shirt. Little flecks of white paint clung to the roughened skin of his hands, but his fingernails were scrubbed clean, apart from the thin rim of paint and glue that always stuck to his cuticles.

'You've got all dressed up, Dad,' I said, a cold worm wriggling in my stomach.

'Because this is a special day,' he said. 'Meeting my daughter. I'm proud of you, Katie. Look at you in your pretty skirt. You've got all dressed up too. You're growing up so fast. I sometimes wish you didn't have to, but there, that's life, isn't it? Can't stop things moving on.'

A blackbird chattered in the shrubbery further down the hill. Someone was crossing the grass towards us, a woman with dark hair waving loose over her shoulders, picking her way carefully in high platform heels with ankle straps. She waved.

'Well, what a surprise,' said my father. 'Who'd have thought it? It's your friend the librarian.'

Janey Legge had a carrier-bag too. 'Hello, there!' she called. 'What a surprise, seeing you both here.'

What a surprise. I wanted to weep.

'Sit down,' said my father. 'Join us, won't you?'

Yes, join us, do. No. I wanted to scratch her smug, over-powdered face.

'Katie, move up on the rug there. Make room for Janey. Well, now, isn't that a funny thing, you being here too?'

'Oh, I always like to come to the park in my lunch-hour.'

Janey Legge was all dressed up too. She had on an

unfashionable little yellow skirt, shorter than was wise for a woman of her age, and a tight white T-shirt. Underneath it her padded bra was too big in the cups so there were dimples where her nipples should have been. She stretched her legs in front of her as she sat down so my father could admire her knees. They were distinctly bony, and her tights were a horrible orangey shade.

'Well, isn't this fun?' she said to me. 'Share and share alike, shall we?'

There were no sandwiches in Janey Legge's carrier-bag. She took out a bag of cherries and a plastic tub. It had brown rice with bits in it, and looked disgusting.

'Get out the rolls, Katie,' said my father.

'I've already put them out.'

'Where are the wholemeal?' He looked dismayed. 'I bought some wholemeal.'

'The brown lumpy things? I didn't bring them. I didn't know there'd be anyone else here.' But you did, I thought coldly. You bought those rolls for her.

'I'm fine with white,' said Janey. Her face said the opposite, as I handed her a ham roll. 'No, sorry, Katie, I don't eat meat.'

'There's tuna,' said my father, quickly. 'You did make some rolls with the tuna mayonnaise, didn't you?'

I wished I'd left that in the fridge too — or spat in it. I consoled myself with the knowledge I'd only brought two yoghurts.

'The open air always gives me such an appetite,' said Janey. 'Macrobiotic rice salad, Katie? Better for your inner workings than those things,' she added, as I shook my head and tore open a bag of crisps. 'Ooh, yes, Col, I will have a glass of that lovely wine. Chilled too, how did you manage that?'

Col. As if I had needed proof that this had happened before. How many times had they met in the park?

207

'My father's name is Colin,' I said. 'Nobody calls him Col, do they, Dad?'

'You can call me what you like,' said my father. He shot me a disappointed look. I knew I was behaving badly, but I couldn't stop myself.

A white sun was trying to burn through the blanket of cloud. It was stiflingly hot. The miserable picnic dragged on, but I knew I was the only one who found it miserable. Janey Legge was bright and coy. My father — I didn't know how to describe my father. I had never seen him like this. He was taller than Janey, but somehow he had positioned himself on the rug further down the slope so he always had to look up at her. She sat very upright, her legs neatly angled to one side, every so often tugging down her yellow skirt, which only drew attention to the darkness between her thighs under it. She stretched her neck a lot, as if she wanted him to see the whiteness of her throat and the little blue veins in it. She didn't need to. His eyes followed her all the time. Sometimes he rubbed the back of his neck as if it itched. When he did that, I could smell the sweat under his arms, and I could see by the way her nostrils curled back that she could smell it too. But it didn't seem to put her off him. Instead her eyes got darker, and somehow brighter.

They didn't talk *about* anything, but they talked and talked. I could tell they weren't listening to each other so much as sucking each other in, absorbing each other. They didn't seem to notice that I didn't say anything. My fingers were in the ground, pulling up blades of grass, scratching, digging.

'Pass us a yoghurt, will you, Katie?' said Janey. 'Oh, Col, these are my favourite. Live and dangerous.' She laughed, and the sound seemed to come out of her flared nostrils. I hoped she'd notice the brown crescents under my fingernails and recoil in disgust, but she was looking at him. 'Like you. A proper live wire.'

My father laughed too, but it was a laugh stuck in his throat, less confident than hers. He was nervous, I could tell. I didn't understand why. I wanted to be gone, to get away from them, but I knew that was what they wanted too, deep down. So I stayed, letting the sight of them cut me over and over again.

'Well,' said my father, eventually. 'Well. I must get back to work.' He didn't move. He was lying practically full length on the rug now, propped on one elbow. Janey, though she was hardly taller than I was, seemed to tower over us.

'Me too,' she said. She didn't move either. Their eyes were locked on each other. I started clearing up the remains of the picnic, hoping that would make them move.

'Well,' said my father again. There was a softness in his voice that I thought must be meant for me, because I had heard it so many times before, when he had put me to bed at night when I was small, when he told me how proud he was of my marks at school. But when I looked up, he was still staring at her.

'You've got to love and leave us, eh?' said Janey Legge. 'Right, Col. You'd better go. Don't want to be late, do you?'

'No,' said my father. He rolled on to his stomach, did a surprisingly agile push-up thing, and was on his feet, gazing down at us both fondly. 'Right, then, girls. I'm off. Katie, I might have to work late again tonight. Janey, I'll . . . ' He touched his mouth with his middle finger. 'I guess I'll be seeing you. Around.' His eyes were saying something else.

I got to my feet too, and picked up the carrier-bag of rubbish. I didn't want to be left alone with Janey Legge. I waited until he had started reluctantly to walk up the grassy slope back towards the house he was working on, every so often glancing back at Janey and doing an embarrassed little half-wave. Then

I said, ''Byeitwasnicetomeetyouagain,' and ran down the grass towards the path out of the park.

* * *

The white sun had elbowed its way through the clouds, and I was boiling, sweat prickling under my peasant blouse, wrists strawberry-coloured as I swung my arms back and forth to keep me going, marching like a soldier. I didn't want to take the bus. I didn't want to sit. I had to keep moving. The more I moved, the less I had to think. I rammed the carrier-bag into a bin as I half ran out of the park. There were two ham rolls left — my father had only managed to eat one, and so had I — but I didn't want to eat ham rolls ever again, and I squashed the bag down hard into the bin, pushing it so fiercely it split.

It was a long way home, and mostly uphill, but I didn't notice how long it took me. Make a plan, my legs said to me, my feet hitting the steep pavement hard enough every time to make my thighbones vibrate. Make a plan. Stop him. My skirt tangled damply round my legs, my muscles ached and pulled. I made a plan.

* * *

'Mrs Owen,' I said, standing on her doorstep. 'I want you to tell me *everything you know* about my mum.'

Mrs Owen looked at me in astonishment. 'You're scarlet, Katie, you've caught the sun. Come in and have a cold drink before you go off pop.'

I was thirsty. I hadn't known it, but my insides felt shrivelled, and all the moisture had leaked out of me into my blouse, which was wringing wet. I followed her into her kitchen. The red and orange and green vegetables on the wallpaper hurt my eyes. Her brilliant white cupboards glared at me. She opened a big, noisy fridge and poured me a glass of cloudy homemade lemonade. I drank it quickly.

'What's brought all this on now?' she asked. 'I *told* you. Not worth digging up things that hurt.'

'I'm going to find her,' I said. 'I'm going to tell her to come home. Dad still loves her, she's got to come home.' It made perfect sense to me, but Mrs Owen shook her head and put a hand on my forehead. When she took it away again she left a headache behind.

'You should lie down,' she said. 'You drank that cold lemonade too fast. Sit down, or you'll fall down.'

'Sorry,' I said. 'I need . . . I think I'm feeling sick.' The fat shiny vegetables on her kitchen wallpaper were dancing.

'You're a funny colour and no mistake,' she said. 'Under that lobster, you're white as a sheet.'

I went and knelt by her downstairs toilet, but nothing came up. Mrs Owen came into the cloakroom behind me and patted my shoulder encouragingly. 'Chuck up, chicken,' she said. 'Better out than in.' But whatever it was, it wouldn't come out.

'Perhaps you better have a lie-down in the spare room,' she said. 'I don't like that clammy look to you . . . ' But I could see what she was thinking. My dad would call it interference.

'I'd rather lie down at home,' I said. 'Dad'll be back soon.'

Mrs Owen looked relieved. 'None of this funny talk though 'bout your mum, mind, in front of him.'

As I walked back up the road from her house to mine, I saw Gary coming the other way in his paint-stained overalls. He'd unbuttoned them to the waist, and he wasn't wearing anything underneath so you could see his pale chest. My stomach twisted again, but this time it was nothing to do with feeling sick. I didn't want him to see me with my pink and white face and the big sweat circles under my arms. I pushed

211

through our gate as fast as I could and up the concrete steps to the front door. Before I got there I heard him shout, 'Hi!'

I turned, hot and cold.

'You dropped your belt,' he said. He was standing by our gate, holding it. I wanted to say, 'No, it's not mine,' and run into the house. But I came slowly down the steps, my eyes fixed on that deep pale V of his chest. It was shiny. He was sweating too. I could smell him when I got nearer, like I'd been able to smell my dad, as Gary lifted his arm and held out the belt to me. But he smelled different. I smelled him in a different part of me. I smelled his sweat not in my nose but in the back of my throat; I smelled him down below in my stomach and in my groin.

I reached over the gate to take the belt. Our fingers touched. I had forgotten my red face, my sweaty shirt — no, I hadn't forgotten them, but I didn't mind my face flaming, I didn't mind knowing he would be smelling my sweat as I held out my hand, just like I'd smelled his.

As soon as I had taken the belt, he smiled, then turned and went. I stared after him. I had forgotten to say thank you, I thought. But I couldn't make my mouth work, it was too dry. I turned round too, went back up the steps and into the house.

★   ★   ★

All evening I felt strange. The heavy June green of the trees in the road outside seemed to seethe with meaning. I didn't understand it, but it was almost in my grasp. My head throbbed, I was still nauseous, and there was a tired, dragging feeling in my stomach. But at the same time I felt oddly elated. Ecstasy was humming somewhere in the world. It hid in the leaves on the trees, it murmured in the hot, pale sky. Its vibrations set

212

my body buzzing too. It hadn't reached me yet, but it would.

The television was on, but I couldn't watch. I read my book instead. I thought about the First Englishman. He was waiting for me, I knew, over the hills, out there in the fields.

It wasn't until half past eight that my father got home. He didn't come into the living room; I heard him go straight upstairs. Then came the sound of the shower.

I went into the kitchen and set the kettle to boil. There was some ham left in the fridge, and I arranged it carefully on a plate with some salad and one of the lumpy brown rolls. He came downstairs, singing under his breath, in clean shirt and trousers, as I was laying a place at the kitchen table for him. His hair was wet and slicked back and he looked younger, like he did in the honeymoon photograph with my mother.

'Oh, Katie, no need. I've eaten. Sorry. I should have said I'd be getting a bite on the way home.'

'With *her*?'

The smile dropped off his face. He looked as if I'd kicked him. 'Don't, Katie. Don't be jealous. There's no need.'

'Jealous? I'm not jealous. I don't know why you can't see through her. And why you had to do . . . *that* to me today. Let me think the picnic was for me. It was for her.'

'No, it wasn't. It was for both of you. I wanted to have lunch with both my special women.'

'Special? Since when has she been *special*?' My insides were winding up like a spring. He looked so hurt. He had not expected me to be like this. I borrowed words I had heard on TV. 'Come on, I'm not stupid. How long has this been going on?' I was watching his eyes, though. I couldn't stop myself, but I knew I had to watch his eyes.

His mouth opened and I thought he was going to speak, but he just looked lost. He let out a little panting breath instead, his eyes flicking round the kitchen as if he might find the right words written on the wall. 'Janey's a lovely woman,' he said eventually. 'She's really interested in you. She cares . . . '

For a moment I wondered how many others there might have been, over the years, lovely women whom I had never heard about because they *weren't* interested in me. It had never struck me before that my dad might have had girlfriends in the ten years my mother had been gone. But I still couldn't stop myself.

'Cares about me? I don't want her to care about me.'

'Katie, please . . . '

'What about my mother? How could you do this to my mother?'

I almost missed it, the flash when his eyes went from open and shiny to flat and blank, and his hand arced through the air towards me. I saw it just in time to skip to one side, putting the corner of the table between us. He almost lost his balance, stepped forward to stop himself falling, and his leg hit the corner of the table. It must have really hurt. My mistake was to think about his pain; I should have made my escape instead. Now everything was very slow and dreamlike. His other hand flailed, knocking the plate off the table, tipping the salad over my skirt. I heard it smash on the floor and felt the shards falling on my feet. Then that hard right hand, the one that always seemed to know where I was, however blank his eyes, swept across and caught me a breath-taking blow on the shoulder. There was an electric tingle through my collar-bone and my whole arm went numb. He's broken it, I thought. Oh, God, he's broken it. What are we going to do now? I stood staring at him, my arm dangling uselessly. But his eyes were all pupil, and he still couldn't see me. I had to get out of the room, but my feet seemed stuck to the floor.

I lunged to one side, like a rugby-player in a slow-motion action replay, feinted, ducked under his arm, and made it past him through the door, up the stairs and into the bathroom because it was the only door that locked.

I sat on the toilet seat, panting. There was sweat dripping down from my hair into my eyes; I was afraid it was blood, and put up a hand to check. He hadn't hit me on the head too, had he? The whole episode seemed so dreamlike I couldn't be sure. Feeling was coming back into my left arm now. My shoulder screamed when I tried to lift my hand on to my lap, but my arm moved. Perhaps it wasn't broken, after all. I could see myself in the bathroom mirror, paper white. My shoulder looked normal. I felt dizzy, and sick, and that heavy dragging feeling in my lower back was stronger, but I thought I'd live.

There was a thin smear of blood on my foot: a sharp edge of broken plate must have nicked it. The gipsy skirt was stained with salad cream and beetroot. Probably it would never wash out. I began to pull it off: it would have to be put in to soak right away. But my arm was working better already. Now there was just a dull ache, which only became sharp if I moved without thinking.

There was a streak of blood on my leg too. I got up and hobbled to the basin, carrying the skirt. The closer I got to the mirror, the whiter I looked. All the sunburn seemed to have leached away. I was salad cream, not beetroot. I turned on the cold tap — 'Always soak a stain in cold water, Katie,' came Mrs Owen's voice in my head — and plunged the skirt in. Thin tendrils of rust crept out of the material.

Oh, no. I lifted the skirt out, turned it over. On the front the stains were transparent and oily, deep beetroot purple. On the back there was a brownish red patch. A cramp shot through my lower body, as if it had been waiting for me to see what was happening. I felt my

215

pants between my legs slippy and wet.

I stared at the blood, oddly detached. So this was it. This was what the fuss was all about. (Oof, another twisting cramp.) This was what Mrs Owen called the Curse, what Trish and Poppy called 'coming on'. All my insides were clenching up and trying to drop out of my bottom. I let the skirt fall back into the water and sat down again heavily on the loo. I had forgotten my arm. Nothing would ever be the same again. I could feel the slow drip of the blood, and with it came so much else that was strange but also oddly familiar. You know what it means to be a woman now, said my body. You *know*.

Trish had started, but Poppy hadn't. At least I had beaten her.

Oh, God, had I been bleeding all afternoon? Had anybody noticed the patch on the back of my skirt? Had Gary seen, when I turned to go into the house? My face went hot with shame as well as sunburn. But surely Mrs Owen would have said if there had been a mark . . . I pulled down my pants and looked at the gusset. It felt as if I had already bled at least two pints, but the dark wet patch on the crotch of my knickers was small. It smelled of meat that had been out too long in the heat, rich and spoiling. That was my insides. The lining of my womb. Maybe an egg too small to see that could have turned into a baby.

But I didn't have anything. If I'd had a mother, she would have known what to do. She would have had something, a pad, a packet of tampons. I had nothing. I wasn't prepared.

I made a wad of toilet paper and stuffed it between my legs. There were clean pants in the airing cupboard, and a clean skirt. I put them on, and listened at the door. There was no sound from anywhere else in the house. What had happened was over now. It was probably safe to go downstairs.

My father was in the kitchen, on hands and knees, carefully sweeping up the shattered plate and shreds of lettuce. I stood in the doorway, different now. I was not the girl he had hit. I was a woman. He could not touch me now.

Slowly he turned and looked up at me. I wanted him to see that I was different. I was not his little girl. Now I was Janey Legge's equal. But my voice came out all wrong, small and scared. 'Dad, I'm bleeding,' I said.

He was stricken, terrified. 'Jesus Christ, Katie, my God, I'm sorry — oh, Jesus, let me see . . .'

'You didn't hurt me. I'm *bleeding*.' He looked at me blankly. 'You know — women's bleeding.'

He sat back on his heels. His eyes filled with tears. Like a reflex, mine did too.

'Oh, my God, Katie. Oh, my God.' He put his arms round my knees and hugged them, burying his face in my thighs for a moment, then flinching away quickly. 'I'm sorry. I'm really sorry.' His face was wet. 'Forgive me. You have to forgive me.'

Now I was embarrassed. He was pathetic. I felt strong again, grown-up. But he was still my dad. I touched his hair, very lightly. 'I need . . . you know.'

'What?'

'Things. Women's stuff. For the bleeding.'

'God, yes.' He looked utterly dazed, completely helpless. 'Things. Right. Mrs Owen?' I shook my head. Too old.

'OK. I'd better . . . You stay here. I'll go . . . Lie down. Does it hurt?'

'Sort of.'

'Oh God. I don't know . . . I'll be right back. OK? Take it easy. I'll be back in a bit.'

★ ★ ★

I lay on the sofa and listened to him reversing the van down the drive. When he returned, half an hour later, he handed me a carrier-bag. Inside it was a belt and some thick, clumsy pads. It was like wearing a bolster between my legs. I knew where he had got them. Janey Legge. *Cow*. Somehow she had managed to destroy even this moment for me.

17

'Kit?' Martin's voice, sounding uncertain for once. 'What happened?'

I can see the flash of his torch, some way off. Now the lights strung along the steel roadway have all gone out, I'm trapped in the small circle of my own torchbeam. Everything else is one big black space — no here, no there, formless and terrifying.

'I don't know. Whatever you do, don't move.' I manage to get my spare torch out of the backpack and switch it on too, for comfort more than anything else. It certainly doesn't illuminate much because I forgot to check the battery before I came out. I'm kicking myself for not making us put on the high-vis jackets.

Darkness itself is not terrifying. You expect darkness underground. What makes you afraid is what might be in the darkness with you. *Long, pale fingers . . .*

'You come back to me, now,' I call to Martin.

The glow of his torch starts to bob through the blackness towards me. It seems to take for ever. How far away *was* he, for God's sake? Somewhere out there is the scary monster Lost, its legs stretching on and on, its hundreds of arms pointing in different directions.

'Well, the only thing you can say for this is that we're getting the authentic Mithraic experience,' says Martin. He's trying for Completely Unworried and not quite hitting it. 'All ceremonies took place in near total darkness, lit by flickering torches.'

'Great.' I can't say I feel too enthusiastic about the authentic Mithraic experience right now. I'd just like to be able to get out of here. I think I know which way the walkway is. I *think*. Carefully I slide one of the loose stones with my foot so that the narrower end points in the right direction.

Martin arrives at my side, reassuringly solid. I can smell his sweat, and I know he feels as uncomfortable as I do. What troubles us both more than darkness is why the lights suddenly went out.

'Nervous?' I ask.

'Of course not, blossom. I'm relying on your extensive knowledge of these workings to get us back to the land of the living.' He sticks the torch under his chin and wiggles his eyebrows. 'It isn't far, is it? Or should I be praying for Mithras to intercede?'

'Get on your knees. I've already promised to sacrifice a couple of bulls.'

'Won't do you any good. He doesn't listen to girls. Strictly men-only cult.'

I cast my torch round hopefully, looking for a gleam of metal from the walkway. Not a twinkle. We've meandered quite a way from it, twisting and turning between massive pillars of rock.

'Did you count steps?' I ask. It's what you're supposed to do, so you always know how far you've come.

'No. Did you?'

No point in saying I didn't expect the lights to go out. Takes two idiots to get really thoroughly fucked.

'Shut up a moment, can't you?' I tell him. 'It could have been a power-cut, but maybe someone's come into the mines and turned the lights off.'

'Off?' says Martin, uneasily.

It's silent, utterly noiseless. Not even the drip of water, though parts of the workings run with it. The earth insulates us from the noise of the world above, and we must be right under the empty offices of the MoD. At least I can't hear what I was dreading: a footfall.

If it's someone turning the master switch off near the

entrance, it will take them a while to reach where we are. And they've turned the lights *off*, not on.

It's a measure of how easily the place can spook you that I'm imagining someone sneaking through the tunnels, in complete darkness, to surprise us. But no — most likely it's a power-cut. Be sensible, Kit — who would be down here on a Saturday?

'Your bat expert,' says Martin. 'Does he work weekends?'

'Maybe. That would make sense.' Relief washes through me. 'He'd have thought the lights had been left on by mistake. He doesn't come right into the workings, just far enough to check on the bats.'

It's quiet, but the darkness is thick and busy all around us, full of ghosts. I'm trying to sit on my nervousness to keep it under control but, like a big greasy beach ball, it keeps sliding away under me.

'We have to move,' I say. 'The longer we postpone it, the more confused we'll get.' I shine the torch down by my feet, to find the stone I moved. 'You stay here, I'll strike out to try to locate the walkway. I'm sure it's this way. Give me your torch, it's stronger than mine. When I locate it, I'll call and you follow.'

'Hold on,' says Martin. 'What are we going to do about the tauroctony?'

'What do you think we should do?'

'We need a photograph, to convince your Dickhead it's here,' says Martin.

I left the camera by the pillar with the raven carving. This time, there's no doubt. I know it's there. I was getting the camera out when Martin called me over to see the tauroctony. I remember setting it carefully down on the ground. Just in case, I check in my backpack but, sure enough, there's no camera.

'We'll pick it up on the way out when we find the walkway,' says Martin, reassuringly. I just wish I had his simple confidence in my sense of direction. 'I'd prefer not to move the tauroctony until we've photographed it . . .'

My torchbeam wanders across the heap of rubble. 'Too right. You pull that stone out, the whole lot might go. The wall's there for a reason, to support the roof, and it's precarious enough as it is.'

As I set out in the direction I think is right, I turn back to give him a cheerful grin. His face is invisible; all I can see is the flare of his torch trained on me. I'm having difficulty putting one foot in front of the other. My knees are shaking. More and more the darkness reminds me of curtains, thick black curtains resisting my groping hands, tangling round my legs, wrapping my face in suffocating folds. The walkway can't be far; provided I don't head off in entirely the wrong direction, I'm bound to strike it soon. All I have to do is keep sweeping the darkness with my torch, and eventually I'll catch an answering glint of metal.

Then why is it taking so long? I must have got the direction wrong. Or perhaps I've veered off course without noticing it.

I stop, and try to activate my personal radar, hoping the walkway might be sending out vibrations to call me in.

'Kit . . . ' Martin's voice, not from directly behind me as I expect, but off to the left. I start to turn towards him, then stop myself, realizing that will only disorient me more. He sounds a bit nervous. 'I think you need to bear more to the left, between those two big pillars over there.'

'Can you still see me?' I ask, trying not to swivel my eyes towards him in case I lose my sense of which way to go.

'Easily.'

'Don't confuse me. I'm sure it's this way. Look at the stone I left on the ground.'

'Which stone? There are about three hundred here, in a big pile.'

'I left one pointing in the right direction. Well, the direction I thought was right. Am I still following that?'

'I can't tell. I don't know which stone you mean and, anyway, they don't have arrows on.'

'Fuck's sake. Try to be a bit helpful.'

'I am being helpful. I think you're off course.'

'You don't fucking *know* I'm off course. I'm doing my best.'

'Don't get shirty. I was just trying to say I think it's a bit further to the left.'

My chest feels tight. He's confusing me. If he'd shut up I might be able to feel it, get back to what I know instinctively . . . But I also know it's easy to lose all sense of direction in the darkness. I sweep the torch round helplessly. I'm really fucked. I've no bloody idea which way now.

'Hold it.' Martin's voice again, this time from directly behind me. Is he moving or am I? 'There! Swing the torch back.'

There it is. Just a wink, between the pillars to the left.

'I think that's it.' I take a tentative step forward, keeping the torch as steady as I can. The wink becomes a glint. Another step, and it's a gleam. Now I can make out the shadowy steel struts of the walkway. Made it. Thank bloody God. Safe.

But experience reminds me that, underground, *safe* is sometimes an illusion.

★ ★ ★

There are individual lighting switches all along the walkway, but they don't work unless the master switch has been set to *On* at the junction box near the entrance. I toggle a couple hopefully as we pass, in case the blackout is no more than a localized cable fault, but

223

no such luck. We make our way by torchlight towards the bats' entrance.

'Sorry,' I say, after a bit. 'I shouldn't have got so ratty.'

'You were way off beam.'

'Wasn't.' I shine my torch on his face to check he's joking. 'Well, a degree or two, maybe, but basically I was going in the right direction.'

'I've never known you to be that much on edge. I thought you'd lost it.'

'Just a bit wobbly.'

'Know what you mean,' he says, to make me feel better, I guess. 'I haven't felt entirely happy underground since, either.'

He thinks this is about the roof fall in the flint mine. Fair enough, we could both have been killed then. He's so big and solid and calm, I forget things can get to him too.

He'll be surprised it's made me quite so flaky. As a rule I don't panic. Even when we got lost in the mist one time on the Derbyshire moors at dusk, trying to find where we'd parked the car — and that was my fault, I'd forgotten the compass and led us round in circles — I didn't panic the way I did today.

'Well. It happens. I wanted us out of there, fast. Sorry.'

'We should have gone back to photograph the tauroctony, though,' he says, with a hint of reproach.

We collected the camera from beside the raven pillar, but I wasn't prepared to take the risk of going back to find the tauroctony without the walkway lights.

'What, and lose ourselves all over again?'

'I could have gone by myself,' he says. 'You could have stayed put to guide me back.'

No way. I've had enough of being on my own with the lights out. We're coming up to a branch walkway and I stop and toggle the switch at its entrance. Still nothing.

'Look, if it's not a major power-cut, we'll turn the lights back on at the junction box and go back, OK?' I'd really rather get straight out into the open air, but I brought him here to find a Mithraic temple — he'll think it's weird I've gone cold on the idea, after all.

Suddenly Martin's fingers are on my arm, squeezing. 'Hold it.' A whisper. 'I can hear voices.'

'*Shit.*' I switch off my torch, and Martin does too. We stand in the total blackness. There's a whisper of air on our faces here, a draught blowing in from the adit not far away, so we must be only a couple of turns of the tunnel away from the Bat Cave. Martin's breath tickles my ear.

'Your bat man?'

'Probably.' Rupert has the kind of high, carrying voice that cuts effortlessly through anything. I edge forward, trying not to make a noise.

' . . . two hundred Greater Horseshoes. In spring the females look for nursery roosts, but with the new incubators we might encourage them to stay.'

'Right through the summer?' It carries less well, but those *r*s have a dismayed Scottish burr: Brendan, horrified at the thought he has to nursemaid all year round a colony of the rarest bats in Britain.

Martin has crept up behind me. 'Can't we get past?'

'They'll hear us.' We're lucky we didn't walk straight into them, flashing our torches. 'We'll have to wait here till they go.'

'So where is it your miners found this bat?' Rupert, getting louder — they're coming towards us. 'I'll show you the incubators on the way.'

Martin's fingers clamp tightly on my shoulder.

'Back,' I whisper. We daren't run: they'd hear us for sure. Martin's boots splash into a puddle but Rupert, bless him, hasn't paused for breath.

'If it was by itself it could have been a Brandt's, though they tend to roost in the colder spots near an entrance. But we haven't managed to log all the ways the bats get in and out, by any means. There are probably plenty of entrances none of us knows about in the woods to the south.'

They're unlikely to overtake us, but the danger is that they'll catch sight of our torchlight when we reach a long straight stretch. If only they'd turn off . . . I don't know this area of the quarries well enough. Which is the roadway leading to the incubators?

'I'd like to get my hands on the idiot who left the lights on. I've told your miners repeatedly I don't want them using the lighting in the areas where the bats roost.' Sounds like Rupert is galloping away on his high horse. 'It's there for emergencies only. They don't seem to appreciate how rare some of these bats are. The junction box should be further in. Then it wouldn't happen.'

I can't hear Brendan's reply, but I can guess the moustache is in the up position and he's saying something along the lines of 'Regretfully, safety requirements dictate . . . ' A steel roadway branches off and Martin is about to dive down there. I grab his fleece and pull him back. Steel makes it a permanent route, one that will be left open after the mines have been filled, so it must be a bat corridor. I'm hoping it's the one leading to the incubators.

Ahead, the main walkway bends to the right, entering one of the bigger voids. If they're still following, they'll see us for sure on this stretch. There's really no choice: I scramble between the struts out of the walkway, and Martin follows me. We switch off the torches and flatten ourselves into a hollow half-way along the rock wall.

'What colour was this bat?'

'Haven't a clue,' says Brendan. Their voices are getting clearer and closer. 'Aren't they all black?'

'Certainly not. Brandt's are mid-brown and silver grey. Of course, it could have been a whiskered bat

— they're virtually identical to Brandt's. You can tell by the shape of the penis.'

'Its penis?' It has clearly never occurred to Brendan that a bat might have a penis, let alone how you might get a glimpse of it. 'You mean you actually look at bat's penises and compare them?'

'A whiskered bat's is longer and thinner. If it's club-shaped, it's a Brandt's . . . ' but Rupert's voice is fading. They've taken the steel roadway to the incubators. I creep back to peer cautiously round the corner: bobbing lights are heading away down the branch tunnel. Brendan is in the lead, and his high-vis jacket with the RockDek logo glows fluorescent in the dark, caught in the beam of Rupert's torch. Finally their lights disappear. It's safe to make our way down the passage again towards the Stonefield entrance.

★　★　★

Martin talks me into eating in the deli, which turns out to be where Mrs Owen's favourite caff used to be. It now has a set of smart beech tables and chairs at the back where you can have lunch. I'm desperate to light up, but not a chance, of course: this is the twenty-first century. I remember those tottering piles of butts, those slagheaps of ash spilling over the foil ashtrays in Mrs Owen's day.

'We *are* going back this afternoon to photograph the tauroctony, aren't we?' Martin says, through a mouthful of panini.

'No. We've already almost been caught twice . . . '

'Twice?'

I forgot I hadn't mentioned the Gary mishap. 'I don't want to risk it.'

'Hey, flower, are you going cold on this? I need that picture to compare it with some of the classic finds from

Mithraic temples. I can't stick my neck out without being sure.'

'You can't stick your neck out without *my* head being chopped off,' I point out. 'If anyone finds out we've been down there today, I get the sack for sure.'

* * *

It's an impossible situation. If we tell anyone what we saw, I lose my job for taking an unauthorized person underground. I lose my *career*. It's the kind of sin that doesn't sit too well on the CV. Without the job, I can't make sure the tauroctony is found.

'It *is* a tauroctony?' I ask Martin, anxiously, on the way back to the car. 'You're absolutely sure?'

Martin snorts. 'It's impossible to be sure unless I can compare it properly. But yes, I think it probably is. The only snag is . . . ' he wrinkles his nose, like a bad smell just hit him ' . . . Mithraism is a soldier's cult. It's very ancient in Persia — dates back to maybe 1400 BC — but it was the Roman Army who brought it back and spread it throughout the empire. All the British temples to Mithras are associated with garrisons — Hadrian's Wall had several. But there is absolutely no evidence of the Roman Army having any significant presence in Bath.'

'What do you mean? There are the bloody Roman Baths, aren't there? Surely the Army passed this way when they invaded?'

'The Romans didn't encounter much resistance in these parts. They probably by-passed Bath altogether and marched straight for the Mendips — they took over the lead and silver mines there around 43, 44 AD, only a couple of years after the invasion. Eventually Bath became a religious centre and a health spa, but by then everything was peaceful. And Mithraism wasn't popular until much later. Second or third century.'

We've reached the car and I press the key fob to unlock the doors. I really don't see why it's impossible. Though I am beginning to grasp why Dickon was so adamant I was wrong about the carving. 'But there must have been soldiers here, if only to heal their old war wounds?'

Martin gives me the look that says I don't know what I'm talking about. 'And another thing. There's absolutely no firm evidence that the Romans took stone from Green Down. It's pretty much accepted they quarried Bathampton Down, but every expert I've spoken to this week says it would almost certainly have been open cast. They never went underground for the stone.'

I get in and slam the door peevishly. 'But if they weren't quarrying Green Down, and there were no bloody soldiers, therefore no temple to Mithras, what's a tauroctony doing propping up a wall underground?'

'Search me, Kit. I need to do a bit of digging myself.' He gets in, and pokes suspiciously at the CD player. 'Can we have Bryan Ferry this time?'

'I don't keep Bryan Ferry in the car. He's reserved for maudlin nights remembering when Nick was nice to me. The Clash?'

'If you *must*.'

I have to put the CD in because Martin doesn't do technology, unless it's a couple of thousand years old. We set off towards Turleigh, Martin staring out of the window, chewing the side of his cheek, always a sign of deep archaeological thought on his part.

★   ★   ★

It's only four o'clock, but Martin insists that dinner is going to take two and a half hours to cook and he'd better get on with the preparation. So we sit in the kitchen, as the light fades in the wintry sky, him

229

chopping things, me on the laptop scooting about the Internet, trying to find pictures of tauroctonies for comparison.

'Where's your garlic press?'

'I shouldn't think for a moment I've got one. Altar stone? Does that sound right? Oh, no, it's mostly writing. '*Deo Invicto Mith* — ' no, '*Mitrae* M.Simple-somebody-or-other VSLM'. What's all that about?'

He comes to peer over my shoulder. 'Marcus Simplicius Simplex, whoever he, fulfilled his vow to the god.' The smell of lemon zest comes off Martin's fingers as he waves them airily. 'They always refer to Mithras as '*invictus*' — unconquered. That's why soldiers thought he was great. It was all about courage and truth, honour and discipline. Also popular, though, with marginal social groups, freedmen and merchants.'

'There — told you so. Why shouldn't there be a Mithraeum at Bath? There must have been freedmen and merchants here.'

He puts down his paring knife. 'Because none has been found in Britain other than in a garrison town. There's one in London, several along Hadrian's Wall, another in Segontium, which was North Wales and always seething with rebellion. OK . . . ' he picks up the bigger knife and starts chopping parsley ' . . . I agree, that doesn't rule it out. *But.*'

'But what?'

'It makes it really hard to convince any respectable academic there could have been one here. Now, if I say breadcrumbs, you are going to be able to find me a loaf, aren't you?'

'What are you cooking?'

'Secret. Man's hidden knowledge. Not to be shared with woman. Like Mithraism. Like freemasonry.'

It's good to have Martin here, in this warm, biscuit-coloured kitchen smelling cosily of crushed garlic and fried onions. I love it when he cooks for me.

'They called the stonecutters in the quarries freemasons,' I say, 'because they cut freestone into blocks.'

'John Wood, who designed the Royal Crescent, was an eighteenth-century Freemason,' says Martin. 'Capital F. That's probably how he got on in life. A poor boy with the sense to make connections.'

I realize I'm looking at a picture of Noddy again on the computer. 'Hey,' I say, 'it's not the same picture. But it's the same chap. In his hat.'

Martin leans over and peers at the screen. 'Oh, yes,' he says. '*Oh*, yes. That's him. Mithras, rising from the Living Rock.'

It's a painting, faint with age, on a plastered wall. He wears a cloak, tunic and trousers. There are faded traces of red on the cloak, and his face is smooth white. He holds a torch in one hand, a sword in the other. Radiant streaks of light shoot out round his head.

'Those rays will be cut through into a hollow niche in the wall,' says Martin. 'They would light a lamp in there. Kind of impressive. The god reborn, rising behind the altar, with a halo of flickering light.'

It reminds me of something, something deep and primitive, that goes with incense and chanting.

'Isn't it a bit like . . . well, *church*?'

'Yes, well, people have made a lot of funny claims for Mithras,' says Martin. 'It's a cult with a saviour, sacrifice and rebirth. He even had a Last Supper. But then other people say he was Lucifer. Fire, dawn, the morning star. The current theory is that it's all to do with astrology. Frankly, it being a mystery cult, it's anybody's guess. Nothing was ever written down about it. Most of what we know comes from the iconography — wall paintings like that one, carved reliefs, altar stones, votive offerings. See those two blokes there, flanking him?'

You can just see them in the painting, two figures in

231

long robes, both holding torches. One's holding his torch up, the other's is pointed down.

'Cautes and Cautopates,' says Martin. 'The Twins. They represent the rising and setting of the sun, or hope and sorrow.'

I know those two. Pushy bastards, once you've met them they keep calling round. I glance out of the window. Cautopates has been doing his stuff: the sun has already sunk behind the hill on the other side of the valley, cold misty darkness is marching up the fields from the river and fierce stars are snapping into an ice-blue sky. I get up and draw the curtains across. That's enough Mithraism for tonight. But Martin is still staring thoughtfully at the screen. 'It would be really something if there is a temple there,' he says. '*Really* something. Very, very big deal.'

'With a very, very big pile of concrete about to be pumped into it.'

'They couldn't. They wouldn't, if we proved it was there.'

I'm not so sure. I think they still would. But I don't say that. I bring him a slice of bread, my handmaiden's offering, and watch him crumble it for the stuffing. There's a distant smile on his face as he imagines the glory of finding his very own undiscovered Mithraic temple.

★ ★ ★

Supper, which turns out to be boned and rolled duck with a mushroom and sage sauce, is simmering away in the oven making my kitchen smell like happy families. Maybe I ought to get Martin to give me cookery lessons one day. He is sprawled on the sofa, a pair of funny little glasses I've not seen him wear before perched on the end of his nose, reading excavation reports he's downloaded. I'm sipping wine, wondering why male-centred religion always seems to be about honour.

'Why do you think your dad said that about marrying me?' I ask.

'Mmm?' Martin pushes his glasses back up his nose, finds that doesn't help him see me, and pushes them so far down they almost fall off the end. 'I can't get used to these bloody things. Do they make me look clever? Or just a sad old queen? Don't answer that. Why wouldn't he want me to settle down with a nice girl?'

'Yes, but . . . ' I try to put my finger on what seems strange about it to me, even though Martin's dad had no idea about his son's sexuality. 'What on earth made him think I was a nice girl? I met him, what? Twice? And the first time I was still very much married to Nick.'

'Actually, I think that was it,' said Martin. 'He thought you and Nick were all wrong. He said to me, 'What on earth made her get tied up with a waste of space like Nick Parry? She needs a nice lad like you, son.' '

'Big on sacrifice, then, your dad.'

'No, dimbo, he must have thought there were advantages for me as well. But he liked dabbling in people's lives, and he was good at summing them up too. Like — well, no.'

'Well no what?'

'No, I was thinking of something else he said. Not relevant. Another time.'

I would press this, but the doorbell rings. This is unexpected. I don't know anyone likely to call. Half past six on a Saturday evening is a bit keen for door-to door salesmen or Jehovah's Witnesses; maybe it's one of the neighbours come to introduce themselves.

It's Gary.

He stands on the doorstep, shifting very slightly from one leg to another like an athlete steadying himself for

233

the run up to the high jump, a bunch of flowers in one hand and a bottle of wine in the other. He's not wearing his nice suit this time, but an equally well-pressed pair of black jeans, and a pale blue crew-necked cashmere pullover. There's a faint and discreet waft of aftershave, and everything about him says Trying Very Hard. My heart goes out to him.

'Hi,' he begins. 'Just thought I'd pop round and welcome you to your new . . . ' And then he sees Martin.

The front door opens straight into the big living space, with the kitchen through an archway beyond, so those lovely happy-family smells are wafting out and hitting Gary's nose at the same time as he spots Martin on the sofa with his shoes off. True, there's an archaeological report in Martin's hand — just drop it gently, Martin, don't let Gary see it says 'Mithraic Temple' in 28-point type at the top — but he's made himself comfortable in a way that suggests I've just got up from twiddling my fingers in the chest hairs poking over the top of his unbuttoned shirt collar.

Matters somehow get worse when Martin does his trick with the glasses again, because he can't quite see Gary properly, and instead of sad old queen, it looks much more like robustly heterosexual, intellectual alpha-male, sizing up Mr Beta who's had the temerity to call on his woman.

'Oh,' says Gary. 'Oh. Sorry. You've got company.' And my heart wrenches.

'Come in,' I say, far too heartily, so that I can hear myself sounding like Frenzied Hospitable *Hausfrau*, with dinner in the oven and the master's sperm in her mouth. 'No, do come in. Let me put those in water . . . ' Shit, shit, shit, I'm making it worse. 'Have a glass of wine. Not Gevrey Chambertin, sorry . . . '

Martin, getting used to the idea of glasses-as-virility-prop, drops them down his nose again and lifts his

234

eyebrows, as if to say, *Gevrey Chambertin? What are you on about? That's posh plonk for nerds who know nothing about wine.* Gary steps over the threshold like a robot, proffering the flowers but clutching the wine as if he's sure I'm going to laugh at the label.

'Lovely,' I say, extricating it from his grasp. 'Ooh, lovely. Rioja. Brilliant. Fab. Adore it. Don't I, Martin?' Shit. 'Well. Gosh, I'm forgetting my manners, let me introduce you. Martin. Old friend . . . ' Martin waggles the glasses again, trying to look like Eric Morecambe, I think, but succeeding only in appearing aggressively possessive. 'And, Martin, this is Gary. From work. The foreman. *Site* foreman, I mean.'

'And what do you do, Martin?' says Gary politely.

'I lecture in archaeology,' says Martin. He catches sight of my frenzied face behind Gary, trying to convey he shouldn't give away any information that would help Gary put two and two together about our little expedition underground. A puzzled look crosses his face. Then he gets it. 'I specialize in . . . oh, this and that. Lots of Palaeolithic work, of course.'

'Palaeolithic, right,' says Gary, so politely this time that it's clear he hasn't a clue what Martin means.

'Which, of course, is the Old Stone Age. But I expect you knew that. Or why should you, of course?' Embarrassment's catching. Martin's got it big-time now, I can see that, but to anyone else it makes him look like a pompous git.

'Of course,' agrees Gary. He stands there looking helpless, as if I took his manhood away when I removed the flowers and the wine.

'Sit down, Gary. Red or white? We've got either on the go.' I'm flapping like a broken umbrella in a hurricane. 'Martin's come down for the weekend.' Short of saying, 'I expect he'd rather your arse than mine any day,' I can't see how to make plain the nature of the relationship.

But what's Martin doing? Oh, God. He's doing his best to help. He's doing his dad the vicar. He's doing *I hope your intentions towards this young lady are honourable, young man*. The trouble is, it doesn't look like that's what he's doing. It looks like he's doing *Fuck off, she's mine*.

'Look,' says Gary, 'I'm interrupting your evening. Sorry. I should go.'

'No,' cries Martin, way over the top. He might as well have shouted, *Yes! Yes! Please go!* 'We hadn't any plans. Stay for dinner. I'm sure we can make it stretch.' He means it, he's longing to show off his cooking to another man, but Gary isn't to know that.

'No, really. I was just dropping by with the wine and flowers as a house-warming gift. I've got to dash, anyway. Some other weekend, perhaps.' He's already backing towards the door.

I catch up with him just as he gets it open. 'Gary, honestly, that was so nice.' I want our eyes to do that tangling thing again, but he won't look directly into mine. 'Really. I'm so touched you brought the wine and flowers. Thank you.'

'That's OK, Kit,' he says, and just for a moment I get a flash of those blue eyes, but he doesn't hold the gaze, and he's off down the pavement, his hands in his jeans pockets and his shoulders all hunched, not looking back at me, heading for the 4×4 parked under Turleigh's one streetlamp. Something seems different. God, he's *cleaned* it. I hadn't realized it was green.

'Jesus, you're useless, blossom,' says Martin, as I turn back into the room.

'Useless? What about you? You frightened the poor bugger away with that glasses trick.'

'I don't know what you mean. I need those glasses. I have presbyopia.'

'You have a bad case of Stage Academic.'

'And you fancy him something rotten.'

'It's not that obvious, is it?'

'Not to him, it isn't. Why didn't you kiss him?'

'*Kiss* him?'

'I don't mean snog him. Just a gentle little peck on the cheek, to say thank you for the flowers. That was all it needed.'

I don't do that kind of kissing. I don't touch people lightly. Martin knows that, because we never kiss, we rarely hug.

He's looking at me, with an odd kind of concern in his eyes. 'You can be such a bloody noodle, sometimes,' he says. 'If you don't want him, stand aside. He's got no dress sense, but a lovely set of pecs.'

★ ★ ★

Fair's fair. After supper, Martin gets the laptop and I do the washing-up, standing at the sink looking out of the window over the terrace since I still haven't bothered to tell the agents about the broken dish-washer.

As I scour the casserole dish, I catch a movement outside in the darkened garden, just a quick flash, something white, like a face beyond the terrace where the apple tree lifts bony arms to the moon. I peer uneasily through the window, until it occurs to me it was my own reflection on the glass; as I reach for the scourer to start scrubbing, there it is again. When my wedding ring catches the light, it looks exactly as if someone is out there, skulking under the tree, watching me, drawing back hastily in case they're seen.

I know who it is. It's Katie. I always knew I'd have to face her if I came back.

I'm not ready yet. Go away.

18

We met at the station in Bath. She said she'd pick me up in her big station-wagon, but I didn't want her coming to the house in case anyone saw and told my dad.

I was waiting by the ticket office when I saw her approach. I knew it was her, even from a distance, by her pale linen dress and the long scarf. Her legs did something odd but elegant when she walked: she placed each foot exactly in front of the other, and it made her hips sway and her legs look very long. She was wearing sandals with low wedge heels and carrying a huge straw bag with leather handles over her shoulder. Everything was in delicate, neutral colours apart from the scarf and her lipstick, but she looked twice as vivid as Janey Legge had in her violets and yellows and ruffles.

My heart was thudding in my throat. This was terrifying. Could I go through with it? I had hardly slept, thinking about the day ahead, what I might discover.

'I'm sorry,' I said, as she drew level. 'Would you mind getting my ticket? I didn't know it cost so much.'

'I was planning on buying it anyway,' Mrs Klein said. 'For goodness' sake, Katie, I'm the one who insisted on us going.' She was already marching towards the counter.

'I'll pay you back.'

'Don't be absurd.'

'Honestly,' I protested.

'It's my treat,' she said firmly, over her shoulder. 'And it *is* my treat. I'm going to enjoy myself.' There was a glint in her eye, something steely. She was a woman

238

with a mission. 'Two, second class, to Paddington, please.'

'Is your daughter a child fare?' said the man behind the glass.

'Oh, heavens. Are you, Katie? I can't remember when your birthday is.'

The man behind the glass gave her an odd look.

'No,' I said firmly. 'I'm adult fare.'

There were still several weeks until my fourteenth birthday, but as far as I was concerned I had come of age.

My legs felt shaky as we went up stone stairs that smelt of pee, and on to the platform. The line stretched in a huge curve away from the station and towards London. Towards my mother, I hoped. Or, at least, towards some idea of where she was.

* * *

When I phoned her, the day after my period started, Mrs Klein had not seemed at all surprised when I asked her to help me find my mother. 'Best possible idea, Katie,' she said. 'It may take us a while but it will be the best thing you ever did.'

She told me the place to start was the Register of Births, Marriages and Deaths. If we knew one useful fact, we could get a long way towards tracing my mother by finding out if she had remarried.

'What useful fact?' I asked.

'Ah,' said Mrs Klein. 'Ah. That depends. But, hey, we'll get there eventually. Find out everything you can about your mum. Full name. Maiden name. Date of birth. Parents' names. Parents' address. Anything like that.'

'But her parents died,' I said. 'They died before I was even born.'

'Anything,' said Mrs Klein, sounding a bit cross.

239

'Anything.' Her voice brightened. 'We'll have to go to London, of course. They keep all the registers at St Catherine's House.'

I'd only been to London once, on a daytrip with my dad. We went to Madame Tussaud's and the Planetarium in the morning, and the Natural History Museum in the afternoon to look at fossils.

'We can go to South Kensington after we've been to look at the Register,' she went on. 'Harrods and Harvey Nichols. Or Bond Street and Fenwicks. I love Fenwicks.' I thought I heard a small sigh from her end of the phone. 'Trish is still up in London with her grandmother, but frankly I can't stand Robert's mother. You won't mind if we don't tell them we're going, will you?'

★   ★   ★

But how was I going to find that one useful fact, whatever it was? I went through the dressing-table drawers in the front bedroom, but there were no letters or documents there to help. When my mother had gone, she must have taken everything with her. I went down the road to Mrs Owen's.

'You still look peaky,' she said, opening one of her gleaming white cupboards to get out the biscuit tin. 'You sure you're not sickening?' I didn't explain why I was still pale. Not telling her about my period felt like another of those growing-up things.

She was my only hope of finding out something more about my mother. Mrs Owen had the relentless curiosity of a society journalist. When anyone new arrived in the street, she was straight in there, offering a pint of milk and a cup of sugar — 'In case you want a brew before you unpack' — armed with a list of questions to establish their antecedents and their social standing in the road. If anyone knew where my mother had come from, she would.

'I really want to know *something* about her,' I said, as Mrs Owen brought the cups to the table. 'I mean, what if she looked for me one day? What kind of a daughter doesn't want to know about her mother?'

Mrs Owen sighed and took a biscuit. 'You in't going to leave this alone, are you, petal?' she said.

'Well, tell me who else I can talk to about her.'

'Course, she was much younger than me,' said Mrs Owen, as if I might not have noticed. 'And she kept herself pretty much to herself. You was tiny when they moved in — I suppose it must've been the same year you was born . . .'

We were away. I dunked a shortbread in my tea, and waited for the rest of the story.

★   ★   ★

The first thing Mrs Klein did once we had settled in our seats on the train was light a cigarette, flipping open the top of a silver lighter and flicking its wheel with a practised thumb. She caught my surprised look. 'Don't tell Trish,' she said. 'I never smoke at home. Robert hates it. And it sets a bad example. Don't *you* ever start.'

'Of course not,' I said piously.

The train jerked once, then began to move away from the station. I peered out of the window to watch Bath going by, but Mrs Klein had already pulled a notebook from her huge bag. 'Fire away,' she said. 'What have you found out?'

There wasn't much. My father met my mother some time in the late fifties, possibly at a dance in Bristol. And Mrs Owen had finally remembered how the name was connected with cards. Playing cards.

'Her maiden name was Trumper,' I said. 'Her first name was maybe Katherine. Kitty for short.'

241

'Katherine with a K or a C?' asked Mrs Klein, writing it down. 'I-N-E or Y-N?'

I didn't know. I wasn't sure about anything. Mrs Owen had been remembering a conversation over thirteen years ago. But Trumper was an unusual name, and that gave me hope she had remembered it right.

'Date of birth?' Mrs Klein asked.

'Sorry. Mrs Owen said she would have been in her mid-twenties, she was sure. No more than twenty-five or -six.'

'Mmm,' said Mrs Klein. 'Dubious. Anything else?'

'Her parents were both killed in the war, in a bombing raid. She was brought up by her gran. She came from Bedminster,' I added. 'In Bristol. But I don't know the address. She wasn't very tall, like me, Mrs Owen said.'

'That's good,' said Mrs Klein, bravely. 'Really useful.' I could tell by the tone of her voice that it wasn't. 'At least she wasn't called Smith or Brown.'

★　★　★

Just before we got into London, long grey streaks of rain slashed diagonally across the train windows. It was the first shower for several weeks, but it didn't clear the heat; when we arrived at Paddington the air was sulphurous and steamy. We took the tube to Holborn, where Mrs Klein produced a folding umbrella from her bag. It matched her reddish scarf exactly. Did she keep lots of them, in different colours, for every outfit?

St Catherine's House was a tall building on the corner of Kingsway and Aldwych. Everything seemed double normal size. Traffic raced by, jerking to a reluctant stop at the zebra crossing, then accelerating away. My heart started thumping again as Mrs Klein pushed through a revolving door into the lobby. It was full of self-important men in commissionaires' uniforms, pacing up and down. Mrs Klein marched straight past them. She seemed to know exactly where to go.

It was a big room like a library, but it made me think of the Tardis, only in reverse, because there was hardly any space to move around so it seemed small and poky. At the far end there were lots of green metal shelves full of tall books, and between them were rows of wooden lecterns, at which people stood leafing through more of the massive books. There was hardly any space between the shelves and the lecterns, and every lectern was occupied. Most of the people in the room were elderly, apart from a few youngish men in scruffy suits, fingers racing down pages and occasionally scribbling in spiral notebooks. The place stank of wet wool and dry, crumbly paper, sweat and stale old-lady perfume.

'OK, deep breath,' said Mrs Klein. 'Dive in.'

I understood what she meant as we neared the shelves. It was nothing like a library, after all. An unseemly scrum fought it out to get hold of the books. Middle-aged women elbowed stout elderly gentlemen in their well-covered ribs to get to the shelf first, and I saw one white-haired but game old lady wrestle a book from the grasp of a younger man in a damp mackintosh.

'I'm sorry,' she said to him, 'I've been waiting *all morning* for the third quarter of 1869.'

I understood. I felt fierce, too, ready to fight off anyone who came between me and the books, because somewhere in there was my mother. We did our share of elbowing to get through and eventually emerged into a relatively calm stretch, 1930 to 1940.

'We'll be all right here,' said Mrs Klein. 'They're mostly researching family history so they're only interested in the nineteenth century when their grandparents were born. We might have to fight off a few probate clerks looking for missing heirs, but mostly we'll have the twentieth century to ourselves.'

My stomach was full of snakes fighting each other. 'Excuse me,' I said. 'I have to go to the toilet first.'

In the cubicle in the ladies' I leaned my head against the door. The grey Formica was cool against my hot skin. For a moment I wondered if I was going to be sick, but it passed as it had the other evening. In my pocket was the ammonite my dad had given me. I ran my fingers over its ridges, counting the bumps to calm myself. I pulled the chain, washed my hands, and went back to Mrs Klein amid the shelves.

The Birth indexes were kept in books with red covers. Marriages were green, Deaths black. There were handles on the spines so you could pull them off the shelf, and each book held a single quarter's worth of records for the whole country, long lists of names in alphabetical order. Mrs Klein had decided we should start looking for my mother's birth well before the war, in case Mrs Owen had got her age wrong.

'Steady,' she said, as I reached up to pull out the red book for January to March 1930. 'They weigh a ton.'

I wondered how the old ladies managed it. They must have muscles like shot-putters'. We were going back through fifteen years of births to try to find my mother's; four quarters per year meant four books times fifteen, which made sixty. Sixty! How long would this take? I hadn't grasped how much there was to do. The only consolation was that Mrs Klein was very quick at flipping through each register. We couldn't get a place at a lectern, so she squatted in a corner at the end of the shelves, balancing the heavy books on her knees. Every now and then someone came past and nearly tripped over her. My job was to trot back and forth with the books. I took her two volumes at a time, carrying them by their handles. I was sure after only a few trips my arms had begun to stretch to gorilla length.

I now saw why it was lucky my mother was called

Trumper. Names like Smith ran for column after column. But there were never more than a dozen or so Trumpers, scattered across the whole country. Sometimes there were none.

'Why do we have to start with her birth?' I asked. An elderly man who had probably strayed into the twentieth century by mistake frowned at us. I lowered my voice. 'It's taking ages. Couldn't we go straight into Marriages?'

'It gives us the detail we need to be sure we find the right marriage. We'll know her exact birthday, her second name and her parents' names. She won't be Trumper after she's married to your dad. She could be registered as Carter, divorcee, on her second marriage certificate, and there are a lot more Carters than Trumpers so we'll need that birthdate to be sure.'

Carter, divorcee. I hadn't thought of my father being divorced. He'd never mentioned it. But he never said anything about my mother. Of course she would have had to divorce him to marry again. I wasn't sure how I felt about her having another husband. I wanted her to be free to come back to my dad, but how else was I going to find her if she hadn't got married? Mrs Klein said she might be on the electoral rolls, but they were harder. You had to know whereabouts she was living and go to that town.

'How do you know all this?' I asked.

She bent over the index as if she was worried about losing her place on the page.

'I traced Robert's family tree for him,' she said. But that was odd, because Trish had told me her Jewish grandparents fled to this country from Germany in the 1930s, so why would Mrs Klein have tracked her husband's family back through the Register of Births in England?

There were few windows, letting in hardly any sun. Dingy fluorescent squares shed a sickly light. The air-conditioning hummed and wheezed but didn't move the air. I went back along the shelves and fetched more volumes. A woman with tarnished silver hair and a whiskery chin threaded her way along the stack, and smiled at me. She passed on down the stack, a grey whisper in her chiffon blouse and Viyella skirt.

I went back to Mrs Klein with the next quarter. She was wearing a pair of half-moon glasses, which perched on the end of her nose.

'We're there,' she said in a low voice, turning the book towards me. 'Here you are. That's your mother.'

I put my finger on the start of the column headed TRUMPER. It was trembling. I couldn't keep it steady as I tracked slowly down the lists of names. Where was she? My mouth was dry, and something cold was creeping through my stomach.

Derek . . . Edgar J . . . Mary . . . My wavering finger moved down the columns. Derby . . . Wolverhampton . . . Luton . . . All over the country, all these Trumpers . . . Michael, Sarah L . . . I couldn't see her.

Start again.

Alexandra . . . Jennifer . . . Ruth . . . Stephen . . .

Overhead the air-conditioning ground away, mmm, mummm, mumm, mum.

And there she was.

TRUMPER, Kathleen . . .

Mrs Klein was holding the big book on a slant, for me to see, so it looked as if the words were running downhill into each other. They were going all blurry.

'Have a tissue.'

That was my mother. My mother, being born.

What had she looked like? Was she one of those babies like a tiny pale bud, or had she been red, crumpled and noisy? Had her mother (maiden name Elaine Billings) cradled her like a precious china doll in her arms, supporting her delicate skull in the crook of her elbow, with her husband (Jack Trumper, fishmonger, m. Elaine Billings 23 March 1932) beaming proudly?

Seeing the names written down, as I now sat cross-legged on the floor and Mrs Klein scooted backwards and forwards bringing more and more information, made my mother real to me for the first time.

She had been a late baby, an only child of parents who were already in their thirties when they married, nearly forty when Kathleen was born. She must have seemed very special, after all those years of trying. Was her grandmother (Kathleen Billings, so Kitty had been named after her, died 18 July 1959) there as well, smiling at the granddaughter she would be bringing up only two years later, after Elaine and Jack died on the same day (2 June 1942) under the rubble of their house? Where had baby Kathleen been that day? How had she escaped?

I would probably never know. Unless I found her.

It was lunchtime. The stacks were almost empty of people, which I was glad of, because the tears kept squeezing under my eyelashes.

Mrs Klein was crying a bit too. There were smudges of mascara under her eyes, and her nose was red. She gave me a big hug. 'Look at the pair of us,' she said, pulling away. I'd left a glistening snail trail on the front of her dress. 'Robert always says he's never known any woman cry as easily as I do. But it is lovely. How do you feel?'

'Weird,' I said. 'Just . . . weird. I can't believe I'm looking at her. It's like I *am* looking at her, really.'

TRUMPER, Kathleen. Known as Kitty. Probably couldn't remember her own mother, just like me, or her father. All she had was her gran, the other Kathleen, who was already in her sixties when her daughter and son-in-law were killed. Then she died too, before Kitty was twenty. Had she already met my father then? I imagined my great-grandmother — I wanted her to look like Mrs Owen, a big, lumbering woman — propped against pillows, holding my mother's hand. 'I'm so glad you've got him, petal,' she gasped. 'I don't like to think of you being all on your own without me . . . '

Kathleen Trumper, m. Colin Carter, electrician, 15 March 1960. Colin, the clever boy, whom everyone thought would do so well in life. Had a trade, see. Kitty loved him, but he was so busy doing well he was never there. She sat at home with her baby, and sometimes went for walks in Green Down, past the sentry guarding the gate at the Ministry of Defence buildings . . .

'Let's take a break,' said Mrs Klein. 'Frankly, we deserve it. And I'm gasping for a ciggie, after all that emotion.'

★　★　★

'And if we find when she got married again, what then?' I said, over lunch in the Kardomah coffee shop next door on Kingsway. My arms ached from carrying the books.

'Lots of possibilities,' said Mrs Klein. 'If her new husband really was a soldier, we can trace him through the Ministry of Defence, once we know his name. They may even still be living at the same address as on the marriage certificate. It's like a hunt, Katie.' Her eyes gleamed with excitement. 'We stalk her through the registers and the electoral rolls.'

Yes, but whose hunt was it? I put down my sandwich. It kept sticking in my throat, and my stomach felt tight and queasy. What would Dad say when he found out what I was doing? Maybe he'd think I didn't love him enough any more. But I did, I did — I just wanted him not to be with Janey.

Mrs Klein smiled. 'Don't worry, we will find her, I

promise. And she'll be so thrilled you came looking for her.'

My fingers crept to the ammonite in my pocket, as reassuring as Mrs Klein's calm voice. She was right. I would find my mother. I had to.

The Kardomah was full of office workers, men who hung their suit jackets on the back of their chairs, girls in neat grey A-line skirts. Mrs Klein towered over most of them, the men as well as the girls, elegant in her pale creamy linen dress that would have looked like a carrier bag on Janey Legge.

And my mother? Could my mother wear a dress like that?

'You must have been very beautiful when you were young,' I said to Mrs Klein.

'Thank you, Katie.' Her mouth did an odd twist that suggested I had said something funny.

'Did you always know you were going to be a model?' I asked.

She laughed. 'Trish always exaggerates. I did a bit of modelling for a couple of years, that's all. I married Robert before I was twenty. And I'll tell you a secret. I only became a model because I ran away from home.'

'You *ran away*?' I couldn't imagine what would make anyone like Mrs Klein do that.

'I had a terrible row with my parents,' she said. 'Awful. So I walked out of school one afternoon and caught the train up to the West End. Never went home again.'

'Never?'

'Well, I did visit, of course. After I was married, after I'd had Marcus, I went back to see them because Robert made me. But once was enough. I saw my mother in hospital when she was dying a few years later, but I haven't spoken to my father in years.'

'Gosh.' I had no idea what to say. It seemed rude to ask more, although I wanted to know why she hated her father so much. Her big sea-green eyes were fixed on me now, and I could tell she was watching to see how I reacted.

'He wasn't a very nice man,' she said. 'He . . . '

One of the office workers bumped into our table as he pulled on his jacket. My glass of orange juice, full to the brim, rocked and slopped over the marble tabletop. Mrs Klein reached quickly to mop it with a paper napkin before it dribbled over the edge, but only succeeded in knocking the glass over altogether.

'Katie, I'm really sorry . . . ' She caught the glass just before it rolled off. The boy in the suit was oblivious, sauntering out of the door. 'My fault. So clumsy. Are you soaked?'

'Actually, no.' I peered down at my legs. I was wearing the gypsy skirt again. Most of the stains had come out, but there were still faint pinkish marks and now a splash of orange near the hem. 'Nothing much, anyway.'

'Are you sure? No, look, it's ruined. I'm so terribly sorry. We'll get you another one when we go to the shops. Robert always says I'm the clumsiest woman he's ever met.'

'No, it's *fine*.'

'No, it's not. Anyway,' she went on, 'let's pay, and get back to the Records Office. I'll bet we find your mum's remarriage within the next half-hour.'

* * *

But we didn't.

'She took her time about getting married again,' Mrs Klein said, as she closed another of the big green books. 'Is that 1972 you've got there?'

My mother had left my father in 1965.

'Maybe I'm wrong, and she didn't keep your dad's name after the divorce, so it's under Trumper. Or

250

maybe she didn't marry her soldier, after all.'

I felt a surge of relief. That meant she could still come back and be with my dad.

'Unless they decided to live together. It was the sixties. We need the divorce papers, of course, I'm so *stupid* . . . ' She took her half-moon glasses off and began to polish them, muttering to herself, 'There has to be an address, that would be a starting point . . . Or children. Maybe they had children, and if they weren't married, would they be registered under her name rather than his?'

Children? Something hot sliced through my chest. 'You mean I could have brothers and sisters?'

'Well, *half*-brothers and -sisters, of course. If she stayed with him she's almost bound to have had more children.'

'But — '

'It could be amazing, Katie. You could have a whole new family.'

'Let's stop. That's enough for today. I . . . want to stop.'

Mrs Klein pushed her glasses back on to her nose and looked over them at me. 'Stop *now*?'

'Yes. Please. I don't know,' I said. 'I don't know if I want to find her, after all.'

'But we're so close.'

I remembered Mrs Owen, talking to her friends the day I had hidden under the table. *She was in the family way when she went.*

If she had other children, why would she want to see me? I closed my eyes to hold in the tears — different tears, now, ones that came blistering up, acid and scalding, from the hard hot lump in my chest. My fingers crept again to the ammonite in my pocket. It felt dead and lifeless. After all, it was only a shell made of stone.

I was nothing to her. She'd left *me*, after all, as well as my dad. There was a new baby, a better baby.

'She's forgotten me,' I said. 'As far as she's concerned I DON'T EXIST.'

A man at one of the lecterns a way off looked up and scowled, put his fingers to his lips. Everything was shifting. Nothing felt safe any more.

'Sssh, Katie. Katie, it's OK.' I felt Mrs Klein's arms go round me. I kept my eyes closed and leaned back, resisting her comfort. 'Don't worry. You're still here. I can feel you.' Her arms tightened to prove it. 'Hush. You're stiff as a board. There. That's it. It's all right.'

I let my neck relax and buried my face in her chest. I could feel the bony edges of her bra, and smelled perspiration through the sweet powdery scent of deodorant. She rested her chin on top of my head.

'I told you before, your mother *would* have loved you. She wouldn't have wanted to leave you behind, but she had to. To give you a better life. Or so she hoped.' Her voice had a crack in it. 'Maybe they didn't have much money. Maybe her soldier had been posted somewhere it would have been difficult to take a toddler. And your father would have stopped her coming back to get you.'

The silence went on and on.

My father would have stopped her? My father would have deliberately prevented me seeing my mother ever again? Maybe she'd tried to write to me, and he'd hidden her letters. Yes, it fitted, I could see that now, but what made Mrs Klein think my father would do something like that? I could hear the rustle of pages as the old men and women looked for their ancestors, the creak of heavy ledgers being taken down from the shelves, the traffic racing past outside on Aldwych.

'Katie . . . '

It was too confusing. There wasn't room in my head for all this.

'I want to go home,' I said.

252

'Hang on,' said Mrs Klein. 'I think we'd better sort this out . . . '

'No,' I said. 'I can't . . . Let's go.' I gripped the edge of the lectern, to stop myself floating away, painfully light, a nothingness. I needed something solid, something heavy to hold me down. I could feel the tug of the ammonite in my pocket but it wasn't nearly heavy enough. Home was not the right place, after all.

'You said we could go to South Kensington.' My voice sounded like one of the old ladies', thin and whispery.

I was thinking of the Natural History Museum: wandering between cool glass cases that held delicately etched stone; gauzy traceries of leaves embedded in sandstone, ferns pegged down in shale, smooth polished ammonites and trilobites and spiny fish skeletons; light coming down from the high windows in strong, clear shafts, unlike this dingy, smelly place full of whispers and lost people. I was remembering how my dad had taken me there. If I could get back there, all of this would be wiped away.

'Harrods,' said Mrs Klein, happily. 'Just what you need. We'll hit Harrods.'

★ ★ ★

At any other time, shopping with Mrs Klein would have been wonderful. You could tell she was fast and decisive, and her ambition for the afternoon was to weigh me down with new clothes.

I didn't want to be rude. I didn't know her well enough to explain that this could not work. She was a force of nature, whirling from rack to rack, flowing unstoppably from floor to floor. It had not occurred to me yet that she might have been trying to shake off demons of her own.

'No,' said Mrs Klein, firmly, when I tugged at a pale

253

blue ruffled top that I had only picked up to please her. 'You're too short. Short looks best in clean lines and plain colours. What about this?' holding out an orange T-shirt. 'And not blue, Katie. Makes you look like a corpse. Your skin's too pale. Go for warmer colours.'

Why was she telling me this? I didn't care. She made me take into the changing room armfuls of clothes and told me to come out and parade everything, whether I thought it looked good or not. I couldn't tell whether the clothes suited me, because I didn't see a girl standing in front of a mirror, I saw something abandoned, mislaid, forgotten. Or something shut away and hidden. Whether my mother had abandoned me, or my father had prevented her getting in touch, it was all absence, an empty space. I was like a vampire who could not be reflected on glass. Fabrics and patterns were transparent, smoke in the air. My eyes looked straight through them to lines of uneven typing in red ledgers; I saw lists of names and none of them truly belonged to me.

'And here's another thing,' she said, tugging at a jersey top to get it to hang properly. 'Cheap doesn't always mean badly cut or nasty material. But if you can't afford much, better to buy one good thing than six cheap ones. Quality shows.' A final tweak. 'Actually, you did well to pick this one out. Looks good. You've got an eye.' I had pulled it off a shelf without even noticing what I held.

There were suddenly a lot of carrier-bags. Where had they come from?

'Are you enjoying yourself?' she said. I could see it was important to her.

'Oh, yes,' I said. 'This is great. Shopping with you, I mean.'

'Well, I wish you'd tell Trish. She won't go shopping with me any more. Screams at me in the changing room, ungrateful child.'

I sneaked a look into one of the bags. It held a skirt, far better than the one I was wearing, which was still sticky with spilled juice. Dimly I remembered trying it on. 'I can't let you pay for all these,' I said, aware it was already too late.

'Don't be absurd. I ruined that skirt,' she said. 'It's been fun. Old New York proverb: 'When the going gets tough, the tough go shopping'. We ought to make a dash for the train. Feeling better?'

The truth was I had no way of knowing, since I remembered hardly anything that had happened since we had left St Catherine's House. I could still hear the air-conditioning humming mum, mumm, mummm, drowning out the soft Muzak in the stores we had visited. I still felt light and dangerously floaty. But I could see Mrs Klein was feeling better, so I nodded.

'We'll get a taxi,' she said, waving her little red umbrella hopefully as we stood on the pavement in Knightsbridge. 'I might even allow myself a teeny little gin and tonic on the train. Horrid without ice, of course, but it has been a bit of a day.'

★   ★   ★

I thought about hiding in the toilet on the train for as long as possible. But there were puddles on the floor and a lot of damp toilet paper so I didn't even go in. The one at the end of the next carriage was the same, and the one after that occupied by someone who had clearly had the same idea as me, and no intention of coming out at all. Perhaps they were hiding from the ticket inspector.

'Are you all right?' asked Mrs Klein, when I got back to the seat. 'You were gone a long time.'

'I'm fine. Tired.'

'Now, I don't want to rush you but we ought to make another trip to St Catherine's House some time soon.

255

And it would help enormously if you could find your dad's divorce papers.'

I was aching to be left alone.

'I'll think about it,' I said. 'It's a lot to take in.'

We rattled through Didcot. Mrs Klein watched the bubbles in her gin and tonic; I looked out at the distant hills. There was a White Horse carved on them somewhere. I remembered it from the train journey to London with my dad.

Was I betraying him? Or had he betrayed me? I remembered the winter walks, digging up ammonites. The ice-cream. The pink blouse. He'd looked after me ever since my mum had gone. She had left me, with her new baby inside her.

'Katie,' said Mrs Klein. I looked away from the window. Her eyes were still fixed on the plastic tumbler of gin. 'Katie, I did want to talk to you about something. Maybe this is the wrong time . . . '

'Yes,' I said. I meant, 'Yes, it's the wrong time, whatever it is.'

'Your father,' she said. 'Trish told me . . . '

'Told you what?' I said. That hot, choking feeling was back.

'I think you shouldn't tell your father what we've been doing today,' said Mrs Klein. 'Knowing the way he is.'

'What did Trish tell you?'

Mrs Klein looked uncomfortable. 'Katie, I know what it's like,' she said. 'I know exactly.' She lowered her voice. 'You probably feel like you're the only person in the world it's happening to but, believe me, it happens to lots of girls. My father . . . Well, why do you think I ran away from home?'

It was obvious now. Did she think I hadn't worked it out? Her need for the baby she'd had adopted was folded in those carrier-bags on the luggage rack above us. But I didn't say anything, just turned away and

256

looked out of the train window for the White Horse.

'Oh, God.' Mrs Klein put her head into her hands. 'I'm doing this all wrong.' She spoke to the tabletop between us. 'I ran away because my father used to hit me. He hit my mother too. I wanted her to leave but she wouldn't. She wouldn't even talk to me about it. I left not just because he was hitting me but because I couldn't bear to see him hit her any longer.' When she looked up there were tears in her eyes. 'It's a terrible, terrible thing, violence, and you have to be brave and stand out against it. Tell someone, Katie.'

'Trish has been exaggerating again,' I said, as coldly as I could. 'I don't know what you're talking about.'

LEVEL FOUR

The Lion

The more you delve into Mithraism, the more you see its resonances in the world we inhabit today. For example, anyone who reads their horoscope in the newspaper would recognize a number of Mithraic symbols. Taurus, the Bull, sacrificed in springtime; Gemini, the Twins, Hope and Despair; while Virgo, the Virgin, surely has something in common with Nymphus, our cross-dressing male bride? Equally familiar will be the name given to an initiate at the fourth level: Leo, the Lion. His element, like the Zodiac sign, is fire.

From *The Mithras Enigma,*
Dr Martin Ekwall, OUP

19

'You have to get me back underground as soon as possible,' Martin reminds me, as I drive on to the station forecourt in Bath. Commuters aiming for the early London train stream across the tarmac, forcing us to a crawl. 'We need a picture of that tauroctony.'

'This is getting too complicated.' There's only a disabled space free, so I slide the car in there. 'I thought you'd just verify the carving on the pillar, then no one would need to know I'd taken you underground. Forget it for the moment, can't you? You're off to California at the end of the week. We'll think about it again after Christmas.'

Someone behind me starts hooting. In the mirror I can see a man in a small red car, waving two fingers and a blue disabled badge. Martin gets out and reaches behind the seat for his bag.

'This isn't like you, Kit. You started it. Why have you got cold feet?' he asks. 'You don't seem to recognize what a big find it would be. You know what my dad said about you? He said you could never bring yourself on principle to believe anything a man told you.' He straightens up, slings his bag on to his shoulder, then leans back in like a lover bestowing one last kiss. 'And that you married a man you knew you could trust to let you down.' He slams the car door, unusually peevish, and walks off into the station.

*　　*　　*

Brendan has made a pot of real coffee, double strength as it's Monday morning and still early. Gary comes into the kitchenette. He gives me a nod, curt enough for it to

261

feel like a rebuff. Not fair: it wasn't me, after all, who turned up unannounced with flowers and wine. I ought to let him know, without making it look obvious, that Martin and I are not paired up.

'Make it look obvious,' says Martin, in my head. 'It doesn't matter if you make a tit of yourself. That's what it's all about.'

At the last count, Martin's been cautioned three times for making it look obvious in public toilets.

'I need to see you,' Gary says to Brendan. 'About the ground-movement monitors. Whenever you've got a moment.'

'Coffee?' asks Brendan, pushing down the plunger on the cafetière.

'No.' And Gary's gone back through to his office at the other end.

'He's grumpy,' I observe.

'Aye, well. He's a quarryman. He's suspicious of mining technology. And, of course, he's got wife trouble,' says Brendan, pouring coffee into his mug, with the smile that says, 'We men understand these things.'

'I thought he was divorced?' I say, before I can stop myself.

'And well rid of her. Seems he can't quite let go.'

That wasn't at all what I wanted to hear, but Brendan's hung the big furry 'shut' sign on his mouth and turns with his pint-sized coffee mug towards the door. When I pick up the cafetière to pour my own, there's about half a thimbleful left.

Outside, the first shift of miners is getting ready to go underground. Big Ted and his crew are shrugging into their gear. They look at me as I walk past, and someone says, just too low to be sure I've heard it, either 'dyke', or 'bike'.

Turning down the narrow passage between the storage sheds to get to my office, I glance back: Gary

262

has joined the crowd of miners round the shaft entrance. I watch long enough to make sure he goes underground, then nip back to his office to sneak the borrowed key back into his desk drawer, relieved to be rid of it.

★　★　★

Green Down is coming to life as I walk to the newsagent's to buy a paper and cigarettes. I sit on the churchyard wall to smoke one, thinking about Martin's parting shot. It's not true. Nick was . . . No, it was the drink made him do what he did, and I didn't understand about the drink when I married him.

Ice still crackles on shallow puddles, but the sky is blue. Across the road, a few last red leaves of Boston ivy cling to the stonework of a Georgian terrace. The years have turned the buttery yellow stone a comfortable weathered grey.

When I was young I walked along this road almost every day. Around me people get on with their lives. Women drive empty people-carriers along the narrow road, pulling in to give way to each other. Children in school blazers trail past with bags of crisps. There are *boys* as well as girls. St Anne's must have gone co-ed. A man with white hair slicked over a pink scalp comes through the churchyard gate; a basset hound with teats that brush the gravel waddles after him. He smiles and raises his hand as if he knows me.

They look remarkably unconcerned about living on top of danger. The mines have been here at least two hundred years: why should they collapse now? In the war years, Mrs Owen told me, the Admiralty stored depth charges in the tunnels, and nobody turned a hair. Every few months, the shells became corroded in the damp, and women and pensioners scraped off the rust as part of the war effort. But I wonder all the same if these people wake in the night, imagining they feel the walls of their houses sway.

I start walking back to the site. Gilmerton. Brendan's right. What happened in Scotland was nearly a disaster. If you lost your home, you might think there was no 'nearly' about it. I've seen those tottering pillars, nibbled away by greedy quarrymen. Why am I even thinking of something that might delay the filling? We need to get it done and dusted as fast as possible. What's there should stay hidden. Let the quarries keep their secrets.

★　★　★

The first website the search engine produces when I type in 'Gilmerton and stone mine' is a newspaper archive. Text and pictures: a row of post-war bungalows on the day of the evacuation. You wouldn't know there was anything wrong, except there are no people, and no cars. One front gate hangs open, a toy horse abandoned on the path beyond it. The curtains have been closed in some of the houses, as if the owners couldn't bear the thought of anyone looking in after they'd left. The street is completely empty. It's like looking at the face of a dead person: something isn't there that should be.

How did they feel when they were told to leave? Was it early morning, women pulling on towelling dressing-gowns, unshaven men in vests, herding their children out of the door, looking backwards as they scurried down the garden path, wondering if they were going to see their home sink slowly into the earth behind them, the kids disappointed when it didn't? Or maybe the police came in the middle of the day, and some people were out at work and couldn't know, so when they came home that night they didn't understand why there were no kids playing and no lights on and nobody there . . .

A shiver takes me. That's what gets me, the thought of them coming home and not realizing anything was wrong. Just for a moment I could have sworn I felt the walls of the office sway.

I'm suffocating. I have to get out. My hand . . .

Easy, Katie. No pain. Two, three and awake . . .

I don't remember standing up, but I'm on my feet when the door opens, rubbing the white scar on my palm.

'Morning,' sings Dickon. 'Good morning, good morning, the world is bright and new, doodley ooh doo, doo doo doo . . . ' He looks puzzled. 'Are you all right? You're a very funny colour.'

'Fine,' I say. I can hear someone's ragged breathing. I suppose that will be mine.

'No, you're not fine at all, are you?'

He comes towards me and I back away, except there isn't anywhere to back to so I end up with my bum perched on the edge of the desk. I want to snarl, 'Leave me alone,' but there are quite enough question marks already over my mental state at work, so I do what I always do in a tight spot.

'Broke up with my boyfriend,' I say. 'This weekend. Sorry, Dickon. Hate being emotional. I'll be OK, honestly.' That bit's true: I *am* OK. The suffocating feeling has already passed. More likely, the proximity of Dickon has driven it out of my head.

'Oh, Kit,' he says, his eyes filling with fake concern. He's still way too close. 'That's terrible. Do you need a hanky?' He fumbles in his pocket. 'I do understand. Thing is, it doesn't get any easier the older you get, does it?'

Fuck *off*, Dickon. He's so completely insensitive — surely to God he can't mean to say these things? — that I don't know whether to hit him or laugh.

'You can't tell me anything I don't know about heartache,' he goes on, finally producing a handkerchief so rumpled and stained even he has the grace to shove it straight back into his pocket. 'Perhaps Rosie has tissues in her desk. Believe it or not, I've had my own share of rejection.'

He's such a tosser.

'But the thing is, you have to go on believing there is someone out there for everyone. I'm sure it feels really bad right now, but I promise you . . . '

Oh, God, no. Make him stop.

' . . . that one morning you'll wake up and realize you spent a whole night not dreaming about him . . . '

The door opens. There is a God, and her name is Rosie. 'I hope you've got that kettle going,' she says. 'It's brass monkeys this morning.'

'Kit has been chucked by her boyfriend,' says Dickon, solemnly.

Rosie's dark eyebrows disappear into her blonde streaks. 'Really?' she says, looking hard at me, the person who told her only last week she was single and not seeing anyone. 'He dumped you, then? Old Whatsisname?'

'It was more mutual agreement,' I say. 'Been coming for some time, really. I'm OK, Rosie. Dickon just walked in at a bad moment.'

'Go and fill the kettle, Dickon,' says Rosie, keeping her eyes on me.

'Right,' says Dickon. 'Understood. Girl talk . . . '

'No, it's your turn to make the coffee,' says Rosie. 'Go.' The door slams as Dickon scurries off. I don't know how she does it, but whatever it is I could do with some of it down the mine with Ted and his crew.

She lifts one eyebrow to indicate an explanation is required.

'Sorry,' I say. 'Monday morning. Not looking forward to facing the miners, but I didn't want him to know that.' Not a million miles from the truth, but still technically a fib.

Rosie's face softens in sympathy. 'Don't worry about it. They'll learn to respect you. Huw thinks you're fine.'

'Your boyfriend is that bit more modern.'

'Tell you what'll cheer you up,' says Rosie. 'Let's go underground. Huw says they're shifting some stone this morning.'

⋆   ⋆   ⋆

Every so often, the miners building the underground roadways come across areas where the old quarrymen have left huge blocks of cut stone. No one knows why they were never taken above ground; perhaps they were felt to be of inferior quality, or maybe the crane had broken down and the quarry owner ran out of money.

Rosie explains all this as we climb down the ladder. As the admin assistant, it isn't part of her job to go underground but, being Rosie, she regards it as one of the perks.

'So, what's special about shifting it?' I've seen enough stone moved in my time to rebuild the Pyramids; I can't imagine why I'd want to bother watching a couple of blocks more.

But Rosie has a big grin on her face. 'You'll see.'

Rosie's boyfriend Huw is working with the Welsh team in a sector where quarrying took place right into the twentieth century. Instead of cavernous voids, the rock has been quarried out of square-cut chambers, reached by the wide passageways the quarrymen call roads. One of these needs clearing. We join the group of miners standing at a junction where two roads cross. The right-hand turning is obstructed by several massive blocks, each practically the size of a double bed.

'Come for the show, then?' asks Huw.

'Incorrigible, your Rosie,' says Cennydd, the shift leader.

A deep primitive growl from far down the roadway to

267

our left. My skin prickles. Something is coming, getting louder and louder. Suddenly there is light, far brighter than that from the bulbs strung above the metal struts. It bounces off the walls as whatever is coming lurches round a corner, then bursts out of the turning with a deafening roar.

Fu-u-uck.

Instinctively everyone takes a step back. It's a beast, a great yellow metal monster with a single brilliant eye, and long, vicious horns. It leaps over the crossroads, head lowered, and buries its horns deep under one of the huge stone blocks. Then, with another mighty roar, it dances back. I swear it's trying to toss the stone, juggle it. It pivots and spins, twists in the middle, bounces on big fat tyres, charging backwards and forwards at what seems like dizzy speed in the confined space, showing us first its big, staring eye then revealing the four blazing lights on its rear. Mud from the straining wheels spatters us. We're all cowering against the wall, open-mouthed, half blinded by the swinging lights, but unable to take our eyes off this extraordinarily primitive contest between machine and rock. All the while the beast growls like an angry dinosaur shaking its prey, until somehow it has balanced the enormous block of stone on the metal forks at its front, then reverses at speed out of the chamber. Its lights disappear up the roadway and the thunder gradually diminishes until we're left in a ringing silence.

Every hair on my body is on end, and I'm tingling all over. 'What the fuck was that?'

'Gary,' says Rosie. 'Pretty good, eh?'

But the thunder is coming back, and drowns us. Back comes the blazing eye, the stabbing horns, charging past us towards the next huge block of stone. This time I can make out a shape in the cab of the articulated loader, dimly recognizable as Gary's profile under hardhat and ear-defenders. I think he's smiling.

Oh, my God.

The long metal forks ram under the stone; he changes up through the gears and the whole machine judders. The four rear lights swing towards us as the back of the loader slides on the muddy surface. We scatter, though Gary seems to know exactly what he's doing and controls the skid; we're not really about to be crushed under the enormous wheels — it only feels like it. He charges at the stone again, and this time the back wheels come right off the ground as the loader strains and roars, trying to take the weight.

'He's showing off,' yells Huw, in my ear.

The loader backs away again, swivelling across the chamber with a screech of gears, and lowers its forks to attack the stone. So far it's been playing with the block, but now it's *serious*, and it looks as if it's thrusting itself right into the stone, pushing and tossing until the engine screams. The block eventually settles on the forks, the machine has what it came for, and it roars again, in triumph or satisfaction, the eye swings round to blind us all, then Gary slams the loader into reverse and disappears up the underground road.

I'm limp, damp, gasping.

'Bloody good little machine that,' says Cennydd. 'Marvellous workhorse. Two hundred and seventy horsepower, hydraulic joystick, shaft-mounted blades. And he knows exactly how to get what he wants out of it, doesn't he?'

Rosie and I look at each other.

★   ★   ★

'It's so *animal*,' says Rosie, as we trudge back along the roadway. 'The first time I saw it, Cennydd was driving it, and I thought of an ant, you know, struggling to lift something that's ten times its own weight. I mean, it has a sort of ant body. I think some of the miners even call it the Ant. But then I saw Gary drive it.'

'Yes,' I say. 'Not really an ant at all, is it, when he's in control?'

'Thought you'd enjoy it.'

★ ★ ★

About half an hour later, Gary sidles into the office. He seems a bit embarrassed. 'What are you doing Thursday evening?'

My face gets hot. Actually, I'm rather warm all over.

'Only that's the night of the public meeting,' he goes on, 'and Brendan's told me to get as many of us along as can.'

Oh. I dimly remember some discussion from my first afternoon on the site; I'd forgotten there was going to be a public meeting.

'Why ever do we all have to go?' I ask.

'PR, really. It makes us look like nice, friendly people. He particularly wants you to be there.'

'Does he want me to wear a dress as well?'

'Pardon?'

'Never mind. I can do the Caring Face of Mining.' Be honest, I've got nothing better to do.

'Would you like me to pick you up? Seeing as we live out in the same direction?'

Dickon's glowering at us from his corner of the office. 'Yes, please.'

★ ★ ★

Luckily they're both elsewhere when my mobile goes: Martin, still on the train by the sound of it.

'Aren't you back yet?' I ask. 'The wrong kind of ice on the line? Typical.'

'No.' His voice goes all garbled and I miss a bit. '. . . curator. Really useful conversation. Lots to think about. I'm half minded to cancel . . . ' The line goes dyslexic again, and I only manage to catch something about 'lonely old queens with nowhere better to go'. 'Sorry,' he continues. 'You still there? I think we're coming up to the Box Tunnel.'

'The Box Tunnel? You're only *five minutes* out of Bath? What've you been *doing* all morning?' I ask.

'I told you. I went to the Roman Baths. I met the curator once at a conference . . . '

The phone goes dead. I imagine the train winding like a worm into the mouth of the Box Tunnel, another limestone scarp riddled with underground quarries.

20

Winter is the best time to search for ammonites, when the fields have just been ploughed and the loose dark soil in the furrows falls easily away.

It wasn't very sensible to go looking for them in a dry summer. The earth was hard-baked under a mat of yellowing grass. I lay on my stomach under the tree in the meadow where Trish had led the biology lesson. Even the cowpats were hard and dry; the cows had gone to another field.

In the winter I had walked this field with my father, and we had come home with two almost perfect ammonites, one nearly as big as a saucer.

I clawed at the ground with furious, savage stabs. But the garden trowel I'd taken from the garage made little impression. The earth wouldn't give up its secrets.

★   ★   ★

I hadn't seen my father since I'd got back from London. Had he stopped my mother finding me? I still didn't know what to think.

After Mrs Klein had dropped me at the top of the road the previous evening, I threw the carrier-bags, unopened, into the back of the wardrobe, but I was too tense to think of going to bed. Instead I prowled through the empty house, a ghost again in my own home. My father had warned me he would be back late. Friday night, with Janey Legge: I imagined them in the pub together, or dancing somewhere, doing stiff rock-and-roll steps like people of my father's generation did in black-and-white films on the television.

I went into my mother's old room. The amber

streetlamp shone on to the window-seat where I had crouched to spy on Gary. I opened the drawers of the dressing-table and ran my hand through the silky scarves. It was like holding my hand in cool water. But after a while the scarves got warm and my arm began to ache. I sat on the windowseat and looked out into the night. There was still a faint glow in the western sky. No light showed in Gary's room across the road. It was Friday night. He must be out with his mates. Maybe with a girl. Something at the bottom of my stomach flipped over.

My father's divorce papers were somewhere in this house, with my mother's address on them. And maybe, if Mrs Klein was right, a bundle of letters addressed to me that had come from her. Which of them had done this to me, mother, father? Did I really want to know the truth?

Where would he keep them?

I had looked for the divorce papers before, when I was hunting for clues about Kitty. There was just one place I had not been able to search: my father's bureau, in the front room downstairs. It was where he did his accounts, every Sunday evening, drawing up invoices in his neat handwriting while I finished my homework at the dining-table.

By the light of the streetlamps, I stood in front of the bureau. There was a keyhole in its sloping front, another in the drawer below, and a locked cupboard below that. When I had hunted for the papers before, my father had been out at work, carrying his big key-ring with him. Tonight he had gone dancing with Janey. Would he have bothered to take all his keys? If he'd intended to have a drink, he wouldn't have gone in the van.

The keys were in his bedroom, gleaming on top of the chest of drawers along with a handful of loose change. I reached out my hand, then stopped. I couldn't. My father would kill me . . . And he would be right. It was a betrayal.

Whose betrayal? Why hadn't he been honest with me? My fingers clamped over the keys.

The top half of the bureau was full of paper: receipts, bills, copies of invoices. But it was easy to search because it was all filed into labelled pigeon-holes; typical of my father. Everything there related to his work.

The drawer below contained nothing but blank stationery, again neatly stacked and separated by drawer dividers he had made himself.

Only the bottom cupboard left. I turned the key; the door swung open, and a jumble of papers and magazines and old shoeboxes slid out on to the floor.

I stared in dismay. How was I going to get this unsuspected chaotic landslide back the way it had been, without my father realizing I had pried? I had been mad to think of going through his papers. It was after ten o'clock: he could be home any moment. I began to shovel the mess hastily back into the cupboard.

As I pushed the last shoebox inside, the battered lid gave way, and I found myself staring into my mother's eyes, instantly recognizable from the photo by my bed. Kitty's eyes, I thought. Kitty, the woman who had abandoned me without a thought and run off with her soldier. For a moment I had no pity, then I thought of the bundle of desperate, tear-stained letters in her handwriting that might lie in the shoebox beneath this picture.

The box was a big one that had once contained a pair of my father's work boots — the label on it said £4.15s.11d. I couldn't immediately see any letters; it held a jumble of photographs and well-thumbed magazines that gave off a musty smell. My mother's picture was tucked under the top magazine, so that only her face and shoulders were showing. It was one of those glamorous, old-fashioned studio portraits, I thought, like the one in my room. Kitty had been photographed with bare shoulders to show the elegant curve of her neck; she had turned her head a little so that she was looking sideways at the camera, instead of full on, and it made her seem shy and vulnerable.

I pulled out the photo to see it better. A cold, liquid thrill ran through me. It was not just my mother's shoulders that were bare. She was completely naked; small breasts with large, dark nipples that seemed to tip up jauntily at the camera, smooth firm belly. She was sitting on a rumpled bedsheet, with her legs apart, the left stretched out straight before her, the right bent, knee raised. One hand was on her thigh, but the other lay gently between her legs, modestly protecting what was there. Around the edge of her fingers there was a dark shadow of pubic hair.

My heart was thumping in my throat. There was something terrible about the picture, in spite of Kitty's apparent modesty, her shy sideways glance, the shielding hand. I couldn't work it out, but it made me uncomfortable. Why had she let herself be photo-graphed like that? And who was the photographer? My father? Or someone else?

The photograph was shaking in my fingers. I didn't want to touch it, but it was also compelling, somehow. The look on Kitty's face: what did it mean? Her mouth was very slightly open, and there was a smile on her lips that might have been forced there, or might have been genuine pleasure. At the back of my head a voice said, *You know, you know,* but I didn't want to listen to it.

I dropped the photo back on to the pile of magazines in the box, and only then understood what they were. Dizziness and confusion swept over me; I felt light-headed with shock. The top one was the worst. Most of the rest could have been bought from the top shelf at the newsagent in Green Down. Trish and Poppy and I had seen others like them there, *Mayfair* and *Forum* and *Double-D-Plus*; once Trish had pulled one down and started leafing through it before the newsagent made us drop it and chased us out of the shop. But the one that had lain on top of my mother's picture was different.

On the cover a naked woman crouched. She was looking back at the camera over her shoulder baring her teeth in something that was more a growl than a smile; her bottom loomed huge in the shot, a big cleft peach, and round her neck was a spiked dog collar, with a man's tattooed hand pulling the lead taut. At first sight it looked quite funny, but I knew it wasn't, really. I couldn't stop myself opening the magazine, and there was the same woman again, still looking over her shoulder, but this time her eyes were squeezed shut and her mouth was hanging open, and her big bare bum was hidden by a pair of straining hairy buttocks.

The thought that came into my head was: Oh, God, they're doing it. Those people are really doing it. And then there was a confusion of images and ideas sweeping through my head too fast to separate: *But he's hurting her — she likes it? Do all men do this does Gary what does it feel like why does my dad have these magazines what's my mother's picture doing with them no not my mother not my father* . . .

I crammed the broken lid back on to the cardboard box and pushed it as far back into the cupboard as I could, and tried to close the doors, but they wouldn't close: something was getting in the way, it was the corner of the box, and I pushed at it until it crumpled and stove in and I could get the doors shut and latched and locked — locked locked LOCKED . . .

I went straight upstairs and put the keys back in my father's room. Afterwards I made myself hot milky Ovaltine, and got into my pyjamas. Whatever else was in that cupboard, I didn't want to know. I sat in Kitty's room, on the window-seat, staring out at Gary's dark window across the road. A little after eleven o'clock my father came down the road on foot. As he passed under the streetlight, I could see a smile on his face. He was a man at peace with the world.

I ran to bed before his key scraped in the door.

★ ★ ★

When I came home from the ammonite field that Saturday morning, my father was back from work early and making lunch. I could hear the radio in the kitchen. He always listened to the local radio station on Saturdays. He liked Old Pete and Big Eval, two Bristol characters who called each other 'my babba' and played oldies.

Bobby Darin, my dad's favourite, was singing 'Dream Lover'. My dad sang along. I could see him through the open doorway, waggling his bum, slicing tomatoes in time to the music. The beat changed for the chorus, and my dad did a little dance, spinning on his toes, swivelling his hips, pointing his knife into the corner of the kitchen at an invisible audience.

I would have to face him some time. I walked into the kitchen.

My dad stopped spinning, an apologetic, guilty grin on his face. 'Katie! Where've you been?'

Well might you ask.

'Nowhere.'

'Is everything all right?'

'Didn't sleep. Too hot.'

He pulled out a kitchen chair. 'Sit down. Are you feeling faint?'

'I'm fine.'

'Only sometimes, the Curse ... ' His voice had dropped. Who did he think was listening? ' ... can be really hard on women. My mother was a martyr to it. I

277

always knew when she had it.'

I pictured a lonely boy, tiptoeing round the house, his mother lying on her bed holding a cold compress to her forehead, moaning faintly. I had grown up without a mother, but my dad had never really known his father.

How could he have kept Kitty from me? He must have understood how it felt to grow up without one parent.

'If you've inherited the way she was when she had her monthlies,' he went on, 'you'll — '

'Oh, stop it!' I shouted. 'Stop this stupid pretence! I know, Dad. I know . . . '

My father gaped helplessly at me. 'That's *exactly* the way it used to take her,' he said. 'Exactly. I always knew to keep well out of her way.'

★ ★ ★

I couldn't find the words to ask him outright if my mother had ever tried to contact me. Every time I said I *knew*, he thought it was something about him and Janey. And Mrs Klein had been right: I had to watch out for that flat gleam in his eye, the first warning glimpse of his dark chaotic side, because I'd seen he could turn just like that if he thought I was criticizing Janey. He was kind and understanding because he was remembering his mother, but I knew the way the muscles tightened round his eyes. Just for a moment I saw it happen and he nearly went, but he pulled himself back.

I shut up.

If I hadn't, would that have changed anything?

Nothing.

★ ★ ★

I stormed out of the house again. I didn't want to be near my father, with that silly fond look on his face every time he said Janey's name.

The music was coming from Gary's bedroom again, the track that sounded like helicopters and desert winds. There he was, leaning against the window-frame, wearing a white T-shirt, looking out over the street.

I was going to scuttle past like an insect, but he saw me and waved.

He *waved*. I thought of pretending I hadn't seen. My face was burning up. My mind gave me a flash frame of the tight hairy buttocks in the magazine. I scuttled even faster than I'd intended.

I was almost past his house when I stopped and turned. He was still at the window watching me, with a grin on his face.

'What's that music?' I called up to him. 'It sounds like aeroplanes or something.'

'It's called 'Silver Machine',' he shouted back. 'It's about UFOs.'

'That's a funny subject for a song.'

'The band's called Hawkwind. They believe in them completely.'

'Oh.' I couldn't think of anything else to say. 'It's very nice.' I flapped a hand feebly and walked on up the road, wishing I knew how to be cool.

★   ★   ★

School started again on Monday after the half-term break.

Trish and Poppy and I sat on the bank overlooking the sports field at lunch-time. Trish was full of where she'd been and what she'd seen in London.

'We went to the King's Road because my father said that was where he met my mother, in a café when she lived in a bedsit near there, and it was amazing, we went in the same café, there was this guy in a ripped black T-shirt and his jeans were held together with safety-pins

279

and he had a safety-pin in his *ear* . . . '

Trish had bought a black T-shirt that said 'SEX' right across the front.

'What, the actual word?' Poppy asked.

Trish nodded, with a wild and happy look.

'You can't wear that,' I said. 'I mean — you'll be arrested.'

'My dad bought it for me,' said Trish. 'He doesn't mind. He thinks it's funny.'

A spider had built a web between the leaves of a rhododendron. It had just caught a fly. It perched on top of the helpless insect, and somehow it was spinning the fly, like a man spinning his rock-and-roll partner, round and round and round so fast the whole web shook in the sunlight.

I thought about setting the fly free but it was probably too late.

★   ★   ★

I couldn't confess to Trish and Poppy the confused stuff in my head. In less than a week, I had moved beyond Poppy and her Barbies, and Mrs Klein had told me not to tell Trish we had been to London. But we were all moving fast.

That week Trish had an idea. She told us on Wednesday, as we were walking home. 'Your birthday's soon, isn't it?' she said to me.

'Well — end of July. Just before term finishes.'

'Let's have a party. It'll be right after the exams. We can celebrate.'

We were coming down the Avenue with its pollarded trees, past the recreation ground. Some boys were playing football. They had left their T-shirts in piles on the grass, and were bare-chested.

'For me?' I said. 'How can we do that? My dad would never let me have a party.'

'Not at your house. Somewhere else.'

'No,' I said. But they ignored me.

Poppy liked the idea. 'We could get people to bring cider.'

'We'll invite some boys. They always know how to get hold of drink,' said Trish. She started waving. 'We could invite Gary.'

There he was, playing football with his mates. We stopped by the railings and watched. That chest was definitely filling out, turning golden in the late-afternoon sun. They took no notice of us, I thought, they were so intent on their game. You could see the tackles getting harder, the dives more extravagant, and when Gary finally scored between the T-shirt goalposts, he did a lap of honour waving his arms and shaking his curls like Kevin Keegan.

★   ★   ★

When I got into the house, the phone was ringing. I ignored it. It stopped, but then, while I was filling the kettle, it began again. It had a hard, jagged sound in the empty house, like a serrated knife-edge, sawing backwards and forwards on a rope. I let it ring, and went upstairs with my tea to curl up on the window-seat in my mother's old room, shutting the door to muffle the sound.

All week long the phone had rung when I was alone in the house. It rang early in the mornings, after my dad left for work. It rang after I got back from school, but it stopped ringing before six o'clock and it never rang in the evenings. I didn't answer it, because it could only be someone I didn't want to speak to. It would either be Janey Legge, looking for my dad, or it would be Trish's mother.

★   ★   ★

'Katie, a word.'

Someone else I didn't want to speak to: Mrs Ruthven, the English teacher. She spotted me as I crossed the school forecourt, alone; I had missed my rendezvous with Trish that morning. Everyone else was streaming past on their way to morning assembly.

'I don't want to be late,' I said nervously.

'This will only take a second,' said Mrs Ruthven. She was standing on the bottom step below the main doors, blocking my way, hugging a pile of exercise books to her chest. With a sinking feeling, I saw they were the ones we had handed in yesterday.

'What exactly is wrong with you this term?' she asked. 'This isn't like you. Your marks were disappointing when I spoke to you last, but now they're ridiculously bad. You got a D in maths, where you used to get straight As — no, don't interrupt. And you didn't even bother to finish the English essay I set you over half-term.'

'I'm sorry, Mrs Ruthven,' I said, keeping my eyes on the ground. 'It won't happen again.'

'It had better not. You do realize, don't you, that if you want to study sciences you need maths?'

'Yes, Mrs Ruthven.'

'Well, buck your ideas up. The exams are in three weeks' time, and you'll have to start doing a lot of work if you want decent marks.' She turned and limped up the steps. We were the only people left outside now, apart from a few stragglers panting through the school gates. One was Poppy.

Suddenly Mrs Ruthven stopped and looked over her shoulder. 'Miss Millichip tells me you were unwell in her biology class earlier this term,' she said. 'Does that have anything to do with this?'

'No,' I said. 'Nothing at all. I will work harder, Mrs Ruthven. Honestly.'

She narrowed her eyes, and disappeared through the

glass doors. There was a sick feeling low down in my stomach.

Poppy caught up with me before I got to the top of the steps. 'What did Ruthers want?' she asked.

'Moaning about my maths,' I said. For once I couldn't lie; I was too worried. What if Mrs Ruthven rang my father? He'd kill me. 'And I forgot I hadn't finished her essay over half-term. I think she's given me an E.'

★ ★ ★

As the week went by, I kept out of my father's way. But was he keeping out of mine too? He left early, and rarely came home before I had already finished my tea. If I was doing my homework, he sat watching television. If I was watching television, he went out to his workshop in the garage.

One night I came awake, very late, feeling the mattress dip as he sat on the edge of my bed. I kept my eyes shut, and tried to make my breath slow and shallow like someone asleep. He stroked my hair, sat there for a while, then went away.

★ ★ ★

The party began to obsess Trish. She talked of little else. She was sure she would eventually come up with the perfect place to hold it.

'If you're so keen on a party, why can't it be at your house?' I said. Not that I wanted a party there.

'It can't be at my house if it's your party,' said Trish. 'Besides, Marcus had a party last year and Dad said, 'Never again'. He saw someone peeing in the birdbath.'

'You'd fall off, wouldn't you?' said Poppy.

'A boy,' said Trish. 'The whole point is to invite boys. What if we broke into school and had it there?'

283

'How?' said Poppy.

'All we need is boys,' said Trish. 'They know how to do that sort of stuff.'

'The caretaker patrols at night,' I said. I had no interest in the party. It wasn't for me, it was for Trish, but I went along with the pretence because I could see it was never going to happen.

'What about the tunnels?' said Poppy.

'The tunnels?' said Trish.

'The ones under our swimming-pool. Katie says there are miles and miles of secret passages underground.'

Trish looked at me doubtfully. But I was Ammonite Girl. I knew what went on beneath our feet.

'Seriously?' she said.

'You can't get in. They're all closed off.'

'A detail,' said Trish, lifting her hand in a weary gesture copied from a Bond film that had been on television last week. 'This is great. We need a planning meeting. Let's meet on Saturday. Come for lunch. My mother keeps asking me if you're all right.'

'I can't,' I said quickly. 'Busy.'

'Busy? Doing what?'

'I could meet you in town earlier.'

'OK. But you've got to find out how we get into the tunnels.'

'Listen,' I said. We were walking along the Avenue. 'And if you won't listen, look.' I pulled her by the sleeve of her blazer into the turning to Stonefield Lane, and pointed down the alley that led behind the undertaker's. 'That's the entrance to the mines, down there. Unless you can do a Dracula and shrink to the size of a bat, there's no way of getting in.'

'There'll be a way in somewhere,' said Trish, sullenly. 'I bet the boys'll know.'

'What boys?' I said. 'Get real, Trish. We don't know any boys.'

'There's Gary.'

'I don't know Gary. I've never spoken to him in my life.'

Your belt. You dropped it —

The smell of his sweat.

'Come on. You live right opposite.'

'I'm not asking him.'

I *couldn't.*

'It would be perfect,' she said. 'No one would know where we were. We could be right underneath their feet, playing music as loud as anything, and they wouldn't know how to find us.'

Like the lost boys, who'd found their way in and never come out ... or the Camera Man. The beginnings of a shiver stroked my skin.

Mrs Owen had no sons, but her daughters had married men who were boys in the 1960s, when the tunnels had been closed and sealed. They would know if there was a way in. One of them was our milkman. He stopped off at Mrs Owen's for a cup of tea in the mornings after he had lined the street with milk bottles.

Trish could see me thinking. 'Go on,' she said. 'Ask Gary.'

'OK,' I said. I wouldn't, but she wasn't to know that. I would ask Mrs Owen's son-in-law.

★ ★ ★

It meant getting up early. George laid his white trail along the doorsteps before six thirty. It was just after twenty-five past when I followed it down the street the following Saturday. My father was still asleep, after another evening with Janey Legge. I had looked in on him to make sure.

The sky was bright blue, the street like a set from a movie about the end of the world, full daylight, no people. The curtains in the front bedroom of Gary's house were drawn tightly. George's milk float was parked outside Mrs Owen's.

Mrs Owen looked terrified when she opened the door to find me on the step. 'What's the matter, petal?'

'Nothing,' I said. 'I was awake, and fancied a cup of tea.'

'Where's your dad?'

'Still in bed.' I was hurt I wasn't getting a warmer welcome. 'Can I come in?'

Mrs Owen's round, crinkled face radiated concern. She was in her dressing-gown, a huge wraparound in tufted pink. 'Are you sure you're all right?'

'Massively fine.' I stepped past her and felt her eyes on me all the way up the narrow hall into the kitchen.

'Here's our George,' said Mrs Owen, unnecessarily. He was sitting at the table, eating a bowl of Rice Krispies with a mug of tea at his elbow. He, too, looked unnerved when he saw me. His eyes shot up from my face to Mrs Owen behind me, his bushy eyebrows knotting in the middle.

'It's all right,' said Mrs Owen. 'Katie couldn't sleep, could you?'

George patted the chair next to him. 'Sit down, my babba.' He was a small man, like Mrs Owen's husband Keith, with a red face under a squared-off fringe of greasy brown hair. He'd taken off his milkman's jacket, and it was draped over the back of the chair. There were damp rings under the arms of his white nylon shirt. 'Gonna be a scorcher,' he said.

It seemed wrong to plunge straight in, so I waited until the tea was poured before I asked about the tunnels.

'What, the underground quarries?' George's eyebrows tangled with each other again. 'Whatever do you want to know about they for?'

'School project.'

'Well, I knows they're there,' said George. 'But I'm no expert. You want someone else.'

'Didn't you ever go in when you were a boy?' I asked.

'What, me? My dad would have had my backside off. He was a quarryman, down Crow Stone, and he reckoned they was dangerous.'

'They are. Don't you go messing round them, Katie,' said Mrs Owen.

'Then we had them lads get lost, in 'sixty-three, and he was proved right. No, they did well to seal up them old tunnels. Couldn't a rabbit get into them now. Every single entrance, tight as . . .'

'A tick,' said Mrs Owen, quickly, but not quickly enough.

' . . . a duck's arse,' said George. 'We watched 'em do it. Lorryloads of cement and breeze blocks.'

'Oh.' I hadn't really wanted the tunnels to be open, but still I felt disappointed.

'Sometimes I think it was a pity, mind. Lots of old stuff in them tunnels. People said they went back to the Romans. Maybe earlier.'

'What, like prehistoric?'

'Before that too. Mind, your dad's the one to ask. He was apprentice electrician at Crow Stone, in his teens, before you came along, and my dad knew him then. Used to talk big about going into the tunnels when he was a boy. Said they wasn't so much tunnels but gurt rooms with pillars, all interconnecting, like a maze down there. Then every so often a dry-stone wall, floor to ceiling. Once when he went inside he found a dead dog.' He took a big swallow of tea. 'My dad said that proved they was dangerous. Animals fell in and couldn't get out, then people couldn't neither.'

'That's right,' said Mrs Owen. 'I told you that, remember? Only person really knew the tunnels was the Camera Man, and he must've died years ago.'

I drank the last of my tea.

'Thank you very much,' I said. 'I'd better be going now.'

Mrs Owen looked up at the clock. 'Stay for breakfast,' she said. 'Keith'll be up in a mo, and I always cook him bacon and egg on a Saturday. You sit and have some too.'

I weighed up the possibility of my dad waking to find me missing while I ate breakfast with Mrs Owen's husband. Was bacon and egg worth it?

'No, thanks,' I said. 'Better not.'

George glanced at Mrs Owen. It looked as if they had some sort of conspiracy going, but I didn't understand what it could be.

'Better not, then,' agreed Mrs Owen. 'You go careful, girl, mind.'

I looked up at Gary's window as I walked back up the street to our house. The curtains were still drawn tight.

★   ★   ★

I had promised to meet Poppy and Trish at half past eleven in the Parade Gardens by the river. But after leaving Mrs Owen's I had crawled back into bed, planning only to stay there until my father got up and left for work. Instead I had fallen asleep, so now I was steaming up Pierrepont Street from the bus station at least fifteen minutes late.

I had done a lot of thinking on the way. For the time being, I would give up the search for my mother. Finding her would either lead to me losing her again, utterly, finally, if she told me she'd left me behind for a reason and didn't want anything more to do with me. Or I would lose my father, if I found out he really had stopped my mother getting in touch.

Eventually, maybe, I might talk to Mrs Klein about it again. But not until the exams were over. I had to work. If I didn't catch up in maths, they might not let me do sciences, and I had to do sciences because I wanted to be a palaeontologist. Or maybe an archaeologist.

Something like that. My future lay in stones and bones. I was going to discover the First Englishman, the one who was waiting for me somewhere in the distant hills.

More immediately, I was going to tell Poppy and Trish there was no way to get into the tunnels, so there was no point in planning this party. They could do what they liked, but I was going to start revising for the end-of-term exams. Forget mothers, forget birthdays, forget boys.

I ran down the steps into the Parade Gardens. I could see Poppy and Trish on a bench by the bandstand. I could tell it was them because Trish was all in black, as she had told me she would be from now on. As I got closer, I was alarmed to see there was a rip in her T-shirt. One sleeve was almost hanging off, her bony white shoulder poking through. 'Are you all right?' I said. 'Did you fall?'

Trish looked at me as if I was mad. 'It's *fashion.*'

'But it's torn.'

'That's what they wear on the King's Road.'

'Oh.'

'You're incredibly late. We've done all the planning.'

'Sorry,' I said happily. 'The tunnels are sealed as tight as . . . ' What was it George had said? ' . . . a tick's bottom. Impossible to get in. I've checked.'

'Forget the tunnels,' said Trish. 'Yesterday's plan. Today's is about ten million times better. We're going to hold the party at Poppy's.'

I stared. Poppy was nodding . . . happily? No, she looked nervous. Trish had obviously steamrollered her too.

'How are you going to persuade your parents?' I asked. I knew very well that her mother didn't like me, so there was no way it was going to be my party.

Poppy looked twice as scared, but also defiant. 'I don't have to,' she said. 'They're going to be away, the weekend before your birthday. Trish has got it all worked out.'

★　★　★

The plan was *simple*, said Trish. As well as being a *stroke of genius*, and *foolproof*. Poppy's parents were going to Scotland again. There was a family wedding. But Poppy couldn't go with them because our last exam was the following week.

'You'll have to stay with Trish again, darling, and revise,' said her mother. 'Can you ask her if that's all right when you see her today?'

So Poppy's house, with its swimming-pool and acres of glass windows, would be empty all weekend. Plenty of space for a party, plenty of time to clear up.

'Brilliant, isn't it?' said Trish.

'No, it isn't,' I said. 'It's stupid. You and Poppy are at your house, right? How are you going to get away from there and have a party at Poppy's? Your mother will go spare when she hears.'

'She won't know either, *stupid*,' said Trish. 'Because Poppy tells her parents she's staying at mine. I tell my parents I'm staying at hers.'

'They'll find out,' I said. 'What happens when your mum rings Trish's mum, Poppy, to check it's all right for you to stay there?'

'She won't,' said Poppy. 'She always gets me to ask. And if she does ring to check — well, I *am* going to stay with Trish on the Saturday night. We'll have the party on Friday night. She's useless with dates so we tell Trish's mother she got the date wrong.'

'It'll never work,' I said. But I could see that it would.

'We tell my mum I'm going back to Poppy's after school on Friday because we want to revise together,' said Trish.

'She'll never believe that.'

290

'Yes, she will, because we're going to tell her you're staying there too.'

'My dad won't let me stay out all night.'

'Yes, he will, if he thinks it's so you can revise.'

Trish had a point. My father wanted me to do well. He was proud of his clever daughter. He didn't like Trish and Poppy much, but he knew that Trish usually got good marks.

'Hold on,' I said. 'The exams won't be over by then. I really have got to work.'

'Oh, *fuck* work,' said Trish.

There was a shocked silence. None of us had ever used that word before.

'I can't do this,' I said. 'I'm sorry.'

'You've got to come to your own party,' said Trish. Her sea-green eyes narrowed. 'Or I write a letter to your father telling him how badly you're doing in maths.'

I shot Poppy, my betrayer, a reproachful look. She had the grace to look ashamed.

'And another thing,' said Trish. 'You've got to ask Gary to come. Don't tell him it's our party, pretend it's Marcus who's giving it, so he knows it isn't for teenyboppers. But you make sure he comes.'

★　★　★

I couldn't ask Gary. I couldn't. I'd never get the words out.

But if I had to go to the stupid party, Gary was the only thing that might make it bearable.

No, there was no way.

I got off the bus and began walking up the hill towards Green Down. Mock orange blossom was blooming in someone's garden; the scent poured over the pavement and made me giddy.

Trish wouldn't tell my father. She knew . . .

She'd told her mother about him hitting me, when

291

she'd promised not to.

I couldn't trust Trish. She'd do whatever suited her. And I remembered how this was, according to her, still my party. So who'd get the blame if things went wrong?

Oh, God. What could I do? I turned off the main road and began to plod down our street. Gary's window was open. Music blasted out. He was playing Hawkwind again, 'Silver Machine'. The one about UFOs. Maybe, if I got lucky, one would land and abduct me.

21

It's Thursday morning, the day of the public meeting, and the frost has been replaced by steady drizzle. While I'm at the sink, I watch a blackbird outside on the lawn. He does a couple of little steps, then a big jump, looks this way and that to check there are no lurking cats waiting to gobble him up, and finally cocks his head on one side and listens to what's under his feet. Then the yellow beak goes stabbing down into the rain-soft earth, and comes up holding a thin, wriggling thread.

He looks very pleased with himself. Stabs the worm a couple more times. Then, inexplicably, leaves it and lands with a rush of wings on the kitchen windowsill. He tilts his head, and that bright bead of an eye looks at me washing up the breakfast things. Then another flurry and he's gone, hopping across the lawn again, looking for his worm.

I'm afraid for a bird so bold. It makes him vulnerable. Next door's cat could get him while I'm out at work, and when I come home I'll find a black feather or two, a drift of fluff, nothing else.

★ ★ ★

Rain always makes me uneasy underground. Old caver's instinct: potholes flood fast. Martin lost a friend who was tumbled through the cracks of the earth like a bundle of clothes in a washing-machine.

The hydrology says the stone mines aren't likely to flood. But prolonged rainfall could make the roof unstable. I don't like being down here when I know it's raining outside. It even smells different, like vegetables kept too long in the bottom of the fridge.

Both teams of miners are in the southern sector today, not far from each other, because yesterday afternoon a new passageway was found. Above ground, boreholes have been sunk, and scientists have stomped through people's gardens with ground-penetrating radar, so in theory we should know what's below, even if the maps are not complete. But the quarries can still surprise us. Ted and his crew have been diverted to build a new section of walkway down the unknown tunnel, with no idea whether it will lead anywhere or not.

Meanwhile the Welsh team, all Valleys men, are putting emergency fill under the road to the primary school. They're a joy, an absolute joy. Nothing too much trouble.

'You think we should start there, Mrs Parry?' says Huw, Rosie's boyfriend.

'Call me Kit.' Has Rosie primed him to boost my confidence? 'Yes. Any chance you'll have it finished today, so we can say it's done at the public meeting tonight?'

'Right-o. Do it in a jiff. We don't hang about, you know.' He casts a glance down the walkway towards the area where Ted's team are working. 'Not like those English bastards.'

'Well, if you've got any spare time at the end of the shift you can come and landscape my garden for me.'

'Sorry, Kit. Queue for gardening services, there is. The boss got in first.'

'What do you think about the wall?' I ask Cennydd, the shift leader. 'Solid? Or should we put some support there at the same time?'

He gives it a long, considered look. 'Looks stable for the time being. No crushing of the top row of stone, see.'

'That's what I thought.'

'And there's quarrymen's graffiti there, so we need

the archaeologist to take a look.' Where the archaeology is worth preserving, the quarries are to be filled with sand instead of concrete, so it won't be lost for ever.

'Let's get him down,' I say. 'He's in the office today, might as well make the fellow earn his money.'

If I wasn't also responsible for Ted and his lot, this would have been a dream job, working with experienced miners who have an instinct for what needs doing. Someone's already gone to call Dickon; Huw is supervising the pump connections.

Out of the corner of my eye I catch a movement back down the walkway where it curves round one of the big pillars. It can't be Dickon already —

It's blond Pat from Ted's crew. He's sweating. No one looks good under these lights, but he seems unnaturally pale.

'We got a problem,' he says. My chest goes tight.

'Accident?' says Cennydd. The Welsh miners have stopped what they're doing, listening, ready to move.

Pat shakes his head. 'Witchcraft,' he says. 'Black-magic stuff. A witch doll, bones and things.'

A shudder goes through me that I can't suppress. 'Where?' I ask, as calmly as I can.

'On a ledge in the side passage. John spotted it. Ted said to call you.'

'The archaeologist's on his way,' I say, feeling the walls closing in on me. 'Tell the others not to touch anything.'

As Pat heads back down the walkway, Cennydd touches me lightly on the arm. 'Superstitious wankers,' he murmurs. 'They'll have made it an excuse to down tools.'

This is the man I saw spitting for luck before he went down the shaft this morning.

'Frankly,' he adds, 'I wouldn't be surprised if they'd put the stuff there themselves.'

* ★ ★ ★

Dickon shines his torch on to the ledge. It picks out the little collection, laid out with as much care as a shop window. 'Witchcraft, my foot.' He starts laughing. 'I hope you weren't taken in by this, Kit. Kids. It's got to be kids.'

I start laughing, too, because I've just spotted the miners' witch doll. It's short and squat and ugly, maybe three inches tall, with long matted hair; the hair is longer than its body, and the pug face is seamed with dirt. 'It's a troll,' I say. 'I remember those. I had one when I was about nine.'

If it hadn't been so filthy it would have been obvious it's made of plastic, not clay. You could get them with different-coloured hair, orange, green, violet, though goodness only knows what colour this one had originally.

'Got to be from the sixties,' said Dickon. 'They sealed up the entrances then, so it has to predate that.'

'No,' I say. 'You could get in afterwards.'

I'm already stretching for the doll, but Dickon puts a hand on my arm. 'Hold on. Got to get a picture first.' Everything found has to be recorded, photographed, plotted, labelled. The camera flash freezes the pathetic little collection on the ledge. Dickon's right: it has to be kids. Feathers, pebbles, a bird's nest. A stub of candle and spent matches. The flash comes again and again, as Dickon captures it from every possible angle. Then he starts measuring the distances between each object.

'Dickon, it's hardly — '

'Just doing my job,' he says tartly, reminding me which of us is the proper archaeologist here.

I walk back to the miners, squatting by the scaffolding and drinking from Thermoses. For a group of men who were complaining about witchcraft half an hour ago, they seem remarkably unconcerned. Ted's sitting on an upturned plastic crate, eating a Mars Bar.

'Kids' things,' I say.

'Really?' Ted couldn't have looked less interested.

It *was* a wind-up. The bastards. They weren't bothered at all, just trying to scare me. As if I'd be frightened of a handful of feathers and a plastic doll. As he raises his mug to his mouth, Ted's tattoos catch the light. They look like faded transfers on his arms, pathetic attempts to be masculine.

'It's a dead end,' I say. 'No point in taking the roadway further in that direction.'

'That isn't what Mr McGill said this morning.'

'It looked like there could be another passage opening up beyond. There isn't.'

'How d'you know?'

I'm standing and he's sitting, but he's so tall there isn't much difference in our height. And he's completely relaxed, whereas my hands are jammed into my jacket pockets. My thumb's sore where I've been picking the skin round the nail. He takes another long, easy swallow of his tea, looking up at me with amusement, to reinforce that he's in charge of the conversation.

'You can see the end of the tunnel now,' I say, more defensive than I intended. 'Just a blank wall of rock.'

'You bin down there?'

'Of course I haven't.'

'So how would you know where the tunnel's to? Hard to see, in't he, from the walkway, even with the big light?'

'Nothing's showing on the geophysics.'

'Geophysics don't show everything.'

'Ted,' I say, biting down hard on his name, 'just do what I fucking tell you. The passage only goes a few metres further. It isn't worth pushing the walkway on. Get it?'

'OK, Kit,' comes Dickon's voice. 'Finished. Can you bring down a crate so we can clear the stuff?'

Ted gets up in one easy movement. For a big bloke he's remarkably graceful. He spreads a palm to offer me the crate he's sitting on.

I don't want to, but it's the nearest. Upending it, the scuffed blue plastic feels unpleasantly warm, like it's oozing the smell of his big masculine arse. I can feel his eyes on my back all the way down the tunnel towards Dickon.

'Righti-o,' says Dickon. 'Careful how you put them in the crate. There's a couple of fragile items at the back.'

I hadn't noticed it before. How could I have missed it? Tiny, perfect, yellowy white; fragile as an eggshell. It's the skull of a bird, maybe a crow, maybe a pigeon, though it's hard to tell because the beak is missing, which makes it look unexpectedly human. I pick it up carefully and it sits on my palm, fitting into the hollow in the centre like an egg in a nest. There's a thick feeling in my throat as I remember the blackbird this morning on my windowsill. Gently I touch the dome of skull with a fingertip, afraid even that might crack it. It has the polish of fine porcelain. I trace the small empty eye sockets, the ragged cavity where the beak has snapped off. My skin is electric, jumping with tenderness, trying to control the jerkiness of my movements, my clumsy stroking, big thick lumpy tears that are pushing their way up and spilling over my lower lids. I feel the bird's soul flapping under my finger, trying to free itself from the skull, from my enclosing hands. I can't let it go, but I can't hold on to it either . . .

'I wonder what this was all about,' says Dickon. 'You know, what they were thinking. Why these things, why here? Like a kind of shrine.'

'Boys,' I say. I hear my voice crack. It feels like it doesn't belong to me. 'Collect anything.'

'Kit, are you sure you're all right?'

'Fine,' I say. There it is in my hand. It can't get away: it doesn't have wings any longer. I'm going to take it out of here, where things get lost, and show it the daylight.

'I'll pick you up at six forty-five,' Gary said, when I was leaving work.

I've cut it too fine. Shouldn't have stopped at the supermarket on the way back.

I take the corner into the village too fast, swerving to miss a ginger cat sauntering across the road. Now the car's at the wrong angle to line up with the garage door. Bugger it, leave it on the pavement.

There's a thick envelope on the mat as I hurl myself across the threshold with my carrier-bags. I kick it out of the way. There'd better be hot water for a shower. No — the clock on the cooker says it's gone half past. The carrier-bags can wait on the kitchen table.

The suede skirt's on the back of the bedroom door, but the matching jumper is screwed up in the laundry basket. Anything will do, so long as it's clean.

The doorbell. Does he have to be early? I hate men who are early.

An orange jumper was a mistake, but too late now.

Why does the zip on your boot always get stuck when you're in a hurry? I hop down the stairs, one boot flapping.

Shit, haven't done my eyes.

'Gary! Sorry, I'm a bit behind. Come in — '

He's in the suit, with a crisp white shirt and an ice-blue tie. There's always something about his clothes that seems to be trying just a little too hard for the occasion. His chin is freshly shaved, and a clean scent of soap and toothpaste comes from him.

I feel like someone hastily assembled from the bits left over after all the other women were finished.

'We'd better get a move on. Brendan said to be there early.'

'Sorry, the zip on my boot's stuck . . . Christ, it won't go up or down, I don't know what I've done . . .'

'Let me.'

Oh — my — God.

But he's too bloody efficient by half. The zip's free, the boot's fastened, and he's back on his feet before I have time to enjoy the moment.

'Come on. It's already ten to,' he says.

Handbag?

'Just . . . '

Keys! Fuck!

'Get the engine started, I'm with you, just . . . '

I'm saying it to his back. He's already half-way down the street. I grab the keys off the kitchen table, find a coat, slam the door behind me and trot after him as fast as this stupid skirt will allow.

★ ★ ★

'What are you doing?'

'Just my mascara.'

'If I have to brake suddenly, you'll poke your eye out.'

I'm trying to concentrate on not losing an eye, but I can't help being conscious of Gary's hand on the gearstick, shifting up and down for the bends.

'Put some music on, if you want,' he says. 'The CDs are in the glovebox.'

U2, Bruce Springsteen, Green Day: stuff that's mostly big and loud but not really my sort of music. A cassette box cloudy with scratch marks makes me smile. Inside is a disembowelled tape spilling loops of shiny brown plastic.

'Hawkwind,' I say, before I can stop myself, and start laughing.

'Haven't played that for years,' he says defensively.

'I don't think it would work. Hawkwind, for God's sake. Music to watch UFOs by. I've never met anyone else with a Hawkwind tape in their car.'

'Well.' He's definitely uncomfortable. 'I ought to

throw it away. Give the car a good clean-out.'

The 4×4 is much tidier than last time, and has the tinny smell of cleaning fluid. He must have polished every surface.

'Don't chuck the tape,' I say, sorry for teasing him. 'It reminds me. Of the seventies, I mean.'

'Reminds me too.' Something makes me think he's smiling, but his face is turned away to check the traffic at the junction.

We've come up a back road I don't recognize, and suddenly there are streetlamps and the first houses on the edge of Green Down, ones that have been built in the last twenty years. Barn conversions and cul-de-sacs of executive homes loop over the hillside where farms and quarries used to be. Gary pulls into the car park outside the primary school. There are hardly any spaces left. Lights blaze from the big timber-and-glass wall of the assembly hall where the meeting is to be held. A polished plaque gleams on the wall: 'Opened 27 April 1982 by HRH The Princess Anne. Architects: R. Klein Partnership.'

'It's a bigger turn-out than the last meeting.' Gary follows me into the packed foyer. 'I hope that doesn't mean we're in for trouble.'

Brendan's standing by the doors into the hall, moustache trying bravely for a lift but only managing half-mast. With him is a brisk woman from the council with pixie-cut hair, and I recognize a man in a suit from RockDek's head office — apart from Gary, the only person formally dressed for the meeting. He has a custard-yellow tie with little maroon spots on it, like cartoon acne.

'Sit near the front,' Brendan hisses. 'I need moral support.'

'No, better at the back,' says the RockDek smoothie.

'Anywhere,' says the woman from the council. She sounds tired.

There's a man with a video camera on his shoulder, filming people going in, and Acne Tie keeps shooting worried glances in his direction.

A girl with a notebook approaches. '*Western Daily Press*,' she says to Gary. 'Are you from RockDek?'

'That's me.' Acne Tie shoulders his way in front of Gary. 'Alan Prince, public relations. If you want an interview, talk to me. I don't want you approaching any of the team directly.'

The pixie-cut woman gives him the kind of look I give Dickon, and extends a hand to the reporter. 'I'm Lucy Mackintyre,' she says, 'project leader for the council. You're very welcome to get a comment from me after the meeting.'

'Catch up with you later,' says the girl. 'Excuse me. I've just seen . . . ' She slides away into the crowd.

'Why are the press here?' asks Brendan, plaintively.

'Look,' says the man from RockDek, 'it's very important we're all singing from the same hymn sheet.'

'For God's sake, back me up,' says Brendan. 'Kit, if I call on you . . . '

'Don't be ridiculous,' snaps Acne Tie. 'We can't have people popping up all over the shop like loose cannons.' He glowers at me. 'Don't say a word.'

Brendan looks desolate.

All the time I'm scanning the faces pushing past us, dreading who might be here, a part of me hoping too. But there's no one I recognize. They'll all be dead, or long-ago moved away. A broad, lurching backside heading up the stairs, following the sign for toilets, makes me think of Mrs Owen, but I'm sure she's gone: a heart-attack, still in her fifties. Nobody would know me now.

It wouldn't take much to remind them.

There's a commotion by the door. An elderly man is trying to push his way in. A woman in a purple pashmina bars his way. 'I'm afraid you can't bring your dog in,' she says loudly.

Behind the man, looking as if it doesn't much want to come in anyway, an elderly basset hound is hauling its teats up the step. Its owner is the white-haired man who smiled at me by the churchyard.

'I can't leave Riley outside on a cold night like this,' says the man, still pushing at the door. 'She's too old.'

Pashmina looks like she wants to say, 'And so are you.' 'No dogs,' she repeats. 'This is a school.'

'Don't see what difference that makes,' says the old man. 'I want to come in and have my say.'

'Well, it's your choice,' says Purple Pashmina. She has the bright saintly smile of a Meals on Wheels lady. 'In, *without* the dog, *with* the dog, out.' Just like she's offering him prunes and custard on a plastic tray. 'Make your mind up.'

The old man looks at the dog. My heart breaks.

'They need to get a move on sorting out that bloody stone mine,' he says. 'That's all I wanted to say. Then maybe some of us can get on with selling our houses.' He turns and tugs at the dog's lead. Riley, who has only just managed to waddle up the step, patiently follows him out again.

'Well, that's one less dissatisfied punter, thank God,' says Alan Prince. 'Every little helps.'

Gary takes my arm and propels me through the glass doors into the hall.

'Hey,' I say, as we shuffle along a row of chairs, treading on people's feet. 'That was a bit sudden.'

'I had to get out of there before I hit that git in the suit,' says Gary. 'For a start, the old bloke was on our side. He wants us to get on with the job, just doesn't understand why we can't fill the lot right away. And poor old Brendan's completely out of his depth. I don't trust those head-office bastards not to stitch him up. There's something going on tonight. I don't understand why the press are around.'

We finally reach two empty seats.

'Who else is here?' I ask.

Gary scans the room, then sits down. 'Not many we know,' he says. 'Rupert's just arrived. Never misses an opportunity to talk about his blessed bats.'

Brendan, Acne Tie and Lucy Mackintyre come into the hall, and make for reserved seats on the platform. Brendan turns and gives us a forlorn little wave as he climbs the steps.

'He's a good bloke,' says Gary. 'I hope they don't let him make a fool of himself.'

*   *   *

At the start everything seems normal. The chairman of the Residents' Association, a tall elderly man who reminds me a little of Poppy's father, introduces everybody on the platform. Lucy does an opening speech about how pleased the council are, et cetera, funding only a matter of time, a formality really . . . Brendan gets to his feet and outlines what has been achieved so far, with the aid of a PowerPoint presentation that only goes wrong twice to leave him peering at the screen in bafflement. But he recovers well, and there's even a smattering of applause when he sits down, after telling us we can sleep sound in our beds thanks to his hi-tech canaries. They'll give us plenty of warning before people's homes drop into the abyss.

'Questions from the floor?' asks the chairman.

There is the usual pregnant pause while everyone waits to see who's got the nerve to speak first. Then it starts.

'Can someone explain why it's been fifteen years since the mines were first declared unsafe, and yet we're still waiting to know whether the problem will get fixed?'

304

The speaker is a man a few rows ahead of us. By his voice — loud and confident — I'd put him among the more middle-class Green Down residents, the type who live in the listed Georgian cottages. He's wearing a creased leather coat that's seen some wear, and dark greying hair curls over the back of his collar. 'You got any idea who he is?' I whisper to Gary.

He shakes his head. Lucy leans forward and explains patiently that the mines will be filled, we're bound to get the funding, the council does take the problem seriously and so do all the partners working on the project . . .

But Leather Coat seems to have articulated something that has been brewing for a while. There are stirrings and mutterings as Lucy answers, explaining again what she explained in her introductory talk.

'Meanwhile we're living on top of disaster!' calls someone from behind us. I suddenly notice the winking red light on top of the TV camera. The news crew have moved from the back of the hall; the cameraman stands with legs apart, braced under the weight of the camera on his shoulder, while its single dark eye roves the audience. Instinctively I lean away from it, which puts me up against Gary's charcoal-suited shoulder. Our arms touch and I want to lean harder. Instead I shift awkwardly away.

'They're so angry,' I say. 'They don't look like angry people, when you see them in the daytime. I don't understand. The mines have always been there.'

'Well, it's hardly surprising,' says Gary. He sounds quite cross with me for not understanding. 'But, then, I guess you didn't know my mum, who couldn't find a buyer for a house she was convinced was going to fall down a black hole any day, taking her with it. She couldn't have got a one-bedroom flat anywhere decent in Bath for what her place was valued at three years ago.'

'Is your mum still in the area?'

'She died in a care home last year. Selling the house just about covered the fees.'

'Sorry.'

The muttering and shuffling are getting louder, and he gives me the stiff little smile that says, 'Thanks for being polite but why should you be?' But I am sorry, though I barely remember her: an occasional presence in Mrs Owen's kitchen, a shadowy figure drawing the curtains across Gary's bedroom windows.

Acne Tie from RockDek has started to speak, to try to calm things down, but the audience is barely under control. Brendan is looking queasy. Now other people are getting to their feet and shouting. Why can't the filling start right away?

'We have to wait for the deputy prime minister's office to confirm the funding,' repeats Lucy Mackintyre, patient and calm. 'You don't think the council could afford this on its own, do you? The work's going to cost more than a hundred and fifty million.'

'I understand we have to wait until routes for the bats have been sorted out,' shouts a woman in the third row. 'Since when have bats been more important than people?' Rupert starts to get up, with the RockDek PR man trying to glare him into sitting down again, but before he has a chance to tell us that, frankly, he'd prefer to save a Greater Horseshoe than the questioner any day, a man leaps to his feet two rows back.

'And who's going to pay for the maintenance?' Someone else starts to clap. 'The work might end in six years, but everybody knows something like this is never really going to be finished. All those underground roadways you've built, who's going to maintain them?'

There's an uncomfortable silence from the platform. The official line is that it will be the people who live above the roadways who are legally responsible, after the stabilization is complete, for their upkeep. Lucy Mackintyre starts to explain this, and unleashes a barrage of angry shouts.

A short man wearing the shapeless creased suit of a small-town accountant gets to his feet. He makes some ineffectual hushing motions with his hands, gives up, takes his shoe off and bangs it on the seat of his chair.

A silence falls.

'My name is Graham Schofield,' he says. 'You say that we are legally responsible for whatever part of the mines lies directly under our houses?'

'That's about it,' says Lucy.

'In that case, why hasn't anyone got me to sign something agreeing to the work being carried out under my home?'

Lucy Mackintyre turns white. There's a huge swell of protest from the body of the hall.

'The fact is,' shouts the little man, over the noise, 'the fact is you have to have my permission. And since by some oversight you have failed to ask me, I want you to know here and now I'm not going to agree to it until I am absolutely satisfied that what you are putting down there is one hundred per cent environmentally safe.'

On the platform, Brendan buries his head in his hands. Acne Tie looks thunderstruck, and turns angrily to Lucy Mackintyre, who's shaking her head. The rest of the hall is in uproar. I wouldn't be surprised if a lynch party didn't storm the platform and string the little accountant up there and then.

'Shit,' says Gary.

'I don't understand,' I say to him. 'What's going on?'

'Graham fucking Schofield has just succeeded in bringing the work to a grinding halt,' says Gary.

★ ★ ★

Brendan explains in the pub, where we meet after escaping what almost became a riot. 'It looks like somebody really fucked up,' he says. 'Pardon my French, Kit. Lucy Mackintyre swears blind it couldn't have been the council's fault, but I bet heads roll. There was a massive consultation exercise a while back, and all the locals should've signed legal forms granting us the right to carry out the work underneath their properties. Seems it was bang in the middle of all that when Mr Schofield bought his house. Somehow he was missed out. Lucy's convinced the previous owner signed before he sold to Schofield, but they can't find the documents, and Schofield swears blind he and his solicitor weren't made aware of the issue. It's all a legal tangle, and nobody's sure who should sue whom.'

'So everything stops?'

'No. We can carry on with the work, provided we don't trespass under Mr Schofield's property.'

'Which is?'

'Just beyond the point Ted and the boys have driven the northern walkway to already.'

'What? That's MoD land, surely.'

'Mr Schofield is the MoD's next-door neighbour. His garden — and it's a big one — backs on to their perimeter fence.'

Brendan sounds like he's known about this all along. How come nobody warned me?

'It was mentioned at the meeting the Friday you arrived,' says Brendan, defensively.

'Well, if it was, nobody spelt it out for me,' I say. 'I don't get it — if you all knew, how come no one's sorted it out?'

'We hoped he'd see reason and come round to signing. Nobody thought he was a closet environmentalist with a grudge against foam concrete.'

'I don't think he is, necessarily,' Gary chips in. 'He's

308

just a pedantic twit who likes wielding the power he's got over us.'

Brendan peers gloomily into his pint like a fortune-teller into a crystal ball. Perhaps he hopes he'll see a little man in an ill-fitting suit drowning there. I take a big sip of vinegary wine. For the moment, the tauroctony and the Mithraic carving are safe.

★　★　★

Neither of us is saying much as Gary drives me home. Maybe he's thinking about his mum, in her little yellow house on the cheap side of the hill before she went to the care home. But I've been thinking about her son.

A car passes us in the other direction, and for a moment Gary's face is lit up by its headlights, sturdy but no longer beautiful the way I remember it, the summer I turned fourteen. He looks solid, and dependable, a man in a suit who cared about his mum. And then I remember the loader roaring through the tunnels, the way he threw it at the stone, making it dance, just on the edge of control.

'I was wondering,' Gary begins. Shuts his mouth again, looks lost. 'Well. You're probably busy.'

'When?' I say, a bit faster than I mean to.

'Saturday morning. Only I'm doing up the kitchen in my place, and I really liked the one you've got in your cottage, and I wondered if you'd come and help me look at tiles and stuff . . .'

What? Look at bloody tiles? Why doesn't he ask me out? Or, better still, jam on the brakes, run the 4×4 into the hedge and shag me senseless?

'Of course I will.'

'Lovely,' says Gary. 'Only you've got really good taste . . .'

The thirty-limit sign flashes past in the headlights as we come down the hill into Turleigh.

'It's not my kitchen. I'm only renting.'

'Oh. Of course. Um. But you did pick that kitchen to rent . . .'

'I'd be happy to help you.'

'Good.' He stops the car on the right, just before my cottage. 'Lovely. See you tomorrow at work, then.'

'Thank you for driving,' I say, hopping out, not sure whether I've done the sensible thing.

'No problem.' He winds down his window as I come round to that side of the car. 'I know it sounds weird, but I enjoyed tonight.' He shoves the car into gear and drives off before I have time to say anything.

As I'm hanging up my coat inside the cottage, my foot nudges the big envelope that was on the mat earlier. Junk mail, I expect. But it's a plain brown envelope, with a typed white label. It must be Martin then, sending research on Mithraic temples. I'll read it while I eat. I bring it with me into the kitchen, wondering what I can cook that's quick. There's a pack of chicken breasts in the shopping and a stir-fry won't take long.

I slit the plastic packaging with a knife, and since it's in my hand use it on the brown envelope as well, walking over to the rack to pick up the frying-pan as I pull out the contents. It looks like a sheaf of downloaded web pages. On top is a single sheet of plain white paper, with ENJOY printed in the middle in big type.

That isn't like Martin.

God.

Going to be sick.

No, just dizzy. Where's the chair?

The pictures are on the floor, and if I pick them up I'll have to look at them again. I don't want to look at them again. But they're in my head anyway now. Vile.

Bastards.

My mouth's dry . . . Water.

No. I'll throw it up.

I'm in the living room now, on the sofa, feet drawn up and arms tucked into my body. Shaking like an earthquake. I can't believe anyone would do that. Even from this distance the pictures are poisonous. I can see them out of the corner of my eye, scattered around and under the kitchen table. In close-up, caverns of flesh stuffed and poked and probed with gigantic instruments and humourless savagery. The chicken pieces are on the floor too, plump, pale cushions that look too much like some of the things in the pictures, moist and flushed purplish-red.

It's not enough closing my eyes. They're still there. It's the women's faces that haunt me most. Dead, burned-out eyes, slack mouths, nobody home. How could they do that? They must be drugged: as sentient as Poppy's Barbies.

I'm going to have to get in there and pick them all up. God knows what I'm going to do with them then. I should shove them straight into the wood-burning stove.

First I switch on all the lights. I want to push back the darkness leaking in from the garden. It's no good, though: the light won't reach any further than the edge of the terrace. Anybody could be out there, watching me, laughing himself sick over how the lady mining engineer reacts to a bundle of hardcore Internet porn. Thinks she's hard, does she? We'll show her hard . . .

For the first time since I moved into the cottage, I draw the curtains.

Then I make myself go into the kitchen and push the pages into as much of a pile as I can with my foot, without looking down. Finally I bend down to scoop them up, and try not to look again, but there's something about the nastiness of it that makes you look and see what you don't want to see. Thank God there aren't any with kids in. Or maybe there are, somewhere in the pile. I've seen quite enough to turn my stomach already.

A woman on her knees wearing a dog collar, the lead pulled tight and grasped by a big, masculine hand . . . For a moment I was sure that was what I had seen but, no, it's a woman chained between four D rings, arms and legs stretched out in an X, a man in a mask with his arm round her throat taking her from behind, while another man kneels between her legs. Who finds this sort of stuff erotic? It's sick. Then I turn the page and her arm is off, hacked off and hanging loose and bloody at the end of the chain. God, I can't believe . . .

I'm trying to bundle everything quickly back into the envelope without straightening it out properly, but half of the pages fall on the floor again and I'm weeping with the frustration of it, I don't even want to touch these pictures . . .

I get the last sheet into the envelope, and go to the sink to wash my hands and face, pulling down the blind first. I'd shower upstairs but I'm afraid of being naked in the house, in case someone outside might be watching.

Where's the tea-towel? I open soap-stinging eyes and turn round to look for it.

There on the floor under the table is a sheet I must have missed and failed to pick up with the rest. Another plain sheet of paper, with one word printed on it right in the centre so big I can't miss it.

SATISFIED?

22

I worked on my maths until I felt myself going cross-eyed. Every evening I stayed up late revising. If I could somehow improve my marks, I thought, perhaps I could duck out of the party because then Trish's threat to tell my father would be an empty one. It didn't seem to work like that, though: I was still having difficulty with schoolwork. Where had all my cleverness gone? The harder I tried, the more stupid I felt. Nothing made sense any longer.

I sat in the front room downstairs with my books spread out on the dining-table, and Gary's music came floating across the road and in through the open window.

My father looked round the door every evening when he came in, and nodded. 'Good girl,' he always said. 'Keep at it.'

I knew he was seeing Janey Legge after work almost every day, because most evenings he didn't get home until after seven, and I could smell beer on his breath. Neither of us mentioned her name now. If I ignored her would she go away? Did it matter if she didn't? I had resolved to stop thinking about my mother, but still the memory of that photograph in the bureau haunted me. And what if her letters had been hidden beneath it?

He came into the front room one evening, and instead of just nodding and telling me to keep at it, he pulled out a chair and sat down at the end of the table, looking at me.

I lifted my head from Ohm's law. 'Yes?' I didn't care if it sounded rude. Tonight, when nothing seemed to sink into my weary brain, I was prepared to run with danger. His eyes were making me uncomfortable.

313

'You're working very hard.'

'I've got exams next week.'

'You can work too hard, you know. You've got to enjoy yourself too.'

I stared at him. He didn't get it. He was too busy enjoying himself to know how I felt.

'You do know I love you very much, don't you?' he said abruptly. 'You're all I've got, Katie.'

No, I thought, you've got Janey Legge now. The curtains stirred in the breeze. Gary's music thudded across the road. Behind my father was the bureau, a neat, orderly pile of envelopes on the top. Below, the cupboard doors seemed to bulge under the strain of holding back the chaos inside. I could almost see the wood splitting.

'Here,' he said. He stood up and rummaged in his pocket. 'You've been working so hard, I wanted to get you something to show you how proud I am of you.' He brought out an oblong box. 'You can use it in your exams. Bring you luck.' He put it on the table and pushed it towards me.

Through the transparent plastic lid I could see it was a fountain pen, with a slim silver body and a gold-plated handle in the shape of an arrow. He had had it engraved with my initials, K.C.C., in curly script.

'Oh, Dad,' I said. I didn't touch it. 'Nobody uses fountain pens any more. They make your fingers messy.'

His eye muscles tightened, but this time it was with bewilderment and hurt. I could see him cursing himself for his clumsiness in buying the wrong thing. I wished I could take the words back, but they were said now. I should have reached out and taken the box — it wasn't too late, I could have said something, told him the pen was beautiful, because it was, and that I would always treasure it and keep it for writing special letters. But I didn't.

He picked up the box with a little smile, trying to make the best of it. 'Well,' he said, 'your old dad always gets it wrong. I'm sorry, Katie. I'll get you something else. Would you like a book token? Get yourself exactly what you want?'

'Yeah, fine,' I said. 'I'd better get on now, Dad. Revision test tomorrow.'

★ ★ ★

I still couldn't bring myself to ask Gary to the party. I desperately wanted him to be there, but I didn't know how to ask him. Trish would never notice, anyway. It looked as if she was inviting half the school — the half that had older brothers.

Trish had never been popular before. I'd heard her called 'yid' behind her back when she first came, and she was easily as clever as I was, which didn't make her much liked either. But everyone wanted to know her now, everyone wanted to come to this party, because everyone knew it was being held behind our parents' backs. Trish had discovered the fundamental truth that being bad makes you attractive.

People kept sidling up to me and asking if they could come to my party.

'It's not mine,' I said.

'Trish says it's yours.'

'Yeah, well, she's organizing it,' I would tell them. 'Ask her.'

Poppy had the same desperate look I caught on my own face in mirrors. But something unstoppable was gathering momentum; too late to jump off now.

★ ★ ★

'Have you asked Gary if he's coming?' said Trish.

Somehow time had bled away and we were in the

week of the party. My mind was on the history exam we had to take that afternoon: I was trying to order civil-war parliaments in my head. There was the Rump and there was the Long but which came first?

'Katie? You listening?'

'Yes. Of course I've asked him.'

'Well, did he say he was coming?'

Then there was the Bare Bones Parliament but that was definitely later. And wallpaper was invented in 1645. Why was it easier to remember the useless bits of knowledge?

'No, he was a bit vague.'

Vague to the point of blissful ignorance. Of course I hadn't asked him. My fingers dug into the bank, pulling at daisies by their roots. They didn't budge. Like Trish, who was giving me a baleful stare that suggested she knew fine well I hadn't spoken to Gary.

'Well, get him to *agree*. I really want him to come.'

Sedgemoor, 1685, last formal battle to be fought on English soil. The Duke of Monmouth is routed, captured and beheaded shortly afterwards.

★ ★ ★

It seemed like fate that as I came down the hill after school I saw Gary approaching from the other direction. Something seemed odd. Heavens, he was wearing a *suit*.

We reached the turning to our road at almost the same moment. He smiled at me. He looked uncomfortable in the suit, which was too large on the shoulders and too flappy round the legs.

'What are you doing all dressed up?' I asked.

'Been for an interview at college,' he said. 'My mum made me wear it.'

316

'College?' I said. 'But you've got a job.'

'I've got a *new* job,' he said proudly. 'Apprenticeship at the quarry. With day-release for college. Started last week at Crow Stone.'

Crow Stone. Trish would have sniggered. The quarry where Gary now worked was, at night, our local Lovers' Lane. It was the place she had suggested for our assignation with Gary, when she'd wanted us to write him a note. Trish and her mad ideas . . .

I would have only one chance. 'Wouldyouliketocome-toaparty?' I said. 'Sortofminebutnot. Fridaynightanytime-aftereight.'

'Oh,' he said. He didn't look very keen.

'It's my friend's older brother who's giving it. His parents won't be there.' Suddenly I was desperate for Gary to come. I'd tell him anything to persuade him. 'He's in a band. He's *met* Hawkwind.'

'All right.' Gary looked a bit stunned by my torrent of invention. I wasn't sure he believed me. But he'd agreed to come.

'Brilliant. Good. See you there.' I turned into my gate and skipped up the steps.

'Hang on,' he called.

'Yes?'

'Where is it? You didn't say where.'

I gave him Poppy's address.

There, done it. Wasn't so bad. My blood felt like it was pumping in time with the opening bars of 'Silver Machine' as I went indoors and laid out my biology and chemistry notes for tomorrow's exams.

★   ★   ★

'Did you say Poppy had asked you over to revise on Friday night?' asked my dad, as we ate our supper that night.

'Mmm,' I said, through a mouthful of new potato.

317

'And to stay overnight?' he continued, his fork poised over his plate.

'Is that OK?'

'It's fine.' He jabbed at his peas and speared them triumphantly. 'Just checking, that's all.'

He hummed all the way through the washing-up.

23

It's got to have been Ted. Only Ted would be such a cunt.

Bad word to use in the circumstances, but there isn't any other combination of letters in the English language with a nasty, jagged enough sound for what he's done.

No, I can't use that word. It brings me down to his level.

Fuck language. It's never there when you need it.

The car smells like I feel. Old ash, tar-stained stubs, unwashed work clothes. I'll never get clean again. Coming down into the valley to cross the river and railway line, the car runs into patches of brownish fog. Even the morning is grimy.

It was a bad night. Didn't sleep much, thinking I heard sounds downstairs. I tried to build walls in my head, but I couldn't stop the images smashing through.

Sick.

So now, driving into work, I've got a headache and a taste in my mouth like —

I don't know what it's like. The words have gone.

The pictures are in the envelope, in the garage. I didn't want them in the house with me. I'll burn them when I get home tonight, in the wood-burning stove.

Tell someone, Kit, says Martin, in my head. *This isn't one to keep to yourself. It's gone a step too far.*

Don't be stupid. I'm not going to Brendan with — well, with those. Suppose he told someone? Then everyone could have a great big laugh. I'm not giving them the satisfaction.

This isn't the seventies. There are laws about workplace harassment and bullying.

319

Go back to university, Martin. It doesn't work like that in mining.

Burn in hell, Ted.

★　★　★

A thousand blessings on the name of Schofield. Because of his divine intervention at the meeting, I don't have to go down the mine today and supervise Ted and his crew.

I'm not afraid of them. I'm *not*.

Brendan has called a meeting of the site-management team and consultants at ten. We assemble, cups of strong coffee in hand, to discuss how to proceed.

'You OK?' says Gary, waiting for me to finish with the sugar. Four spoonfuls, but this is a bad morning. 'You . . . look a bit rough.'

Well, then, I must be looking very grim indeed. I peer at my face in the shiny surface of the kettle. It makes me look like a pixie with toothache, of course, but also reveals dull stringy hair, a scary whiteness and big dark circles under my eyes.

Dickon's reflection appears next to mine, a goblin leering over my shoulder. 'Not sleeping, Kit?' He lowers his voice and his hot breath tickles my ear. 'It'll get better, really it will. Girl like you won't have much difficulty finding another man.'

Alan Prince, the RockDek PR man who was at the protest meeting, and another bloke from Head Office are already sitting at the long table in the meeting room, laughing just a little too self-consciously with a third man in a suit. As the consultant engineering company in charge of overall strategy, someone from Garamond has to be here every time there's a major hitch: this is the man who will call the shots. Lucy Mackintyre is sitting as far away from the rest as she can. She lifts her eyes as I come in, and I wonder if she's looking for an ally in this hostile room, but there's nothing to read in her calm politician's gaze.

'So,' says RockDek's man from Head Office, when we're all seated, 'we're at an impasse. Lucy?'

'That's about the size of it, Peter,' she says.

'So, can we have any indication from you when this is likely to be sorted out? I'm sure you acknowledge it's the council's cock-up?'

'I don't think you can make that assumption. The consultation exercise was a joint-partnership venture, the way this project has been conducted since its formal constitution five years ago. RockDek's inept filing is not the council's responsibility.'

'Don't fuck around, Lucy,' says Brendan. 'Save that for the press. I need to know when I can get on with the work in the north-western sector. I'm sure you know it's been designated an HHA.'

'I'm well aware,' snaps Lucy. 'But I had a meeting with the solicitors first thing and, high hazard or not, we can't proceed under Schofield's house until this is sorted out.'

'Any word from English Partnerships and the DPM's office about the funding?' asks the man from Head Office.

'Nothing,' says Lucy. 'Officially. Unofficially I've been warned that there will be no decision until we get this sorted.'

'This is ridiculous,' says Peter. 'We've got men hanging around doing nothing. The costs . . .'

'In PR terms, it's a disaster,' says Alan Prince.

'Has anyone spoken to the Inspector of Mines? We have a legal obligation to proceed with the work in the HHAs . . .'

They have faces like wolves, circling Lucy. She's not afraid.

'Didn't you hear me? I've spoken to the lawyers. You *cannot* proceed with work under Mr Schofield's property. What I'm here to find out is if you have any ideas on how to get round the problem. Can you make the void safe without trespassing under his land?'

'Kit?' says Brendan. 'Any thoughts?'

'The easiest way would be to curve the roadway more directly north, so we swing round Schofield's property and miss it altogether. I'll need a map showing the exact boundaries.'

'Surely — ' begins Lucy.

'I think you'll find Mrs Parry's been supplied with one of those already,' says Peter, smoothly.

Bastard. I know I haven't. This is the first time anyone's talked specifically about the Schofield problem. Are they setting me up? But what for?

Now I know how the bloody bull feels, about to be led out to the Mithraic sacrifice.

'I think you'll find I haven't had a sight of that information,' I say as calmly as I can.

'It's in the package of information I emailed you in your first week, Kit.' *Et tu*, Brendan? You bastard.

'Whether Mrs Parry checks her inbox or not is neither here nor there,' says Lucy. 'Will safety be compromised if we have no access to the area beneath Schofield's property?'

'No,' I say.

'Yes,' says Brendan, at the same time.

Lucy raises her eyebrows. 'Why are you so sure, Mrs Parry, when you haven't seen the map?'

'Because I disagree with the original decision to designate the void as a high-hazard area,' I say. 'I've checked the load calculations, I've seen the geophysics and the results of the test bore holes, and I can find absolutely no reason to think that that area is significantly more unsafe than the mines as a whole. Of course it has to be filled eventually. But I don't agree it needs filling right away.'

There's a silence. I keep my eyes on Lucy

Mackintyre. She's looking right back at me and this time there's something a little warmer in her eyes.

'Mr McGill?' she says.

'Mrs Parry has not worked on limestone stabilization before,' he says. 'Her predecessor Dan Brotherton had, and so have I. He convinced me the area was one of greater risk.'

I shift my gaze from Lucy and catch Gary's eye. He looks like he'd prefer to retreat to a safe distance while the madwoman sets light to her petrol-soaked garments. But he's hanging in there bravely, and crinkles his eyes just a bit, showing some support, I hope.

Lucy Mackintyre must have caught the look, because the next thing she says is: 'Mr Bennett? I know you're not an engineer, but you have worked in the quarries. What do you think about Mrs Parry's suggestion?'

'It isn't my area of expertise,' says Gary. 'And I've never quarried these workings — they were closed in the nineteenth century and sealed some years before I started at Crow Stone. But I was surprised when the north-eastern void was designated high hazard. I think there are far more worrying spots in the mines. Like under the primary school, where Mrs Parry has been concentrating her efforts this week.'

'With all due respect, Mrs Mackintyre . . . ' says the man from Garamond, quietly, his first intervention in the meeting. Everyone shuts up. ' . . . the issue isn't whether or not we should change the designation that's already been accepted by the Inspector of Mines. The point is do we stop all work in that void for the time being, until someone pulls their finger out and gets Mr Schofield to sign on the dotted line? Frankly that's our decision, not yours, and I'm inclined to go for stop.'

So Mithras gets to keep his secrets, for the time being.

★　★　★

Brendan grabs my arm as the meeting breaks up.

'Kit, I'm not at all happy — '

'Neither am I,' I cut in. 'I think I'm being set up.'

'What on earth do you mean?' He looks completely sincere, but he always does.

'Why haven't you discussed the Schofield problem with me before? You've let me carry on in that void without a word. I refuse to let you make me the fall-guy.'

Around us, the arguments are continuing. The Garamond representative isn't happy with Lucy's report from the lawyers. He seems to think he can find lawyers who will slap a court order on Schofield on grounds of public safety, and compel him to sign. Peter from RockDek has cornered Gary and, by the look of it, is bawling him out for disloyalty. Rupert, who wasn't invited but turned up anyway, is haranguing Alan Prince about bat routes. The only person who has managed to make a smart exit is Dickon.

'Look,' says Brendan, in a low voice, 'I know you're having personal problems . . . '

'What?'

'The job's hard on partners. We've all been through it. You're lucky if a relationship can take the pressure of being apart. When it breaks up — well, maybe it's for the best. Look at Gary. Look at me, for God's sake. Just try not to let it show while you're at work.' With a heave of the moustache the tombstone teeth flash supportively. 'You aren't being set up, Kit. I promise you.'

★   ★   ★

Crossing the site back to my office, I pass Ted and his miners. Gary's given them the job of sorting and shifting some timber that's been delivered to the wrong place.

They all turn and look at me. Their eyes are burning into my back as I somehow keep my legs firm enough to carry me past. Someone laughs softly, triggering a flash frame of those folds of purplish-red flesh, those wet lips and dead, humiliated eyes.

Burn.

★   ★   ★

I can't find any reference to Schofield's boundaries in the set of maps on my computer, but that won't satisfy Brendan because he will only say I accidentally deleted the relevant map, in a fit of grief for the departed boyfriend. I email him, asking for a copy of the original. It comes back almost instantaneously, an attachment without a covering message.

I superimpose it on my own mapping of the work. We're well short of the boundary of Schofield's land, thank goodness. But another day, and it would have been a different story.

Accidental, or deliberate?

'Want me to fetch you a sandwich from the deli, Kit?' Rosie perches on the edge of my desk. 'Hey, look at me. You're miles away. Deep underground.'

'Sorry. Thinking.'

'Bad habit.' Her open face, still tanned from her last skiing holiday, radiates concern. I'm tempted to tell her about the porn, but what's the point? Nothing she can do.

Besides, seeing her in her shiny red Puffa jacket and matching lipstick, I couldn't. She's so young and fresh. You can't work in masculine environments without coming across pornography at some point. But this was in a different class. Twisted. Violent. Grotesque.

Burn.

'Coming to the pub?' Now Gary's in the doorway.

'No. Trying to get myself up to speed on the memo I never got.'

'It's not like Brendan. He's very conscientious.'

'You're saying I'm making it up too?'

'Hey, I supported you in there, in case you hadn't noticed.'

'Sorry. Thank you. I realize you didn't have to stick your neck out.'

He sits down at Dickon's desk, somehow managing to look entirely comfortable on the posture stool. 'For what it's worth, I thought you were right. I've never understood why that void is an HHA. But Dan was in the Territorial Army. He probably signed the Official Secrets Act, in blood.'

'You're joking.'

'I hope so. Anyway, you still on for tomorrow?'

Chicken breasts, purpled and bleeding. Dazed faces spattered with curdy white.

'Not sure,' I say. Disappointment floods his face. 'I didn't sleep properly. Could be coming down with something.'

I feel awful because his blue eyes are full of concern.

'Look, I understand. Take it easy. Would you rather not?'

What I'd rather right now is a hug, a big Martin-type cuddle. No snogging, no shagging, just an uncomplicated squeeze, from someone who'll prove to me that all men aren't shits.

'Ring me tonight. I might be feeling better by then.'

There's a rush of cold air as the door opens and Dickon comes in, carrying a bag from the deli and blowing his nose. Gary leaps up from the posture stool so fast he nearly falls over.

'Don't mind me,' says Dickon. 'Am I interrupting something?'

★ ★ ★

There's a roaring blaze in the wood-burning stove. The curtains are drawn tight against eyes and the night; only half past eight and I'm bathed and in my pyjamas. On the coffee table is a mug of hot chocolate, too hot yet to drink, and cinnamon toast, made the way it should be from white bread dipped in egg and fried.

Cinnamon toast sticks back together the bits of you that are falling apart.

Eat this, Katie. Dear God, you have to eat something. You can't spend the rest of your life —

Sometimes I wonder if my whole psyche has been constructed out of cinnamon toast.

The toxic brown envelope lies on the floor by the stove. I fetched it from the garage before I had my bath. It's already acquired a damp, mildewed smell, and is smeared with cobwebby dirt from the woodpile.

Open me, it says. See all the things men can do to women. See how you can be shafted, fucked, abased, desecrated. We can do this to you whenever we want and, so complete is our power over you, you'll even put a sad, slack grin on your face.

I'm not going to open the envelope again.

Instead, I take a bite of cinnamon toast, closing my eyes. There's a lot to cinnamon toast. The sugar crunches but the eggy bread is soft and slippery. It's sweet and spicy but also buttery and savoury from the frying.

I open my eyes and reach out to turn the handle on the stove door, remember how hot it gets just in time and take the tongs instead. A blast of heat slaps me in the face.

It's evidence, of course. Proof I'm not imagining Ted's hostility.

I could keep the envelope . . .

. . . or let it go.

You've got to let it go.

It's on the flames, lying there helplessly, as surprised

as I am that I moved so quickly. The edges are turning a darker brown, smoking a little, then a yellow flick of flame laps around one corner. I almost expect to see the envelope gather its strength and leap out on to the rug at my feet. The tongs have found their way into my hand again, but I tighten my muscles and keep my arm by my side, and the flame whips across the envelope, peeling it back and exposing the corners of blackening pages.

The phone rings. I get up and go into the kitchen.

'How are you feeling?' says Gary.

'Better.' The floor tiles are cool under my bare feet. I walk back into the carpeted living room with the phone. 'Loads better.'

I kneel down by the stove, with the phone at my ear. I should have fed the pages one by one to the fire. It has taken uneven bites out of the envelope, unable to consume the stack of paper all at once. I catch glimpses of a charred breast, a shackled ankle, a crinkling penis. I pick up the tongs and, one-handed, close the stove doors. *Let it go.*

'I'll be fine for tomorrow,' I say. 'What time?'

⋆   ⋆   ⋆

Gary picks me up at ten. The 4×4 smells even more strongly of polish. To my regret, Hawkwind has disappeared from the glove compartment.

'You do know I've no idea what your kitchen's like?' I tell him. We're coming up to the traffic lights where we turn right on to the main road for Bath. 'Big? Small? Square? L-shaped?'

'Oh.' He pulls on the handbrake. 'You mean I should have taken you to see it first.' He indicates left instead of right. 'I never thought . . . '

'No, it doesn't matter. It's your decision, anyway, how it looks.' I imagine him buying a neat, blond kitchen from Ikea, with a lot of stainless steel.

The car behind starts hooting: the lights have changed. Gary turns right and gets more hoots as a consequence. He gives me a helpless smile, and waves apologetically to Mr Angry.

It's a white, misty morning, brighter than yesterday — though perhaps it's me that's brighter, Saturdayish, relaxed, easy. Something burned out of me last night. I slept dreamlessly and woke clear-headed, just as it got light. I felt good enough to go for a run along the canal tow-path, not a very long run, and more like a stagger by the time I came back up the field into the village, but after a hot shower and breakfast I'm glowing still.

Traffic is strung out in a long rope, cars with that Saturday look, carrying families towards the shops. Gary and I seem somehow to have leaped a stage. Shouldn't we be doing drinks, dinners, cinema, tickets to watch ageing rockers at the NEC before going to look at kitchens? This is the kind of thing I do with Martin.

Gary's eyes are on the road. He has the tired winter tan of people who have spent a long time in hot climates, and there are faint freckles where the skin stretches tight over his cheekbone, just under the fantail of lines at the corner of his eye. His driving is patient, controlled; he goes fast when there's space, slowing down easily when there's not — none of the impatient, jerky stuff that Nick used to do when he met traffic, slamming his foot on the brake as if he'd really prefer to ram the other cars up the backside.

But gentle and patient wasn't how Gary drove the loader. I drop my eyes to the gearstick, where his hand rests, and a tingle starts in me just thinking about those long fingers with their scrupulously neat nails.

'There're a couple of kitchen places I thought we'd look at.' The hand comes off the lever and waves towards the back seat. 'I picked up some brochures last week.'

I'm leaning over to see if I can reach them when suddenly the brakes hit and the seat-belt practically takes my arm off.

'Fuck,' says Gary. He's gone white.

A huge silver sod-off American-style SUV is sliding in front of us from a side-road. It has a long wheelbase and rides high on the road, though any creature taller than a ferret would end up as hamburger on the bull bars at the front. It's probably called something like a Chrysler Destructor, or a Ford Planetcrusher. It makes Gary's 4×4 look like a Mini.

'I missed that,' I say. 'Didn't they indicate?'

At the rear of the SUV, the owner has put in one of those mesh dog guards. Instead of a dog caged in the back, a boy is crammed in, lying half on his side staring out at the road, all knees and elbows. He's a young teenager and there's something about him that doesn't look right. His head lolls like that of a nodding dog and he's making faces in an odd way too, mouthing like a goldfish at the world outside. He starts waving.

'Fucking *bastard*,' says Gary. His hands are clenched on the steering-wheel and the veins are standing out in his neck.

'What's the matter?'

Gary can hardly speak. There's something wrong with his eyes too — shit, he's almost crying. He lifts a hand off the wheel and waves back at the boy, trying to smile.

'What is it?' I ask.

'I can't believe he'd do this. It's barbaric.' The lines at either side of his mouth have deepened, like fault lines in rock.

'You mean the kid in the back of the car?'

The traffic lights have changed to red and the SUV's brake-lights blaze on, bright enough to reach for sunglasses. To the right is an empty lane for city-bound traffic to filter and turn. Suddenly Gary swings the wheel hard right and shoots into the filter lane, so that we draw level with the SUV. He hauls on the handbrake and then he's hopped out of the 4×4, Careful Driver metamorphosing into Road Beast, rounding the bonnet and heading for the other vehicle. It's happened so quickly I can't think what to do to stop him. He's bristling with aggression. He hauls on the handle of the driver's door, trying to get it open, kicking futilely at the front wing of the vehicle, but the driver must have seen him coming and snapped on the central locking.

He does wind the window down, though, which is brave of him, the way Gary looks. I let mine down a crack to hear what the hell is going on.

Gary's still hauling on the handle, which makes him look rather silly. SUV Man has the advantage because his vehicle rides so high on the road. He doesn't look exactly pleased that someone's trying to inflict grievous bodily harm on his wraparound bull bars, but he's a lot more in control than Gary.

'You fucking bastard, Jeff,' spits Gary, and it all falls into place. This must be the South African driving instructor Mrs Gary ran off with.

'I'll have you if you scratch my car,' says Jeff. A long, stubble-shadowed chin, and short, tight *as*.

'You treat him like one of your bloody dogs,' says Gary. 'Bastard. If I had my camera . . .'

'He likes it in the back,' says Jeff. He sounds vaguely amused. 'Come on, Gary, think, man. You're only making it worse.'

'You've put him in a fucking cage,' says Gary. 'Like he's not — '

'Well, he isn't, exactly, is he?' says Jeff. 'Go on, say it, Gary. Jamie isn't what most people would call normal.'

I'm sure Gary's about to hit him, but somehow he makes a superhuman effort and steps back, but he can't stop himself swinging a kick at the side of the SUV.

There's an enormous clang. Gary must be wearing his steel toecaps. Jeff's face goes dark red.

Meanwhile the green filter arrow has lit up and the cars behind us are starting to get mad with Gary too. The one behind gives a long toot and a couple of others join in.

It looks like Jeff's going to get out of the SUV and have him, as promised. I wouldn't blame him because when Gary steps back there's one hell of a dent in the door. But this has gone far enough. I wind my window right down.

'STOP IT. JUST STOP IT.'

Two astonished faces. More hoots from behind. In the wing-mirror, a man in the green Renault behind us is opening his door so he can join the party.

'I saw that boy in the back and Gary's right,' I yell. 'It's humiliating, and I'll be his witness if it comes to court.' I have no idea what I'm talking about, but I'll do anything not to have to pick up the bloodstained bits after a fight in the middle of the Lower Bristol Road.

The hooting behind us rises in a crescendo. Gary gives me a grateful look, and skedaddles round the front of the 4×4. He hops in, revs the engine and does a screeching right turn.

Jeff guns his SUV and tries to cut across the traffic after us, but the man in the green Renault is having none of it. Everybody must be feeling brave today: I wouldn't fancy tangling with those bull bars. Fortunately Jeff stalls, which is one up to us.

The right turn has taken us into the one-way system leading to the city centre. We're both breathing hard, and the adrenaline's pumping like a geyser. I want to laugh, because we got away with it, but the thought of the boy in the back of the SUV sobers me. Gary's *son*? I don't need to ask what Jeff meant, *not normal*. Anyone could have seen that the child is different.

I can't help myself. I reach out and squeeze his wrist.

It's OK, I want to say, it can be sorted, whatever it is. But, of course, one look at the boy would tell you it can't be sorted. Gary takes one hand off the wheel and squeezes back. The car lurches to the left, and we cross the river again.

'Sorry. Sorry, Kit. What must you think of me?'

'Nothing,' I say. 'Don't worry. Nothing. Let's go and sit down somewhere. You can tell me all about it.'

★   ★   ★

In the end, we go to Gary's house. He drives on auto-pilot. I'm quite grateful to get there alive.

He lives in Bradford-on-Avon, about seven miles out of Bath. Terraces of Georgian houses sprawl down a steep hillside. There's an ancient stone bridge, a Saxon church, and a lot of swans. Gary's house is about half-way up the hill, with views that stretch across Wiltshire.

'How did you afford this?' I ask, bowled over. The house goes on and on, up and up. You could easily fit in four families, one on each floor.

'No garden,' says Gary. He flings open a door at the back of the kitchen. It leads on to a tiny walled courtyard. There's just about enough light to keep a small shy fern alive.

'It's better in summer,' he adds apologetically. 'You get a bit of sun at midday.'

A lion's head fountain dribbles a thin greenish trickle down the wall. Raised flowerbeds spawn some rare species of pebbles. There's a bench, and a redundant copper sundial. 'I love it,' I say. 'The perfect low-maintenance garden.'

'I quite like it too,' he says, pleased.

He makes coffee in a tiny L-shaped kitchen with painted wooden cupboards that might have come out of a barge, and a geriatric electric hob on which only one ring works. We take our mugs upstairs to a first-floor living room painted buttercup yellow.

'This house is at least three times too big for you,' I say. His face falls. 'Don't get me wrong,' I say hastily. 'It's a brilliant house. But why did you buy one so huge?'

'It was for Jamie,' he says.

Ah.

'Tell me about Jamie,' I say.

* * *

By the time he has finished, I want to be on the other side of the room, giving him a hug. But between us is ten clear feet of worn but scrupulously vacuumed carpet. It's the kind of story you can't forget.

In 1982, the year Nick and I started going out together, Crow Stone quarry closed. The good stone had finally run out. Gary tried to get a job at one of the other local quarries, in Combe Down and Limpley Stoke, but Maggie Thatcher's dole queues were long and no one was hiring. It was the summer of the Falklands War. Everyone, apart from lefty students like Nick and I, loved a soldier. Dazzled by the glory of the battle at Tumbledown, Gary joined up, just as the British took Stanley. Instead of the South Atlantic, he got sent to South Armagh. When he came back, he met Tess at a disco in Warminster.

'It happened to be Tess, but it could easily have been someone else,' he said. 'I was twenty-three. I'd spent six months being more scared than I would have believed possible, not knowing when I'd turn a corner and have my head blown off by a sniper in a block of flats that didn't look that much different from parts of Bath. Seen it, done it, wiped the blood off my boots. I thought I was old enough to get married.'

That I can relate to. Round about the same time, I

was in a Princess Diana lookalike dress, coming out of Brighton register office with Nick.

'Tess was lovely-looking,' said Gary. 'Still is. Bit of a good-time girl, but I was a good-time boy then. She'd been going out with squaddies since she was at school. Might be going out with them still, except I got her pregnant.'

'Not Jamie,' I said, working out the dates.

'Jamie was much later. Tess told me she'd missed her period. I said, 'Well, we'd better get married then,' ' said Gary. 'Because that was what I wanted, really. A different kind of good time. A wife and a baby. Something that said *Gary was here.*'

'You've got two children, then.'

'No. It was stillborn.'

Down the side of the room is a long bookcase, floor to ceiling, with more videos and DVDs than books on it. One title, in the middle of a shelf of paperback thrillers, catches my eye: *Coping With Loss.* Unlike the rest, its spine is glossy and uncracked. Gary doesn't strike me as the kind of bloke who reads self-help books, but I can imagine him buying it for Tess, urging her to read it.

'She didn't want a baby after that. Not for years. And I don't think I noticed when that changed. In fact, I didn't notice nearly enough. I'd left the Army by then and gone back to quarrying. The best jobs were abroad. I got one in Zambia, and I was there when Tess met Jeff. When I came home, she was pregnant again.'

'So Jamie's not yours?'

'Tess let me think he was. I don't come out of this very well — absent husband, absent father. I was there for the birth — Caesarean, the cord had twisted round the baby's neck — and I held him and kissed him, then flew straight back to Zambia. Tess was left to cope with everything. To cut a very long story short, she and Jeff carried on behind my back for something like ten bloody years, Jeff rightly figuring that his life was going to be easier if good old Gary went on thinking he was Jamie's dad and banking a nice big overseas pay cheque.'

On the wide shelf next to me there is a photo in a pale wood frame: Gary, more hair, arms full of toddler. The toddler's not looking at the camera, he's looking up at Gary and laughing, smiling into a future that's all love and aeroplane mobiles.

The Early Learning Centre catalogue. That was why he had it in his desk drawer.

'How did you find out?'

'Mum was diagnosed with Alzheimer's. I came home to be with her while she could still recognize me. I got a job in the quarries at Corsham, and I bought this house for all of us, or so I thought. Stupidly, I expected Tess to help me look after Mum. It was a bit of a shock when she announced she and Jamie were going to live with Jeff instead.'

'And you had no idea Jamie was his?'

'When I didn't believe her, Tess said Jeff had already taken a DNA test. My lawyer pointed out I didn't have a leg to stand on with custody, and it wasn't even worth fighting for access because Jeff had seen far more of his son than I ever had. I did fight, though, not that it did me much good. I made the mistake of going round to confront Jeff and I lost my temper and threw half the rockery through the front window. Jeff wanted to sort me out, or at least set the dog on me, but Tess persuaded him otherwise. Instead they called the police, and eventually got a court order banning me from going anywhere near them or Jamie.'

There's another picture of Jamie on the bookcase. He's older in this one, nearly the age he is now. The plumpness is gone, and his face is all awkward angles, his hair messed up and his collar skewed. He's posing for the camera but he hasn't quite got the hang of it.

336

His blue eyes are anxious, confused. *Am I doing this right, Dad?*

'Sometimes I think it's my fault anyway,' says Gary. 'I thought I was doing the right thing, earning more money for us by working abroad. But I should have been here. Maybe we could have done more for him when he was small. You know, these alternative-therapy places . . . They say you can help the neural pathways grow in the brain, if you keep moving their limbs. Maybe he wouldn't be so helpless if we'd made more effort.'

'Don't be daft,' I say. 'You can't know. You certainly can't go back. None of us can.'

'Then to see him like that in the back of Jeff's car, like an animal. That's how he thinks of Jamie. You saw it.'

'Maybe he's right, though, and Jamie *likes* riding in the back. You know how kids — '

'He shouldn't *let* him,' says Gary, knuckling the side of his eyes. 'It's degrading.'

It might look that way, but no judge is going to take it as evidence that Jeff and Tess are bad parents. Gary's eyes meet mine. He knows he's lost his son. I can tell he's about to say, 'Come here. Hold me'. And if he doesn't I will anyway. My leg muscles are tensing to lift me out of the chair and across the room.

Muffled in the depths of my bag, the phone goes, with its irritating tinkly chorus of 'There Must Be An Angel (Playing With My Heart)'.

'They'll ring back,' I say, my eyes fixed on Gary. 'Or leave a message.'

But his face is alert, worried. 'It could be work. I left my phone downstairs. Better answer.'

He's right. This is how we'd hear if there had been a collapse underground. My fingers hit tissues, Tampax, mascara, ballpoint pens. Where the fuck's the phone?

It stops ringing.

Gary gets up from the sofa. 'I'll go and check mine.'

My phone starts up again.

It's wrapped itself in the lining of my bag, while ambulances, fire engines, helicopters could be converging on Green Down. Houses sway and crumble. A huge chasm yawns in the high street, with a minibus full of children tumbling into it. My heart's thudding. Somehow I get the phone out of the bag and to my ear.

'You took your bloody time.' Martin's voice.

'Jesus Christ. What are you ringing for? You're in California.'

'Actually, no,' says Martin. 'I'm at the railway station in Bath.'

Gary has stopped half-way to the door. He must have worked out by now that Green Down hasn't sunk into the bowels of the earth after all, but he still looks anxious.

'What the hell are you doing there?' I ask the phone.

'Waiting for you to pick me up.'

'Hang on.' I take the phone away from my ear. 'It's all right. It's only Martin. *My friend.*'

Has he picked up the emphasis? He's got that polite, helpless, blank look again.

'Kit!' Martin's voice comes tinny out of the handset. 'Where are you? Don't tell me — '

I jam the phone back against my ear.

'Doesn't matter. But why — '

'You're with him, aren't you? You naughty girl. That was quick work.'

Surely Gary can't hear any of this. I'm practically screwing the phone into my head in the hope Martin's loud voice isn't spilling out.

'Bring him along to the station. Only fair to let me squash into the back of your car with him since I've selflessly given up San Francisco for you.'

'No,' I say. 'I don't understand . . . ' Gary discreetly leaves the room. 'Why are you here? I thought you were going away.'

'I told you. When I phoned from the train on Monday. With what the curator showed me, I reckon there's enough evidence, after all, to turn received scholarship on its head, and justify blowing out the California trip. I decided last night this is more important. I have to come and look for a Mithraeum in your quarries.'

'Look,' I say. 'This isn't a good time.'

'I'm here, Kit.'

'You should have warned me.'

'I did.'

'The line broke up. I didn't hear you.'

'Sorry. I should have phoned to tell you what train I was getting, but I thought, Fuck it, I'll just come.'

'Well, if you're here, I suppose I'd better come and get you.'

Gary is downstairs in the bargee's kitchen, washing up the coffee things. He doesn't look at me.

'Sorry,' I say. 'Martin's just arrived in Bath. I wasn't expecting him.'

'I'll drive you back so you can go and pick him up.'

'He's not my boyfriend,' I say.

Gary picks up the tea-towel and starts drying the mugs. 'I know. Dickon told me.'

'Dickon told you what, exactly?'

'That you and Martin had broken up last weekend.' He sounds quite angry now, betrayed.

'Gary, it's not like that.'

'I'm sure.'

'Really. Martin and I are friends.'

'Come on, Kit,' he says, hanging the tea-towel to dry on the radiator. When he turns to face me, he's stiff and polite. 'You don't owe me anything. Dickon told me you were crying in the office. You should give it a chance again, if Martin's come all this way.'

'No,' I say. 'You've got it completely wrong.'

He's being deliberately obtuse. He doesn't want to

hear that I'm not having a relationship with Martin. I can't make it much clearer unless I spell out that Martin is gay.

Why don't I, then?

Because I've suddenly realized I don't know Gary at all.

How can I be so sure he was going to say, 'Come here'? How do I even know he was telling the truth about him and Tess? What would have happened if I hadn't been with him this morning on the Lower Bristol Road?

I used to think I knew Nick, until the day I came home and smelt perfume and sex in the hall. And opened the bedroom door. *Why don't you join us?*

It still hurts.

'Oh, forget it. Drive me home.'

But as he locks the front door behind us, I remember the anxious smile on Jamie's face in the photo. *Am I doing this right, Dad?* My heart lurches.

★   ★   ★

'I despair of you, Kit,' says Martin.

We are sitting on a stone seat at the side of the Roman Bath, our feet on a limestone pavement that's been there for nearly two thousand years. Honey-stone columns frame a pale, wintry sky. The bases are Roman, the tops nineteenth-century reconstruction.

'You mean you let him think we were a couple who broke up last weekend and right now are making up again?'

'That's about it.'

'So stupid.' He hunches his shoulders, rests his chin on his hands and stares out across the murky green water. Wisps of steam rise from it and are eaten by the sunlight. 'What is it with you and men?'

'I'm sorry?'

'You're such a fuck-up sometimes. Anyone would think you set out deliberately to destroy your relationships.'

'That's not fair. Nick wrecked our marriage, not me.'

Martin doesn't reply. A family of African tourists wander in to the bathhouse, wrapped in about three cable-knit cardigans each on top of colourful robes. Two tiny children start a jumping game back and forward over the channel, rusty red with deposited iron, where the hot spring water flows to fill the bath.

'He didn't want to hear me,' I add. 'You weren't there, I was.'

'Are we back with Gary or still talking about Nick?'

I'm not sure. I kick my heels against the pavement, then remember I'm taking my frustration out on an archaeological relic. Luckily Martin hasn't noticed. He's focused on the statues that look down from the terrace above.

'I've always hated those statues,' he says. 'Crappy nineteenth-century stonemasonry. The Romans probably never had any statues up there, and if they did they would have looked a damn sight better. God's sake, I swear that one's Frankie Howerd in *Up Pompeii*.'

'Excuse me,' says the African lady, in her tribal best and Scottish woollies. She has perfect English, with an American accent and intonation like birdsong. 'Would you mind . . . a photograph?'

'Delighted,' says Martin. 'Now . . . oh, I see. It's digital. Fine. Hang on a sec. You all shuffle a bit that way and I can get you all in with the steam rising off the Great Bath in the background.' The family, Mum, Dad, two older boys and the two little tots, obligingly shuffle as one along the Roman pavement. 'No, back a bit that way.' They shuffle back and forth, now in a line, now in a bunch, an elaborate dance as Martin squats, stands up, jumps on to a low wall, almost steps back into the water trying to find the best angle. I love the way he takes things so seriously.

Reluctantly he hands the camera back to the Africans. Just for a moment, he wanted to produce their entire portfolio of holiday snaps.

'Excuse me,' says the lady again. 'Thank you very much, and can you tell us where we will find the Sacred Spring?'

Martin explains and off they go.

'They'll be sorely disappointed,' he says to me. 'Nothing to see but a few bubbles on the surface of the King's Bath.'

'That's us British, innit?' I say. 'We don't like to make a big fuss.'

Martin glances at his watch. 'No wonder I'm so bloody hungry.' He puts out a hand and hauls me to my feet. 'Come and look at what I brought you here for. Then we'll have lunch somewhere and I'll give you Uncle Martin's Complete Guide to Men.'

*   *   *

The inscription doesn't say much. It's a slab of plain stone, kept in a back room at the museum alongside a lot of other similar blocks. This is the stuff that the public doesn't see, things that look like nothing very interesting but bring archaeologists and historians out in a hot sweat.

'Coffin lids,' says Martin. 'One of the things I like about the Roman period is that they were good recyclers. Some time around the late third century, somebody spotted this thumping great block of stone, and thought, Hey, that'd make a lovely coffin lid. Just the job for our mum. So they nicked it.'

'Nicked it from where?'

'Ah, straight to the point as ever. I'll make an archaeologist of you yet. Before this stone was recycled for funeral use, it was a plaque commemorating the restoration of a building destroyed in a fire. What's really interesting, though, is what kind of building it was. Look at the inscription.'

On the stone a lot of spiky Roman letters mean little to me. Except one word. INVICTO.

'Isn't that the word you said crops up on Mithraic altar stones?'

'What? Oh, the *invicto*. Yes, that's true. 'Unvanquished'. No, what I was thinking of is the other bit. The inscription refers to 'PRINCIPIA' — a word that usually describes a military headquarters. Basically, this plaque tells us that a chap called Naevius restored a building that was used by the military. So although we don't know exactly where it was, we can guess it wasn't a million miles from where the coffin lid was dug up.'

'Which was?'

Martin gives me a big beaming *invicto* smile. 'On the hillside just below Green Down.'

★　★　★

On Sunday, we go walking.

Martin has an Ordnance Survey map that he has persuaded his friend the curator of the Roman Baths to mark up, showing us where the coffin lid with the Naevius inscription was found. We park the car in the road by the church in Green Down, and set off on foot along one of the ginnels that criss-cross the hillside between the rows of cottages. It takes us steeply downhill, ending in a flight of steps that emerges on the lane not far from the primary school. The view is breathtaking. Below us lies a steep, wooded slope, plunging to a brook that cuts through the valley. All around the land is full of folds and pleats, like a piece of material gathered together by giant hands. The rock underneath would look like marble cake, the swirls of

343

strata dotted with fossils. The sky is low and heavy, and the air smells of rain on its way.

Set Martin down in front of a landscape, and he's like a man in front of a row of top-shelf magazines — he has to stop and look. I can see him taking it all in, *reading* it, the tramway from the quarries taking the stone down to the old Somerset coal canal; the ridges of a medieval field system on the far side of the valley . . .

'Hang on, Kit, don't belt off into the blue. You're walking down an old drover's road . . .'

I'm walking down the road Trish and Poppy and I used after school, to reach the field with the cows where I dug up ammonites. In the summer, the branches from the trees would lace together to form a green roof over it. Now the barns of Vinegar Farm have been converted to houses, and the trees have been cut down to give them a view.

Martin follows me down to the bend in the road, looks round to make sure no one's watching and hops over a low wall.

'Here. Let me give you a hand.'

'I can manage.' I haul myself over the tumbled stones, grabbing on to a hazel bush. 'Are we supposed to be here?'

'Of course not. This is extreme archaeology. Add to the list of thrills the chance of being shot for trespassing.'

We clamber up a hillside carpeted with beech leaves. It levels out eventually into a shallow bowl beneath a cliff. Vines and creepers hang down over an old quarry face. There's something naggingly familiar about it, the beech trees knitting their branches overhead, the tall holly bush rooted in a crack in the rock, and a pang of something between fear and a sweet, early-morning sadness hits me. But Martin ignores the quarry, and sets off up the slope to the side.

'Where are we going, exactly?'

'Almost there,' he says. 'Ah. Yep. Wriggle past me — hang on to that holly tree, if you can.'

There's hardly any room. We're perched precariously on the hillside overlooking what used to be Vinegar Farm, peering down through the trees at the old farmhouse. Beyond, a high stone wall encloses a landscaped garden, a series of terraces laid to lawn and shrubbery, cascading down the slope from a large Victorian house.

'That's where they dug up the coffin lids,' says Martin. 'The garden of Hope House, when they were landscaping the lower terraces round about the end of the nineteenth century. Such a bloody shame — just before archaeology got careful. We don't know nearly enough about exactly what they found or precisely where they found it. Things got lost because the Victorians kept the bits they liked for themselves.'

'So was this whole area a Roman cemetery?'

'No, no. They only discovered a few burials. It was normal practice in Roman times to bury the dead along the roadside just out of town. This lane was probably a well-used track in Roman times. Of course, the villa was higher up, between Hope House and the farm buildings, I reckon.'

'There was a villa here as well?'

'Oh, yes. Definitely. The Victorian excavation wasn't complete, by any means, but we know it's here and, anyway, the name of the farm gives it away. 'Vinegar' is a corruption of 'vineyard'. In the Roman period, when the climate was a degree or two warmer, this would have been an ideal slope for growing grapes. Still is, probably.'

A car swoops down the lane where bullock carts used to sway slowly up the hillside. I can almost hear a troop of soldiers marching past, *sin dex*, *sin dex*, left right, left right, leather straps creaking and sunlight winking off buckles and spears and polished metal helmets.

'History's all layers, really,' says Martin, reading my mind as he often does. 'It's still there if you peel them back.'

'Including a Mithraic temple?' I ask. 'Do you really think there is one, somewhere underground?'

'Fuck knows,' says Martin. 'I think we found a tauroctony, but what would I know? I've only read about these things or seen them in museums. I've never excavated a Mithraic temple in my life.'

There's a hungry look on his face. He has to find his temple. He wants to believe there is one. He feels about it the way I once felt about the First Englishman.

* * *

We make our way past the creeper-hung quarry face and down to the road again.

'See?' says Martin. 'For a change, we didn't almost get caught.' He sounds faintly disappointed.

'You want to go on walking?' I ask. It's still early in the day; we're booted and waterproofed and it seems a shame to go home yet. Martin nods, and we set out along the lane winding gradually down the slope towards the valley bottom. The sky has darkened and it has begun to drizzle. I pull up my hood, and the world reduces to the rustle of Gore-Tex and the thud of my boots on the road. Drops of water fall from the rat-tails of my fringe and ski down my nose. Martin's hair is hanging round his face in damp ringlets, raindrops glistening in his beard.

Towards the bottom of the hill we come to a dog-leg crossroads. The road turns back on itself and plunges down to a village on the old coal canal. Martin gets the map out, frowns at it, then points sharp left uphill, where a kissing gate lets us through on to a mossy asphalted footpath. We climb it slowly, turning every so often to look back over the rooftops to the valley. In the

346

distance the river Avon slides under the Dundas aqueduct, winding towards Turleigh and Bradford. Somewhere in that direction, Gary will be sitting in his big lonely house with the photograph of his blue-eyed not-son.

Near the top of the path is a bench, and Martin parks himself on it with a sigh. I sit down next to him and we inspect the view, rapidly disappearing into misty drizzle.

'Sitting down was probably a mistake,' he says. 'My bottom's wet.'

Even getting my backpack off is an effort after the climb. 'I made some sandwiches. They might be soggy, though.'

They are.

'Very good,' says Martin. 'Wet sandwiches and a wet bottom. Weekends with you are such fun, Kit.'

'I didn't actually invite you,' I point out. 'Which reminds me — when were you thinking of going?'

'Well.' Martin pulls out the slice of cheese from the middle of the sandwich, pops it into his mouth and throws the bread away. 'Mmm. That's a good question.' He chews for a bit to let the suspense build. 'When can you smuggle me down your stone mine again?'

'No,' I say. 'Not on. We nearly got caught last time.'

'Cold feet?'

'Fucking frostbite.'

'Come on. You can't quit now. This could be one of the biggest archaeological discoveries of the century.'

'We're hardly very far into the century.'

'I'm taking the long view. This could be so big they'll still be talking about it in 2104. Seriously, Kit. This is potentially fucking amazing. I don't understand why you've suddenly gone cold on it.'

I don't know why either. Maybe it has something to do with the sweet, sad feeling that stole over me in the hollow in the woods. It reminded me I came here to close the tunnels, not to dig up history. 'I can't get you in,' I say. 'Nobody gets in who doesn't work there.'

'Officially, you mean. You can sneak me in like before.'

'It's too risky.'

'Please think about it.' He leans back on the bench and almost topples off. 'Anyway, I've cancelled California — nowhere else to be now. Can I stay with you this week?'

The other side of the valley has disappeared in the rain; the sandwiches have the texture of damp blotting-paper. Martin gets to his feet. 'Onward and upward, flower.'

I chuck the sandwiches into the hedge for the birds, heave on the backpack and follow him, the rain finding its way down the neck of my cagoule and sending chilly fingers to touch my throat and shoulders.

He thinks he'll talk me round. He reckons I'm a sucker for the old boyish charm.

He thinks wrong.

At the top of the path we come out through another kissing gate on to a lane. Martin consults the map again. There's something familiar about this junction too, though I'd be hard pushed to say exactly where we are. We take a left up a track past some cottages, cut right behind a barn and come out on to another lane in front of a set of high solid metal gates.

It jolts me. I have to stop.

Jesus. Here.

Just breathe deeply and normally. In two three, out two three. Again.

In a moment I will count to three and you will awake completely refreshed. But first, I want you to put those pictures back behind the gate. I want you to lock the gate. The gate is now locked. Nothing can harm you, Katie. You did nothing wrong.

. . . two, three, and awake.

Martin, in front, hasn't noticed and plods on past the

gates. He has no idea that all the demons in my personal hell are hurling themselves at the other side of those gates, screaming for me to open up and set them free. For a moment I thought the metal was starting to buckle and dimple like the side of Jeff's SUV. But everything's quiet.

There's a huge padlock on the gates, just like the one I used to imagine there, on a heavy chain looped round and round the handles. A faded notice says: 'Crow Stone. For sale or rent, prime industrial opportunity. Contact Richard Chaney and Partners'. Weeds are shattering the concrete driveway. The gates are two thick slabs of metal, crusted with brown rust. Buddleias poke their arms like hopeful prisoners round the sides. Nobody has taken up this prime industrial opportunity for a long time.

Martin is disappearing round a bend in the road. I walk on after him.

24

We went to Poppy's house on Friday straight after school. Her parents had left for Scotland first thing that morning. They thought she was spending the weekend at Trish's house. Trish's parents thought the McClarens weren't leaving until Saturday, and Trish would be staying with them tonight. All three of us had carried overnight bags to school; Poppy's was empty, since she was going back to her own house that afternoon.

The estate was quiet as we walked down from the main road. The afternoon sun slanted down through tall umbrella pines; the houses were set in big gardens far enough away from each other to be completely private. As Trish had said, it was the perfect place for a party. But Poppy was looking tense. I couldn't blame her. My stomach was churning too. The only one of us who looked unconcerned was Trish, sauntering along with her book bag over one shoulder and her case in the other hand.

It was going to be a warm evening. There wasn't a breath of wind. My school dress stuck to my back.

The hall was cool and silent, apart from the click of the keypad as Poppy reset the burglar alarm. We dropped our bags on the parquet and went through to the kitchen.

'What are we going to eat?' asked Trish.

'Eat?' said Poppy.

'There is something to eat, isn't there?'

Poppy's mother had cleared out the fridge before they left.

'Well, for God's sake,' said Trish. 'They're only going away for the weekend. Has your mother got some weird thing about bacteria? Or does she chuck food away to show she can afford to?'

Poppy blinked nervously, looking for a moment as if she might cry. She wasn't used to Trish mocking her family to her face. She rummaged in the freezer, stacked full of steaks and ice-cubes, and came up with some frozen bread and ice-cream. We made toast and Marmite and broke open a packet of custard creams, but neither Poppy nor I were very hungry.

How slowly time moved. We had nothing to keep us busy because we didn't know how to prepare for a party. Trish had told people to turn up with something to drink, maybe some music too. Because we had never been to anything other than the children's parties parents had organized for us, we had no concept of what a party really was. We did move all the furniture back towards the wall in the living room, with its cream-leather sofas and ivory carpet, and opened the patio windows to the terrace. Poppy laid out some ashtrays in case anyone smoked, but that was all we could think of. Then we went to get ready.

We had all brought more than one outfit so we could ask each other what looked best. Trish was determined to wear the SEX T-shirt, even though Poppy said it might get her more than she bargained for. Poppy wore a long white dress, with a glittery owl on the front, that looked like it had escaped from Abba's touring wardrobe.

I looked at myself in Poppy's mother's mirrored wardrobe doors.

'Where did you get those trousers?' asked Trish. 'They look pretty good.'

Your mother bought them for me. Better left unsaid. They were black and silky and flowed round my legs when I walked. With the stolen bra plumping out my chest, I did look good. 'Orange T-shirt or black?' I asked.

'Black,' said Poppy. 'Much more sophisticated.

Especially with the belt.'

'I'd go for the orange,' said Trish. But I knew that was because she wanted to be the only one all in black.

'It's nearly eight o'clock,' said Poppy. So we all clacked in our high heels down the polished steps, sat in a line on the cream sofa and waited.

'We need music,' said Trish. Thankfully, Poppy must have hidden the Donny and Marie records, but her taste ran to the dull end of pop — Hot Chocolate and Billie Joe Spears. Trish stomped off upstairs and fetched a Roxy Music cassette from her bag and we all sat down again to wait.

'Nobody's going to come,' said Trish, at a quarter past eight. Poppy and I exchanged a hopeful glance.

At twenty past, the doorbell rang, announcing two girls from the year below us in identical sequined dungarees. Nothing to drink. No music. Not a good start. Trish put on the other side of Roxy Music, and the girls had a glass of water each, then started jigging self-consciously around the centre of the living room.

At eight thirty, another group of girls arrived, with a bottle of cider and *The Partridge Family's Greatest Hits*.

'This is hopeless,' said Trish, dragging me out on to the terrace. 'I can't even be in the same room with them. We're a social disaster.' The doorbell rang again. More girls, with a bottle of gin this time, nicked from their parents. Poppy poured herself a large, fortifying glass.

At nine o'clock we were up to fifteen girls, and a rather more impressive array of drink, most of it stolen. Someone had sensibly brought crisps and Twiglets. Poppy was on her second large gin. Trish had produced a packet of cigarettes and was chain-smoking. But we all knew this was a disastrous party. The first boy had arrived, with his sister, but he didn't count because he had glasses and spots and sat on the sofa reading a

Howard the Duck comic.

Then everything changed. One minute the party was fifteen girls dancing round their bags to Hot Chocolate. The next, David Bowie was blasting out of Poppy's father's quad speakers at double volume, and the kitchen was full of boys pouring beer and rolling joints.

Poppy — third gin — was looking shell-shocked, but bearing up bravely and handing round Twiglets. Trish was up and dancing with a tall guy who said he was at Bristol University, but I was sure I had seen him by the bus stop outside the technical college. He flailed his arms like a bad swimmer, and a sad-faced porcelain clown spun off the wall unit and shattered.

I was on the sofa, squashed up at the opposite end as far away as possible from Howard the Duck, and wondering miserably if Gary was ever going to come.

Trish flopped down next to me. 'Bad breath,' she said, meaning the boy she had been dancing with.

'Where did all these people come from?' I asked.

Trish shrugged. 'Search me.'

'Didn't you invite them?'

'You know how it is — word gets round.'

'But there are so many of them.'

'Good, isn't it?' She bounced back to her feet. 'So many boys, so little time. See ya.'

Howard the Duck leaned across the sofa towards me. 'I like your friend's T-shirt,' he said. 'Fancy a snog?'

★ ★ ★

It was after ten o'clock. Gary would have come by now, if he was coming. For a desperate moment I even considered taking up Howard the Duck's offer, in the way that a fast train approaching a station platform always makes you think of jumping. Instead I went out to the terrace. Groups of boys and girls sat cross-legged, cigarettes glowing in the dark, talking and drinking, flicking their fag ends and beer cans into the still empty pool. On the lower terrace, where Mrs McClaren had sunbathed, someone had rigged up an extension speaker from the hi-fi, and people were dancing. There was still a little light in the sky; the umbrella pines loomed over the house like watchful gods.

I had never felt more alone.

I walked round the side of the house, past a row of dustbins that leaked a foul smell into the hot night. Through the lighted kitchen window, I could see Poppy talking animatedly with a group of boys. Her white dress had a pale brown stain across the front, and one shoulder strap had slipped down. Her face was quite pink.

I didn't like the looks on the faces of the boys. They laughed when she laughed, which was often, but they watched her like cats watching an insect, trying to work out whether or not it will be good to play with and maybe eat. At some point, a curious paw will reach out to pat the creature. I felt so detached from the party I could have stayed there in the shadows by the smelly bins all night, but I didn't want to see what would happen to Poppy. As I sidled past the window, I saw her hold out a glass — one of her mother's best crystal — to be filled.

There was a patch of lawn to the side of the house, overhung by trees, and Poppy's parents had put a wooden bench in their shadow. My platform heels wobbled on the uneven ground; I stopped and slipped them off. They hurt like hell anyway. I sat on the bench and wished I had one of Trish's cigarettes to smoke. Or that I was drunk, like Poppy. Trish had poured me a glass of cider at the beginning of the evening, but it had tasted metallic and I hadn't finished it. I watched the moon rising through the branches of the pines and felt sorry for myself until I heard a high-pitched laugh cut through the muffled beat of the music indoors. A couple were coming round the side of the house. I slipped off the bench and pushed through the rhododendrons to avoid them.

At the front the outside lights were blazing, illuminating the wide driveway curving down from the road. Someone was hunched over, vomiting into a terracotta urn holding a bay tree while a girl crouched beside him, patting his back.

Dear God, what had we done? How would we ever clear up tomorrow morning?

A car stopped at the top of the driveway. It reversed slowly: someone looking to see if they had the right address, perhaps. My heart was beating hard in my throat. Then the car drove past again. But I heard it stop, further up the road. There were voices, footsteps.

I ran back round the side of the house and in through the patio doors. The darkened living room was a chaos of leaping bodies, music thudding from the stereo so loud you could feel it pulsing in the flow of your blood. Pale arms and legs tangled on the pale sofa. There was a thunderous smell of beer and sweat. I paused to slip into my platform heels again, then walked as coolly as I could into the hallway.

No one in the living room could possibly have heard the doorbell, but it was chiming, although the front door was open. Gary stood on the step with his finger pressed politely on the button, three or four others behind him. I pulled the door wide open. I wanted to hug Gary, but stood there instead with a stupid grin on my face.

He looked surprised to see me, as if he had forgotten who had invited him. Then he stepped over the threshold. I felt his arm go round my waist, and he pulled me against his chest. He smelled of soap and tobacco. Then he let go.

'Come through to the kitchen,' I said. My voice sounded squeaky in my ears, almost drowned by the music from the living room. I couldn't meet his gaze, and I looked down, then hurriedly raised my eyes again in case he thought I was staring at his crotch. 'There's lots to drink.'

One of the boys at the back raised an arm and I saw they had brought drink too, cans of lager. I recognized a couple of the boys who had been playing football; there was one with frizzy hair, and another with an upper lip so downy it was wishful thinking rather than a moustache. Gary was carrying a bottle of wine. He was wearing jeans and a black T-shirt with 'Led Zeppelin' in Gothic lettering across the front. 'Lead on,' he said. My back tingled as I walked across the hallway. I hoped the trousers Mrs Klein had bought me looked as good from the back as they did from the front.

The kitchen was packed solid with bodies jostling to get at the drink. I stopped at the door, but Gary plunged in, grabbing my hand, and fought a way through.

'Corkscrew?' he said. 'Want some wine?'

I knew I would be able to live for weeks on those words, replaying them over and over. Great bubbles of feeling were swelling in my chest. Even if nothing else happened, he had held my hand, however briefly. I rinsed a glass under the tap and held it out. He filled it, and took a beer for himself, holding the can up in a toast.

I felt someone grab my arm.

'Katie!' hissed Trish, in my ear. 'For God's sake. You'd better come. It's Poppy . . . '

I could have killed her. 'Sorry,' I said to Gary. 'Got to go. But I'll come back.' Trish was tugging at my arm.

Poppy was in the swimming-pool, at the deep end where there was still a low reservoir of stagnant water. That part of the pool was in deep shadow, but the glimmering white dress, soaked now, gave her away. She was sitting in the water, apparently without the will or physical ability to move.

'She jumped in, I think,' said Trish. 'Or maybe she slipped. I don't know. I don't think she's hurt herself.'

'We're going to have to get in to get her out,' I said. 'For God's sake, what happened to all those boys she was with? Can't they help?'

The boys had vanished. There were some people peering over the balcony above and laughing, but the terrace itself had emptied.

I took off my shoes and rolled up my trousers above my knees, then climbed down the pool ladder at the deep end where Poppy sat in about six inches of water. It was blissfully cool on my hot, sore feet but it was better not to look down to see what was floating on top. I was half-way towards Poppy when I discovered Trish wasn't following.

'Hey,' I called to her, 'give me a hand, will you? I can't manage her on my own.' Poppy had seen me coming, and started to giggle. She was swaying like a cartoon drunk; I was terrified that at any second she would pitch forward on her face into the water and drown.

'We need someone stronger,' said Trish from above. 'We'll never get her out otherwise.' She sounded scared too.

'Well, get somebody, then.' I shouted up to the people on the terrace. 'Stop gawking and get down here. We need help.'

The faces above melted into the night. I hoped that meant they were on their way. One trouser leg had come unrolled. I could feel it dragging in the water.

Poppy started patting the water with the flat of her hand, sending sheets of spray my way.

'K-k-kk-Katie,' she slurred. 'Come on in, the water's . . . sslovely.'

'Stop that,' I said to her. 'Can you stand up?'

I could just see her face in the glow from the lights

round the pool. There were panda circles of mascara under her eyes, and the ends of her hair were wet.

'Can't stand up,' she said. 'Legs melted.' She started giggling again.

I got my arms under hers and tugged. She was a dead weight. 'How did you get here?' I said.

'Ssssllppped.' She must have fallen with the boneless good luck of the drunk. 'But, hey, what a night for a swim.'

I heard splashing behind me. Someone had come down the ladder and was wading across the pool towards us.

'She's had a bit, hasn't she?' said Gary. 'Here, let me.'

He picked her up effortlessly. Poppy hung over his back but somehow managed to get her head up and wink at me.

''Sssllovely,' she said. Gary waded away towards the shallow end, where wide, gentle steps rose to the terrace. I followed.

'What shall I do with her?' he said.

'I don't know. Do you think she's OK?'

'I think she's just very drunk. Maybe we'd better lie her down somewhere.'

'It's her house,' I said. 'We can take her up to her bedroom.'

We dripped water through the patio doors and the press of bodies in the living room, then up the polished stairs. Trish was nowhere to be seen. I turned on the light in Poppy's room.

A couple were on the bed, snogging amid a pile of coats.

'Out,' said Gary. 'The lady of the house wants her bed back.'

Howard the Duck and one of the girls in sequined dungarees scuttled out. Gary lowered Poppy on to her bed while the Barbies watched. Under the light, her white dress had become transparent. Her nipples stood

358

out as pink circles, and you could see her knickers had little blue roses on them.

'I decorated this room,' said Gary. 'I remember having to move all those bloody Barbies.' He was looking around proudly. 'I didn't do a bad job, did I?'

'Do you think we should put her on her side?' I said. 'Just in case.'

Poppy had gone from cheerfully drunk to comatose. We rolled her over, and I pulled her hair back off her face. She couldn't have been completely out of it because her arm crept up and she put her thumb into her mouth.

'It's very hot in here,' I said. The sliding-glass doors to the roof terrace were already a little open, but Gary pushed them wider. He stepped out and I followed him. Over the tops of the shadowy pines, stars had pricked holes in the sky. Music was blasting from the room below. People had crept back to sit round the swimming-pool, now the embarrassing drunk girl had been removed. Cigarettes glowed in the darkness.

'Lovely night,' said Gary, leaning on the rail at the edge of the roof.

'Lovely night,' I agreed. God, was he never going to kiss me?

'What's your name?' he said, turning round. Suddenly he was very close. I smelt soap and tobacco again, and I could feel the warmth radiating from his skin. 'I don't even know your name.'

There was a terrible crash, and the tinkle of glass hitting the floor.

'Fucksake,' said Gary. 'You certainly know how to hold a party, Whatever'syourname. What's happened now?'

A girl screamed. We peered over the edge. A boy was on his knees by the pool, clutching his arm. There was a dark streak across his white T-shirt.

'Oh, my God,' I said. 'He's bleeding to death.' I ran

back into Poppy's room and downstairs.

Trish was in the hallway.

'Should we phone for an ambulance?' I said.

'Don't be stupid,' she said. 'We do that, we'll be in real trouble.'

'What if he dies?'

'Of course he won't die. He just nicked himself. Someone closed one of the patio doors and he walked straight through it, that's all.'

But she sounded panicky. I pushed past her and went through the living room on to the pool terrace. There was a crowd round the kneeling boy. A girl had taken off her T-shirt, I noticed with shock, and she stood in her bra dabbing at the boy's arm. Someone else had used a handkerchief as a makeshift tourniquet.

'It's not stopping,' the girl was saying. 'Jesus, it won't stop.' Drips of blood spattered the flagstones around them.

'Oh, fuck,' said Trish, beside me. 'How the hell are we ever going to get that cleaned up before Poppy's parents come home? What do you use to get blood out of stone?' She started giggling hysterically. 'Blood out of stone. Did you hear what I said? Blood out of stone . . .'

'Shut up,' I said. 'Trish, we've got to call someone.'

'No,' she said fiercely. 'They can take him themselves. Someone must have a car. Take him to Casualty. It'll be quicker.'

'Gary and his friends came in a car,' I said. 'It's parked up the road.' I turned round, expecting to see Gary, but he wasn't there. He'd followed me down the stairs, hadn't he? But I hadn't looked back. Maybe he was still upstairs.

'I'll go and find him,' said Trish. 'Do you know what his friends look like?'

'I think so,' I said. 'They were the ones he played football with, remember?'

Trish looked blank, and shook her head.

'OK, OK,' I said. 'You find Gary, I'll go and get them. It wouldn't be Gary's car anyway. He doesn't drive.'

I went into the house. The music still thudded out; people were still dancing in the living room, oblivious to what was happening by the pool. I'd last seen Gary's friends in the kitchen; maybe they were still there. Leaving Trish to look for Gary, I pushed my way into the crowded kitchen.

I could see Gary's friend with the frizzy hair by the window. I waved to make him notice me, but his attention was on getting his roll-up to light. I had to elbow my way through.

''Scuse me,' I said. 'Was the car you came in yours?'

He looked at me, puzzled. 'No, it belongs to Carl. Why?'

'Which one's Carl? There's someone bleeding to death, and we have to get him to hospital.'

'Fucking hell,' he said. 'I think he's over there by the door.'

I followed him, thankful he seemed prepared to help. Carl was the one with the wispy moustache. I couldn't hear what they were saying, but I could see Carl shaking his head, and my heart sank. But he dug in his pocket, pulled out some car keys, and handed them to Frizzy Hair.

'He said he's had too much to drink,' explained my saviour as we elbowed our way out to the pool, 'but I was going to drive back anyway. Oh, Jesus, what a mess.' The boy who'd gone through the glass door was still kneeling at the poolside, and there seemed to be a lot more blood over the flagstones. One of the girls in sequined dungarees was trying to sweep up the broken glass with a dustpan and brush.

'We've got it under control,' said one of the others. He was bare-chested, and had torn his shirt into strips to bandage the boy's arm. 'But he's got to go to

361

Casualty. It needs stitching.'

'If you can get him out to the front, I'll bring the car down the drive,' said Frizzy Hair, and disappeared through the house at a run.

Two of the boys persuaded the injured lad on to his feet. I'd assumed the girl who'd taken off her T-shirt was his girlfriend, but it turned out she was his sister. She was shivering violently.

'You can't go to hospital like that,' I said, as we waited at the front of the house for the car. Frizzy Hair seemed to be having a problem starting it.

She looked at me blankly. I think she had forgotten she was wearing nothing but a bra.

'I've got a spare T-shirt upstairs,' I said. 'Hang on, I'll get it.' The car engine on the road above caught, and I saw the headlights flick on.

I had left my spare clothes in my overnight bag in Poppy's room. I pounded up the stairs. My bag was on the stool by the dressing-table. Poppy was still curled on the bed, her thumb in her mouth. The sliding doors on to the roof terrace were still open and the voile curtains stirred in the breeze. I bent to unzip the bag and heard a laugh from the terrace.

I pulled the orange T-shirt out of the bag. I was half-way to the door when I heard the laugh again, and a male voice saying something I couldn't catch.

I knew that laugh.

Downstairs Steve Harley and Cockney Rebel were singing 'Come Up And See Me, Make Me Smile.' There was a boy bleeding, and his sister shivering in her bra.

I parted the voile curtains and stepped on to the roof terrace.

They were by the rail, overlooking the pool, under the sharp white stars. He had his arms round her and she had jammed her crotch against his. He was kissing her throat. He had his back to me, but there was no mistaking who it was. She saw me over his shoulder, and although there was no way I could properly have seen her eyes I knew they were sparking with triumph, like those hard white stars.

I felt ripped in half. My throat closed up, and I wanted to spit, 'Bitch', but no sound would come. The blood swirled into my head and for a moment I was blind and deaf. Then the world punched me in the gut, and I was gasping for breath.

Blue eyes, blue eyes. It's just a test, a game for us to play.

Ooh lala. Come up and see me, make me smile.

He moved his hand to her breast.

I pushed my way back through the curtains, my eyes hot with tears. I would not let them spill out. I would not. Poppy stirred on the bed, and farted.

I looked at the orange T-shirt in my hand. What the hell was I holding that for?

Ooh, lala. Blue eyes, blue eyes.

Bitch.

I scrubbed furiously at my eyes. No, I would not give her the satisfaction. But I couldn't stop the big gulping sobs. She had stolen him from me. Bitch.

'Sorry,' said a voice behind me. 'Only we've got to go now.'

I wheeled round. The girl in the bra stood in the doorway.

I looked at the T-shirt in my hand. There were mascara smears all over it.

'I've got another,' I said.

'That one's all right.'

'No, I've messed it up.' I pulled the bag off the stool, and its contents spilled over the floor. I seized the long-sleeved green T-shirt I had planned to wear tomorrow, and thrust it into her hand.

'Thanks,' she said. 'Got to go. By the way, the police have arrived.' She went out, pulling the T-shirt over her head.

Slowly, I went over to the dressing-table and peered at myself in the mirror. Panda eyes, as bad as Poppy's. Nose glowing like an electric cherry. Below, the music cut off abruptly. There was some cleanser and a jar of cotton-wool balls. I cleaned my face as best I could, and went downstairs. My ears were ringing with the sudden silence.

In the hallway, all the lights were on. A uniformed policeman was talking to one of the boys from the kitchen, the ones who had been crowding round Poppy. The boy pointed at me, and the policeman turned.

'Do you know whose party this is?' he asked.

'It's mine,' I said.

'And who might you be?'

'My name's Trish Klein,' I said.

★   ★   ★

It was nearly two in the morning. I sat in the devastated living room waiting for Mrs Klein to arrive. One policeman was out in the garden, trying to track down the last partygoers. The other had gone to phone Mrs Klein — I'd given him the number. He popped his head round the door. 'You're in big trouble and no mistake,' he said. 'If you were my daughter, I'd tan the hide off you. Not even your house, eh? They could sue you, you realize that?'

I turned my head away and looked through the shattered patio window to the pool terrace. He snorted and went out to join his colleague.

There was blood all over the flagstones. There were beer cans at the bottom of the swimming-pool, and probably vomit too. The cream-leather sofa had brown pockmarks where cigarettes had been stubbed out, and sticky splashes of red wine and beer. Twiglets and fag ends had been trodden into the ivory carpet.

All I could think about was Trish and Gary. Where were they?

He was having sex with her. They were on Poppy's bed — they had pushed her on to the floor, she was completely oblivious — and he was on top of Trish, pushing into her, and she was laughing, and panting, and gasping, and lifting her long legs into the air . . .

My guts twisted.

The house was silent, apart from the odd distant shout as the policemen chased partygoers through the rhododendrons.

They'd done it. Her eyes were closed, and she was smiling. He was lazily tracing one finger over her belly. 'You've got wonderful breasts, Trish,' he was saying to her.

No, no, no.

I heard car wheels on the gravel outside. Hard, sharp footsteps on the parquet.

Mrs Klein stood in the doorway. Her hair was uncombed and her dress crumpled.

'Jesus fucking Christ, Katie,' she said. 'I didn't expect to find you here. Where the hell is my daughter?'

'I don't know,' I said. I was beyond tears by now.

'Did you have anything to do with this?' she asked. 'Does your father know you're here?'

'Yes,' I said. 'No. I mean, it was my party. They said it was for me. And my dad doesn't know. He thinks . . . '

'I can guess what he thinks,' said Mrs Klein. 'Same as I did. He'd bloody well better not find out.' She pulled a packet of cigarettes out of her bag and lit one. 'I would ask where the ashtray is, but I see it's the entire room. Anyway, you're coming home with me. We'll sort this mess out in the morning. God knows what Di and Philip will say when they get back. Where's Poppy?'

'Upstairs,' I said. 'She passed out.'

'Christ!'

365

'She's all right,' I added hastily. 'We put her on her side.'

'I'd better go up and check on her. Have you any idea where Trish might be? This was her idea, wasn't it?'

For a moment the habit of loyalty persisted and I was about to deny it. But then I remembered the flash of triumph in Trish's eyes. I nodded.

'Doesn't surprise me one bit,' said Mrs Klein. 'And tell me, is she with someone, do you think? A boy, by any chance?'

I nodded again.

'Yes, well, I know my daughter,' said Mrs Klein, grimly. 'Upstairs?'

I nodded a third time.

'Follow me,' she said. 'I need you there in case I decide to murder her.' We went upstairs. The door to Poppy's bedroom was closed. I hung back, but Mrs Klein marched straight in. Poppy lay asleep on the bed, just as I had last seen her, thumb still in mouth. Mrs Klein bent to listen to her breathing, then pulled the sheet over her, her mouth set in a hard, straight line. 'You stupid girls.'

She crossed the room and yanked back the voile curtain.

They were doing it against the wall. Trish had hooked both legs round his waist and was shouting oh oh oh as he bounced her against the brick-work.

But although the sliding windows were still open, the roof terrace was empty and silent.

We searched the other bedrooms on the first floor. No sign of them.

'What's his name?' Mrs Klein asked me. 'Has she been seeing him before?'

I shook my head miserably. 'I don't know.'

'Just a moment, Katie,' said Mrs Klein. She stopped half-way down the stairs and turned, her face on a level with mine. 'Let's get one thing clear. You have no

366

obligation to protect either my tramp of a daughter or your miserable excuse for a father. Why on earth you should feel any loyalty to either of them, God only knows.'

'Really,' I said. 'I don't know where Trish is. Last time I saw her she was upstairs.'

Mrs Klein clicked her tongue but said no more.

Poppy's parents had a bedroom and bathroom in a separate annexe downstairs. Although the bed was rumpled, and Mrs Klein picked up something off the floor, holding it at arm's length before wrapping it in a tissue and throwing it down the toilet, there was no sign of Trish and Gary there either.

'Right,' she said. 'That leaves the garden. I'm going out to introduce myself to the police and find out if they've seen hide or hair of that little madam. You stay here. We'll all be going home to Midcombe, then we'll come back here first thing in the morning to clean this house from top to bottom.' She swept out towards the pool, her wedge-heeled sandals crunching on broken glass.

I needed air, then remembered I wasn't wearing shoes. I couldn't think where I had left them. Behind me on the white carpet I saw a smear of blood: my own. I must have cut my feet on the broken glass without noticing. Immediately, it began to hurt a lot. I limped upstairs to find my school shoes, then went into the bathroom to clean my feet and find some sticking plaster. I sat on the toilet seat to inspect the damage.

'You should put antiseptic on that.'

A dark shape flickered behind the frosted glass of the shower cubicle, and I looked up to see an eye peering through the gap between the sliding doors. Trish pushed them wide and came out. I registered that the SEX T-shirt was on back to front before I bent my head to study my foot again.

'Is there glass still in there? Want me to take a look for you?'

'No.'

'What's the matter?'

'I think you know.'

'No, I don't.'

'Where's Gary?'

'Ah. So that's it. He's gone home.'

'Left you to face your mother, then. Very brave.' I stood up and hopped on one foot to the medicine cabinet to look for TCP.

'I did ask him to take me with him,' said Trish, in a lost little voice. 'He said his mother wouldn't like it.'

I turned round. She was sitting on the edge of the bath, huddled up like a bird on a frozen branch.

'Don't ask me to feel sorry for you,' I said. 'We're all in trouble.'

'Who called the police?'

'No idea. The neighbours? It was pretty loud.' I found the TCP and a roll of cotton wool, then sat on the toilet seat to apply it.

'We'd have been all right if they hadn't.'

'All right?' I said. 'All fucking right? Get real. How did you think we were ever going to clear this up so Poppy's parents didn't know there'd been a party? Not to mention someone nearly bleeding to death. *Ouch.*' The TCP stung.

'You need tweezers,' said Trish. She got up and rummaged in the cabinet. 'Here. Give me your foot.' She knelt in front of me. 'See? There's a bloody great splinter of something in there. Now, I can do this, or you can get my mother to.'

'You do it,' I said. As she probed my foot with the tweezers, my tears dropped on to her bent head and lay twinkling in her dark hair.

★ ★ ★

368

When Mrs Klein came back from talking to the police, she was not pleased to find Trish had been hiding in the house all along. She clearly suspected us of collaboration, and assumed that I must eventually have persuaded Trish to give herself up.

Poppy had been roused just enough to shamble downstairs and fold herself up again on the back seat of the car, with her thumb in her mouth. Trish was in the front and I sat next to Poppy, her feet in my lap.

'If she's sick you can all three clean the car tomorrow morning as well,' said Mrs Klein. 'Now, as for you . . . ' She turned her head to reverse the car on the McClarens' gravel. 'I can't believe a daughter of mine would be so stupid. After all I've told you. Have you no concept of what it would do to your life if you got pregnant at your age?'

'No,' said Trish.

'You're fourteen, Trish. Just fourteen. What did you let him do to you?'

'Nothing.'

'Come *on*.' Mrs Klein let out the clutch and the car shot up the drive in a spray of gravel.

'He kissed me. That's all.' I had a clear view of Trish's profile as we passed under the streetlamp at the end of the McClarens' drive. Unseen by Mrs Klein, she closed her right eye in a wink.

Bitch.

* * *

I couldn't sleep at the Kleins' house. Mrs Klein put Poppy and me together in a spare room with twin beds. The night breeze came up the valley and through the open window; I was by turns too hot and too cold. Poppy lay in the bed next to me, snoring. I may have dozed, but I saw the curtains flush yellow as the sun rose. I was flooded with wretchedness because it was a new day and I had to face the fact that I hadn't dreamed the party, or Gary and Trish.

My mouth was dry and I wanted to pee. I got out of bed and plodded across the corridor to the bathroom. Suddenly I was desperate not to be there, but to go home and wake up in my own bed, as if that might wipe out all the miseries of the night before. Please let me start again, I thought. Please.

I rubbed my hot, sore feet on the cool porcelain pedestal of the toilet, and imagined breakfast in the Kleins' big kitchen, sitting at the pine table as Mrs Klein poured me strong coffee and tried to persuade me to go looking for my mum again.

No.

Breakfast would mean watching Trish's smug, kissed face, as she ate her cereal, stretching her neck so I could see her love bites. Had they done it? Until last night, I wouldn't have believed Trish would dare, but now I wasn't sure.

I had to go home.

I slipped back into the bedroom and dressed in the jeans I had packed to wear today. My black T-shirt smelled of smoke, but the orange one was unwearable since I had used it as a handkerchief. I left my bag on the bed, and wrote a note telling Mrs Klein I would come back later in the day to help clear up.

Outside it was fresh, with a pale blue sky and a sun that promised to be hot when it rose higher. The last of the roses still nodded in the garden, and a blackbird sang. I carefully closed the Kleins' front door behind me and let myself out into the lane. Already my spirits were lifting, although my head was muzzy from too little sleep. There was no one about. It was not yet six.

I thought the blackbird stayed with me, moving from tree to tree as I walked up the hill from Midcombe. It was probably several birds, singing their boundaries. The breeze kept me cool as I climbed towards Green

Down. Things didn't seem so bad in sunlight. I would get home, and although life could never be quite the way it had been before the party, I would get by. I would see Gary leave his house in the mornings for his new job at the quarry and I would smile at him and wave like friends do. Seeing him would be enough. Tears pricked behind my eyes, and I ground my teeth to stop myself crying until my cheeks ached.

Perhaps he wouldn't go out with Trish for long. I didn't mind if he never went out with me, so long as he didn't go out with Trish.

Yes, just seeing him from a distance would make me happy. I'd been happy when that was all it was. I couldn't hope for more.

I reached the top of the hill and turned to look down at Midcombe and the grey-green slate roof of the Kleins' house. I would go back, of course I would, to help them clean up. But I needed to be in my own bed.

What would I tell my father? Nothing of what had really happened, of course. I would creep in quietly and when I got up I would tell him I hadn't been able to sleep at Poppy's, I had missed him. I crossed the main road and began to go down the hill on the other side, with all of Bath laid out below, golden in the early light.

The walk had cleared my head and woken me up. I was not sure I'd be able to sleep when I got home. Something about this lovely morning filled me with optimism. Last night had been a temporary setback, that was all. I felt a deep-down conviction that, in spite of everything, I would end up with Gary.

Our road was full of long shadows. It was too early even for George the milkman. Gary's curtains were drawn tight. I remembered how it had felt when he had put his arm round me at the party: that was what I wanted to hold on to, not the sight of him with Trish. If I went and sat on the window-seat in my mother's old

371

room, I could gaze across the road and imagine how he would look asleep.

I let myself into the house, and began to climb the stairs. I was so preoccupied with thinking of Gary that the sounds didn't register until I had already opened the door of my mother's room.

I knew what they were doing, of course. It just didn't look like my idea of how it was supposed to be. My father was like a blind animal, pushing at her, trying to burrow into her, grunting, his back shiny with sweat. Her eyes were turned to the ceiling, and she was panting, jolted back into the pillows as he scrabbled away. Her hands were on his shoulders — why didn't she push him off? The sheet was tangled round his legs and he kicked it awkwardly away, and there was no mistaking now what was happening.

In my mother's bed. How could they?

I closed the door quietly and went back down the stairs to let myself out into the sunlight, my face running with tears.

25

Tuesday is Brendan's birthday. He's decided to celebrate in style, in the pub: not our usual pub but an inn just off the A36, not far from where he lives in Bathampton. Disco, karaoke, generous float behind the bar, licence extension until two in the morning. I've never been keen on parties, but there are some occasions it would be impolitic to miss, especially since this is also doubling as the works' Christmas do. Martin has decided to tag along.

'Time I had a man-to-man chat with this Gary of yours,' he says, getting out of the Audi in the pub car park.

'He's not mine.'

'More's the pity. Look, I'm not asking you to marry the bloke. Just do us all a favour and shag him.'

There are coloured lights strung in the trees around the vast car park, and an illuminated reindeer on the lawn. Martin's dressed up in his best Calvin Kleins and a red bow-tie. Perhaps it's some kind of signal to other gay men who understand these sartorial messages. Something along the lines of I-am-available-but-bunking-up-in-someone-else's-house-therefore-can-we-do-it-in-the-car-park?

He'd better not embarrass me tonight.

'I don't want to sound rude, but when are you leaving?' I ask him, slamming the driver's door.

He shrugs and looks a bit sheepish. 'I thought you might want some company over Christmas.'

'Christmas? That's ages away.'

'Er, no, Kit. It's the end of next week. Don't you want me to stay?'

This is tricky. Of course I want Martin to stay. Best

373

best friend, et cetera. But . . . 'Of course you can stay.'

'Goody. I know you don't do Christmas. I'll plan our Mithraic feast instead.'

'What Mithraic feast?'

'December the twenty-fifth. Big day on the cult calendar. Mithras's birthday. Born from the living rock, remember?'

'You're kidding.'

'Want to take a guess how many websites I found protesting Mithraism and Christianity were not linked in any way?'

'Too many.'

We start across acres of floodlit Tarmac. We've arrived fashionably late, so the only space left was at the far end of the car park. It's a long hike, and my spike-heeled sandals are killing me already.

The pub doors open, emitting a cloud of steam and a tall, bulky figure, already unzipping his flies. He relieves himself into the shrubbery. In the winking light of Santa's reindeer, I recognize Ted. 'Jesus. See what I'm working with?'

'It's a man thing, Kit. Very important ritual. Drinking to mighty excess, then watering the ground. We all do it.'

'Not *quite* so publicly.'

'I do hope you'll introduce me to the gentleman in question.'

Ted lurches back through the pub doors, ignoring us. We follow him in.

The main bar is packed, the noise deafening. There's an over-whelming smell of beer, aftershave and not-quite-clean socks. Some wives and girlfriends are here — there's Rosie over by the bar with Huw — but most of the team are only living in the area temporarily, their womenfolk left at home in Wales, Cleveland or the Forest of Dean.

'Want a drink?' I yell over the hubbub.

Martin looks at the heaving crowd by the long mahogany bar. 'I'll get them.'

'White wine, please,' I tell him.

'What happened to our agreement? It'll be vinegar, anyway.'

'OK then. Bitter lemon. Double.'

The agreement was that I would drive. Normally I'd trust myself in a car after a couple of glasses of wine, but I'd promised Martin I wouldn't drink anything alcoholic; he's such a nervous passenger. After years of driving Nick it's not a problem. I loathe parties so much that even booze doesn't make them bearable.

While Martin's pushing his way to the bar, elbows raised like a swimmer breasting through surf, I look for someone to talk to. Rosie's too far away; no sign of Gary; Brendan's moustache is visible over by the jukebox but he's surrounded by Ted's crew.

'Hello,' says a voice, rather too close to my ear.

'Hello, Dickon.'

I've never seen Dickon dressed up before. He's all in black — ill-fitting shirt buttoned to the neck, tailored trousers — and with his stooping shoulders it turns him into a seedy vicar.

'You're looking very nice, Kit. I like that jumper. Is that what they call a Bardot top?'

For once his gaze isn't on my breasts. It's roaming the hollows of my bare shoulders, above the red mohair. Now I wish I hadn't worn something off-the-shoulder. His eyes feel like fingers. Martin's still at the bar. I can't see anyone else who will rescue me. 'Is your wife at the party?' I ask hopefully.

'Lord, no. Too far to come from London, even if she wasn't on duty. She's a nursing sister at the Middlesex.' He takes a swallow of his beer. 'Not drinking, Kit? Can I get you something?'

'Someone's fetching me one.' Out of the corner of my

eye I see Martin, drinks aloft, wading back through the crowd.

'Oh,' says Dickon. 'Who's this, then? A mystery man?' He leans forward, and I can feel his breath on my neck. 'Don't tell me you made up with your bloke?'

'Actually, yes,' I say, as Martin arrives. 'Martin, meet Dickon. He's our archaeologist.'

'Really?' says Martin, handing me my bitter lemon. 'I admire anyone who can stick rescue archaeology. So depressing. You must always be looking at huge office blocks, thinking, I know what was under there, all gone now. We academics have it easy. Sorry, Kit's useless at introductions. Martin Ekwall, senior lecturer in archaeology at Sussex Uni.'

Dickon looks somewhat disconcerted to discover he's talking to another archaeologist. 'Well,' he says uneasily, 'I have managed to save quite a lot of sites as well.'

I've seen Gary come through the door.

He's looking round, hasn't noticed me. Now he's making his way through the crowd towards Rosie and Huw at the bar. I catch up with him just before he gets there.

'Hi.'

'Oh. Hi.'

He takes in my bare shoulders above the ruby red mohair. Doesn't say anything, just looks.

It's enough, that look. It's like the night of the party at Poppy's house; I could live for weeks on that look. I give him the look back.

We're caught in the middle of the shouting crowd. Can't hear a bloody thing. Can't see anything except him, looking at me, looking at him. Could be stuck here for ever.

He puts his hand on my elbow, the way he's done before, to steer me through a room, and shocks run up and down my arm.

We're at the bar somehow.

'Hello,' shouts Rosie. 'You look smart, Kit. I like the velvet trousers.'

'Karaoke's going to start in a mo,' says Huw. 'You up for it, Gary? How's your Noel Gallagher?'

'Not a chance,' says Gary. He hasn't taken his hand away from my arm. 'I leave that sort of thing to Brendan.'

'What about you, Kit?'

'Not likely.' Actually, I could out-sing Annie Lennox right now, with Gary's fingers pressing gently through the mohair. Never thought of the elbow as an erogenous zone before, but my whole arm is throbbing. I move a step closer to him, so that my leg is touching his.

'Drink, Gary?'

'St Clement's will do.'

'You're very good,' says Rosie. 'One wouldn't hurt, you know.'

'Not tonight. Too icy on the roads.'

Martin is pushing through the crowd towards us. As he arrives, Gary's hand slips off my arm.

★   ★   ★

In the main bar Brendan, rather red in the face, is on stage, doing a very bad Bruce Springsteen. He's taken off his shirt, and is whirling it round his head like a demented male stripper, pale belly wobbling. The rest of the room is revving imaginary motorbikes and roaring the words with him.

The pub is a rabbit warren of side bars and nooks, so we've managed to escape the worst of the noise, though not the occasional glimpse of Brendan's doughy, sweating flesh, alternately flashing pink then yellow under the spotlights. Gary seems politely absorbed in Rupert's account of how the female Greater Horseshoe bat suckles her young.

I lost sight of Martin altogether until I spotted him in

the next bar along. He is deep in conversation with an old chap, whose beaky purple-veined nose juts into view every so often.

Martin catches me looking and beckons me through. The sound of the karaoke falls away as I round the corner, blessed relief; I bet this is the snug the pub regulars retreat to on party nights, poor blighters. There's a log fire and three or four tables, only one occupied. Martin and the old bloke are perched by the bar.

'Kit, this is Roger Morrissey. He used to live in Green Down.'

He smiles at me, extending a hand politely. He's not actually that old, maybe late fifties or at most sixty, with thinning white hair and the leathery face of someone who's spent a lot of time outdoors. A muscle keeps jumping under one eye, a sort of tic. 'Haven't we met before? Your face looks familiar.'

'No,' I say, parking myself on a bar stool, relishing the relative quiet. 'I've only been in the area a couple of weeks.'

'You came down to be with Martin? That's nice.'

'No, it's Kit who works on the stabilization,' says Martin, patiently.

Roger nods, clearly imagining I have a secretarial job.

'Roger used to work for the water board,' Martin continues. 'But get this — he knows the stone mines.'

For a moment I *don't* get it. We're in a pub full of people who know the mines, who go into them every day.

Then the penny drops. This guy would have been still at school when the mine entrances were bricked up in the early sixties.

'You're one of the lost boys,' I say, before I can stop myself.

★   ★   ★

378

In 1963, when he was fifteen, Roger Morrissey went into the stone mines one October afternoon with three other boys. The story wasn't quite the way Mrs Owen and other people had told it later. The boys did get lost, but they came out alive. One had a broken leg, but otherwise they were unharmed. Afterwards, all the known entrances to the underground workings were closed and sealed.

Most of the underground quarrying in Green Down had ended midway through the nineteenth century, and by the start of the Second World War there were only a few surface quarries left cutting stone from the open hillside, Crow Stone among them. As for the disused tunnels underground, there were gates, padlocks and bars on the entrances, but that had never deterred local boys from trying to find a way in. Roger and one of the others, his best friend Paul, had been into the mines many times before. They must have explored all those passages and voids where we have now driven the walkways. Their preferred route was to slip into the system via the adit to Stonefield Mine, where Rupert's bats roost.

'We thought of those tunnels as our den, when we were young,' says Roger. 'You know what boys are like. We kept our secret stuff there, cigarette cards, lucky cricket balls, that sort of thing.'

'Did you leave the troll?'

'The troll?'

'The doll, with long hair. And the bird's skull.'

Roger shakes his head. 'I don't remember that. But lots of other kids used the tunnels. Mostly the same way we did, through Stonefield. I'm sure we weren't the only ones to leave stuff.'

On the October afternoon that Roger and Paul went in for the last time, they hadn't been underground for a while. They were fifteen, no longer as interested in dens and gangs and the kind of games they had once played

379

there. Perhaps they might have found other uses for the tunnels when they were older, somewhere to take girls to scare them before slipping off their knickers, or to smoke dope. The only reason they went there that particular Saturday afternoon was that Paul's cousin Trev and his friend Johnny had come over from Bristol, and they badgered Paul and Roger to take them underground.

But when they got to the Stonefield entrance, it wasn't fenced, as usual, with wood palings and wire that could be easily lifted out of the way. It had been bricked up completely apart from a gap at the top big enough for the bats: far too small for fifteen-year-old boys.

If they had given up and gone straight home to play Paul's Beatles records instead, everything would have been different. *Everything*. Paul would never have broken his leg, the mines would not have been sealed that year, and my own life would have taken a different course. But instead of going home they walked down the hill, along the old drovers' lane that Martin and I had taken on Sunday.

'Have a crisp,' says Martin, pushing the bag towards Roger. 'So you'd already seen the raven symbol in the mines, when you were young?'

'There'll be at least a half a dozen in there that Paul and I scratched into the walls,' says Roger. 'We saw one carving of a bird like that on a pillar, with the whaddyacallit, the staff thing you drew for me just now . . .'

'Caduceus,' says Martin.

'Whatever. We thought it was a quarryman's symbol. And we made it the secret sign for our gang. But we'd grown out of all that, and that afternoon we were just going to take Johnny and Trev in a little way. Since we couldn't get in through Stonefield, we thought we'd go and show them the old abandoned open quarries in the wood up by Vinegar Farm.'

'Where we were walking on Sunday, Kit,' says Martin, not realizing I already know that area like the back of my hand.

'There was another entrance up there,' says Roger, 'an old adit at the back of an abandoned quarry face, covered with creepers in the summer. We didn't even know it was there — never been in that way. There's dozens like that, and it just depends on you coming across them by accident, which was what we did that afternoon. October, it'd all died back, see? And we were messing about in the woods, where we shouldn't have been, as usual, and Paul came across it and guessed what it was and gave a big shout to the rest of us, so we all piled up there.'

They beat down the nettles in front of the adit with sticks, and tore back what was left of the creepers to expose the low stone arch. They had torches, three between the four of them, and one of those had a dodgy bulb. It was already late afternoon; the sun was dropping fast down the sky. None of them had ever been that way into the mines before.

But someone else had.

'You know what it's like in there,' says Roger. The muscle under his eye is jumping faster. I feel a pressure on my elbow. Gary has joined us; he's listening as intently as Martin and I. I lean back, returning the pressure with my shoulder. He feels warm and solid. 'You come round a corner, and suddenly you're in a damn great cavern, all sorts of passages off, walls here, ledges there . . . Trouble is, we'd not been that way before, see? We come into this big void, floor all flattened out and levelled off with what they call gobs, the discard stones, and the first thing we see is this altar.'

Martin leans forward.

'Altar?'

'Well, pretend altar, like. It looked like an altar, with a

381

cloth on it, and a couple of candles, and all these
. . . like *offerings*.'

Martin's looking puzzled. This isn't his idea of a
Mithraic temple. But I know exactly what Roger's
talking about.

'And you'll never guess what these offerings were.'

Martin narrows his eyes, thinking he can smell
wind-up a mile off.

'Cameras. Bloody cameras. Dozens of them. Leicas
and Nikons and old Box Brownies. Every make you can
think of, lined up looking at us like so many eyes.'

Gary's squeezing my arm now. He can't know how
comforting it feels.

'There's this feller called the Camera Man, see? He
was an old tramp who used to shelter in the mines in
winter, and he had a thing about cameras. Used to
break into the photographic shops in town and nick
'em. Steal from people's houses too, sometimes. We'd
all heard about him, it was a local story. But we hadn't
come across one of his stashes before because we'd
never been into those southern tunnels.'

He looks around, knowing he's got us all hooked on
the story.

'It was where the Camera Man used to hang out.
He must have heard us coming and hidden, but
when we found his stash it must have upset him
because next thing we knew there's this thing rushing
at us, wrapped in dirty old rags like something out of
a horror film. It's only the Camera Man running
down the void towards us, not the Curse of the
Pharaohs, but we were terrified. We legged it. In
several different directions. Johnny, Trev's friend from
Bristol, is the only one who makes it out of the adit
and into the wood. He's too scared to go back in,
blunders about a bit in the trees, eventually comes
across a telephone box in the lane and dials 999. Of
course they don't believe him at first. They think it's

a kid winding them up, talking about ghosts in underground tunnels.'

'But what were the rest of you doing?' asks Martin. 'Who had the torches?' He must be remembering how it felt when the lights went out on us in the mine.

'I had one,' says Roger. 'Trev was with me, and we thought we were going in the same direction as Paul, but we weren't sure. We didn't have a clue where we were, or which way was out, and although I'd now worked out that what we'd seen was no ghost, only the Camera Man, I wasn't going to go back and ask him. There were other stories about him, about the reason he'd lost his job and gone off his trolley in the first place, and why he liked cameras, and I didn't want to risk finding out that they were true.'

'I thought he was supposed to have suffered a broken heart?' I say. 'Some woman rejected him.'

Roger laughs. 'How did you hear about him?'

'Talk in the village,' I say — which is true, after all.

'So what happened?' says Martin, impatiently. 'How did you get out?'

'Well, next thing we hear moaning. Trev's all for going in the opposite direction, but I thought it could be Paul, hurt hisself. We don't want to call out to him in case the Camera Man comes after us, but we try to work out where it's coming from and follow the sound. Turns out to be from behind a big pile of loose rock, which scares me rigid — for a moment I thought the roof had come down on him. Then I realized this is old rubble, a collapse that happened a while ago. Took us a while to figure out how to get round it — bloody miracle Paul managed it at a run, must've been sheer chance he didn't break a leg this side. But on the other side there's an archway, and a couple of steps down, and that's where Paul was. Must've come barrelling through there in the dark, lost his footing on the steps because he wasn't expecting them, crashed down in some blessed pit on the other side and snapped his leg like a dry stick.'

'This pit,' says Martin. 'How deep?'

'Not very,' says Roger. 'There was two in there, one either side, just past the doorway.'

'Anything else?'

'Couldn't see much. By that time our torch was a bit weak, and Paul's was broke. But there was stone benches, like, either side. Painted walls. Another roof collapse in one corner.'

'What was painted on the walls?'

'To be honest,' says Roger. 'I can't remember.'

'You *can't remember?*' Martin is scandalized. He's found a man who may or may not have stumbled into an undiscovered Mithraeum, and he didn't take notes of what was on the walls.

'I was paying more attention to my mate,' says Roger, with some dignity. 'He was in a lot of pain. The bone was right through the skin, there was blood and stuff. I thought we had the Camera Man after us, and I wanted to get the fuck out.'

'More than one chamber?' asks Martin, almost pleading.

'Maybe. It was too dark to see what happened at the far end.'

'Anything else you can remember about it?'

'Not a sausage. Trev and I somehow got Paul upright and on to one leg, arm round each of us, and we half carried, half dragged him out of there as best we could. I had some notion this was another of the Camera Man's places — didn't occur to me it was anything else.'

'But you must have told people about it when you got out? Why didn't they go in there and look for it?'

Roger shakes his head. 'I told you, didn't think then it was anything out of the ordinary. There was all sorts of odd corners in those mines, the quarrymen's breakfast

384

holes, the places they stashed their tools, loads of old stuff left after the quarrying stopped. I wanted to get Paul out of there because I didn't want us trapped in a dead end if the Camera Man came. We got him back round the other side of the roof fall and were in a big void. Couldn't tell how far it went. The roof had come down in several places.'

'Unstable area,' says Gary. 'Once one pillar goes, domino effect.'

'Maybe,' says Roger. 'Anyway, I thought our best bet was to keep moving, and hope we came to somewhere we recognized.'

'What do you reckon?' says Martin, to Gary and me. 'An area that's unstable? A void with a lot of roof falls? Surely you ought to be able to identify that.'

But Gary's shaking his head. 'Doesn't match up with anything we've found,' he says. 'Either Roger's remembering more roof falls than there were, or it could be some area we haven't come across because the whole lot's collapsed in on itself since. This must all have happened more than thirty years before we started digging bore holes and surveying.'

'This is in the southern sector — you're sure?' I say. 'How far north had you gone?'

'Not a great distance, by that point,' says Roger. 'Hard to be sure, mind — it's a long time ago and I wasn't exactly paying attention to where we'd run to. That was how come we got lost.'

'How did you eventually get out, Roger?' asks Martin.

'We kept going till the torch battery failed,' says Roger. 'Still nothing we recognized. Then we sat down and waited to be rescued.'

'You must have been shit scared,' says Martin.

'Funnily enough, not really. I didn't doubt for a moment we'd be found. We'd been in there on our own so many times, see, it was more an adventure. I was sure someone would find us. I just hoped it wasn't the

Camera Man. Anyways, Johnny succeeded in convincing someone it wasn't a wind-up, and the police came out, still a bit worried they was being made fools of, mind, because Johnny didn't even know Paul's or my surname or our addresses — he'd come along with Trev on the bus from Bristol and didn't have a clue where any of us lived.' He rubs the side of his eye, where the tic is still jumping. 'No, it's now I get scared . . . I still sometimes wake in the night, thinking what could have happened.'

He rests his hand again on the bar, and it's shaking. I think of covering it with my own, because I know how he feels, but I don't want to embarrass him.

'It was only when my mum got worried after I didn't show up for tea and rang Paul's mum, and they both rang the police station, that there was confirmation of Johnny's story.' He gets out a handkerchief and wipes the corner of his eye. 'But they didn't know where he'd gone into the mine, and neither did he, he was that disoriented. All he could tell the police was that it was in a wood, so they went up to Paradise Woods, the north-eastern side of the workings, miles away from where we'd gone in, and they went in through the adit there, even though it was padlocked and clear that couldn't have been the place. Then they got lost themselves. They had to regroup and wait for one of the old quarrymen who remembered a bit about the tunnels. But even he didn't know the whole system, just the sector where he used to work. Eventually, though, they must have found a way through — all them tunnels join up somehow, and we'd staggered a long way ourselves. Turned out we'd got quite close to the Stonefield entrance in the end, way over to the west, and hadn't known it in the dark. It was three o'clock in the morning before we heard them shouting a way off, and we started shouting back, and they eventually found us and got us out.'

'And after that they sealed the tunnels,' I say.

'Yep,' he says. 'Sealed 'em for good, all the entrances they could find. Except . . . '

That tight feeling in my chest. The log fire is pouring out heat. The room's suddenly airless. I've got to get away before he goes on.

'I'm going to get some cigarettes,' I say loudly, before he can finish his sentence. Martin glares at me. 'Run out. Sorry. You carry on without me. Is there a machine here?'

'Round the other end of the main bar,' says Roger. 'Where the sign is for the toilets. Out in the passage there. You know, it's funny, love, I'm sure I *have* seen you before. Or — have you got a daughter?'

'I stayed at the hotel by the weir when I first arrived,' I say. 'The one just down the road from here. Maybe you saw me then.'

Ted is giving his all on Tina Turner's 'What's Love Got To Do With It?' as I pass the karaoke stage. Something looks weird. My God. He's wearing a dress, sequined, low-cut, knee-high and far too tight. That's *scary*.

The cigarette machine's half-way down the corridor between the ladies' and the gents' at the far end. I have a nearly full packet in my bag, but I feed coins in anyway and pull the lever for a packet of Marlboro. As it falls into the tray I lean forward and rest my head on the front of the machine.

The door out to the bar swings open behind me, bringing another blast of Ted/Tina, hitting what I would have thought was an impossibly high note for a man of his size.

Gary pulls me away from the cigarette machine, and turns me round to face him. My hand curls up in his like an animal playing dead. He keeps his eyes on my face, and slowly uncurls my fingers from my palm, one by one. Then he lifts my hand to his mouth and sucks my middle finger.

A bolt of electricity zaps right down through my body, hot, cold, white, red, hard, liquid, all at once. I can't take my eyes off him. His tongue slips round my finger, licking it from tip to root, tracing little wet circles on it, his lips opening and closing softly round it, sliding it over his teeth, backwards and forwards. I can't tell who's moving the finger — him or me. Everything that happens to the finger goes right through me.

The door to the gents' opens. Dickon comes out, his fringe wet as if he's just splashed his face with water, droplets clinging to the front of his vicar's shirt. His eyes widen as he takes in what's happening.

Gary sees my eyes flick away but he doesn't take his gaze off me. He removes my finger from his mouth, and smiles at me.

We're blocking the corridor. Dickon tries to shuffle awkwardly behind Gary.

'Sorry, Dick,' says Gary. 'I'm in your way.' He steps forward and his body presses lightly against mine. It's all I can do to stop myself grabbing him and pulling him hard against me, Dickon or no Dickon.

Over Gary's shoulder Dickon gives me a hard, contemptuous stare. As he reaches the door to the bar, it opens again.

'Thank Christ,' says Brendan. 'Gary. I've been looking all over for you. You been drinking?'

It's clear Brendan has. He's red-faced, red-eyed, damp-moustached, and there's lipstick on the collar of his shirt.

'No,' says Gary. He's stopped smiling. A question like that means only one thing.

'The alarms are going off at the mine,' says Brendan. 'Somebody's got to get down there.'

★   ★   ★

I get my working gear out of the boot of the car and we go in Gary's 4×4, all three of us, leaving Martin at the pub with my car keys in case it takes all night to sort out whatever's happened. Brendan insists on coming although he can't go underground, the state he's in.

Bathampton to Green Down, at least fifteen minutes in normal circumstances. Gary does it in five. It helps that it's after midnight, hardly any traffic on the road. I'm doubled over in the front seat trying to get my boots laced without strangling myself on the seatbelt, agonizingly conscious of Gary next to me, making the engine scream as he takes the hill in third. When I think about it I can still feel his tongue slipping round my finger. Brendan's moaning in the back that he shouldn't have been so stupid as to invite everyone to his birthday party, he should have had the sense to know that if something went wrong it would happen when anyone qualified to do anything about it was rolling drunk and therefore not only incapable but legally barred from going underground.

'Shut up, Brendan,' says Gary. 'We don't know what's happened yet. That system's always generating false positives. Or it could be an electrical fault. And neither Kit nor I have had anything to drink so we can get down there and sort it out between us.'

'What if there's an inquiry?' says Brendan. 'Jesus, they'll hang me from the nearest pithead.'

'There won't be an inquiry,' I say. All I can think about is Gary's body pressing against mine as Dickon shuffled past, and it makes me almost sick with excitement. But for Christ's sake, Brendan's right, this could be an emergency. 'If there'd been a big collapse, we'd have had the police on to us. The only person we've heard from is the security guard.'

It doesn't have to be a collapse. All sorts of things could have set the alarms off. An intruder. At a pinch, one of Rupert's bloody bats, waking up early. Or somebody doing a tap dance in their kitchen above. Microseismic analysis is fine in deep mines under the Australian outback, where the heaviest thing up top is a bouncing kangaroo, but I've always thought it's dodgy in an urban setting.

'Can't Dave tell where it is?' asks Gary.

'He says the whole system's gone berserk.'

'Bound to be a fault, Brendan.'

Nonetheless, we have to go and check.

We draw to a halt outside the green fence. Dave comes belting out of the security hut and lifts the barrier. The 4×4 bounces over the ruts on to the site.

There's a soft but insistent whoop-whoop-whoop coming from the security hut. All the lights on site are blazing. Mist hangs under the big floodlights, and darkness as usual seems to gather over the top of the shaft.

Gary disappears into the hut with Dave. Brendan paces up and down. I lean on the sill of the 4×4 and tighten the laces on my boots.

The whoop-whoop stops.

'I'm sure it's electrical,' says Gary, coming out of the hut again. 'Brendan, you get in there and ring the police just in case. They've probably had complaints already about the lights. Kit and I will go down and see what's what. We'll check the whole system through, in case, so we'll be a while.'

'It could be an intruder.'

'I doubt it. The shaft's still padlocked.'

'Maybe you shouldn't take Kit down, though.'

I give Brendan a look that ought to sober him up on the spot.

'Sorry,' he says. 'Old habits. I'll get some coffee on for when you get back.'

'We'll be a while,' says Gary again.

★ ★ ★

390

Night makes the shaft far more sinister than it is by day. Or is it Roger's story that has put us on edge? Gary feels it too, I can tell. He goes down first. He double-checks the lighting board at the base of the shaft. Three times he looks at me to make sure I've got my self-rescuer attached to my belt, and checks his own.

We set out down the walkway, swinging torches like searchlights to check for any sign of a collapse.

Nothing, nothing, nothing. The mines are utterly silent, now the alarms have been turned off. There's just the occasional drip of water. My head buzzes with the silence, the whoop-whoop of the klaxon still reverberating in my head.

'It'll be quicker if we split up,' I say. 'You do Mare's Hill and Paradise Woods, I'll go south-west to Stonefield, and then the primary school.'

'No,' says Gary. 'We'll stick together.'

We don't talk much after that. There can't be anyone here, but it feels as if someone's listening.

We head first for the northern quarter, for the void under the Ministry of Defence where I found the raven mark on the pillar. The welding gear lies at the end of the unfinished walkway, exactly where I remember seeing it when work was abandoned here after Schofield's intervention at the meeting. Nothing has disturbed the piles of metal and timber struts. Gary turns over a bucket and finds a plastic sandwich container, but the date stamp is last week. It's one of ours.

As we start walking back, he flicks his torch along each pillar, looking for the one with the raven carving.

'I was right,' I say. 'There is something here.'

'I know. I had a word with Dickon about it last week.'

'You talked to Dickon?'

'He still refuses to see any significance in the carving. Says you shouldn't question his professional judgement. But I think you and Martin are right.'

He stops, holding the torchbeam on the side of a pillar. 'There.' In the yellow light I can make out the crudely carved bird, the circle and horns of Mercury's magic staff. It has never struck me before that it looks like the male and female symbols fused. 'And if there's more than one of these carvings . . . But, hey, what do I know about it? I leave that stuff to clever blokes like Martin.'

He's very still, the torchbeam utterly steady.

'Martin doesn't know so much,' I say. 'Archaeology's all guesswork.' I start walking again, conscious of Gary's eyes on me, the sound of my boots loud in the silence. 'Come on, there's still the southern part of the mines to check. And if *Roger* is right, we haven't built the walkways yet into the part of the workings where the lost boys were chased by the Camera Man.'

'How did you know?' says Gary.

'Know what?'

'About the Camera Man. You already knew about him, before Roger explained.'

'Martin has a friend who is curator at the Roman Baths. He told me when he heard I worked at Green Down.' Not a very good fib, but the best I can do at short notice. 'He seems to be a local legend.'

'One of many.' Gary's eyes are unreadable under the brim of his hard-hat. He points the torchbeam at the ceiling and strides on ahead. *Shit*. I've just remembered I told Roger, in Gary's hearing, that I'd heard about the Camera Man in the village.

The empty mouth of another walkway looms to the left. We take the loop to Stonefield. On the ceiling of the big void, Rupert's bats hang sleeping in dense black clusters, their claws hooked into cracks in the rock. Nothing has disturbed them.

The noise of our footfalls bounces back at us from the rock. It sounds as if other feet are coming up the branch walkways towards us. We go down each tunnel

392

to meet them: nothing. Finally we cut south, towards the primary school.

Gary sweeps his torch round another void, across another dry-stone wall. 'This all looks fine.'

'Would the sensors pick up a collapse further in, where we haven't reached yet?'

'Maybe. But my money's on an electrical fault. We'll have to get someone to check the cabling and fix it as soon as possible. Brendan will go spare if his precious system's down over the Christmas holiday.'

We've reached the end of the last section of southern walkway, the area where Ted and his crew found the witch doll. The dead-end tunnel looms to our right, dark and ominous. The miners didn't bother cabling it for light.

Gary points his torch down there. Empty. I can see the ledge where the witch doll sat.

Gary takes my hand, and leads me into the tunnel. He stops just by the ledge. He pushes me back towards it, very gently, quizzically.

I let myself be pushed. I feel his mouth on mine. It's a while since I tasted another person's saliva. His is mint and tobacco and orange.

He sets the torch down, where it illuminates us both. The hats come off. He takes off his jacket and folds it, laying it carefully on the ledge. He kisses my throat. 'Oh, Kit,' he says. 'Oh, Kit.'

His hands on my arse, lifting me on to the ledge. Then his finger strokes the crotch of my velvet trousers.

'The best sex feels like this,' he whispers in my ear. My jacket snags on the rock wall behind. 'Something you really shouldn't be doing, right here, right now.' He's opening my jacket, pushing his hands under my mohair jumper.

My hands are lifting his sweater. Undoing the button at the top of his trousers. 'You did switch off the microseismic sensors?'

'No,' he says, all innocence, and pushes hard against my hand.

★ ★ ★

'You reek of sex,' says Martin, in the car on the way back from the pub.

He sounds grumpy.

'I gather *you* didn't score, then?'

'And get kicked to death the minute I raised so much as an eyebrow? It was look, don't touch, in there tonight. In spite of the man in a dress.'

'Well, don't take it out on me. You wanted to go to the party.'

'I didn't expect to be left there on my own, with no one to talk to by the end but that plonker Dickon.'

The car takes the corner at the top of the hill into Turleigh, and I wince. Rock ledges are hard on the bum. A little bit of Gary trickles out of me as I shift on the car seat.

'Serves you right if you can't walk tomorrow,' says Martin. 'And you've wrecked those velvet trousers. What did you do? Roll them up in the mud and jump on them? There's a bootprint on the arse. They were Joseph, too, I saw the carrier-bag in the bin.'

'So buy me another pair for Christmas.' It comes out sharper than I meant it to.

Martin touches my arm. 'Look, I know I said I wanted you to shag him, but what I meant was, I want you to be *happy*. You ought to be ecstatic. What went wrong?'

I change into third as we come down the hill. Nothing went wrong in the mines. I would be happy, if it wasn't for what Martin had said to me in the car park, as Gary's tail-lights disappeared down the road.

'I found a text message on my mobile, Kit,' he said. 'I thought we'd sorted this out last year. I know you and your sister don't speak, but for Christ's sake, at least give her your number so it isn't always me she has to call.'

My not-sister. Bloody Trish. It's like she *knows*.

26

My head was still full of the sight of them. Little lights sparked behind my eyes as I ran along the road, like the drops of sweat that glistened on my father's back as he grunted and burrowed into Janey.

Mrs Owen's was too close to home. I didn't have any refuge, that morning after the party, except the white house at Midcombe. When I came down the hill into the village, there in the garden was Trish's mother, sitting on her wrought-iron bench under the roses with a cup of coffee and a cigarette. She might have been waiting for me; she didn't seem surprised when I came through the garden gate. Perhaps she had already looked in to check on Poppy and me.

'Another insomniac. You could be my daughter, Katie Carter.' She patted the bench beside her. 'But you're not, more's the pity. I'm not exactly overjoyed to be Trish's mother this morning.' She blew a cloud of smoke into the bright air. 'Have you been home? Are you all right?'

I nodded.

'Nobody awake?'

It was easier to nod again. We sat there in sunshine and silence, until the kitchen door crashed open and Trish demanded bacon and eggs.

★　★　★

Poppy threw up breakfast immediately after she'd eaten it, so we left her pale and shivering on the bed with a hot-water bottle. Mrs Klein telephoned my father to say I was spending the day with Trish.

'I'm not going to tell him what you're really doing,'

she said to me. 'It might be better if we kept what happened last night between us, don't you think?'

She piled buckets, mops and a carpet-cleaner into the back of her station-wagon, and loaded Trish and me on to the bench seat.

I didn't want to sit that close to Trish and edged up against the door.

'If you're going to try to fall out, please put your seat-belt on, Katie,' said Mrs Klein.

'Not like that,' said Trish scornfully. She reached over and pulled the belt across my chest, snapping the buckle into its slot. I'd never worn one before; my dad's van didn't have any. 'You're such a divvie sometimes.'

That's all you think I am, I thought. Stupid. Stupid enough to let you snatch Gary from under my nose. I'll show you.

We swept and scrubbed Poppy's house, hard at it all morning, but the house still looked like a disaster area, with burn marks in the white carpets. At lunchtime, Trish's father turned up with sandwiches and Poppy, who was still shivering. He tacked plywood over the shattered patio window. Trish helped him, passing him the nails. Poppy went to be sick upstairs. Mrs Klein and I left them to it and sat on the bench on the lower terrace to eat our lunch.

'Katie,' said Mrs Klein, staring at the pine trees instead of looking at me. 'I owe you an apology. I forget sometimes how young you are. I shouldn't have put so much pressure on you to look for your mother.'

'I know why you did,' I said. I could hear Trish's father bashing the plywood into place. He was an architect, but he didn't know how to use a hammer. He didn't have my father's precision. Bang, bang, bang, like gunshots. 'You had a baby. Before you got married. You had it adopted. That was why you ran away from home and went to London.'

Mrs Klein swung round to face me, panic in her eyes.

'You haven't told Trish, have you?' she whispered. 'They don't know.'

Bang, bang, bang.

'That's why you wanted me to find my mother,' I said, making my voice deliberately loud. For once I felt powerful. I wanted to hurt Trish, but instead I could hurt her mother. 'Because you couldn't find your own daughter.' I knew I was right by the pain in her eyes. I ignored a twist of guilt, and pressed on. 'Or maybe you did find her and she didn't want anything to do with you. Well, I don't want to find *my* mother. She left me behind, like you gave your baby away . . . '

Mrs Klein's face was rigid with grief, but she reached out a hand and lightly touched mine. 'Katie, I'm so sorry. Of course you must loathe me.'

Bang, bang, bang from the upper terrace, where Trish and her father were working together. I got up, and walked to the edge of the lawn. Through the pine trees I glimpsed the green humps of distant hills. I wanted to be there, anywhere but here. In this garden last night I had waited for Gary, hoping he'd come, then losing hope, then finding it again, then having Trish snatch it from me. Could you ever trust hope? Was it better not to hope for anything at all?

And my mother — was she ever going to come back to look for me, like Mrs Klein had looked for her lost daughter?

Mrs Klein came and stood next to me. She put her arm round me and gave me a hard, fierce hug. 'You're a little soldier, Katie,' she said.

★   ★   ★

We were still cleaning when Poppy's parents turned up at half past four. Mrs Klein had called them that morning and told them everything was under control, but they had still got straight into the car, furious at having to miss the wedding in Scotland.

I knew from the look Poppy's mother gave me whom *she* blamed for the party.

'Listen, Di, I understand it was all Trish's idea,' said Mrs Klein to her, 'so don't be too hard on Poppy, will you? We'll pay for the window, by the way.'

'The sofa's ruined,' said Mrs McClaren. 'And the carpet . . .'

Mrs Klein's lips went thin. 'We've got most of the marks out. Come on, girls, let's get out of the McClarens' way.' She ushered Trish and me into the car.

'Miserable cow,' she said, as she let out the clutch and accelerated up the drive with a screech of rubber. 'She ought to take at least half the blame for having had the bad taste to buy a cream leather sofa.'

We drove back through Green Down village. I remembered walking this exact route the day the swimming-pool had emptied. The car passed the entrance to the alley that led down to Stonefield, where the bats flew in and out of the mines. If we had found a way to hold the party there, would things have turned out differently? Would I have got off with Gary, or would Trish still have managed to steal him from me?

She would not do that again. I had made up my mind. Gary was *mine*, even if he didn't know it yet.

★　★　★

Trish was craning her neck to look for Gary's window as we approached my house. I was glad there was no music blasting from his house; I wouldn't have put it past her to leap out of the car and hammer on his door while Mrs Klein was dropping me off.

The car drew to a halt, and Mrs Klein got out to retrieve my overnight bag from the back of the station-wagon. I saw our front door open. My father

399

stood there. A smell of cooking filtered out into the late-afternoon air: roast meat and vegetables. To my relief there was no sign of Janey Legge, and my father came slowly down the path alone.

He was whistling.

'Hello,' called Mrs Klein. 'One daughter, delivered safe and sound.'

'So, you got lots of revision done?' my father asked. Quiet voice, dangerous voice.

'Not as much as I wanted,' I said, trying to avoid lying because I knew what was going to happen.

Mrs Klein didn't know. She had only met my father a couple of times, so how could she understand what that gentle, patient tone meant?

She handed me the overnight bag. 'There you are, Katie. We'll see you soon.'

Trish was leaning out of the car window, scowling at Gary's house. Perhaps if she had not been with us, I might have turned and run back to the car.

But perhaps I deserved this. I started to climb the steps to the front door, the cloudy lozenge of glass looking down like a one-eyed god. I heard Mrs Klein's car door slam, and the cough of the engine starting.

'Poppy's mother called,' said my father, pushing back the front door and shoving me through, 'so don't bother to lie. I know exactly what's been going on.'

The door swung shut. I was alone in the hallway with him.

'You little tramp,' he said. 'Just like your fucking mother.'

Fourth level of initiation: Leo, the Lion.

Dressed in a long scarlet cloak, the Lion has an arid and fiery nature. A fire-shovel is his symbol; and fire-shovels for carrying hot coals were

400

discovered during the excavation of the Mithraeum at Heddernheim. So we might conjecture that this level of initiation involved some sort of ordeal by fire — a baptism of fire, perhaps. Classical writers suggest that initiates were branded either on their forehead or their hand. The purifying force of fire burns away the old and transforms the Lion into a new person, a companion of Mithras who hunts at his side when he seeks the bull.

Having been through the fire, the Lion will for ever be immune from its consuming power.

Dear Gary,

I'd really like to see you again. It's hard to explain, but things aren't good at home. Don't come round. I will be at the quarry at Crow Stone on Thursday night. Seven o'clock. I can get in through the fence by the allotments. Don't reply to this note. Just nod when you see me.

Katie

27

When I ring through to my answering-machine at the Cornwall cottage, there are nine messages from Trish and two from Nick, in the vain hope he can persuade me to answer even if she can't.

I know what this is: they've run out of money.

'Are you going to call her?' asks Martin, as he shoves a cooked breakfast under my nose. 'Get that down you. Just what you need after a hard night.'

'I wasn't drinking.'

'I wasn't talking about drinking.'

'Did I really reek of sex?'

'Of course not. You just had a smug smile on your face. As did he.'

'Are we a teeny bit jealous?'

'You didn't answer my question. Are you going to phone Trish?'

I look glumly at the bacon. The thought of talking to Trish makes me lose my appetite. 'There's no point. She'll only be spinning another hard-luck tale. Nick will have some ghastly disease. The car fell into the river. Welsh Nationalists burned down the pub. God knows.'

'Maybe it's true,' says Martin. 'Nick might be ill.'

'Pull the other one. He's indestructible.'

'Every ten minutes, someone dies of an alcohol-related disease.'

'You're full of cheer this morning, aren't you? He's got a liver of steel.'

What Nick doesn't understand is that Trish won't stick around much longer if their financial situation doesn't improve. I'm almost tempted to write them a big cheque: they deserve each other. But the truth is I

402

haven't got it to spare. The bastard bled me dry.

All the same, I will call.

★ ★ ★

The site is hung-over. Cars are parked at angles. Piles of timber and metal struts are balanced skew-whiff. Office doors only shut if slammed. There are pallid faces, bloodshot eyes. Nobody stops to talk, because talking hurts too much; the miners disappear quickly underground and stay there, leaving it unusually quiet above. Rosie hasn't turned up.

Gary is leaning on the bonnet of a white van in the car park, head down over wiring plans with a man in overalls whom I presume is the electrician. As I walk past, Gary lifts his head and looks. Just looks. It goes through me like a hot knife. I'm melting round the edges. Neither of us winks, smiles, or says anything; we only gaze. The Americans used to talk about a thousand-yard stare, but there are miles of tunnels in our look.

I'm smiling to myself as I come round the corner and see Dickon, skipping down the steps from the office. 'Just the person,' he says.

Just my luck.

'There's something you ought to see,' he goes on. 'In the Mare's Hill void — one of the miners told me last night. Something they saw there right before the work got stopped by Schofield.'

'Oh, yeah?'

'Seems your funny bird symbol might be more interesting than I thought.'

'Really?'

'Really.'

I'm bounding up the steps into the office and grabbing my torch. 'You got the camera?'

'You want to go right now?' He looks a bit taken

403

aback by my eagerness.

'You bet.'

'OK, then.' He comes into the office and reaches for his waxed jacket. I check the work schedule on the computer. While the Schofield situation remains unresolved, both crews are concentrating their efforts in the south-western quarter.

'So whereabouts is this . . . what, exactly?'

'Wait and see. It's not far from the pillar with the carving.'

They must have come across the tauroctony, although God knows how. No. The wall where we found it was way off the walkway. Perhaps they found *another* fragment of it, in a different wall . . .

We leave the office, and I head back towards the car park to tell Gary we're going underground.

'Hey, hold on,' says Dickon. 'Where are you off to?'

'To tell Gary where we're going.'

'No need. I already buzzed through to Security and let them know.'

'You did?'

'Just before I saw you. Let's get down there. If it's as interesting as it sounds . . . '

'Hey, come on, Dick, what is it? Don't be a tease,' I say, over my shoulder, walking down the narrow space between two of the storage huts, our usual short-cut from the office through to the shaft entrance in the centre of the site.

'You won't be disappointed.'

There's something in his tone that makes me hesitate. I haven't thought this through. If the miners have found something, why didn't they tell Dickon until last night? I stop and turn, suddenly aware of how dark it is in this narrow cut-through. I can't see his face properly, because the low winter sun is behind him, but he's so close I can hear his liquid breathing. Too close. A sour whiff of last night's beer reaches me. I take an uncertain step backwards.

'Hold on,' I say. 'Seriously, I'm not going underground without knowing what it is you're taking me to see.'

Some way off, a compressed air line chugs and hisses, but there are no voices; everyone else must be underground or in the offices. Dickon's lips part, showing his teeth, but I still can't make out his eyes; can't decide if I should stand my ground or run for it, looking like a complete fool. What am I afraid of? It's Dickon, for God's sake, you could spread him on toast, but he's basically harmless . . .

His hand whips out and grabs my wrist, slamming my arm back and pushing me up against the side of the tool store, where the metal ridges dig viciously into my spine. I'm limp with the shock of it, caught off balance, my heel skidding on the muddy ground as I try to stay upright.

'Hold on.' It comes out as a squeak, not at all the way I want it to. I can hardly get my breath. His face is right up against mine now, so close I can see the glistening hairs in his nostrils, the thready veins at the tip of his nose. His breath is hot and moist, and I turn my head to avoid it, but it's like damp fingers on my cheek and neck.

'I saw you,' he says, in a hiss right up against my ear. 'You know I saw you. You enjoyed being watched, you whore.'

'Hey,' I say, trying to push him away with my free arm, but he's much taller than I am, and surprisingly strong. His left hand catches mine and he wrestles me back against the metal wall. Alarms are running through my blood. I'm trapped. This can't be happening. 'Let me go. Of course I wasn't enjoying — '

'You were. And how's Martin going to feel about that?'

He's forcing my arms apart and pressing himself

405

against my tits; I try to shrink away but the wall is unyielding. My breathing's getting quicker and quicker as the panic rises. 'Don't be absurd, Dickon. Let *go*.'

'Your boyfriend's in the bar, and you get off with Gary . . . ' Every word comes out in a little pant.

'You're so out of line,' I say, wriggling frantically to get free, but he seems to like that and lays the whole weight of his body against me so I'm almost suffocated by his chest.

'You enjoyed it,' he hisses again, right up against my face. 'You like people watching, don't you?'

Everything goes black round the edges. Time is slowing down. The stubble on his chin grazes my forehead. A long way in the distance, a woman on the recreation ground calls to her dog: 'Inky. Inky! Come *here*, you little bastard.' I have to fight to breathe, pushing my chest against his heavy body to create an airway. Dickon grunts with either effort or pleasure, attempting to force his hand down the back of my trousers. He's not a rapist, I say to myself, to calm my breathing. He hasn't got the guts. He's only a fumbler. I can feel his erection against my stomach: it makes me want to heave.

'I won't tell Martin what went on last night if you're nice to me.' His breath is moist and warm on my cheek again. Then he's jamming his face into mine and forcing his fat wet tongue into my mouth.

Fucksake.

'Ooof.'

Hard enough, I hope, to turn his testicles inside out and push them back up wherever they dropped from. Hard enough that my knee's vibrating, anyway. Anger blazes through me; why should I take this?

He grabs at my breast as he folds up, nails digging painfully into flesh that is already tender from what Gary and I did last night, and suddenly I'm raging so white hot I lash out a steel toe-cap, wanting to catch him in the balls again and do real damage this time . . .

Too wild. Missed by miles. Got his shin, though. Bet that fucking hurt. Shit, he's still standing, coming back at me —

'Bitch.' He drags my jacket half off my shoulder and tries to pull me close so I can't get another swinging kick in. He's wrong, though: his eyebrows meet in outraged surprise as my knee connects with the side of his thigh, and his lips part in a little rosebud.

'Aah.' He loses his balance and skids on the mud, hauling on my jacket to take me down with him.

I twist to one side to avoid falling, and the jacket comes off. Everything cascades out of my pocket, torch, handkerchief, cigs, biro, into the mud next to Dickon. But he's given up, all the fight suddenly gone. He lies there doubled up, knees to chest, with those wet cow eyes squeezed shut, waiting for the next kick.

I'd like to, but I can't. The blinding white rage is disappearing, evaporating with every ragged breath. I lean back against the wall and try to stop myself shaking. He looks so pathetic I feel bad already about having kicked him.

'You dare ever try anything like that again,' I say. 'You dare . . . ' I bend down to scoop up my jacket and the stuff that fell out of my pocket. My cigarettes are in a puddle, just behind him, and I snatch them up too, even though they'll be unsmokable now. 'Think yourself lucky.' My legs are still shaking as I walk off, but maybe he's got his eyes squeezed shut and doesn't see.

★ ★ ★

Instead of going back to the office, I head towards what passes for the ladies' on site — a single Portaloo a little away from the others for modesty's sake. Inside, its fogged mirror reveals me flushed pink, my chest heaving in great gulps of smelly chemical-toilet air. My eyes are chips of serpentine, cold, hard, glittering green.

That bastard. I breathe in the eye-watering stink and imagine myself pushing Dickon's head down the bog, or wadding handfuls of paper towels into his vile mouth to choke him. But instead of satisfaction, I feel soiled.

I shouldn't have let him see us last night by the cigarette machine. Shouldn't have given him the ammunition . . .

Sick, twisted bastard. *His* fault. Not mine. Still, I shouldn't have given him the excuse . . .

No, HIS FAULT. Get it? Not yours, Kit.

And how could I be so naïve as to think he really meant to show me something in the mine? He probably thought he *was* going to show me something. Jesus, how could he be so deluded? What did I . . . ?

Men.

Should I tell Gary?

Of course not.

★ ★ ★

I walk cautiously back through the cut-through, where there's no sign of our scuffle apart from a churned-up patch of mud, and my dark red plastic cigarette lighter half hidden under the edge of the storage container. As I'm reaching down to retrieve it, someone comes into the passageway between the containers. I straighten up quickly, slipping the lighter into my pocket, heart a jackhammer in my throat, ready to defend myself if it's Dickon again.

No, a broader silhouette. It's Brendan.

'Ah, Kit,' he says. He has the pained expression of someone trying to line up both eyes to look in the same direction. 'I was looking for you . . . You must be the only person on site without a headache, apart from Gary, of course. I just saw Dickon puking his guts up in the car park — told him to go home, poor chap.'

'It was a very good party, Brendan.'

'Aye, it was, wasn't it?' He closes his eyes. 'Too good.' Tries to open them again, but his eyelashes have become superglued. 'Until the end. I just wanted to say thanks.' The eyelids prise themselves apart at last. 'We were lucky. Could have been much more serious.'

'Is the alarm system fixed?'

He shakes his head and winces. 'If Gary and the electrician don't find the fault, we'll have to get somebody over from Australia to take a look. That'll mean it can't be sorted till after Christmas.'

'It won't make much difference,' I say. 'It doesn't really work, does it? It's not the right thing for an urban environment.'

'Well, maybe,' says Brendan, the closest he's ever come to admitting his beloved system is flawed. 'I still don't like leaving the quarries unmonitored over the holiday. Especially as Ted's team found a crack in the rock this morning.'

★　★　★

Brendan, Gary and I go down to take a look at it. In spite of their hangovers, Ted and his crew have been busy pushing forward on a new section of roadway. They found the crack in the roof at the end of it, a jagged line a couple of metres long, at its widest only a couple of centimetres.

'How long do you think it's been there?' I ask.

'Impossible to tell,' says Gary. My arm is throbbing where Dickon's fingers dug in; I want Gary to look at me and twig there's something wrong, but his eyes are fixed on the ceiling. 'The thing that worries me is that there are no signs of the old quarrymen having done anything about it. That could mean it's recent movement.'

The sensors would have been useful here, after all. We

409

could have inserted a couple to monitor whether the crack's still moving. I have to forget the nauseous sensation of Dickon pressing against me and concentrate on the job.

'Is any part of the alarm system salvageable?' asks Brendan.

'Not according to the electrician. He thinks there's too much water down here, getting into the connections. A bugger, isn't it?'

'What would the old quarrymen have done?'

Gary sighs. 'We spend a small fortune on high technology. They'd have used a couple of pieces of wood and a hammer.'

★ ★ ★

I haven't seen this done before so I hang around to watch. It's simple but effective — roof support and early-warning system all in one. The miners shape a set of timber wedges, the same width as the crack, and hammer them into the ceiling. Provided the crack doesn't open any further, they're enough to keep the roof from falling down. When the wedges drop out, it tells us the rock is on the move again.

'There,' says Ted grimly, as he bangs the last wedge into place. 'If I find this bugger on the floor tomorrow morning, we'll know we're in trouble.' He gives me the Ted glare I'm used to by now, the one that says it'll be all my fault, because I'm a woman messing where I shouldn't.

★ ★ ★

Afterwards I go back to the office. If Rosie were here, instead of hung-over, at least there'd be someone I could tell. Although I'm not sure I'll tell anyone. I feel a fool, soiled by my own stupidity as much as by Dickon's

410

dribbling lust. The member of the hideous plaster Priapus on his desk points accusingly in my direction. I'd like to smash it to smithereens, but instead I put the spare hard-hat over it and glower for a bit at the phone.

While no one else is around, I ought to be able to find the courage to ring Trish. But which telephone? If I use the mobile, she'll have my number. If I use the one in the office, she'll know where I am.

The mobile. At least that way I can pretend I'm abroad.

It's the first thing she asks me: 'Where are you?'

'Doesn't matter. What do you want?'

'How about 'How are you, Trish? How's Nick? Long time', etc?'

Fact is, I don't care. Since the day I found them in bed together, I really don't care. 'I suppose you want money.'

'It would help. If you're feeling stingy, Nick could always write the story. That kind of thing sells really well these days, and I can help him with some juicy quotes.'

She's trying it on, of course, to scare me. I still trust Nick to keep his promise: about the only honourable thing he ever did was agree he wouldn't write about me. Even in the bitterness of our divorce he kept his word, though maybe giving him half the house helped.

Trish is still blathering on about what they'd get for first British serial rights, quite the businesswoman. If anyone keeps that pub going, it's her. 'We'd split it with you, of course. Fair's fair. But that isn't why I tried to get hold of you.'

Dickon's left his computer on. The screen-saver is hypnotic, stars erupting from the centre. I've never been to the flat above the pub in Aberystwyth, but I can picture it. Trish will be on the scuffed-leather chesterfield they took from the London house, shoes kicked off and long legs tucked to one side. The sticky

411

smell of chips from the pub kitchen downstairs hangs in the curtains, and there's a bottle of wine already open on the coffee-table though it's not yet lunch-time. Nick's the one with the problem, but Trish can put it away too. Though she prefers a few lines of the white stuff.

'So why did you call?'

'Just thought I'd ask how you like the thought of being an auntie.'

'What?'

'I'm going to have a baby, Kit. Unexpected, completely bloody unplanned, to be truthful, but I've grown to like the idea.'

The phone folds up in my hand with the *zap* noise it always makes. I'm falling into the black hole where the stars are being born.

★   ★   ★

Trish big-bellied. Somehow unimaginable. She'll be wearing low-slung jeans, like a singer in a girl band, a deep V-necked top to show off her enhanced cleavage. Big hoop earrings and red streaks in her hair.

How long's she been pregnant? Not that it matters.

She texted again, immediately afterwards: 'We could do with some dosh'.

Trish with a baby. It just doesn't seem possible.

'Jealous?' asks Martin. He pours more wine into my glass, and opens the doors of the wood-burning stove to throw in another log.

'No,' I say. 'I never wanted children. Let's face it, that was half the problem between me and Nick.'

'I know I'm only a sad old queen, so what would I know, but if this isn't jealous, it's a very good imitation.'

'Yep, what would you know?'

Martin gets up and goes through to the kitchen. The oven door bangs open. Rich, buttery smells pour out. There are sounds of pouring, stirring, scraping, but he says nothing more. The silence creeps over us, and I refuse to do anything to push it away.

★ ★ ★

It's the saddest old cliché: wife always the last to know. Comes home early one day and opens the front door to find that special quality of silence in the house, the silence of two people upstairs frozen in mid-fuck, listening for a footfall on the stairs.

Nick and I had already fallen apart, really. I spent most of my time in Cornwall. I came back that weekend to pick up some winter clothes, thinking I'd timed it so he wouldn't be in the house.

He didn't know I was coming to London that afternoon, but Trish did. In my innocence, I'd called her to suggest we meet up and left a message on her answering-machine.

I went up the stairs, seeing a blouse hanging on the banisters, a shoe kicked off on the half-landing, following the trail Trish had left for me, a drag hunt tracking the smell of perfume and desire. They must have heard me coming, but they didn't get out of bed. I pushed open the bedroom door and out came a wave of that thick, sour smell, sweat and unchanged sheets and fucking.

Nick was so drunk he suggested I join them.

For a moment I saw fear in Trish's eyes, as if she only then understood the consequences of what she'd done. Then she sat up, the sheet falling away from her tits as I backed out of the door. It's a set of snapshots now; I've reduced it to that. Pictures I never bother to look at most of the time. I take them out occasionally to remind myself of what I left behind. I can't even remember what Trish said. The last close-up is of her lazy, triumphant smile, carrying in it fifteen years' worth of retribution.

LEVEL FIVE

Luna

Think of the holy cave as a soldier's camp, the night before the final battle — a camp of darkness. The only illumination is the moon: Luna, which represents the fifth level of initiation. The ancient Persians believed that honey came from the moon, and that the semen of the bull slain by Mithras was purified there before being returned to the earth to engender fruitfulness. Thus from cold white death comes new life.

From *The Mithras Enigma*,
Dr Martin Ekwall, OUP

28

Thursday it had to be, because my maths exam was on Wednesday and I wasn't going to waste all that revision. A scientist would need maths — even if she ran away with Gary on Thursday night.

Meanwhile, though, I had to be a little soldier. I sat very straight in the chair at school, not letting myself lean on the back. I wore my cardigan all week, in spite of the heat. I didn't turn up my dress over my belt. Most of the bruises were on my back, but there were enough on my arms and thighs to make someone ask questions. But I made sure no one saw them.

The person I had to avoid was Mrs Klein. She might have recognized the stiffness in my shoulders, the careful way I walked and sat down.

Trish and I were avoiding each other. Poppy was off school. She showed up for the maths exam on Wednesday and gave me a pale smile as we filed into the gymnasium. She pointed to her stomach. 'Still being sick,' she mouthed.

'No talking, girls,' said Mrs Ruthven, who was invigilating. 'Turn over your papers. You have ninety minutes, starting from now.'

Mrs Ruthven liked to patrol the rows, checking for cheats. Halfway through the exam, she stopped next to my desk. I raised my eyes from the paper. She was looking at the bandage on my left hand.

★   ★   ★

As I was leaving the gym after the exam, she stopped me. 'What have you done to your hand, Katie?'

'Nothing, Mrs Ruthven.'

'Well, it's clearly not nothing, since it's bandaged up.'
'It's a burn. I — I did it when I was ironing.'

★   ★   ★

My father was holding my hand just above the glowing hotplate on the cooker. The heat was blasting up, searing my fingers. I was wriggling, resisting as hard as I could, but he forced my hand down.

I screamed. Fire needled through my skin right to the bone. I had never felt anything so bad. For one terrible moment my hand was the only part of me that existed. It was enormous, throbbing, stretched to bursting point with pain; it was my hand that screamed, not me.

My father let go. I snatched away my hand, panting, supporting it just above the wrist because it was too huge and heavy to hold itself up.

'Oh, my God, Katie,' said my father. 'Oh, Jesus, Jesus, I'm sorry, what have I done?'

He cried, not me.

★   ★   ★

'Really, it's not so bad, Mrs Ruthven.'

'Burns can be nasty. You don't want it infected. Get some antiseptic ointment from the nurse. And you might find it's better left open to the air.'

'I'd rather keep it wrapped up.'

★   ★   ★

My father had been very careful with me since Saturday, when he'd bandaged my hand, tears running down his cheeks. I'd tried to pull away, not wanting his tears to touch me.

'You should let me run it under the tap,' he said. 'Take the heat out of it.'

418

'No,' I said. It hurt worse than anything I had ever felt, worse even than the time he'd put my shoulder out of its socket, but I wanted it to go on hurting. I hoped it would scar. I wanted it to remind me, always.

You're a little soldier, Katie.

On my own, I unwrapped it. There was a red weal across the pad of flesh where my thumb joined my palm. In the centre it was puffy and white. It hurt less now, but it hurt enough.

Why do you do it, Dad? I wondered. This is how it's been all my life. Why do you do it, when I know you love me?

He always said sorry, but he never explained.

When Mrs Klein's father hurt her enough, she ran away. I didn't really think Gary would run away with me. But I didn't know how you ran away on your own at fourteen. Talking to Gary might be a start, so long as my father didn't find out about it.

You little tramp. Just like your fucking mother.

But there was no sign of Gary all week. I looked for him on my way to school, but the shifts for his job at Crow Stone started early. After school I sat in the window-seat in my mother's old room, watching the street. Every evening it was my father I saw coming down the road first.

On Wednesday, walking home after the maths exam, I saw Gary on Green Down high street. He was coming out of the newsagent on the other side of the road, stripping the Cellophane off a packet of Embassy.

I willed him to look up and see me.

He looked up.

Yes!

For a moment I thought his eyes were going to slide over me. Perhaps he didn't recognize me in my school uniform. There were a lot of other girls walking along the road. I waved.

He looked puzzled for a moment, but then he

recognized me and gave a quick embarrassed nod.

Yes!

Tomorrow night I would meet him at the quarry.

★ ★ ★

On Thursday evening, my father had told me, he and Janey were going to the social club in Odd Down where she lived. They were going to play poker with some friends of hers.

'You will be all right?' he said to me. 'You're sure you don't mind being left on your own?'

'I'll be fine.'

'You know what we've decided to do for your birthday?' He was hovering awkwardly on the threshold of my room. His hair was damp and curly from the shower, and he was wearing a pink shirt I'd never seen before. 'We're going out, the three of us, somewhere really posh. Janey's going to book it. She said to keep it as a surprise, but I wanted you to know we hadn't forgotten that Sunday's the big day. She said lunch, but I said, no, dinner. Our Katie's old enough for a proper night out. We'll all wear our glad rags, and go out like a proper family.'

His eyes were anxious. He wanted me to tell him how wonderful that would be.

I wish I had, now.

★ ★ ★

If you walked past the churchyard and the school to the end of the road, then took the path beside the allotments down the hill, you came to Crow Stone the back way. It was one of only two working quarries left in Green Down. The stone was good, but not top quality. Better building stone came out of Randall's quarry on the eastern side of Green Down, but Crow Stone was always busy. During the daytime, lorries and vans crawled up the steep lane, and the air screamed with the sound of the huge saws that cut the stone into blocks. You couldn't live in Green Down and not know about the place.

I walked to the bottom of the path and out on to the lane. The verges were grey with stone dust; the trees overhanging the banks looked tired, their leaves coated like old men's tongues. In front of me were the high metal gates. 'Crow Stone. All visitors report to site office'. They were shut and padlocked. No matter.

The quarrymen started work at eight in the morning and finished at six. After that, the quarry was deserted. Building stone is cut out of the beds, not blasted, so there were no explosives and therefore no need for a security guard. At the end of the day, smaller tools were locked in the sheds, the forklifts and diggers parked neatly in the centre of the site, and the gates fastened. But you could slide through the rhododendrons that bordered the allotment path, then wriggle through a hole in the fence and climb down the side of the quarry. The owners didn't bother to repair it: it was impossible to carry out stolen gear that way. Besides, every time they replaced the fencing, kids cut through again.

Everyone knew that that was where boyfriends and girlfriends went. I had been through the broken fence just once, a year ago, by myself, because I knew the quarrymen often found ammonites in the rock. My father told me they had collections of fossils to show visitors. The way he described them made me think of specimens laid out in rows on the ground, but they must have locked up the collection with the tools because there was nothing to be seen. I rummaged in a heap of gobs, but the discarded stones showed only a few broken fossil shells. I'd found better in the fields.

It was a quarter to seven — early still. I walked back up the path and cut off into the bushes, where a trail of

421

empty beer cans and crisps packets marked the way to the place where the green mesh fence was bent back from the post. It wasn't difficult to slither through. Would Gary come that way too, or did he have a key to the gates now that he had a job there?

Crow Stone was a huge quarry. It had been worked for years, the quarrymen cutting deeper and deeper slices into the hillside. On the eastern edge, where I came through the fence, I had only to scramble a dozen feet to the quarry floor. But to the west, the oldest part of the workings, where the sun was already dipping towards the trees at the top of the cliff, the quarry face was high and sheer, stretches of it covered with creepers and ivy. No stone was taken from there. The area below was used as a stacking yard, where the newly cut blocks were stored while they dried.

I checked my watch again. Just on seven. Already the area under the high cliff was in deep shadow. He should be here any minute.

I settled down with my back against the wheel of a forklift truck in the middle of the site. The sun was still warm on my bare arms. Everything was utterly quiet. No traffic, hardly any birdsong. A plane crawled over the sky on its way to Lulsgate airport. Shadow fingered blindly across the quarry floor.

Seven fifteen. He was late.

No need to worry. He'd been late coming to the party.

I wound the bandage off my left hand. A blister had come and gone, and the burn had turned a darker, duller red. It was healing quickly, but still sore to the touch.

I pictured Gary in his room, washing at the basin. Soap bubbles popped on his chest. Droplets of water glittered in the tufts of hair under his arms.

The shadow had reached the centre of the quarry already. It was getting chilly now, out of the sun. I began to count the goose pimples on my arms. I was a long time counting, and still Gary did not come.

I saw him with Trish in the shadows on the balcony. He was kissing her throat, and I saw him put his hand on her bottom, rub it, then move on casually to her breast. I shifted uncomfortably on the hardpacked ground.

I wanted him to do that to me. Cupped in the bra I had stolen, my breasts itched, as if his fingers were only inches away.

Rooks were flapping towards the trees where the sun had hidden. They were calling to each other. Time, gentlemen, please. Time to go home. Gary. Gary Gary. Gary. I repeated the name quietly to myself until it sounded like the calling of the rooks.

It was getting late. I looked down and my fingers were trying to burrow into the earth. Dust streaked my black trousers.

Suddenly I saw myself as anyone else would have seen me. A child, really: a silly, ridiculous child, with a cardigan tied by its sleeves round her waist, scrabbling at the soil, dreaming of digging the First Englishman out of the dirt. I'd never even found a complete ammonite, only bits. And now I was kneeling in an empty quarry, imagining my hero was going to rescue me. The cliffs crowded round to get a good look at this stupid girl who thought Gary Bennett was going to come and kiss her.

For a moment the whole quarry seemed alive and stretching its wide mouth to snigger. The sleeping machines looked ready to wake up: all the things that rumbled and moaned and shrieked in the daytime, the grumbling winches, the pulleys, the singing belt, the screaming saws, the hoses like water snakes, the stone-crushers, the forklifts shaped like crouching grasshoppers.

A big white moon hoisted itself into the sky over the

lip of the lower cliff. I was cold and pulled my cardigan round my shoulders. My knees hurt, and one foot had gone to sleep. I tried to get up, but my foot felt like a sock full of sand at the end of my leg. I didn't dare put weight on it, so I sat back instead with my dead foot resting on my other thigh, and tried to rub some life back into it.

It was hard to see my watch now, but I crawled out of the moon shadow of the truck, and realized it was already half past nine.

He wasn't coming.

Thus from cold white death comes new life

I stood up.

I started pacing round the forklift trucks and the bulldozer, a yoyo on a string, walking a little away, then being pulled back. The quarry walls hung like stone curtains in dark folds and creases, but as the moon rose it frosted the western cliff with icy light. I could make out clefts and cracks and tufts of grass.

Thinking about the cliff stopped me thinking about Gary. It was like a puzzle, a lovely absorbing equation that I knew I was clever enough to solve. Every time I paced past the bulldozer's scoop, the yoyo's string stretched a little further.

My parabola took me now beyond the semi-circular stacks of drying stone, propped on blocks of waste stone so the air could circulate beneath them. I kept getting closer and closer to the old quarry face.

Towards the top of the cliff there was a patch of shadow. It was so dark it didn't look like stone. I wasn't sure what it was. A ledge?

I flicked out past the stacks towards the cliff, then back to the bulldozer and trucks.

If I could get up there, it might be somewhere to hide.

I was quite clear. I was not going home. I wanted my father and Janey to get back — I was sure they would come home together tonight: it was only a matter of time before she began to stay — and find me gone. Then they would be sorry. Then *everyone* would be sorry. The news would run through the street, and Gary would know what had happened because he had let me down.

The yoyo's string snapped. I came to rest at the foot of the cliff.

It didn't look so difficult from here. The moonlight shone full on to the rock, and what seemed smooth from further away was pitted, scored and uneven. There were fault lines, toeholds and tiny ledges where a whole foot could rest. All I had to do was stretch one hand up and begin to climb.

★   ★   ★

At first it was easy. The cliff was a chess problem that distracted me from what I was feeling. I thought carefully about every move. If I took it steadily, one step at a time, I would reach the solution. I covered twenty-five feet quite quickly. Then it got harder, because the rockface was both smoother and more vertical. I liked the challenge; I knew I could get higher. There was a fine handhold just above my head, and out to the left a little a good place for my foot, a jutting knobble of rock with a tuft of grass spilling over its sides.

I was about thirty feet above the ground now. Dreadlocks of ivy hung from the brow of the rock above. I remembered what my father had told me when he took me to the climbing wall: three points of contact. The climber's triangle. My fingers curled into a crack. My other hand gripped a nipple of rock. I winced as it pressed against the healing burn. Then my left foot had

425

to come up. It was quite a stretch to the next foothold, the knobble of grass-covered rock. I had to bend my knee up until it felt as if it was nudging my armpit.

Now my right leg was extended below at its fullest stretch. I had to pull myself upwards, at the same time transferring my weight to the left foot on the grassy knobble. Then I could bring my right leg up and find a new foothold. This was going to be the last tricky bit; then I could clamber sideways on to a diagonal fault line leading upwards, a good wide crack I would be able to shuffle along without much trouble. Think ahead. Like chess. Bishop's move. Easy.

I pushed off with my right foot, shifting the weight to my left, bearing down on the grassy tuft. Easy. Chess.

No, snakes and ladders. The tuft of grass gave way, a sharp flake of rock split from the cliff, and my left leg shot away below me. There was no foothold for the right. My breasts and belly slammed against hard stone.

I was dangling, fingertips screaming. All that stopped me tumbling to the bottom was the just-maybe-enough strength in my upper body, keeping my hands clenched on the holds above. It felt as if all my weight was on my fingernails. My arms ached and burned. My toes scrabbled for a crack in the rock.

Going to have to let go . . .

My right foot found enough purchase on the rock to take some of the weight off my screaming arms. My head cleared of panic, so that I could feel more carefully with my other foot for another toehold. There was another tiny crack. I pressed myself on to the rock, trying to sink right into it, Spiderman's clumsy little sister.

The moonlight poured down. I clamped myself to the indifferent rock. I might have been a puppy hanging ignored on to a leg.

I couldn't move. My muscles were locked. One leg was burning, where I had scraped it down the rock, flaying my trousers. My nose rested against stone, and all I could see were sandy granules of limestone, like the pores on an over-magnified face. I wondered if I could turn my head, even slightly. I didn't think I could.

There were dwarfs inside the rock, digging for gold. Thud, bang, thud: I could feel the rockface bulging in and out against my chest to the rhythm of their hammers. No, it was my heartbeat. I thought of the picture of the weeping Jesus in our living room, knocking at the door of the human heart.

Oh, Jesus Jesus Jesus, I said to myself, over and over. Please, Jesus, let me find a way back down.

But when I managed to unstick my nose from the rockface, and peer between my starfish legs, I found I couldn't go down. My knees had jammed solid, and my elbows trembled.

Jesus, I thought. Jesus, help me. Or I'm stuck here until the cold air takes all the strength out of my fingers and toes.

— Go up.
— What?
— Go up.
— I heard the first time. You mad?
— Go up. It's the only way.

It wasn't Jesus, of course. It was my mother. She was sitting at the top of the cliff. I couldn't see her in the darkness, but I knew she was there.

— Go on. One hand at a time, one foot at a time. Like your father said.
— I can't.
— You don't have to do it all at once. Just relax one fingertip. You won't fall. I promise you.

I relaxed one fingertip. She was right. I didn't fall. I could feel a toe starting to relax too, without me having to tell it. Gradually my muscles were loosening and, to my surprise, instead of weakening they grew stronger.

My mother had come down the cliff now to help me.

427

She was clinging to the rockface beside me, whispering in my ear so we didn't wake the machines below.

— Let go of the cliff with your right hand now. Just move it an inch or two to the right. See? You can do it. There's another hold. There are lots of them, all over the cliff. You don't even have to look. You can feel them. I'll help you.

My confidence was growing.

— Now let's move a foot up. Right foot. Not too far. Maybe three or four inches. To the right a bit. The crack is wider there. It's a good hold. Don't shift your other foot yet, press down with your weight, make sure. Good. Easy. It will take you. You can move your left leg now . . .

And so, slowly, gradually, we inched our way up the quarry face, two frosted spiders in the moonlight.

The patch of darker shadow I had seen from the ground was about twenty feet below the top. My groping hand reached over a lip of rock and on to a proper ledge. I automatically turned my head to tell my mother, but she had gone.

Never mind. I was sure now I'd find her again when I needed to. I grasped the rock, pushed up with my foot, and up again, a heave, another push, and I was flat on my stomach on a ledge that extended eight feet deep under an overhang of rock.

I had been right. It was a good place to rest, a fine place to hide. All I wanted now was to lie down and sleep. I crawled deeper into the shadow, propped my back against the ivy-covered rock wall, and fell backwards into the stone mine.

★   ★   ★

The adit must have been part of the earliest workings at Crow stone. On that part of the hill, the strata twisted back and forth. After the underground workings had been exhausted, in the nineteenth century, the quarry owners had discovered there were still good beds of stone beneath their feet. They cut down, carving out a vast open bowl, until the adit was suspended more than half-way up the quarry face. Vines and creepers had grown down to cover it, and it was eventually forgotten. Even after the lost boys nearly vanished in the mines in 1963, no one had thought to seal it.

I pushed myself wearily to my feet and took my first blind step into the darkness, fingers brushing the rough-hewn tunnel wall to keep me straight. I won't go far, I told myself. Just a few steps. Just far enough. Then I'll find somewhere to curl up against the wall and wait until sunlight fingers its way between the strands of ivy. I walked forward, testing each step on the uneven floor with my toes.

I turned round to look back. I couldn't see the entrance.

In my panic my fingers lost contact with the tunnel wall, and I snagged my foot on a rock. I stumbled forward, lost my balance, and ended up on hands and knees. When I managed to get to my feet again, the tunnel wall had vanished too.

I could hear my breathing in my ears, tight and harsh. The sound of it had changed, and the sound of the silence around me was different too. It seemed hollow, vast, empty. I knew I must be in some large space; perhaps a huge cavern the quarrymen had cut out of the rock.

I reached out, groping empty air. I could see nothing. The darkness was smothering. It wrapped itself more tightly round me the more I struggled. I told myself the wall of the tunnel had been only inches away when I fell. I had to go back a pace or two and I would be able to reach out and touch it. I turned, took one tentative step, terrified I would stumble again. Then I took another, my hands waving uncertainly in front of me, blind man's buff. Still nothing. And nothing. And nothing. And nothing again. Then I understood I could no longer be sure which way I was facing.

Oh, Jesus Jesus Jesus. There was nothing to tell me which way I had come or which way to go, and the darkness wound round me so tightly it was crushing the air out of my body. *Please, God, let me find a way back. A safe way.*

29

Friday morning, Gary catches me in the car park. 'Are you avoiding me?'

'No,' I say, surprised. 'Of course not. Why would you think that?' But I can't meet his eyes. The smell of Dickon's berry breath, the pressure of his erection against my belly, like a perversion of everything that had happened between Gary and me. Hissing in my ear, *You like people watching* . . . My fault. His long, pale fingers like worms reaching for me in the dark. Click, click, click. And now Trish, with her one-woman campaign to get back at me for something I'd never meant to happen. Trish and Nick. Come to bed. Come and join us . . .

He puts a hand on my arm, and because I'm not expecting it, still thinking of Trish and Nick, I flinch. 'OK,' he says. 'Sorry. I must have misunderstood.'

He walks away, his hands in his pockets, his back stiff.

* * *

You can tell the weekend's almost here. 'Land of My Fathers' comes floating up the tunnels from where Cennydd and his team are working, putting the finishing touches to the walkway Ted's crew pushed forward yesterday. With two crews on the southern stretch, the miners have made good progress. By this time next week we'll have stopped for Christmas, and they'll be back in Wales for a good long holiday. The harmonies are beautiful underground, echoing through the voids.

The singing ends abruptly. I stop dawdling and hurry round the corner. 'Problem?'

'Maybe,' says Cennydd. 'Take a look at what we found this morning.'

'The wedges?'

Above, my torchbeam scans the long dark crack in the mine ceiling. It looks just the same as yesterday, but two of the wedges are lying on the floor below.

'Reckon it must be widening quite fast,' he says. 'Ted told me he'd jammed them in good and tight.'

Brendan: *If one pillar goes, domino effect . . .*

'Must be your singing.'

He laughs, but I can tell he's as uneasy as I am.

'Seriously, Cenny, I don't like the look of this.'

'Let me show you something else.' He leads me on to where the miners are constructing the next section of roadway, parallel to a drystone buttress. 'This is what shut us up just now.'

Cennydd shines his torch up to the top of the wall. The stones in the top row have crumbled, under pressure from the rock above.

'See there?' he says flatly. 'I haven't seen stones crushed as badly as that anywhere else in the workings.'

'I want to get Brendan down to take a look at this,' I reply. And call in the hydro-geologist. Picturing Brendan's big map of the workings, my guess is that this part of the quarries cuts into the steepest part of the hillside. The whole lot couldn't be on the move, could it?

★　★　★

Steam hangs in the cold air under the walkway lights as Brendan pours coffee from his Thermos into an insulated mug. I take it gratefully; a grizzling, anxious headache has set in behind my eyes.

'I've phoned the hydro-geologist,' he says. 'He assures me the slope's perfectly stable, even in a small hurricane.'

432

'I still think he ought to come and see for himself.'

'He's coming, don't worry. He wanted to leave it till Monday, but I persuaded him my team wouldn't panic unnecessarily. He'll be here first thing tomorrow, and we'll keep a crew on stand-by over the weekend. What's your feeling?'

Mining's as much an art as a science. You can measure and calculate as much as you like, but in the end it comes down to instinct.

'I'm uneasy. Don't you think — '

'I'd really like Gary to have a look before we take any decisions,' Brendan says. 'He's worked with these rocks longer than any of us.' He swallows the last of his coffee and upends the mug. 'You seen Dickon this morning?'

My hand is shaking as I give him my cup. We start walking back towards the shaft. My head's pounding; I still feel soiled by what happened in the alleyway, but it's too late now to say anything. Not that I would to Brendan, anyway. 'No. Maybe he started the weekend early.'

'His car's in the car park. He must be around somewhere. Oh, there's good news, by the way.' He takes a victory punch at the air. 'We're back in business in the northern sector. There's a way round the Schofield problem. Lucy took further legal advice, and apparently the lawyers think the council can slap a notice on him under section eight of the Mineral Workings Act to get access for emergency work. Doesn't need the landowner's consent after all. So once that's been done — after Christmas, now — we can get moving again under Mare's Hill. Shall we go back up top and do some projections?'

It's hard to take in what he's saying because my head feels like it's been split by that long zigzag crack. We shouldn't go on working while the crack's on the move. We ought to clear the mine until the hydro-geologist gets here, alert the council, get the emergency services on stand-by for an evacuation . . . As I start climbing the ladder back to the surface, I can see that none of this is going to happen. Brendan's face below me shows vague concentration, but is otherwise relaxed.

'Brendan,' I call down, 'what triggered the Gilmerton collapse? I know a pillar could have gone any time, but did you manage to pinpoint anything above ground that started it?'

'It was difficult to be sure,' says Brendan. 'Building work, maybe — well, that was one of the official explanations. My own theory is weather, though most of the consultants wouldnae have it. They like something big and solid to blame, like a lot of heavy plant, digging foundation trenches. But quarrymen will tell you winter's a killer. There's a lot of water in this rock — a hard frost can cause cracking in the upper layers.'

The headache throbs with every step up the ladder, making it harder and harder to think straight. Wavery images swirl in my head, nothing solid I can grasp, the people at the public meeting with their tight anxious expressions, the old man and his dog, red watery eyes, dog, *he found a dead dog*, doggy paddle, something reminding me . . . I pause on the middle platform to ease the pounding and get my breath back before starting up the second ladder. 'We've had some hard frosts the last couple of weeks,' I say.

Brendan heaves himself on to the platform, puffing a little. 'True.'

'And if you follow that with heavy rain, we could get slippage because we've got quarries cut into a steep slope that's already unstable.'

'Now, don't you worry . . . ' He catches himself before he can come out with 'your pretty little head'. 'That's why we'll be leaving some of the walkways open, after we've filled, to allow groundwater runoff. You should look at the geomorphology report.'

'I have,' I say. 'Don't you think we should at least put

the emergency services on stand-by?'

His soft toffee eyes go hard. 'No need to overreact. My high-tech canaries would have alerted us if there was serious movement.'

'Maybe they did.' When I look up, the circle of sky at the top of the shaft is ominously grey. 'What if the alarm on Tuesday night wasn't entirely down to an electrical fault?' Gary and I didn't find anything when we checked the underground roads — but that's not to say there hadn't been some movement further in, in a part of the workings we haven't reached yet, which set off a reaction in the sensors. 'And it's going to rain again.'

'No,' says Brendan. 'It's too early to run off with your arse in your hand.' He winces and checks himself. 'Sorry. What I mean is, we don't know enough yet to start worrying people unnecessarily.'

'But they live right on top — '

'Wait for the hydro-geologist's report.'

I start climbing again, my head thumping. My hard-hat seems to weigh a ton, and the straps inside feel too tight, squeezing out thoughts droplet by droplet. Frost damage, water swirling through the passageways, pile drivers overhead thudding monotonously on to the weak earth . . . No, no, that can't happen. No building is allowed on the surface above the stone mines until they have been stabilized. Water running down the sides of the passages, the rock sweating like damp crumbling cheese . . . Why do I keep thinking about building work? Brendan's words have set something tapping at the back of my mind. No, I can't get hold of the notion. It's running through the cracks in my head, like the water out of Poppy's swimming-pool . . .

Roger talking about the roof fall, blocking the void where they found what might have been an underground temple. A recent collapse, he thought; the lost boys went into the workings in 1963.

I've been thinking of the Mithraeum as being in the

northern part of the workings, perhaps somewhere under the Ministry of Defence, because that was where we found the raven carving and the tauroctony. But the lost boys went into the mine from the south side, somewhere in the woods above Vinegar Lane. The big question is, how far did Roger and the other boys run through the mines to get away from the Camera Man?

Suppose the temple itself was much further south, in a part of the workings we haven't yet reached? Maybe . . .

★　★　★

. . . in a branch of the workings we don't even know is there?

The computer screen in Brendan's office shows a lot of wiggly lines and cross-hatching: the map of where we think the workings lie under Green Down. Fifteen years ago, after a gale flattened trees in Paradise Woods and exposed a couple of mine shafts, the local authority commissioned a detailed survey of the extent of the quarrying. It was carried out from above ground, using bore holes and ground-penetrating radar. The results were plotted on to this chart: our crib sheet, in the absence of better historical maps.

'Click there,' I say. 'Can you enlarge that sector for me?'

'That's the *southern* sector,' says Brendan. 'Get your bearings, Kit. We're supposed to be planning the schedule for the northern voids.'

'I'm curious about something, in the light of that roof crack.'

'I told you, wait for the hydro-geologist.' Nevertheless Brendan zooms the image.

'Down a bit,' I say. 'Sorry, I mean south.'

'Can't go down a bit,' he says. 'Nothing there. See?'

Click, click, click.

In the centre of the screen, a meandering loop of road, a scatter of squares representing houses, widely spaced, each with a generous plot of land. 'High Pines' is written across it. There is none of the heavy cross-hatching that represents underground workings.

'Was it surveyed?'

'See — there.' Brendan points to red dots on the right of the screen. 'Bore holes. They obviously found nothing.'

'But if there was a collapse underground?'

'I can't see how they'd have missed it. The bore hole would have shown loose earth and rubble.'

'But suppose they did?'

'Well, anything's possible.'

They missed it. I'm sure they missed it.

When was Poppy's house built? Those clean modern lines, the flat roofs and big windows . . .

'Do we know when that estate went up?'

Brendan brings up another chart, cross-references. 'Nineteen sixty-two.'

The year I was born. The year before the Lost Boys went into the mines. Foundation trenches. Digging. Heavy plant. The estate cut into the southern slope, with views through the pines out across the valley.

Fourteen years later, the crack in Poppy's swimming-pool. And the pool repairman had said there were mines underneath. Where else had the water gone?

★　★　★

The pine trees are even higher than I remembered. The last time I was here was the morning after the party, the day we cleared up the mess at Poppy's. In the weeks since I've been back in Green Down, I haven't come this way. But, then, I haven't been down to Trish's old house in Midcombe either.

It looks different, and for a moment I can't work out

437

why. Of course — the wall. There wasn't a wall round the estate when Poppy lived here. I can't quite see the point, since it isn't high enough to stop a determined burglar, but when I round the corner and see the gated entrance I understand it's not to deter burglars: it's to deter people like me. So much for the gentle stroll I'd planned round the estate. There is an automatic barrier, with an electronic eye to read residents' passes, and a CCTV camera on a tall pole. The people who lived here always thought themselves a cut above.

I lean on the yellow stone wall — not even decent local stone, this is reconstituted rubbish — and look down the hillside. The trees cut off the view, but far below is Vinegar Lane. From here, I can't see Poppy's house. Her parents could still be there, of course, but somehow I doubt it. I've no intention of going and introducing myself to find out.

There's no way of telling what's under here. But I wouldn't mind betting that there's a void, with several roof collapses. And not far off, maybe even quite close to the surface, a double chamber with two pits by the entrance, and a niche in the wall where fire burned and danced in the headdress of the god.

★   ★   ★

'The temple won't be in great nick,' says Martin. His voice on the phone sounds tinny and distant, but the crack in it gives him away: he's trying to sound cool but he can't suppress his excitement. 'We already know somebody had taken the tauroctony and smashed it and used it in a wall, so the chances are it's been vandalized. It was probably broken up by Christians towards the end of the Roman period — the Theodosian edict at the end of the fourth century banned pagan worship throughout the empire.' I can hear him filling the kettle. 'And plenty of quarrymen could have been in since and

438

trashed the place without knowing what they were looking at.'

'If you're not doing anything else this afternoon, can you check out whether High Pines was the only development built on Green Down in the late fifties or early sixties?' I ask. 'The planning department must have records.'

'I'm supposed to be meeting Roger in Bath for a drink, so I'll call in at the council offices beforehand.' There's a clatter of what sounds like cupboard doors at his end of the line. 'Sorry, I'm making a celebratory cuppa. Amazing, isn't it? There was John Wood going on about his lost temples to the sun and moon on Lansdown, and all the time there really is a Roman temple to the god of light, here on Green Down.'

'You don't think maybe he *knew* it was there?' I ask. 'He was a freemason. Suppose the eighteenth-century quarrymen found it, a secret space with pictures on the walls of handshakes and terrible ordeals?'

'Now, that would be interesting. Nobody's ever proved any sort of direct link between Mithraism and freemasonry, but there are certainly claims that the two are connected. D'you fancy another underground expedition this weekend?'

'No,' I say, reminding myself I have to meet up with the hydro-geologist tomorrow, and that will be quite enough excitement, especially if it rains again tonight. 'There's no need to go charging at this, Martin. If the Mithraeum's under High Pines, it's not under threat at the moment. We're nowhere near tackling that section, and I don't think anyone even realizes there's been quarrying there.'

'I've got a good feeling about this,' he says, as if he hasn't heard me. 'Southern slope, not far from Vinegar Lane and the site of the Roman villa. Where they found the inscribed coffin lid, commemorating a military establishment. Less than half a mile as the crow flies.'

439

I look at my map. They form a triangle on the hillside: Poppy's house, the Roman villa and the disused open quarry at Crow Stone. My heart clenches.

★　★　★

Darkness has fallen, a sliver of moon like a rip in the sky between the scudding clouds. Martin told me Luna was one of the higher Mithraic grades. Also known as Perses, the Persian, carrying a sickle shaped like the crescent moon, and — like the Roman mother goddess Cybele — the divine reaper gathering the harvest.

Earth goddess, sky god — as usual with Mithraism, impossible to tell exactly where male shades into female, dark into light.

As for our own little tear in the fabric of the universe, I've been underground again, as the miners packed up for the day, to recheck the crack. But it looks exactly the same as it did before.

Because Martin's gone into Bath to have a drink with Roger Morrissey, there's no reason for me to rush home. He'll make his own way back later, on the train that chugs along the valley bottom. Rosie's left early for a weekend of rock-climbing with Huw in the Brecon Beacons, and there's been no sign of Dickon all day, thank God. I'm still not sure how I shall react when I see him.

To stop myself thinking about the feel of his hands clawing at my jacket, I bring up the maps of the workings again on my computer screen. Suppose the Mithraeum is where we think it is, under High Pines . . . in an area that doesn't exist, as far as the project is concerned. How do we reach it?

There must be a way to get there from the north-eastern sector, if that was the way the boys headed after they found it.

If. So many ifs. We can't even be sure where they

440

went in. Does that entrance still exist, or was it bricked up years ago?

A faint pattering against the window; the rain has begun. Deep inside, my gut churns — I should have made Brendan talk to the council, alert the emergency services. I'm already reaching for the phone. He's gone back to his lodgings, but I could ring him . . .

And confirm everything he thinks about nervy, over-cautious women engineers?

Shit. A black wedge of the hillside slides down towards Vinegar Lane, Poppy's house disintegrating into a set of Lego bricks that go tumbling over and over . . . No, of course it's safe. Nothing's going to happen. For God's sake, this isn't the first time it's rained in the last couple of centuries.

I stare at the map in frustration. Suddenly there it is again, leaping out at me. *Crow Stone*. A cold, sick feeling in my stomach, and I can't stop the shudder. However calm I've learned to be underground, I still find it hard to let myself picture the adit half-way up the cliff at Crow Stone.

The office door opens. Who the . . . ?

I spin round to see Gary, trying to back away down the steps.

'Sorry, Kit. Thought everybody'd gone, saw a light. I'll leave you to it . . . '

'No, don't.' I can't see his eyes properly: the light makes dark hollows in his face. There's stubble round his jaw. When I move on my chair I can feel the bruising from the ledge in the mines. 'I was just finishing. Only working late because Martin's . . . ' No. That's not the right thing to say. 'You haven't got a cigarette on you, have you? I forgot to get some at lunch-time.'

He comes into the office. There's a site rule that we don't smoke indoors, but it isn't strictly observed, and there's a whole weekend for the smell to disappear before Dickon comes back to sniff disapprovingly.

Dickon, shit, what am I going to do about Dickon?

'Look,' I say, to get it out before I lose courage, 'I should have made it clear. Martin isn't my partner and never could be. He's gay.'

'Uh-huh,' says Gary, holding out the packet of cigarettes. 'So what are you trying to tell me, Kit?'

I take one, not letting my eyes meet his, and play for time by fumbling for my lighter in the pocket of my coat. Gary laughs when I proffer it to light his cigarette first. 'You won't get much of a spark off that.'

It's not a lighter, although it looks like one at a distance, same size, same dark red see-through plastic as mine. It's a flash drive for a computer, a memory stick, the sort you can hang on a key ring, with a USB connector that allows you to download a couple of hundred megabytes of files.

'Where did that come from?' As soon as the words are out of my mouth, I know. Of course, it was yesterday, the tussle in the cutthrough, coming back afterwards and seeing what I thought was my lighter lying in the shadow of the tool store . . . 'It's Dickon's,' I say. 'I picked it up by mistake.' It already feels greasy in my palm so I get up and put it on his desk.

Gary leans over and picks it up. 'Incredible,' he says, turning it in his fingers. 'You'd never have believed it possible a few years ago. The contents of your computer on something you can shove in your pocket. I ought to get one of these — they're only twenty quid or so. Memory's cheap, these days.' He holds it up to the light, as if you could see everything that's on it through the transparent red plastic. 'I wonder what old Dickon keeps on his.' Before I can move he's slotted it into the USB port on the front of my computer, leaning over my shoulder to control the mouse.

'You can't do that,' I say, panic rising though I don't know why. 'What if it's private?'

'Exactly,' says Gary.

What action do you want Windows to take with this device?

Open it using Windows Explorer.

There are only two folders on the memory drive. One is called Download 1, the other Download 2.

Gary clicks on Download 1. A set of jpg files: pictures. They appear as thumbnails, too small to make out clearly . . .

'Oh, no,' says Gary. He doesn't sound surprised. He clicks for a full-screen view on one of the thumbnails.

I've seen this picture before, curling brown round the edges as I pushed it further into the flames. I don't want to see it again. I push back my chair and get up, shoving past Gary, folding my arms, walking away into the corner of the office to turn my back to the screen, determined not to see what else is there. No, no, no. The smell of burning; the cast-iron thump of the wood-burning stove's door. I should have known. Why was I so stupid? Not Ted, after all. It feels like Dickon's fingers are tightening round my throat, his erection butting my belly again.

'Dirty boy,' says Gary, behind me. I want him to stop looking at the pictures. I can't bear the thought of it, those vile images, those chicken-flesh folds and crevices and shackles and ropes and eyes that are sometimes dull but sometimes terrified . . . Her eyes. Oh, fuck, her eyes. What was in them, looking into the camera? To shut the eyes out, I stare at the office wall, bland grey melamine pockmarked with dried up Blu Tack, an old work rota, torn at one edge, a memo from the Health and Safety Executive, 'Personnel are reminded before going underground . . . '

His hands on my shoulders. 'You've seen these before, haven't you?'

I don't want to say anything.

'Did he send them to you?'

'I didn't know it was him.'

443

'You should have told me. It's not acceptable. You know that. Have you still got them?'

'Of course not. I burned them.'

'It would have been useful if you hadn't.'

He strokes my hair, but I still can't bring myself to turn round and look at him. I'm scared of seeing desire in his face. But part of me wants him to put his arms right round me. I want him to make it all right, after everything that's happened.

'How did you know what was on there?'

'Because last time we had the computer consultant in, he asked me who'd wiped the hard drive on Dickon's computer. They look out for it these days; it's a sign someone may be downloading stuff they shouldn't.'

'And you didn't do anything?'

'We only recovered a couple of file fragments. He'd wiped it rather well. And — sorry, Kit — this sort of thing may be unpleasant, but it isn't like downloading child porn.'

'Get rid of it,' I say. 'If this stuff isn't illegal, it should be. Those women got hurt, you can tell. There was one . . .'

'It's safe,' he says, into my hair. 'They're not on the screen now. He wouldn't have known why they would upset you so much. It wasn't personal, in that sense.'

The walls are shaking. If one pillar goes . . .

'What do you mean?'

'I've known who you were from the day you arrived. *Katie*.'

When everything goes, it's a relief. One by one, the walls come crashing down in my head — domino effect — stones cracking and tumbling and bouncing over the ground in slow motion, raising puffs of dust as they crumble into nothingness. The haze settles, and it all comes clear: all the stages between *I was* and *I am* and — maybe — *we are*, and some of those stages are about

444

Martin and some are about Nick and some are about Trish, but really they are all about me not looking at what happened that summer when I was nearly fourteen, knowing but refusing to know, Crow Stone and the Camera Man and the First Englishman, lying in wait for me in the dark . . .

'Come home with me,' I say. 'Please. I don't want to be alone.'

LEVEL SIX

The Runner of the Sun

Earth goddess, sky god: think of it as the most ancient drama, the battle between darkness and light, being played out in the cave. At the bleakest, blackest hour — the ordeal of the sixth level — the initiate seeks Heliodromus, Mithras's deputy on earth, the Runner of the Sun. In his fiery chariot, with his whip, he urges on the horses that pull the sun across the sky. Where he leads, the Father went first; we have almost reached his domain.

From *The Mithras Enigma*,
Dr Martin Ekwall, OUP

30

This was darkness like nothing I had ever experienced; darkness, in fact, like *nothing*. There was not the slightest glimmer anywhere. I reached out a hand, but there was nothing to touch, except more empty, velvety air. I had crossed into another dimension. I was in the void.

In daylight, there might have been a glint of light reflected on the curve of a wall, or at least a patch of lesser darkness to tell me which way led back to the outside. But outside it was night; not the glowing orange night of the streets I was used to, but the silent darkness of the countryside, with the moon too high now to shine into the adit. The quarry was cut into the side of the hill that faced away from the city, looking across the valley towards another lightless hillside. There were no streetlamps at Crow Stone, no houses nearby, no busy main roads: nothing but a lane that dead-ended at the gates.

The only thing that convinced me I had not been spirited away into another universe was the rock floor beneath my feet, reassuringly solid, if uneven and chilly.

I had to think. *Think*. I had panicked long enough to get myself lost. Surely — *nonne*, I thought irrelevantly, a question expecting the answer 'yes' — surely I could use my brain to find myself again? I sat down to put more of myself in contact with the reassuring floor.

What did I know about the place I was in? At school, a couple of years ago, we had done a project on the stone mines. A local historian had come into the classroom and given us a talk on quarrying methods. He'd shown us photographs, talked about wrist stones, chog holes, Lewis bolts, none of which seemed very useful now.

I didn't know which way I had come. I didn't know which way was out. I didn't know how big this cavern was. I couldn't see my watch, so I didn't know what time it was. I didn't even know how long I had been turning in panicky circles, or how far I might have come from the entrance. That was quite a lot of things not to know.

So, was I going to die?

Of course not. No one I knew had died, let alone died three days short of their fourteenth birthday. It simply wasn't possible. God didn't let that sort of thing happen. He certainly wouldn't let me die of ignorance, especially if he saw me making some kind of effort.

But God didn't even exist in this place, because there was *nothing* here, I was surrounded by *nothing* . . .

For a long, long while I lay shaking on the floor, the rock grazing my cheek, my hands clawing and scrabbling, squeezing and unclenching on the hard clammy ground.

★   ★   ★

I slept. When I woke up, it was as dark as ever. I was cold, and I felt light-headed: hungry and thirsty, with a foul-tasting mouth. But I was no longer afraid. Sleep had taken me right through fear and out the other side. All that was left was a steely determination that I would get out alive.

I thought of staying where I was. If I moved, there was a greater chance of stumbling *away* from the entrance than towards it — only one way back, but three hundred and fifty-nine degrees of wrong direction I could spin through. I could wait till morning and hope I was close enough to the entrance to be able to see a way out. But the chill persuaded me I should move. The void seemed a lot colder than it was outside, and now I couldn't stop shivering. Moving might warm me up. Moving would give me a purpose.

My legs felt numb and stiff but rubbing them put some feeling back, and I managed to get to my feet. I reached out a shaky blind person's hand — no, that was no good. I had to have faith. I took a deep breath, strode confidently forward and cannoned straight into hard rock.

The force knocked the breath out of me and spun me round; I put up a hand to save myself and pain shot across my palm as I caught the place where the burn had begun to heal. My breast had taken the main impact, and that hurt like hell too.

I felt my way along the rock, shuffling round the corner with the squared-off edge. It might be the entrance to a tunnel, like the one I had followed into the void. I held on with my right hand and stepped away as far as I dared, stretching out my left arm and groping for another wall, but there was nothing. So I felt my way back round the rock as far as I could, and realized I had hit a thick, solid column, with the girth of an ancient oak tree. No, even bigger than any oak tree I had seen. I had walked into one of the pillars supporting the roof of the void. But it wasn't possible to walk right round it, because abutting it was a different structure: something that felt like an uneven wall. That made sense: ' . . . gurt rooms with pillars, all interconnecting,' George had said. 'Then every so often a dry-stone wall, floor to ceiling.' That made me remember my father had been in here when he was a boy. He'd worked at Crow Stone. It consoled me to think he might have walked through this same cavern before me. He might hurt me, but he would never abandon me.

Once when he went inside he found a dead dog.

My toes curled inside my shoes. I told myself to tread carefully.

451

Having the wall to trail my fingers along was extraordinarily comforting. I kept the other hand warily in front of me, in case I was about to bump into something else. The wall seemed to go on and on.

The silence had become very loud. There were people calling in it, singing, dogs barking, conversations, music, machinery, the sound of picks on stone, chipping away the edges of a block, taking the cut back, saws scraping to, fro, to, fro, the razzers and the frigbobs deepening the cut as the pickers dripped water into the groove from a tin can with a hole in it to lubricate the blades. There was the sound of hammering, driving in the wedges to separate the stone from the bed; the squeak and creak of heavy iron bars forcing the blocks out. Chains rattled through winding gear. Iron-wheeled trucks ground over iron rails, hauled slowly up the incline by jinny rings and horse-powered windlasses at the top of the slope.

And there was light. Most of it was coming from behind my eyes, welling up under the lids but not quite spilling over strongly enough to dispel the dark. If only I knew how to turn up the power, my eyes could have been torchbeams blazing in the void. But there were also lights moving at a distance from me, candle flames, oil lamps, tiny squat saucer shapes only a couple of inches high, whose flickering light sometimes showed me a hand or a moustachioed profile or a dusty peaked cap at a rakish angle.

The wall was endless. For a while it stopped being a wall made of loose-piled stones and became a solid rock wall. Then it was a drystone wall again. Then it ran out altogether, terminating in another solid rock pillar.

I was reluctant to let it go. I felt round the corner. There was a ledge. There were things on it.

I hesitated. What kind of things?

Did I want to find out?

Cold, a little damp, all of them. Something smooth,

very smooth, moulded, curved. A knob or a dial on the side, ridged along the edges. A smaller protuberance on top, a button that yielded to the touch.

My fingers moved on. Something small, squarish, metallic, with a polished surface, a ridge across it a finger's width from the top. Or the bottom. Or the side. Impossible to tell.

Something stippled to the touch, bumpy, clammy, like skin. I let that go quickly, in case it moved.

Something that *did* move when I touched it, rolling across the ledge until it caught in a shallow depression: something small, cylindrical, a little sticky, waxy.

A candle.

In my shock, I knocked it off the ledge; I heard it drop and roll away. But already my fingers had met another. There were at least four or five at one end of the ledge. I could feel the wicks.

A candle wasn't much good without matches.

No matches. Matches would be damp anyway, useless if they had been here any length of time.

My fingers hovered, uncertain. Moved back along the ledge. Found the small square thing made of metal. Got the pad of my thumb against the ridge and pushed.

I felt it flip open, could smell petrol. There was a tiny indented wheel underneath the flip top, and I flicked it, like Mrs Klein.

A flame shot up and dissolved a small patch of darkness, enough to show me my hand, my startled reflection in the polished metal of the lighter, and a ledge far bigger than I had guessed, piled with cameras. Shadows jostled as I stepped back in shock and almost lost my footing again on an uneven patch of ground.

The Camera Man was *real*.

There must have been thirty or more cameras. Some were in scabby leather cases. A couple of old-fashioned ones had bellows lenses, the material rotting at the edges of the concertina folds. I didn't know enough about cameras to recognize the makes, but even I could tell this was a collection that spanned decades. Most were covered in greenish mildew and thick grey dust. Apart from the ones I had touched in the dark, they looked as if they hadn't been disturbed for years.

I was afraid of losing the light, now I had found it. There were lots more candles, stubby yellow things maybe three inches long, so I lit one and stuck it in a pool of wax on the ledge, closed the lighter, then stuffed the rest of the candles into my pockets and into the waistband of my trousers, like so many small guns.

I looked round. Candlelight revealed a curving dry-stone buttress, stretching back the way I had come, ending in the thick squared-off pillar with the ledge and the cameras. Beyond that, more darkness, in which I could just make out the dim shape of another pillar.

It was all very well having light, but it only showed me how hopelessly lost I was.

Two candles would be better than one. There was a cracked china saucer on the ledge, at its centre a blackened wick in a solidified pool of wax. I lit another candle and stuck it into the wax, a makeshift lamp. I held it up. It seemed to push back the darkness, but that might have been wishful thinking. I left the first candle burning on the ledge, cast one last glance over the cameras to check there wasn't anything else I could use, then set off for the pillar I could see ahead.

In that fashion I moved on through the voids, navigating pillar by pillar. Sometimes I lit another candle, and left it burning on the floor, or on a ledge, so I could look back along the way I had come, a trail of small flames in the dark. Walking was easier now I could see the ground, and didn't keep tripping. From *pillar*, I told myself, to *post*.

From pillar . . . to post.

Pillar . . . to post.

To pillar.

No posts. It would have been nice to see a post occasionally, to break the monotony.

To *pillar*.

On and on.

Every so often there would be another wall. Behind me the trail of candles receded into the distance. Sometimes I felt I was still, and it was the flames that moved further and further away. After a dozen candles, I began to regret using so many. I might need the rest for light if I didn't find a way out soon.

I wondered if my father and Janey Legge were home yet. Whether they had noticed I was missing. What they would be doing about it. It occurred to me I could look at my watch now I had light.

My God. It was three a.m.

But that was good because it was high summer and dawn couldn't be far away. When the sun rose, light might penetrate into the mines, only a gleam, maybe, but enough to give me an idea of the way out.

Some hope. I'd been walking for ages. I might be half-way to the centre of the earth by now. Perhaps I should stop, for a while at least. Maybe people were already looking for me, like they'd looked for the lost boys, and I should stay still so they could find me more easily . . .

You blithering idiot, Katie Carter. *Nobody knows you're in the mines*.

The only person who was going to get me out of there was myself.

Since I had lit the candles, the voices and the sounds had gone, and the other lights. But every so often there was a rustling in the darkness. It might be *rats*.

It might be worse.

What had happened to the Camera Man?

I had assumed the stories I heard were true; that the mines had been blocked up, every entrance, and the Camera Man could no longer make his winter home in the underground tunnels.

But if I could get into the mines, so could he.

What if he was following me in the darkness?

I wanted to run, as fast as possible, outrun him between the pillars because I was young and fast and he was old and creaky. But that was how I had got lost in the first place. Besides, how could I outrun him when he knew the tunnels and I didn't?

I sank down beside the next pillar, trying to stop my hands shaking and spilling the candle. He could be watching me right now, out there in the darkness. He could see me, but I couldn't see him.

Click. He had raised the camera to his eye and captured my picture. *Click.*

Only a drip of water.

Maybe.

Click.

'Leave me alone,' I said. 'LEAVE. ME. ALONE.'

Click.

He had long, spidery fingers, which flickered over the settings on the camera, twisting the focus ring on the lens, clicking through the stops, hovering over the button as he waited to find the perfect shot. He was moving round me now, choosing his angle, flitting silently from pillar to pillar just beyond the reach of the candlelight.

Click.

'GO AWAY. *Please.*'

He was an eye on legs, and a mouth that hung slackly open. His lips spun a long, thin thread of drool.

Click.

His fingers would be cold and sticky at the tips. He would leave wet fingerprints on the camera. And when he had taken enough photographs, he would put it down and come towards me, his damp fingers fumbling at his trousers, releasing the long white worm with its single oozing blind eye . . .

The candle flame shivered a little, as if someone had breathed on it from not far away.

No. None of this was true. There was no one here. It was all in my head.

I thought of my poster girl in the dark wood, head bowed, waiting for the clammy fingers to caress the back of her neck. *Some are born to sweet delight, some are born to endless night.* Like me, trembling, terrified of the click of the shutter, the footfall in the dark.

All in my head. I made myself get up again and go on.

★   ★   ★

Endless night. In the distance I saw a gleam. There was a light ahead, between two rock pillars.

At last. I hurried forward.

But I think I already knew before I got there that it would be one of the candles I had left burning behind me earlier.

★   ★   ★

That was the worst, the very worst. I knelt between the pillars, like my poster girl between the trees, bleak, hopeless. I would never get out.

Give up.

No.

Where was my mother? She surely hadn't brought me here to leave me lost in the dark. Her presence on the quarry face had been so strong.

Mum. Please, Mum. Come back.

I called on all the things that might make me strong in the dark, my lost mother, my beautiful coiled ammonites that lay all around frozen in the stone, the plaster statue of the Virgin Mary that stood on the windowsill in the front room, our weeping Jesus, and did those feet, bring me my bow of burning gold, bring me my arrows of desire, and we shall build, in England's green and pleasant, and did those feet, the First Englishman, walk upon England's pastures green, some are born to sweet delight, some are born to endless night, the Son of Morn in weary Night's decline, the lost Traveller's Dream under the Hill . . .

And we shall build. The lost Traveller's Dream.

The lost Traveller got to her feet again, picked up the candle and stumbled on through the darkness.

★ ★ ★

I tripped, putting out my burned hand to save myself again, feeling the jolt of it through every nerve. This time I did lose the candle. It flew through the dark and upended itself so the saucer acted as a snuffer.

Not to worry. My teeth already felt ground down to the jawbone from being gritted, but I did have the lighter safe in my pocket, and there were still four more candles tucked into the waistband of my trousers.

I lit one, and looked for the saucer. It had cracked right across and was in two neat halves. Never mind. I could still use one as a candle-holder.

Then I realized what had tripped me; not uneven rock, this time, but a metal rail, embedded in the floor of the mine. In the light of the candle it was dark orange with rust.

Chains. Winding gear. Trucks on metal tramways, horse-drawn or hauled up the incline by jinny rings and windlasses. I remembered the local historian's description of the underground quarries, and a picture he had shown us of proud men in their caps posing with their dogs by a line of wagons.

If this was the tramway, it had to lead somewhere. Out.

Or further in.

There was a fifty per cent chance of being right. And if I was wrong, all I had to do was retrace my steps, and follow the tramway in the other direction. *Some are born to sweet delight* . . . I was going to get out. I lifted the candle higher, to see if there were any clues to help me choose which way. To the left was a tall dry-stone buttress, ending in a pile of rubble and earth — a small roof collapse.

And there it was, at the foot of the rubble. For a moment in the wavering candlelight I thought I was just looking at a smooth, rounded stone. But there was something about the shape. I had found —

★　★　★

'I know what you found, Kit,' says Gary, quietly.
　'I found the First Englishman.'

31

The wood-burning stove, in which a week ago I burnt Dickon's vile porn, is alight and the lamps are on in the living room, pushing back the darkness. There is nothing to see through the window except beads of rain, blurring the reflection of Gary and me on the sofa. Somewhere out there is *tonight*: Martin, drinking with Roger and talking about the Mithraeum; Brendan, driving back up the motorway to his wife and family for the weekend; Dickon, with his sad dirty fantasies; the stone mines that are going to be filled and laid to rest for ever with all the stories that are trapped in them.

In here, *then*, and the thing I haven't been able to tell anyone.

'It wasn't your fault,' says Gary. 'Really, Kit, you had nothing to do with it.'

'How would you know?' I say. 'You weren't there.'

'I thought your funny little note was from the other girl. The pushy one. The one who jumped me at the party.'

'Trish.'

'Was that her name? I didn't take it seriously. I didn't know what you were called, not then, anyway. You were just the girl who lived across the road, who used to watch me from the front bedroom of her house.'

'You saw me?'

'Of course I bloody saw you. What do you think all that performance was about? Leaning half out of the window while I towelled myself dry. I was showing off.'

I shake my head. 'I don't remember it that way.'

'Take it from me, I was showing off.' He squeezes my shoulder gently. 'Go on. What happened after you found the skull?'

'You didn't fight her off,' I say, still stuck in another part of the story. 'You let her jump you.'

'I was seventeen,' he says. 'For God's sake. You're not exactly in control at that age.'

You can control it, Katie. You can close the gates. We're going to let it out and look at it, just for a while, then I'll show you how to lock it away again behind the gates. Backwards now, from a hundred.

Ninety-nine, ninety-eight, ninety-seven . . .

Crow Stone.

★ ★ ★

In the candlelight it was golden-yellow, like the stone. I remember it being smooth, polished, glossy, though later when I saw it in the daylight outside it was anything but smooth, grey-white, not yellow, and there were scratches on it and tiny scraps of flaky stuff. But in the mine, at the foot of the pile of rubble, in my memory of that moment, it was smooth, creamy yellow. The eye sockets were deep shadowy discs, and when I put the candle down on the rubble and picked up the skull, they looked right through me and out the other side.

I held it in both hands, one on either cheekbone, and I made myself look into the eyeholes.

The First Englishman.

The jawbone was missing, but I could see the upper row of teeth, long but surprisingly dainty. I traced my finger over them. So *old*. A quarter of a million years old, half a million maybe. This smooth, golden thing that had once been a person, that had once sat by a fire, feeding wood to the flames, had once eaten, laughed, made love. Had run across the hilltops, had hunted in wooded valleys, had dandled children.

My First Englishman.

I love you, I said to the skull, without forming the

461

words. I came all this way, through all this darkness, to find you.

Katie, said my father, I'm so proud of you. You were right. The First Englishman *was* here on Green Down. You found him.

Katie, said my shadowy mother. Katie. I love you.

I was *crying*. Why was I crying? I was holding the First Englishman in my hands and my tears were dripping on to the polished dome of his skull. I brushed them off with my sleeve, and some of the little flaky bits stuck to my jumper, but I didn't notice then.

You are going to be famous, Katie.

I balanced the skull on my palms. I had to carry it out of here safely. It was the most precious thing I would ever hold. The shadowy eyes looked at me.

'I'm sorry,' I said. 'It's the easiest way.' I slipped my fingers into the eye sockets; the tips tingled inside the darkness of the skull. Inside my head, something reciprocally stroked the underside of my own skull. I picked up the candle with the other hand, stepped away from the rubble and between the iron rails of the tramway.

★   ★   ★

'Oh, Kit,' says Gary, into my hair. 'Oh, Kit.' Just the same as underground, the night of Brendan's party. His arms tighten round me as if he's trying to stop me flying away.

'I'm fine,' I say. 'It's all right.'

'Of course it's not all right,' he says. 'You'd been wandering for hours, you were lost, by yourself. No wonder . . . '

'I'm not sure I was by myself.'

★   ★   ★

462

Which way?

I hoped the iron rails didn't lead back to Crow Stone. The skull was too fragile, too valuable; how could I carry it down the cliff, even supposing I was capable of getting myself safely down the old quarry face? I didn't remember rails on the way in, but it had been pitch dark. I had been wandering underground for a long time. Surely these would take me to some other away out.

But what if they had blocked up all the other entrances?

They had missed one. They might have missed others.

Which way? Left, or right?

'It is a common misconception that Early Man lived in deep caves,' my book had said. 'Deep caves were the haunt of bears and hyenas. Man lived close to warmth and light, near the cave entrance.'

There you are, I thought, with wonderful but entirely misplaced logic. I can't be far from an entrance. I lifted my face. There was the faintest sense of an air current coming from the right. I looked back doubtfully at the roof fall and the tall dry-stone buttress, stretching away to my left. At least that way there was something to see. Ahead, where the air seemed to flow, I could see nothing beyond the fizzing halo of light round the candle.

And how much good had sticking to the walls and pillars done me so far? The iron rails had led me to the First Englishman; now they would lead me out of the mines. I gripped the skull in one hand, raised the candle with the other and set out into darkness again.

Almost immediately I thought I heard rustling, a footstep behind me, perhaps. I stopped and listened. Nothing. No — there. Was that a dog barking in the distance?

It was gone. Everything was quiet again.

A whisper?

The earth settling.

I lifted the candle higher. Nothing, nothing, nothing. A dancing shadow —

A wall. I was coming to another buttress. No, more rubble — another roof collapse. But there was a way round it, and two pillars set close together in the void beyond, and between them I thought the darkness seemed less intense . . .

I heard something stir behind me.

Run. Got to *run*. *Go*. Don't let it —

If you run, you'll fall. The floor's too uneven. You'll smash the skull.

Walk.

I held the candle lower, to make sure I could see where I was treading.

I won't run. It's *nothing*.

I. Will. Not. Panic.

Something fanned my hair, like a breath. It passed over the top of my head and I saw it in the candlelight, a small dark speeding thing. I raised the candle again. The roof above me was dense brown-black with the folded-umbrella shapes of bats.

I followed the bat, along the tramway, towards the patch of less intense dark. On the left-hand pillar was a carving, on the side parallel to the tram rails. Someone had chipped into the stone a kind of sun symbol, one that didn't look exactly right, like a bonnet with radiant spikes coming out of it. I stopped to look at it, wondering if this was a quarryman's sign that the way out was not far ahead. The shape was quite neatly chiselled, about the size of a man's fist.

There was another movement overhead, another hurtling body. I stepped between the pillars and followed the rails as they curved to the left. The darkness changed from black to deep grey, then fuzzed paler and I was in a narrow, winding passage with gleams of light on the walls. Thank God. Thank God and the soul of the First Englishman. This *was* the way out. The passage bent again, sharply right, and I saw a waterfall of yellow dawn running through long strands of ivy.

★   ★   ★

'Oh, my God,' I say, remembering now something else I had forgotten. 'I came out into the woods right by Vinegar Farm. Where Martin and I stood the other day to look for the site of the Roman villa.'

★   ★   ★

The strands of ivy parted and I came out of a low arch at the back of the old quarry face in the woods. I was maybe half a mile from Crow Stone, no more. God knows where I had wandered all night, like someone who had strayed under the hollow hills into the realm of the fairies.

I left the saucer and the rest of the candles just inside the adit. The air outside was fresh, and smelled of wet grass and warm cows. Through the tree-trunks I could see them plodding up the meadow towards the farmyard, their coats steaming in the early sunlight. Filled with that wild exhilaration that comes with staying up all night and seeing the dawn, I started running down the slope under the beech trees, with the light bouncing off the leaves.

In my hand I was holding a skull.

I stopped and thought about it. Perhaps this wasn't such a good idea. It was very early, but there was a cowman awake at Vinegar Farm. There was no knowing who else I might meet on my way up the hill into Green Down.

Where could I safely hide the First Englishman?

I should go back, put him inside the adit. But I didn't want to leave him behind. He was my discovery. Against the wall that bordered the lane there was a pile of rubbish someone had fly-tipped. A plastic carrier-bag was caught on a rusting fridge door. There were dead leaves inside, but the weather had been dry for weeks. I emptied out the leaves and a few surprised woodlice, checked the bag to be sure it wasn't torn, then laid the First Englishman carefully inside. No, not safe enough. I scooped up the dry, crumbling leaves again and packed them round the skull to protect it.

As I walked up Vinegar Lane, with all the birds going mad in the woodland and the generator chugging in the farmyard, I felt like swinging the carrier-bag joyfully to and fro. Instead I cradled it carefully in my arms.

★   ★   ★

The fire in the stove is dying down; Gary crouches by it to open the door and throw in another log. Like that long-ago morning, I should be hungry but I'm not.

'Where's Martin?' I say. 'He ought to be back by now. What time is it?'

★   ★   ★

It didn't occur to me to go anywhere but home. The First Englishman was my talisman. He was a protection against any harm. My father would be thrilled when he saw what I had found. And I was so tired; all I wanted to do was curl up on my safe bed and sleep, with my curtains wide open to let the daylight fall on me.

When I turned into our road, I thought I could hear the whir of George's milk float in the distance. But there was no one about. I didn't even bother to glance up at Gary the Betrayer's curtains. Let him sleep. He would see my name in the papers, the girl who had discovered the First Englishman, and he would know then what he had missed.

My eyes felt dry and gritty. So tired. The euphoria was wearing off. As I let myself in through the front door, it struck me that I might not be thinking straight. What if my father was waiting for me in the hallway?

You little tart, just like your mother. *Thwack*.

No. I'd done this for him, to make him proud of me. You're a clever girl, Katie, I don't deserve a daughter as good as you.

You little tart.

The hallway was deserted and silent. I pushed open the living room door, in case he was waiting there; dust motes spun in the golden air. No one. I went back into the hall, and started to climb the stairs. The house was holding its breath. One foot after another, the carrier-bag clutched in one hand, hardly weighted at all by the skull, bouncing gently against my thigh.

His bedroom door was open. Light poured through the uncurtained windows and lay in squares on the faded brown carpet. I went right in, to be certain, but I already knew he wasn't there. I checked my mother's old room too, peering through the crack where the door was hinged to the frame, in case he and Janey were in bed together.

The house was empty. He hadn't come home.

I went into my own room and lay down, clutching the carrier-bag to my stomach. The bedside clock told me it was five thirty. He'd spent the night with her.

I was hungry and thirsty, with sore, scratchy eyes and the beginning of a headache, but I lay still and stared at the ceiling. Over and over, one thought repeated itself. He hadn't come home. It was the first time he had ever left me by myself in the house overnight. Janey was winning. But she didn't know I had found the First Englishman. That would bring my father back to me.

After a while, I heard the sound of a key in the lock; I should have known he wouldn't stay away without coming back to check on me in the morning. I leaned over the side of the bed and tucked the carrier-bag underneath so he wouldn't see it — not now, later was the time to show him — then quickly pulled the bedclothes over me to hide the fact I was still fully dressed. Downstairs, he went through to the kitchen; I heard him fill the kettle. I wriggled further down the bed and rolled on to my side, facing away from the door.

His feet on the stairs. The creak of a floorboard on the landing; the hush of air as he pushed the door wide and came in.

I could feel him standing there, looking. I wanted to turn and show him I was awake, have him come over and give me a hug. But, like before, I kept my breathing slow and shallow. The door closed quietly. His footsteps crossed the landing into his bedroom; the wardrobe door opened, a drawer was pulled out, and I guessed he was changing into his work clothes. Then he went downstairs again to make himself a cup of tea.

I didn't hear him leave for work: I had already fallen asleep.

★ ★ ★

'It wasn't your fault,' says Gary again. 'Stop blaming yourself.'

'How do you know I'm blaming myself?'

'It's written on your face.'

'You can't see my face.'

'It's always been written on your face.'

'What time did you say it was?'

★ ★ ★

I woke with a start. Something had disturbed me. The clock told me it was just after ten o'clock; outside, the dustbin lorry was grinding along the road.

I was still light-headed. After last night's ordeal, the world seemed unreal: the dustbin men, the clock and the sunlight stood at a distance, and I moved through an area of mist, disconnected from everyday life.

I had already decided what to do.

Half an hour later, I was on the bus heading into town. On my knees was a carrier-bag — a better one this time, a Harrods bag from the clothes Mrs Klein had bought me in London. It contained a shoebox, and in there, tucked like an egg into a nest of cotton wool, was the First Englishman.

The bus stopped. A fat woman got on and stood in the aisle panting and glaring until I shuffled along the seat, protecting my carrier-bag from her bulk. She opened her handbag and took out a powder compact; her elbows flailed as she peered at her moon-face in the tiny glass, and applied powder to her damp cheeks. What would she say if she knew what was in my carrier-bag? I hugged the First Englishman close.

The museum was in Queen Square, one of John Wood's triumphs. I had been there on school visits, but I'd never been in alone. Just inside the entrance, a woman sat behind a desk. She was about the same age as Janey Legge, with a blonde perm that was growing out and a downy skin. She looked surprised to see someone my age, on my own.

'Hello,' she said. 'Shouldn't you be at school?'

'I've got something the curator ought to see,' I said, dredging up what I hoped was the right language to make her take me seriously. 'An archaeological relic. Of great antiquity.'

Her pale eyebrows twitched. 'The curator is rather a busy man,' she said. 'Perhaps you'd let me take a look . . . '

I looked at her doubtfully. Was she trying to fob me off?

'I've got a degree in archaeology,' she said.

'He'll want to see it.'

'Of course.'

'It's very old.'

'Is it in that bag?'

I put the Harrods bag on to the desk, and lifted out the shoebox. The lid didn't quite fit over the First Englishman, and I had wrapped it round with sticky tape to keep it on. I pushed it over to her.

'Like pass-the-parcel, isn't it?' she said. Her forearm was furred with long pale silky hairs that caught the light as she picked at an end of the tape. She took off the lid. Her eyebrows shot up, and she caught her breath with a little whinnying sound. 'I see.' The First Englishman seemed diminished, lying in his nest of cotton wool. There were more flaky bits than I had remembered, and some wiry black strands I had not noticed before, caught on the back of the cranium. She was looking at him with a puzzled expression, lifting the skull out carefully and turning it in her hands. 'Where did you find this?'

If I told her, would I get into trouble for being in the mines last night? Probably. But which was more important: me or Science? I looked into the First Englishman's blank eye sockets. Maybe he wasn't the very first Englishman; this morning, I could admit that. He might not be quite a quarter of a million years old. But he was part of history, and the place I had found him gave him what my book called the archaeological context. The experts would have to know that.

'It was in the stone quarries on Green Down,' I said. 'Underground. He'd fallen out of the ceiling, I think, when it collapsed. That makes him prehistoric, doesn't it?'

470

She looked at me. 'Possibly,' she said eventually. 'Yes, possibly.'

'Good.' I relaxed.

'Would you like to wait here?' she said. 'I just have to ... ' Her eyes slid away from me. 'The curator's office is through there. Would you mind if I take your skull away with me to show him?'

'Of course not,' I said, trying to sound dignified.

'You can sit over there.' She pointed to a couple of chairs by the wall. 'Give me a shout if anyone comes in, will you? I won't be long.'

She disappeared through double swing doors into a long corridor. No sooner had the doors shut than they opened again. 'This roof collapse. Did it happen while you were there?'

'Oh, no. It was an old one.'

She vanished again. The double doors batted to and fro for a while, then became still. I hoped no one came in; I wished she had suggested I go through to the museum and look at the exhibits instead. Something didn't feel right. The minutes crawled by, and I shifted uncomfortably on the hard chair, unable to work out what was making me uneasy. Of course she would take the First Englishman to show the curator. But what was taking them so long? Why wasn't I invited to go with her?

The doors bounced open.

'Sorr-ee,' she said, with a curious singsong intonation that made her sound not sorry at all. 'The curator was a bit tied up. But he's very interested. I wonder if you'd mind hanging around a while — we're going to call in some other people to look at it.' Her eyes were bright and excited, darting everywhere; droplets of sweat shone in the pale fuzz on her upper lip.

It was what I had hoped for: excitement, respect, experts flocking to see what I had found. So why did I feel like backing out of the doors and telling her I couldn't wait, I had to be somewhere else? 'Well, I ought to be at school . . . '

'Oh, I don't think your teachers would mind for something like this.' She sounded almost breathless. 'Which school do you go to?'

'St Anne's.'

'I'm sorry, I've forgotten what you said your name was.'

'You didn't ask me.' Suddenly I didn't want to tell her my name. But it was my discovery, and she had come back without the skull. I had to tell her my name, I had to stay, or how would I be able to claim the discovery as mine?

'What's your name?' she pressed.

Reluctantly I told her. She wrote it down.

'And where do you live, Katie?'

The doors from the street opened. Two uniformed policemen came in.

★　★　★

'I should have run,' I tell Gary. 'I wish I'd run.'

'Of course you couldn't have run,' he says. He lights another cigarette for me. My throat hurts with smoking, talking, the effort of not letting myself cry because it's far too late to cry about it. I ought to laugh, really. It was a black comedy. But I can't find it in myself.

He lights one for himself, and gets up to empty the ashtray into the wood-burning stove. 'Actually . . . ' he says, his back to me. His shoulders are tense and hunched, like he's expecting to be hit. ' . . . it's me you ought to blame.'

★　★　★

Crow Stone. All the work had stopped. There were men standing round the silent machines, men eating

472

sandwiches and smoking, staring as the two cars came through the big metal gates. I looked for Gary but didn't see him, although he must have been there.

The police cars stopped in the middle of the yard. Alec and Mike — the two uniformed policemen had told me to call them that — got out of the front of ours. I tried to get out too, but the door at the back of the police car wouldn't budge.

'Sorry,' said Alec, coming back to open it for me. 'We left the kiddie locks on. Not that you're a dangerous criminal, Katie.'

Mike laughed. He had crooked teeth. I didn't trust either of them, though they kept trying to make friends.

I had tried to brush the quarry dust off my best black trousers that morning, but as I got out of the car I could see there were still faint white streaks on the material. DCI Savile was climbing out of the passenger seat of the plainclothes car, a maroon Ford, only an M registration but it looked ready to be scrapped. The other one, whose name I had already forgotten, the detective sergeant, was closing the driver's door.

DCI Savile came over to me. He was a large man who walked like an elephant, rolling from hip to hip. Even in the sunshine he was wearing a grey mac. 'So where was it you found the tunnel?' he asked.

I pointed to the old quarry face behind the stacks of drying stone.

'Fuck a blinking duck,' he said. 'How do you expect me to get up there?'

★ ★ ★

'I was there,' says Gary. 'Of course I was. It was very hot that morning, I remember. Hot and dusty. I was on the big saw, coughing a lot. It must have been about a quarter to twelve, maybe a bit later, they told us to down tools. The police were on their way. Something had happened, they said, inside the underground quarry. Somebody had got in there last night. No one seemed to know exactly what was going on. They had us checking the sheds and counting the tools in case there'd been a break-in.'

'So did you see me?'

'I saw you.' He comes back to sit on the sofa, and takes my hand. 'As soon as you got out of that police car, I was practically shitting myself, because then I knew it must have been you who sent the note, not the other girl. All these thoughts going round in my head — what had happened to you? What if I'd been there? And — sorry, this really isn't very nice, but I was only seventeen — what had you said to them about me?'

'You thought I'd said something about you?' He can't meet my eyes. 'Like I'd told them that you'd raped me or something?'

'That's exactly what I thought. In fact, I couldn't understand why I hadn't already been arrested, because you knew my name, you'd put it on the note. But then when they clearly weren't interested in any of us, and started pointing up at the rockface behind the stacking yard, I guessed it must be something else. And then I began to think that I should have been there, and maybe stopped whatever happened to you. Because I thought I knew what it was. I was remembering that note, how you'd written that things were bad at home. We all knew, you see. Everybody in the street had a pretty good idea what was going on. So it was me who told them, Katie. That was why they arrested your father.'

★ ★ ★

So where exactly did you find the skull?

I don't know.

Have you got any idea which way you went after you got into the mine?

No, I told you, I was lost.

Perhaps we could take her in and get her to show . . .

Don't be absurd, Tom. Put her through that again?

He gets up, and they go over to stand behind the half-open door of the interview room. They're whispering, but I can hear them.

I don't think she realizes, sir.

No, no, no.

* * *

'It's all muddled,' I tell him. 'I can't remember what order things happened in now. They were experimenting in those days with hypnotizing witnesses, because they thought it would help dredge up details that had been suppressed. They took me to a woman at the hospital, a proper psychiatrist. She was very nice, but she didn't seem entirely comfortable with what she was doing. What she found out wouldn't have been admissible in court anyway. Everything got really muddled after that, and I think maybe she was trying to help by making me forget some of it.'

* * *

No pain, Katie. No pain. I want you to count backwards from a hundred.

I don't want to forget.

You won't forget. But I can take away the pain.

Ninety-nine, ninety-eight . . .

* * *

'Everybody knew,' he says. 'But no one was ever willing to come out and say it. People liked your dad. They felt sorry for him, having to cope on his own. We'd all heard about your mum running off. My mum used to call you

475

'that poor little girl over the road'. Telling the authorities that he hit you would have been crossing a line that nobody felt certain enough to cross. It was the 1970s. Of course, people still smacked their kids then, I mean walloped them, sometimes, if they were naughty — when my dad was alive, he took his belt to me more than once. And you were never off school. You never went to the hospital. We thought it couldn't be that bad. But sometimes the neighbours heard you scream. They'd started talking about it. It was getting to the point when someone was going to have to say something. That morning in the quarry, I thought it'd better be me.'

★   ★   ★

All the people, waiting silently in the quarry. Alec and Mike, the two coppers, moving round talking to the quarrymen, asking them if they'd ever found anything as special as this in the rocks.

Somebody had fetched a long ladder. Some more policemen had arrived, in plastic boots and overalls.

One appeared on the ledge where the adit was, pushing through the creepers. He called down. 'Sir, you'd better come up and see this.'

'What've you found?'

'We've got a thigh bone.'

When my dad got home, he was going to be really, really proud.

★   ★   ★

The way I remember what happened next, I was by myself in the house, waiting for my dad to come back. I was going to tell him about the First Englishman. The stir it had caused. All the policemen in the quarry.

I *know* I wasn't really alone, though. I was in my

bedroom, with the social worker in the green blouse, packing my case. My hand hovered over Beau Bunny and my other old toys heaped on the chair. Sometimes, if I wasn't well, I still took them into bed with me for comfort. But, no, I wouldn't take them. They'd be safer here. And my ammonites. Too heavy to carry. I slipped into my pocket the little polished one my dad had given me, careful not to let it touch my palm: the burn had gone red and angry again after the night in the quarries. Just a small case, for the moment, the social worker said. It wouldn't be for long, anyway, a night or two, until the fuss died down and the journalists went away.

I pushed my dressing-gown over the top of everything. Tucked my slippers down the sides of the case. Then I reached over to the bedside table and picked up the photo of my mother, in the frame my dad had repaired so carefully. I was afraid of it getting damaged if I tried to squash it into the case as well.

'If you like, I'll take that for you,' said the social worker. She put it into her briefcase. I think she gave it to the newspapers because I never saw it again. Then we went down the narrow stairs and out of the house and got into the big black car with the dinosaur body.

★ ★ ★

'Say it, Kit,' says Gary. 'You still can't say it, can you?'
Tears are running down my face.
'I can't.'

★ ★ ★

The psychiatrist's room in the hospital was painted pale blue. 'Crow Stone, Katie,' she said. 'We have to talk about what happened at Crow Stone.'
I was sitting on a low chair upholstered in mottled

red plastic. There were little grooves scratched into the wooden arms, and my fingers picked at the varnish.

'I'm going to put you into a very light trance. You'll still be in absolute control. You can ask me to stop any time you want. Just look at this light, please. Concentrate . . . '

The light was yellow like the sun through the curtain of vines.

'I'm going to take you back, Katie. A long, long way back. Let's go back to what you can remember about when you last saw your mother.'

'It's Christmas,' I said. 'I can see the lights on the tree. There's washing drying on the rack in front of the fire. My clothes: they're wet . . . '

★　★　★

How did they get wet, Katie?

We've been out in the snow. I went out with my mum, to the recreation ground.

The firelight, golden and red on the silver ornaments on the tree. The smell of wet wool. I'm full and sleepy and milky, and Wynken, Blynken and Nod are sailing the skies in their boat that is the crescent moon.

Voices in the other room stop me drifting away with them.

I saw you. You little tart.

Something smashes. The wall shakes, the wall where weeping Jesus hangs.

But it's no good, I can't remember. Perhaps the glass balls on the tree shiver, and perhaps the firelight on them bobs and flickers.

I start to cry, because I want my mother to come back. Instead I see my father, and his eyes have that lost, helpless look.

★　★　★

478

In the candlelight it is golden-yellow, like the stone, but smooth, polished, glossy. I turn it in my hands and look deep into the shadowy eye sockets. They look right back into mine.

I love you, I say. I love you and I've missed you. I know it wasn't true. You didn't leave me.

This smooth, golden thing that had once been a person, that once sat by a fire, hanging my wet coat and mittens to dry, telling me the story of Wynken, Blynken and Nod. Had once wheeled my pushchair past the recreation ground and kissed a soldier.

My mother.

Katie, said my shadowy mother. Katie. I love you.

LEVEL SEVEN

The Father

The seventh and highest grade of enlightenment ... The bull is led into the cave for sacrifice, and at last the adept is at one with Mithras.

From *The Mithras Enigma*,
Dr Martin Ekwall, OUP

32

It's been spoken out loud.

I found my mother's body, where my father had left her ten years before, hidden under a roof fall. Because I found her, I lost him: he was arrested, and sent to prison for life.

'I've still got the newspaper cuttings somewhere,' says Gary. 'My mum kept them. She even took them to the home with her. Isn't that funny? She didn't know you, really, and by the end she didn't even know me, but she kept those cuttings with her until she died.'

In Green Down, people still remember the different stories that came out of the stone mines: the lost boys, and the Camera Man, and the little girl who went underground and came back with a skull.

'Why didn't you say something when you recognized me?'

'Come on. How do you say to someone, 'Hey, don't I know you? Aren't you the girl who found her mother's skull?' What if I'd been wrong?'

Now it's been said, the noise in my head has stopped. I feel limp, but in a good way, like after a long, hard run or a pummelling massage. The firelight plays on Gary's face. He chews a thumbnail, his eyes turned away from me, looking out into the dark.

'Did I do the right thing?' he asks.

'I don't know.'

'Better out than in,' Mrs Owen would have said. But after so many years it doesn't really all come out. It's still stuck in there, scar tissue on the soul.

The rain's falling in sheets now, sending long, thick dribbles down the windowpanes, and the fire is dying.

'Where's Martin?' I say again. 'It's gone half past

483

nine. He said he was going for one quick drink.'

'He'd have phoned if there was a problem.' But Gary doesn't know Martin.

'He'd have phoned if there *wasn't*.' I get to my feet, trying to remember where I left my mobile.

'Do you mind if I make us a sandwich or something?' Gary heads for the kitchen.

'Go ahead. I'm not hungry.'

There's a sick feeling in my stomach. My phone is at the bottom of my bag. 'Message', the screen tells me. A text. I must have missed the beep. The idiot didn't call me because he knew I'd talk him out of it.

You'll be sorry to have missed this. We're going in.

'Shit. They're in the quarries.'

'How long ago?'

'It says five thirty.'

'Call him back. See if there's a reply.' He stands in the archway to the kitchen with the butter-dish in his hand. 'They won't have got in. They're probably back in the pub by now. What on earth would make him risk — ' He sees my face. 'Oh, no, Kit. I don't want to know about it. You fucking idiot.'

My fingers are trembling as I key in the number. He can't still be in there. The stupid bastard. What does he think he's doing? He knows how easy it is to get disoriented. He must be relying on Roger — but it's forty years since Roger went into the mines.

While the phone rings I go to the cupboard under the stairs where I keep my caving gear. Everything's jumbled, instead of neat and ordered the way I keep it. 'He's taken my ropes. And my spare hard-hat, and the head-torch.'

Martin's phone rings on and on. Eventually voicemail cuts in: *I'm sorry, the person you are calling is not available . . .*

'Phones do sometimes work underground,' Gary says, through a mouthful of bread and cheese, wandering out of the kitchen. He's kicked his shoes off, settled in for the night.

'Not this one. Martin, ring me at once, you idiot.'

'Don't worry. I'll bet they never got in. Sure you don't want a sandwich? They could't possibly get access from the site.'

'They wouldn't need to. The entrance the boys got in by was never sealed — I'm almost sure it must be the same way I got out in 1976. Roger will have taken him up through the woods.'

'In the dark?'

'It was probably only just getting dark. I'll bet Martin had this planned all along.'

'Hang on.' Gary puts his sandwich down. He's gone white. 'If they went in off Vinegar Lane, that would mean they're in the southern part of the workings.'

'Did Brendan get you to take a look at that crack this afternoon?'

'I told him I thought we should shut down all work in that area until the hydro-geologist's seen it, then get some emergency fill in quick.'

★ ★ ★

We run out to his 4×4 through pelting rain, hauling on jackets as we go. The spare torch batteries fall out of my unfastened rucksack and I scoop them out of a puddle, hoping they'll still work after a soaking.

The tyres slip as we take the hill out of the village.

'We'll have to get help, Gary. There's got to be something wrong, hasn't there, if they're still in there?'

Four hours, at least, they'll have been underground.

'They'll be lost, won't they? There's something about that area of the mines. People always get lost there.' I know I'm babbling, but it stops me having to think how this really is all my fault. I told Martin about the raven. I made him obsessed with finding a Mithraic temple, just as I had been obsessed with discovering the First Englishman. 'Something always goes wrong when people go into that part of the mine.'

Gary doesn't say anything, just puts his foot down and the 4×4 roars up Brassknocker Hill, the back wheels sliding away on the bends. Clutching the dashboard to keep steady, I send another text to Martin in the hope he can respond.

★   ★   ★

It's already past ten o'clock. The lights of the barn conversions round the old farmhouse are fuzzy in the sheeting rain. Gary parks at the bottom of Vinegar Lane and we scramble up the bank under dripping trees.

'I think we should get help,' I say. 'We can't do this by ourselves. We might not even be able to find them.'

'If we call someone out, you'll lose your job for sure,' says Gary. 'People have seen you and Martin together.'

'If you try to protect me, *you* could lose *your* job.'

'Let's find out what's happened first.'

Underfoot is slippery with mud. We are following the path, such as it is, that Martin and I followed last Sunday. Gary has a head-torch, but Martin took mine and my big flashlight so all I have is the little Maglite I keep for household emergencies. It's already looking ominously yellow.

'Are you sure this is the right way?' asks Gary.

'I have no bloody idea. It all looks different in the dark.'

'Did you see the entrance when you were up here on Sunday?'

'I didn't even remember it existed last Sunday. And I can't promise it's the same one Roger was talking about. We could be barking up the wrong tree entirely.'

'Paddling up the wrong creek might be a better metaphor.'

486

The path is now doubling as a small milky stream, yellow white in the light from the torches, giving off that wet-cement smell I have grown used to in the last few weeks. 'This is limestone runoff,' I say. 'It must be coming straight out of the quarries.'

'I don't know if that's good news or bad,' says Gary.

'Well, at least it suggests we're going the right way.'

The little quarry where Martin and I had stood last weekend is hardly more than a dip in the hillside, only twenty feet deep, the rockface about thirty feet high. We follow the stream to the back of the quarry, where it gushes out under a mass of sodden ivy and creepers. Just for a moment I see myself pushing through the strands in the yellow light of dawn; Gary must sense it because he gives me a quick wet hug as he pushes past and starts tearing away the vegetation from the low archway hidden behind it.

'Someone was here before us,' he says. 'This has already been partly cleared. They went in this way.'

'Thank God we got something right.'

'Before we go in, try phoning again. You never know, they might have come out. We didn't see a car parked in the lane.'

I flip open my phone, hoping for another message. The mailbox is empty. I tap in the number, feeling sick, praying he'll answer this time.

It starts ringing. A plane rumbles far overhead, probably heading for one of the Wiltshire RAF bases, and for a moment I imagine someone's picked up, but I must have moved the phone away from my ear: as the plane fades into the distance the sound of ringing comes back, and goes on and on and on.

Gary's jacket is a bright yellow and silver splash against the dark wall of the quarry, but his face is shadowed under the head-torch. 'He'd have picked up by now,' he says.

'The voicemail hasn't yet cut in.' Suddenly the

ringing stops, and I wait for the female voice to say, 'I'm sorry . . . ' but it doesn't come. There's silence on the line; I can't hear anything now but the rain on the leaves, and Gary's breathing.

'What's going on?' says Gary. 'Someone there?'

'I don't know. The ringing just stopped. Could be his voicemail is full, or unavailable . . . ' I take the phone away from my ear and look at the screen. 'No, I think it's connected. But no one's saying anything.' The screen goes blank. 'Shit, no, it's cut off now.'

'Right,' says Gary. 'We'd better go in.' He starts pushing through the ivy, then stops. 'I don't want you doing anything dangerous, Kit. If there's a rock fall I want you to get out right away and call for help. OK?'

'Not OK,' I say. 'He's my friend. If I find him, I stay with him. *You* go and call for help.' I try to get past him and into the adit, but he grabs my arm where Dickon's fingers left a set of small painful bruises.

'This isn't about you being a woman,' he says. 'Or only in the sense that I care about you as a woman. I don't want you hurt too.' He touches my face; his fingers are cold and wet from the rain. 'In fact, I'd quite like to kiss you but as usual the fucking hats are in the way.'

I find his fingers with mine, and pull them to my mouth.

'There,' I say. 'That'll have to do.'

He takes my hand and lifts it to his face, so I feel the stubble on his cheek, and he sucks my middle finger as he did in the pub. That cold spear of longing goes through me again. I wish I could see his eyes, but the head-torch is shining right in my face. He lets go of my hand. 'It'll do until we come out.' I can tell from his voice he's smiling. 'But do what I fucking tell you, OK?'

'Sod off.'

We go into the darkness under the archway.

Everything feels different underground now. There are no safe, shining steel roadways here; just narrow, winding passages of bare rock opening out into pillared voids, and beneath our feet the tram rails I followed that night to get out. This is no longer Kit's environment, where I am a professional doing a job. It's my mother's place. Not far from here I found her skull.

The Christmas my mother disappeared was a couple of years after the lost boys had been found, and the mines had been sealed for good — or so people thought. But there are always ways in, like the forgotten archway under the vines in the wood, and the adit I discovered at Crow Stone. My father had found another, by accident, not long before he killed my mother.

He was rewiring one of the cottages at the top of Vinegar Lane; late-nineteenth century, two-up two-down, built like so much else in Green Down on the site of an old quarry where the good stone had been exhausted. A developer had bought two to do up and sell on. They were built hard up against the old quarry face, which was effectively their back wall, and they had long, narrow gardens to catch the sun in front of them, instead of behind. The fuse box was in a shallow cupboard in the back room; when my father was working in there, he accidentally knocked through the single skin of brickwork and found himself staring down a flight of steep stairs into a dark tunnel.

The cottages still stood empty at Christmas; the developer was asking too much and hadn't managed to sell them. My father rolled my mother's body in an old piece of carpet, loaded it into the back of his van and drove to Vinegar Lane. He parked outside the cottages, and let himself in through the front door with the key the developer had given him in case the pipes froze. If anyone saw him, they thought nothing of it: the neighbours were used to seeing his van there. Perhaps there had been a burst in the empty, unheated house. Carpet? Why not? The places were being done up, after all.

My father knocked through the brickwork again, and carried my mother's body into the underground quarries. He buried her under a roof fall; he must have thought it unlikely she would ever be discovered. Flesh doesn't last long in wet limestone. My mother was bones years before I found her, scattered by foxes.

I can't remember who told me all this: the police or the psychiatrist. Nobody else ever talked to me about it. They couldn't think of what to say. Not even Mrs Klein.

But I didn't want to talk about it either. I understood that my father was in prison, not only because of what I had found but also because of what I had said. My buried memories of my mother's last days could not have been brought as evidence to the court to convict him, but the police used them, and me, to make him confess what he had done.

There's a splash from behind me and I swing the torch round to see Gary ankle high in liquid mud. There's a lot of water in the narrow passage, running down the walls and forming deep, creamy puddles on the ground.

'How far in was the pillar where you saw the sun carving?' he asks.

'When it opens up into a void, that's where the pillar should be, the first we come to.' I close my eyes to imagine it but it's so long ago. 'I remember it being on the left as I was coming out that night — so our right — but I could be wrong.'

'Are you all right about this?'

'Are you mistaking me for someone who's sensitive?'

'Kit.'

'Sorry. Force of habit. I'm OK. A bit wobbly, but

more because I'm worried about Martin. The rest is
. . . still like a story that happened to someone else.'

'What happened to your father? He must have come
out of prison eventually.'

'No,' I say. 'He never did.'

★ ★ ★

Usually, the mandatory life sentence for murder means
nothing of the sort. People get out after ten or eleven
years. But life meant life for my father, who was
convicted of assaults on me as well as my mother's
murder.

Gary wasn't called to give evidence in court. It was
the nurse from school, who stood witness to the bruise
she'd seen on my hairline and the burn she'd dressed on
my hand.

My guess is that my father's temper kept him inside.
I can't believe he learned to control it in prison when he
couldn't stop himself hurting the people he loved.

He died there, of a stroke, last March. I didn't hear
until August. The letter from the National Victim
Liaison Service took a long time to find me.

'I understand why you couldn't write to your father,'
says Gary. 'It would be impossible to forgive him.'

Impossible? I don't know. I never got so far as trying.
The truth is, it was impossible to forgive myself.
Nobody suggested I should visit him in prison, but the
real reason I never went to see him was because I
couldn't bear to see the hurt I imagined in his eyes.

DCI Savile, who retired years ago, was proud of how
he persuaded my father to confess. 'He wanted to see
you,' he told me, when I tracked him down last
September. 'He said to me, 'Let me talk to my little
girl.' I said to him, 'I'll make sure you never see your
little girl again if you don't tell us the truth about what
you did to your wife.' So he told us. Then he said, 'Can

I see her now?' And I said, 'Look, mate, what makes you think she ever wants to see you again?' ' Savile took off his steel-rimmed glasses and polished them. There was a flicker of uncertainty in his little elephant eyes, but only for a moment. 'And I was right, wasn't I? You never did see him again.'

I never visited. I never wrote. I should have. He was still my father.

Fucked up or what, Gary? Now do you understand why I never take this out and look at it?

Instead, I say, 'This is the void now. But I haven't a clue which way to go from here.'

Gary shines his flashlight round it. It's a much smaller space than I remember, but I know it's the same one because there's the mark on the pillar, the radiant sun that I can now recognize as the Mithraic symbol for Heliodromus, the Runner of the Sun. It's much cruder than I recall. Martin must be right, and these aren't Roman carvings at all; they're eighteenth- or nineteenth-century copies.

'You know what I think this is?' says Gary. 'It's exactly what you thought it was in 1976. It's the exit sign.'

'What? Nothing to do with Mithraism or freemasonry?'

'Well, that might be where someone copied the images. But this is the equivalent of what we used to do when I worked underground at Corsham. You paint road signs on the wall so you don't get lost. The quarrymen probably couldn't read in the eighteenth century. They used pictures.'

You can tell these are old workings. The pillars have been heavily robbed of stone and they look twisted and fractured, seamed with fault lines. On the ceiling miners' candles have left sooty black circles.

'The bats have gone,' I say. When I was last here, the ceiling was alive with them.

'Your policemen disturbed them?'

'Who knows? But it might explain why this entrance isn't on the site maps. If there were no bats coming out this way, Rupert and his students, roaming the hillsides at twilight, wouldn't have spotted it.'

The police never found it either. I showed them the way in at Crow Stone, and they followed the trail of melted candles I had left from the Camera Man's altar to my mother's burial place. I don't remember anyone ever asking how I got out. They must have assumed it was the same way I went in.

'So which way would Martin have gone?' asks Gary. 'How does he think underground?'

Martin thinks like me underground, because usually I'm there to tell him the safe way to go. But he also thinks like an archaeologist. Metal tram rails wind off to the right — the rails I followed after finding my mother's bones, though that wouldn't influence Martin, as he doesn't know about it. But they belong to a more recent period: nineteenth century, not eighteenth.

'Left,' I say. 'Martin would have stayed in the older workings.'

'Are you sure? You came along the tram rails; so the Camera Man's stash must have been in that direction.'

'The Camera Man knew the whole of the workings.' I'm already setting off to the left, shining my torch along the pillars. 'He was obsessive — stole plenty more cameras than I found. I don't believe that was his only stash. And when the lost boys came in this way, they would have been aiming for the part of the mines they knew. They would have headed north-west, not towards the east. That's the way Roger will have taken him. Besides — ' I stop abruptly. 'There. I'll bet that's Martin.' My torch beam rests on a pink chalk mark, chest height on a pillar — an arrow pointing back the way we've come.

'He left that for us?'

'No, for himself. He's been in the quarries before, knows how confusing it can be away from the roadways we've built.'

Gary says nothing, but I know what he's thinking. If he's been here before, then it was indeed me who brought Martin in; if something's gone wrong, it really will be my head on the block. We splash on through the milky puddles. On every pillar, at every junction, Martin has dashed a pink arrow. Because the arrows point backwards, it's not always clear which way he went.

'Not that way,' says Gary, grabbing my arm.

'How do you know?'

'You're starting to veer east again. You've got a lousy sense of direction, Kit.'

There's the next chalk mark. He's right, damn him.

'Never mind. You can't help it.' He's wearing a smug grin under his hard-hat. 'Women are wired differently.'

'Fuck off.'

'How far have we come, then?' he asks.

'What?'

'Do you know how far we've come from the entrance?'

He's right. I never have been much good at this. Martin can do it, but I've never got a clue. 'You tell me.'

'Nine hundred and eighty metres, give or take a couple of strides.'

'You can't be that exact and hold a conversation.'

'I can. Old quarryman's trick, counting pillars, counting steps. Always know exactly where you are underground. It might save your life one day.'

Or someone else's. Was that Martin, answering the phone? Why didn't he speak? Where are they?

'Have you got any idea where we are in relation to the rest of the workings?' I ask. 'Could you get us right the way through to where we've built the roadway?'

He narrows his eyes, rubs his forehead just above the

nose. The place pigeons are supposed to keep their homing gland.

'Don't know. Maybe. It's no big mystery, Kit. It's just counting, remembering the turns and thinking about the layout of what you already know . . . ' His torchbeam picks out a gleam in the darkness ahead. '*My God.*'

I've seen this before, or something very like it, in a different part of the workings — the Camera Man's stash, a jumble of mouldy Leicas and Kodaks piled on a narrow ledge. Time and the damp haven't been kind. Everything is filmed with mould, or caked with grey dust. Metal is corroded, red brown and flaking. Just one uncapped, unseeing lens returns our torchlight, or we might have missed the collection altogether.

'Well, at least we know we're on track,' he says.

'Remember, the lost boys scattered from here. This is where the Camera Man nearly caught them.'

'So we're looking now for an old roof collapse.'

'One of Martin's little pink arrows would do for a start.'

Gary casts his torch around above the ledge.

'Nothing.'

'On the other side?'

We each take a different side of the pillar — 'Got it,' says Gary — but as we meet up in the next void I feel uneasy immediately. I can't put my finger on it; something's not right.

'Oh, shit,' he says. He sweeps the flashlight in a wide arc. 'I don't like the look of this.'

There's a fine haze in the void, fogging the torchbeams. You might mistake it for water vapour in the chill, but it catches in the back of the throat, filling your nose with that cement smell.

'There's too much dust in the air. There's been a collapse.'

33

'Martin! Where are you?'

Nothing. Our flashlights stab through the haze. It's not so much a fog as a blurring of the beams, almost unnoticeable but utterly terrifying.

'Martin! Are you there?'

'Roger! *Anyone* there?'

Gary raises a hand: has he heard something? We stop moving and listen, but there's only the ambient hiss of silence. I step forward but Gary shakes his head: he must be able to hear something I can't.

The hiss stretches out into component sounds; still mostly hiss, but also our breathing, the occasional plink of water and a gentle ticking sound. It's such a big silence, in such a big darkness. Above our heads, there must be normal life, ordinary sounds: wind in the trees, rain on pavements, cars rolling to a halt in garages, keys in front doors, people running taps, setting off their dishwashers, cleaning their teeth ready for bed . . . But this is the underworld. Normal rules do not apply. I try to visualize Brendan's map: are we yet under the houses in the pine trees where Poppy lived? We can't be far from the old roof fall that Roger told us about, and behind it the chamber with the pits where his friend broke his leg.

Gary shakes his head again, in frustration this time, and we move forward, adding the sound of our footsteps to the silence. The cement taste is in the back of my throat again. We've gone about three steps when there's a rumbling sound.

A hand on my arm jerks me forwards — my feet tangle with each other, and I almost trip — everything is in slow motion, the earth vibrating, the air full of dust

496

and small stones bouncing off the ground and hitting the back of my legs, my arms windmilling trying to keep myself upright, a flash frame of Dickon blocking the low sun in the alleyway, Dickon going down into the mud and dragging on my jacket, torchbeams bouncing every which way, gasping and sucking in cement air —

And then, just as suddenly, all still, all hiss, and the sound of earth trickling down the heap of ceiling that's growing out of the floor behind us.

'Uuh, uuh . . . ' Big, heaving breaths. No words. The pile of ceiling — a couple of tons, maybe, of earth and stones — is right where we were standing before, listening to the silence. My feet are on strike — reasoning rightly that if they take me anywhere my knees will only fold up and collapse under me — and I have a strong urge to giggle. I grab Gary's hand, and he grabs back, and we stand about three feet from our graves clinging to each other and laughing like lunatics. Then he hauls on my arm and we stumble away from the roof collapse — except where do you go? Where's safe?

'Is more going to come down?'

'Fuck knows,' he says. 'I've seen that kind of thing happen before. A piece of ceiling falls out, just goes, no apparent reason, no warning. No visible damage up top. What bothers me is that it isn't the first collapse in this area tonight. And the more goes, the more unstable it all becomes.' The haze in the torchbeams is visibly thicker, and our faces are yellow-white with dust.

'You think that's what's happened to Martin?' My voice surprises me by being quite level.

'Maybe. Look, Kit, one of us is going to have to go back. I'd rather it was you.'

'No,' I say. 'No way am I leaving you both down here. Bloody Mithras isn't going to get you both.'

'Well, someone's got to get help — the sooner the

better. We might have to evacuate some of the houses on top.'

'You go, then. I have to find Martin.'

Gary shakes his head. 'No wonder the miners said you'd be trouble. OK. I'll give it ten more minutes. Then one of us goes for help.'

We aim for the gap between the next two pillars, hoping for another pink arrow on one.

'No,' I say. 'Dammit. We've come the wrong way. They weren't this far over.'

'Don't be so sure,' says Gary. 'Look.'

He points with the flashlight. The beam plays over an uneven surface, forty or fifty feet away.

The debris from another roof collapse.

I'm already running forward. The debris stretches for more than thirty feet across the void; enormous blocks of stone are jumbled in with the smaller rubble. If they're under this lot . . .

'Slow down. This has been here for years.'

He's right. The hammering in my chest stops and my heart slows down almost to normal pace again. There's even a clump of small, pale mushrooms growing out of the debris. This has to be the old roof fall Roger told us about — but which is the way round it? I walk slowly along the edge of the rubble until Gary pulls me away.

'Just because it's been here a long time doesn't mean I trust the rest of it not to come down.'

'This isn't just a roof collapse,' I say. My torch has picked out neat, squared-off edges, dressed surfaces. 'There was a wall here. These are discard stones from the quarrying, not loose rock. It looks like it stretched right across this void. Someone built it to wall off whatever's behind it.'

Gary has his mobile phone in his hand. 'What's Martin's number?'

'You're mad. The phone won't work here.'

'I've got a booster on the antenna. It's patchy, but you

can sometimes get a signal.'

'Give me the phone.' I snatch it from him and key in the number. There's a pause, then —

A phone starts ringing, somewhere behind the collapsed wall.

We both start running, trying to work out how to get to the sound.

'Bloody hell,' says Gary.

Between the end of the roof fall and the rock wall of the quarry, someone has pulled away the stones, leaving a narrow gap. We have to clamber over rubble to squeeze through, only to find in front of us another stone wall. This one is different, though. Unlike the drystone walls built with discarded stones, it is made of neatly chiselled blocks, mortared together with a pale cement.

'This isn't right,' I say. For a moment, it even strikes me it might be modern. 'The quarrymen didn't bother with cement.'

But the Romans did.

In the centre of the wall is a low archway. Beyond it, two steps down — the Mithraeum. It has to be. Jesus, it *is* here, we *were* right . . . Somewhere at the back of it is a low, flickering light that fills me with superstitious dread and, incongruously, the sound of a phone, ringing and ringing.

Gary holds me back. 'No. There may have been a collapse in there.'

'Stop being so fucking protective.'

'I'm being sensible. If I get buried, I'd quite like you still to be alive to go and get help.'

'Oh.'

He goes in, a silver glow in the darkness. His torch beam plays over shadowy walls, heavy blocks of stone that form two rows of solid benches and two statues flanking them.

Cautes and Cautopates. The gatekeepers of the

temple: Hope and Despair.

Martin . . .

At the end of the chamber is the roof fall. Somewhere underneath it, the phone rings and rings. Gary shines his torch up at the ceiling. It's not a big fall, but on the ground beside it lie heavy blocks of stone at a canted angle. He kneels, puts down the big flashlight, and carefully starts removing rubble. Almost immediately, the light from his head-torch picks out a dusty red waterproof.

That's Martin's jacket.

I'm straight in there, kneeling beside Gary, scrabbling away at the debris.

'You won't be told, will you?' he says. 'Look, you're not helping. It's not as bad as it looks. Got any water in your backpack?'

I'm already unzipping it. At some point, the phone must have stopped ringing; I'm aware instead of the sound of Martin's breathing, fast, a little uneven.

'He's unconscious, but see if you can wash some of the dust off his face, get an idea what kind of colour he is underneath it.'

A section of ceiling has come down: mostly earth and small stones. Martin is lying on his stomach, his face turned to one side. His hard-hat is off, lying on the floor beside him.

'I think he's taken a blow on the head, but he could be bleeding internally. No other obvious injuries . . . ' The way Gary's voice trails off makes me look up. 'Ah, shit. He's trapped. Give me the phone, I'll see if there's still a signal.'

A big slab of rock has been dislodged from the roof. It missed Martin, but smashed instead on top of a couple of tall, heavy blocks of carved stone, which look as if they were part of the altar. They lean at drunken angles, balanced precariously, and Martin's right arm is underneath.

'Is his arm crushed?' I feel quite dizzy in the strange, flickering light, coming from somewhere behind the canted blocks.

'I don't think so. The blocks are wedged on top of each other and the arm's caught between them.' Gary shakes the phone in frustration. 'Lost the signal altogether now. I don't want to move him until we've got some support under the blocks. There's some blood, but I think most of it is from a cut on his scalp.'

I unscrew the water-bottle and pour some on to my hankie. My hands are shaking as I start to wipe the dust off Martin's cheek. He looks pale, but it's hard to know in torchlight.

'Can we get him out? Is there something we could use as a crowbar?' But even as I say it, I see how impossible it is. The blocks are delicately balanced; the wrong movement could tip them off Martin's arm, and on to his head.

'We need something to prop it. Airbags, preferably. Then lifting gear.' Gary stares round the chamber, chewing his thumbnail. 'There's both on site. But the crane's too big to bring in here.'

'We'll have to wait for the emergency services. They'll have the right kit.'

'I could get the loader in.'

'It'd be like picking up butterflies with boxing gloves. You'd kill him.'

'But I could use the loader to shift those blocks down the sides.' He points to the stone benches. 'With those out of the way, we might get the crane in.'

Martin groans suddenly.

'There, you old bugger,' I say to him. 'Thought that'd bring you round — threatening to destroy some good archaeology.' But his eyes are closed. He doesn't seem to be conscious at all.

'We've got to keep him still,' says Gary.

'He hasn't moved.'

501

'But he might. Look, I'll give you my phone. Keep trying it as you make your way back — as soon as there's a signal, call for help.'

'I told you, I'm not leaving Martin. You go.'

He looks helpless. 'It isn't safe.'

'One of us has to stay. There has to be a route connecting this area to the main workings; the lost boys took it because when they were eventually found they were nowhere near here. Didn't Roger say they got almost as far as Stonefield? You stand a better chance of finding the way than I do, and it'll be a lot quicker if you bring help back from that direction.'

He's thinking it over, chewing the thumbnail again. The tunnel from Vinegar Woods is narrow: far too tight to bring the crane through, and the climb up from the lane is steep.

'You said you thought you knew where we were.' I have to press him; I'm the one who got Martin into this mess so I'm the one who has to stay. 'We're wasting time. We have to get help right away.'

'OK.' He gets to his feet. 'Oh, God. Where's the other one?'

We completely forgot Roger. There's no sign of him, but Martin surely didn't come in alone. Gary is eyeing the pile of rubble. If he's under that, it's too late.

'Maybe he went for help.'

'In which case why didn't we come across him on our way in? He had Martin's arrows to follow.'

'Could he have gone the other way?'

'And got lost again? Great. So now we'll need a search party as well as a rescue team. Always assuming he's not buried under that lot.'

'Go,' I say. 'Be careful. Keep counting.'

'I'm going.' He bends and touches my lips again with his fingers. 'And you keep safe.'

He casts one last glance around — a different kind of look, this time, not one that is assessing risk, but a puzzled gaze that takes in the carving on the altar stones, the faded frescos, the flickering light somewhere towards the back wall. 'Is this it?' he asks. 'Your temple of whatsit?'

'Mithras.'

He nods, raises his eyebrows, purses his lips. Noncommittal. 'Very nice.'

'It's not worth it, though, is it?'

'Oh, I don't know. I leave that sort of judgement to you experts.'

He squeezes my arm quickly, then he's gone, patting Cautes or Cautopates on the head before he strides through the archway. It was the one on the left; I don't know which is which. Hope, or sorrow?

⋆   ⋆   ⋆

There's not much I can do for Martin, now I've sponged the blood off the back of his head. It's just a cut, I think; scalp wounds always bleed like buggery. I give him a little kiss, on the top of his head. It's the first time I've ever touched him with my lips, and I'm glad he's not awake to feel me do it or he'd take the piss mercilessly. His hair is clogged with dust, and I'm aware of how the heavy altar stones loom over us both, the huge block from the roof balanced precariously on top. His breathing sounds steadier now, only a little faster and shallower than you'd expect of someone asleep. But being unconscious is hardly a good sign.

To distract myself, I stand up and walk round the altar stones to track down the source of the flickering light. Either Martin or Roger lit a candle somewhere. It's a miracle it wasn't snuffed out by the dust after the roof fell in.

No, it's not one candle, but three. The massive central altar stone, still standing but half covered with rubble, has a niche hollowed in the back. On its front is an elaborate carving. Under a frieze of leaves, Mithras rises from the living rock, the signs of the zodiac round him. He wears a billowing cloak, with stars carved into it, and on his head is a radiant crown, like the Statue of Liberty, a halo of light, the rays cut right through the limestone so the candlelight shines out from behind. I suppose in Roman times it would have been an oil lamp, creating this eerie pattern on the walls and roof of the chamber. Are there traces of paint left on the carving? I can't tell in the dim light. It would certainly have been coloured: a deep blue cloak, perhaps, green on the leaves, white plaster on the god's face.

The damp has almost entirely obliterated the frescos on the plastered walls: they're no more than faint outlines. The tauroctony is gone, in pieces under the Ministry of Defence. But there's still something powerful about this place. Mithras, god of light, born from the living rock, worshipped in dark places.

How did it come to be here? The quarry in Vinegar Woods must be much older than anyone realized. This must be where the stone was taken for the Roman villa and its outbuildings. Perhaps the villa owner was a retired soldier. And the inscription on the coffin lid that was found suggests there was some sort of military establishment nearby. The cult's followers must have thought the passages quarried into the rock ideal for a temple site.

I imagine them arriving by night, torches flaring in the wind as they climb the hillside to the adit. Wrapped in thick soldiers' cloaks, scurrying through the passages, as we did. Kneeling to wash their hands in one of the hollowed pits in the antechamber. The older men punching each other lightly on the arm in greeting. The young initiates nervous, unsure what to expect. There wouldn't have been more than thirty of them, no room for more on the stone benches down either side of the nave.

At the end of the antechamber, a wicker screen. The doorkeepers, Cautes and Cautopates, painted statues, one holding his torch aloft in triumph, the other trailing it in despair. A drum begins to beat. The chatter of voices in the antechamber dies. One by one, the men file between the Twins and enter the darkened nave.

I am a star that shines out of the depths

He bursts on them like a supernova. Mithras, god of the airy light between heaven and earth. Flames flicker in his halo; the Father has lit the oil lamps in the recess behind the altar. One of the young men is trembling violently. He doesn't know whether he will have the courage for the ordeal.

I sit down, a woman on benches built for men, where they ate the ritual feast — if that's what they did here. Nobody really knows, not even Martin. It's all rumour, conjecture by outsiders, the classical world's equivalent of the conspiracy theories that hang around freemasonry. Which may or may not have been connected.

There ought to be an angry god around somewhere, drawing back his hand to strike me down for violating this male sanctuary. But it's oddly peaceful, in the wavering light, only the sound of Martin's breathing disturbing the silence.

I unzip my jacket. There's a concealed pocket inside on the left, which other people use for maps or their phone. I reach down into it. It's deep; I only open it when I wash the jacket, or transfer what I keep here into my overalls when I go caving. It always goes underground with me.

Smooth on one side, rough on the other. I draw it out, and lay it on the stone bench beside me. The candles give out just enough light for me to see the polished spiral. It's the only thing I have left that my father gave to me. I wrote to the prison after I heard he'd died, and asked for his things. He must have owned something: books, maybe even a photo of me or my mum. But they told me Janey Legge had taken his stuff. She had his ashes too. Turned out she'd visited him every month all the years he was in prison, even moved up to the Midlands to be nearer. I thought about asking for her address, but they probably wouldn't have given it to me, and I didn't want to see her anyway. She'd never tried to find *me*, after all.

As I look at the little ammonite, he's suddenly with me: not the angry god, but the flawed, bewildered man. What would he think if he saw me now?

Katie, he'd say. You were right, after all. There is something here.

It's Kit, now, Dad, I say. I had to change. I was pretty fucked up for a while, you know.

I know. I thought of you all the time.

I thought about you, too.

We're sitting at the kitchen table. My father reaches out and places a finger on the ammonite. He pushes it tentatively across the table towards me. Our eyes meet.

I pick up the ammonite, and trace the spiral, the way I used to when I was Katie. The polished rock is smooth and comforting under the fleshy pad of my thumb, imprinted with its own ridged whorl.

I missed you, Dad.

★　★　★

The light seems dimmer as the candles burn down. It's a good twenty minutes since Gary went. I slip the ammonite back into my pocket and get up to see if there's any change in Martin. He seems paler in the torchlight. I kneel beside him and touch his hair again. To my surprise he grunts.

'You awake?'

'Flower?'

'Keep still. No, I mean it. Don't try to move. You're under some rock that isn't very stable.' I keep my hand lightly on his head. Stupid, really: it makes me feel I'm somehow protecting him from the crushing weight of the stone blocks.

'My bloody head hurts.'

'I bet. Do you remember what happened?'

'Were you here?'

'No. Do you know where you are?'

'In the temple?'

'Very good. What happened to Roger?'

'Can I phone a friend on that one?'

'So what's the last thing you remember?'

'I was shining my torch over the back wall, trying to work out where the tauroctony would have fitted. That's it. Fuck, my arm's sore . . . ' The muscles in his back tense. Something makes a scraping noise under the big stones.

'DON'T MOVE!'

'I can't move it.' He sounds surprised. 'Why can't I move it?'

'It's trapped under a couple of altar stones, which are just about balanced against each other. They might come down.'

'*Shit.*' His back stiffens again.

'Just relax. Gary's gone to get help. You'll be out in no time, if you keep still.'

'Come round this side, so I can see you.'

'It's better if I sit here.'

'If you don't take your hand away from my head you'll get hurt too.'

'The rock's not going to come down if you stay still.'

'I can see your knee. It's not your best feature. I want to see your face.'

I shuffle round, with a cautious glance at the altar stones. Something has shifted underneath, I'm sure. They look more precarious than ever. I hate taking my hand away from his fragile head. Cunning bastard, he knows I can't protect him so well from this side.

507

Because he's lying prone, with his head turned, only one of his eyes is visible; in the light of the torch it scans me disapprovingly.

'I can't see you if you shine the torch on me. Shine it on yourself. God almighty, what do you look like, woman?'

'Look, mate, I've battled through fairly adverse conditions to effect a rescue. Should I have left Gary here instead?'

'So I could die happy with a hard-on? That wouldn't be very dignified.'

His left hand is groping my thigh.

'Lie still, dammit. Stop trying to touch me up. Wrong gender, remember?'

'I was just feeling for your hand.'

I take his. He squeezes, and closes his eyes — eye, rather, since I can't see the other. I squeeze back, and the light goes all sparkly and fuzzy and the shape of his face blurs.

'Kit,' he says, 'I saw seven golden candlesticks.'

I blink and look round, puzzled. There are no golden candlesticks here, just three half-melted cheap candles in the niche behind the altar.

'The first and the last,' says Martin, and it comes out as a kind of sigh. 'Like my dad always said, it ends with Revelation. Good old St John the Divine.'

'It's not ending. Gary's on his way. and Roger's probably beaten him to it, by now, and called nine-nine-nine.'

'Roger?' he says. 'Roger wasn't here.'

'Who lit the candles then?'

'The first and the last,' he repeats.

'You came in alone, you silly bugger?'

'There was a rainbow, and a sea of glass, and beasts full of eyes.'

'You're rambling.'

'Terrible having a vicar for a father. He was always

right. Bible to back it all up, chapter and verse. Made me learn huge chunks by heart. I'm going to open my eyes and he'll be standing there, between a pair of fucking great pearly gates, wagging his finger, saying, 'I told you so.' '

'You'll be all right. They've relaxed the rules on sodomites.'

'I always envied you having a father who was an architect.'

'My father wasn't an architect,' I say. I squeeze his hand very tightly. He squeezes back.

'Cut my arm off,' he says.

'What?'

'Cut my arm off. I don't want to die.'

'I'm not cutting your arm off. It's your trowel arm. You'd never manage as a left-handed archaeologist.'

'There's a Swiss Army knife in my pocket. Cut the fucker off and get me out of here.'

'I can't.' I feel sick thinking about it. 'Stop being silly. I told you, Gary's on his way.' My hand is being crushed under the pressure from his, but I don't think I could do it, not even if it were the only way to save his life.

'I'm afraid,' he says. 'Anything's better than lying here waiting to die. You know that, don't you? You must have felt the same, in the flint mine, when the tunnel gave.'

'I'm not going to let you die.' With my other hand I stroke his beard. 'I love you, you stupid old git.'

'Save it for Gary,' he says. 'It's wasted on me.'

'No, it bloody isn't.'

'Dad,' he says. 'I told you she was crazy.' He opens his eye and looks up at me, then sighs and closes it again. 'I saw him, you know. 'He had in his right hand seven stars . . . and his countenance was as the sun shineth in his strength.' '

'Stop going all mystic on me,' I say. 'It doesn't end with Revelation. Or Mithras.' But his cheek feels cold and clammy, and his breathing's changed, shallower and

509

more ragged. His eyes stay closed and he doesn't say anything else.

The chill of the place is getting to me now, and it can't be doing Martin much good, so I take off my jacket and fleece and tuck them round him. I lie alongside him as best I can, trying to warm his body with mine. How did the followers of Mithras manage? They must have lit fires; if Martin was conscious and on his feet he'd be pegging out the ground looking for the burn marks where the braziers stood. And if they lit fires, there must have been a chimney of sorts. But, like all the other ventilation shafts from the workings, I suppose it will have been capped long ago.

I'm so cold now I'm afraid my shivering could disturb the delicate balance of the altar stones, so I get up and start pacing the chamber again. Where's Gary? Surely he's out by now? Or is he lost too, in the Bermuda Triangle that is this part of the workings? I'm shaking quite violently. No need to ask how they organized the ordeal of cold for the Mithraic initiates. Just strip the poor buggers off and leave them naked here for the night.

The old quarrymen must have known this place was here. And kept quiet about it. Someone has to have built that long wall across the void to hide it. Because they were afraid of it? The quarries in the early days were small concerns, each owner working his separate patch with maybe only one or two men, possibly his own sons. This could have become someone's family secret, walled up and left to moulder because it was a heathen place, the devil's temple, bad luck. Eventually even nature helped conceal it, when part of the quarry roof fell in.

And who pulled away the stones years afterwards to rediscover it? My money's on the Camera Man.

The Camera Man. Funny, really, that all my fear of what happened to me here that summer focused on someone who had had nothing to do with my mother's death, who was probably dead himself before I ever came here. I have been drawn back over and over again to the underworld, but I always feel him in the dark with me, watching me through the lens, his long, pale fingers reaching out for me. The beast full of eyes . . . Odd how Martin picked that image from Revelation, as if he plucked it out of my subconscious mind.

The candlelight flickers, making me uneasy. I thought I'd faced all that, exorcized it, tonight. But I can still believe I'm being watched, the Camera Man creeping back after all these years.

The first and the last . . . I can't believe Martin had the nerve to come into the tunnels on his own. It goes against all sense. Of course Roger was with him.

Roger wasn't here.

Who lit the candles? It must have been Martin, then. But to come in alone . . .

You'll be sorry to have missed this. We're going in.

That was the text he sent — *we're going in*. There *were* two of them.

Roger wasn't here.

Who else, then?

The beast full of eyes . . . I can feel the back of my neck prickling. I could swear it's got colder, and that the light is dimming. No, no, no. It's my imagination. There is no beast. There are no eyes.

The tiniest, softest . . .

CLICK

'Who's there?'

I swing round, and there he is, the camera in his long, pale fingers.

34

'Well, Kit.' Dickon steps between Cautes and Cautopates and into the chamber between the stone benches. 'Looks like you were right, after all.'

Now I can see who it is, I feel strangely calm. He's wearing his old waxed jacket, its pockets bulging with handkerchiefs and the usual Dickon pharmacopoeia, a camera slung round his neck, a big blind third eye.

'It was you who came in with Martin, then. I didn't realize you two knew each other that well.' I move casually behind the remaining half of the altar to keep something solid between us.

Dickon shrugs. 'We talked at the party after you'd left. He was buying drinks for that bloke Roger. The pair of them made a fairly convincing case for there being something here. I met up with them this afternoon when Roger showed us the way in.'

'I can't believe that.' Why would Martin want to go underground with Dickhead, of all people? 'He didn't say anything about intending to meet you.'

'He wasn't planning to meet me. I phoned Roger — found his number in the directory — and he told me they had arranged to take a look at the adit in the wood. Invited me along, when I reminded him I was the archaeologist on this project.'

Tick, tick. Water dripping somewhere in the corner of the temple — or rock settling into a new, unstable configuration.

'Why wasn't Roger with you when the roof collapsed?'

'He didn't want to go exploring.' Candlelight throws shifting shadows on the walls. Dickon moves a step closer between the stone benches. 'Said he'd got lost once, he wasn't going to risk it again. He went home for his tea, and it was only after he'd gone that Martin and I decided to get some proper gear and come in.'

Jesus. How could Martin do that? He let the bastard into my cottage, pawing through my kit. It's my fault for not telling anybody about the porn, or Dickon's attempt to grope me. Martin must have thought that going into the mines with him was safer than going in alone, and infinitely preferable to not going in at all. Though what the pair of them thought they were doing, with rain bucketing down and making the tunnels even riskier than usual . . .

'You left him,' I said. 'You left him when the roof fell in.'

'I was going for help, Kit.'

His cow eyes are wide, his body easy and relaxed. But I don't believe the fucker.

'If you went for help, where is it? You left him to die.'

'I got lost. Couldn't find the way out, realized I was going round in circles . . . '

'How long have you been watching me?'

'Watching you?' There's a little smile on his face, like something I've said has delighted him.

'You don't seem exactly surprised to find me here. You were hanging around waiting for Martin to die so you could be sure no one was going to know you came into the mines together. You were going to pretend he went in alone so you wouldn't lose your fucking job.'

'Don't be ridiculous.' But I can see it in his face. He must have heard Gary and me arriving, must have been waiting in the dark all this time . . .

For what? His arms are hanging loosely at his sides, but one knee is flexed and his weight is on the other leg as if he's getting ready to run. He looks relaxed but I know that kind of body language. I grew up with it. It's the coiled spring that looks as if there's no tension on it at all until it explodes into movement. I can imagine him crouching in the darkness, fingering his balls in panic, trying to work out what to do now that someone else has come along and found Martin still alive. He must have watched Gary set out for help, hoping Martin was already too far gone, wondering how he could save himself with rescue on the way and me sitting there holding Martin's hand.

There's only one way, of course.

'I told Martin about you and Gary,' he says suddenly. He's trying to distract me, stop me working it out. If there were *two* bodies under a fresh roof fall, no one would guess that Dickon had been anywhere near here. His eyes are flat and blank in the candlelight, unreadable. My breathing begins to quicken, watching him for the slightest sign.

'He was pretty bloody upset,' he adds, his eyes fixed on my face, determined to convince me he's not lying. He can't have heard any of the conversation between us, or he'd realize Martin would have been the absolute reverse. 'My guess is it made him careless. He needn't have been under that roof fall, you know.'

He's trying to wind me up. My heart's going faster and faster, trying to judge when he's going to make his move. He wants to catch me off-guard, of course, but in the end it doesn't matter because, unless I can get past him, there's no other way out. The altar stones may feel reassuringly solid between us, but in the end it will come down to brute strength.

I was faster than him last time.

He wasn't really trying then. Nothing like so much at stake.

'Poor old Martin,' says Dickon. 'The Americans have a word for it, don't they? Pussy-whipped.' The word comes spitting out, like a gob of venom from an injured snake.

Then I understand how much he loathes me — loathes all women. How scared he must be of us.

514

'Pussy-whipped,' he repeats, his eyes flat and dark. He's psyching himself up. 'You even make him *cook* for you.'

'He loves cooking . . . ' Even though Dickhead's scaring me shitless, this is absurd. But something's nagging for my attention, something I ought to have worked out long ago. 'How the fuck do you know he cooks, anyway?'

'I've been watching,' he says, and suddenly everything slips into place like cold jelly. 'You leave the curtains open when it's dark — don't tell me you aren't inviting it.'

'You've been staking out the cottage?'

'I've got photos.' He sounds absurdly proud, as if he expects me to praise him for it. 'Hey, Kit, come on, that's how the world is divided — the watchers and the watched.'

Hunting me, like Mithras stalks the bull. I feel sick. 'No,' I say. 'You've got me wrong, Dickon. You've got it all wrong. You're fucking *mad*.'

'I don't get things wrong.' His eyes go hard, like that first day underground when I contradicted him. 'I know what you like, Kit. And I'm wondering if you might like watching too.'

'Whatever you're going to do, you'll have to be quick.' I want him to think I've got his number, I'm in control, but my voice sounds tight and squeaky in my ears. I keep thinking about the violence of the porn he sent me, the woman chained and spreadeagled, her arm hacked from her shoulder . . . Blood and semen. 'Gary will be back any minute. He's been gone long enough.'

'What makes you think he's not lost?' he says, but there was a flash of uncertainty this time in those eyes. In mine, too, maybe — am I playing this wrong? My hope is that I can bluff it out, make him face up to the fact that killing anyone is crazy. But should I be keeping him talking instead, hoping rescue will come in time before he finds the nerve to do what he's planning? I've no idea how long it's been since Gary left, no idea how long it might take him to get back. I want to glance at my watch, but it'd be a dead giveaway. No, I'm going to go for broke, shoot the moon, face him down. It's Dickon, Dickhead Dickon, he's not a murderer, for fuck's sake, he's a watcher, by his own admission, not a doer. I can make him collapse and back off, maybe, if I keep my cool.

'Roger knows you were with Martin this afternoon, even if he didn't see you come into the mine together.'

'Hmm,' says Dickon. Bored, impatient. Christ, he's not taking in a word I'm saying. Stuff's whirring inside, the little orange light's flashing, but it's all internal processing and it doesn't matter how many times I thump the keyboard, the program's not responding. He lifts the camera, aims it at me, then shakes his head and lets it drop on its strap. There isn't enough light in here for a decent shot.

'I'd like to have seen you fuck,' he adds, almost wistfully. 'You and Martin, or you and Gary. But I was never there at the right time. A pity.' The past tense. Jesus. He *is* going to kill us, he really is. He reaches into the pocket of his waxed jacket and pulls out a heavy torch.

'I wouldn't use that,' I say. 'You're even more of a pillock than I thought you were. No one will be convinced it was accidental.' He turns the torch on, and starts moving the beam over the plastered walls of the Mithraeum.

'There were frescos,' he says, surprised. 'Not much left, but it looks Roman. Amazing. Who'd have thought . . . ' His gaze switches back to me. 'Of course, the central symbol of Mithraism was the sacrifice of the bull.' He takes another step, this time towards the corner of the altar where Martin lies trapped.

'I know it was you who sent me those pictures,' I say quickly. Have to distract him from Martin, somehow.

'Gary knows too. He's got your flashdrive. They'll get you for that . . . '

Mistake. His eyes go the way Dad's used to. He's round the side of the altar so fast I'm completely unprepared, swinging the torch and at the same time making a grab for my jacket with his other hand. I . . . Jeez. Too slow. My shoulder vibrates with pain where the torch just caught it a slamming blow — waking an old, old injury, reminding me of how powerless I really am. I'm stumbling, and he's already drawing his arm back to swing again, the camera bouncing on his chest with its big, blind eye winking at me.

Dad . . .

At least I've got him away from Martin . . .

Fu-u-uck. This time, my breast — mashed into my ribcage. Jee-sus. His eyes are as blank as my father's — no, there's a flash of cunning in them that I never saw in Dad's. He's calculating where to land the next blow. This isn't about finishing it yet, it's . . .

'I'm going to crush his skull and make you watch.' It comes out between his teeth, a rusty creak more than a voice.

'No,' I say, trying to put myself between Dickon and the fallen half of the altar, to stop him getting to Martin. 'No.' Every muscle screams at me to back away, but instead I make myself go forward to meet him, keeping my eyes fixed on his. Snake, snake. Make it attack me, not Martin. 'You've got no idea, have you, of what a pathetic cunt you are? Pussy-whipped? That's not Martin, that's you. Too scared even to rape me the other day. Collapsed like a used condom.' I'm shaking — oh, God, let it not hurt, I don't know if I'm strong enough if it hurts too much — but I'll say anything, the uglier the better, to make him go for me first and hope to hell it will buy us time, while he does what he wants to me. Where has Gary got to? 'That's a damp little finger in your trousers. I don't believe you can even get it up. It's all in your warped mind. You know the miners call you Dickhead, don't you? But I expect you've been called that all your life.'

The torch is swinging back again, its beam flashing over the ceiling, revealing fragments of fresco, raw rock, blue plaster, a flying cloak, a circle of stars . . .

I am a star that shines out of the depths

Help me, Mithras, now at the hour of my death . . . Make him do it slowly, slowly, so Martin has a chance.

Invicta —

I lash at the candles in their niche behind the altar, the flames waver and bend horizontal and, for one moment, everything seems to go dark, except Dickon's torchbeam sweeping inexorably across the ceiling towards me.

Did they ever sacrifice a bull in here? It would have to have been a very small one. A very docile one. I suppose there might have been ways of doping it. Bit of a con, really . . .

And then I hear it, the great roaring, sweeping through the tunnels, growing closer and closer, and the light gets brighter and brighter until the brilliant eye of the god comes swinging through the tunnels and shines into the temple.

★ ★ ★

The articulated loader charges through the archway into the temple, spattered with mud, the headlight blazing on the front. Its huge tractor wheels bounce over the steps and the shallow ordeal pits, treads sliding. The roar of the engine is deafening in the confined space. I jump away from the altar and take refuge in the back corner of the Mithraeum. Dickon stands transfixed, mouth gaping, torch hanging limply in his fist.

The back end of the loader slips away and Cautes or Cautopates goes flying; Gary fights the steering and gets control back, though something suggests he doesn't give a fuck for the archaeology. He brings it to a halt well short of the altar, just as four tall figures, shining in silver and yellow high-vis, charge through the archway carrying airbags.

I'm waving my arms, trying to warn Gary.

'Back off! It's too dangerous . . . '

He's mad. The noise and vibration will bring the altar stones down on to Martin.

'The stones have SHIFTED.' But I might as well be shouting to myself. They can't hear me over the noise of the engine. Gary is backing the loader, lowering the arms of the forklift and pointing them at the heavy stone benches. The four others are at the back of the chamber by the roof fall. As the loader swings its Cyclops eye round again, I can make out Ted's heavy features, the tattoos curling up from under the neck of his sweatshirt. They kneel around Martin like monks. Ted turns and yells something: one of the others runs past me and back out of the chamber.

There's more noise coming from beyond the chamber, scraping and grinding. They must be using a digger to pull away the collapsed wall outside, to get the lifting gear through on its heavy caterpillar tracks. Gary's loader roars, and charges at the stone bench, the forks forcing their way underneath it, the back wheels bucking and rising off the ground as the machine struggles to lift the load. He backs off, hits another gear, the engine screams, the forks pitch and toss the stone, the wounded bull dances in the flickering light, kicks out, lowers its horns again, bellows and roars, the priest rides it, hauling its head back, the knife poised for the sacrifice . . .

The engine cuts out. The silence is like a shockwave hissing in the ears. The stone bench is gone, a heap of

519

blocks on the far side of the chamber, leaving room for the crane to come through. Gary leaps down from the cab, running towards me.

And in the silence there's the lurch of something heavy shifting and settling —

— a vibration felt as much as heard —

— the thunderous impact of the huge block sliding off the altar stones —

— hitting the ground where Martin lies.

35

The smoky smell of Gary's sweat. My face against his chest, remembering, but it's too late, I'm pummelling my fists against his shoulders. 'You fucking killed him! I told you it was too dangerous, you bastard, you fucking killed him — '

'Shut up — ' He catches my flailing wrist, gets an arm round me. 'Stop it, Kit. Sssh.'

'You had to do it. You had to bring that thing in here and play the hero. Jesus Christ. How could you? He was my friend.'

I'm crying now, real ugly crying, snot and tears melting my face into a red lumpy destroyed thing, the hopeless crying of someone who's come to the end of everything.

'You and that fucking . . . god. Fucking Mithras killed him.'

I am a star that shines out of the depths

No.

Destroyer.

'How could you do this to me, you bastard, you . . . '

My free hand batters on his chest, on the faded old sweatshirt he always wears for work. My palm stings and my tears soak into the oil stains and the paint smears, and the smell of him overwhelms me, the smell I love so much, as he tightens his arms round me.

Sssh, sssh, now . . . It's all right.

Out of the corner of my eye I see him grab my hand, the one that hurts after he burned it, and his nails are clean except for that thin white rim of paint round the cuticles that he never quite manages to soak off.

Katie, he breathes into my hair. Katie.

How could you do this to me, you fucking bastard?

Katie. Don't be like this. I love you.

You bastard, you killed her.

'Kit. Fucksake, Kit. I'm not your father.'

But it's too late. They're all dead now.

'I didn't kill anyone, Kit. He's still alive. They got him out.'

He's lying. I saw the stone go. Martin was underneath.

'No, he's OK. Really. It's true.' He strokes my hair. 'Sssh. The paramedics are with him now.'

'He's right, Mrs Parry. We got the airbags under them littler stones — the big stone shifted when we inflated them, but we got him out, I promise you.'

Bloody *Ted*. I'm weeping into Gary's sweater and proving everything the free miners ever thought about women engineers. I straighten up and pull away, trying to rub as much of the snot off my face as I can.

'Is he all right, Ted? You really got him out without hurting him?'

'Don't know how he is, Mrs Parry, until the paramedics have done their stuff. But we didn't hurt him, and he's breathing.' Job done, as far as Ted's concerned. His eyes are already roving the ceiling anxiously. 'Not much more we can do until they move him, but I think we should get some support under that corner of the ceiling before the night's over.'

'Thank you.' It seems an inadequate thing to say. 'Really, thank you.' I seem to be holding on to Ted's hand, shaking it up and down. God knows what I'm doing that for. I let go. 'Sorry. I'm a bit upset. It got . . . rather tense waiting here.'

Fucking Dickhead. Where's Dickon?

'That's all right,' says Ted, wiping his hand on his jumper to get rid of my snot. ''Spect I'd have been a bit tense myself. Sorry it took so long, but it was a bugger getting the Ant started. The paramedics and fire crew went up through the woods, but Gary reckoned we'd be quicker with the loader and the airbags from the top end.' He nods and shambles off to join his crew, just a big bear of a man, not the Balrog I'd made him out to be.

'Dickon was here,' I say to Gary. 'He . . . he left Martin to die.' I can't quite bring myself to say *and I really think he was going to kill me too.*

'I saw him. Pillock.' Gary's eyes look flinty. I can tell he hasn't quite taken in what I said, let alone what I didn't say. 'But he was number two on the list.'

'List?'

'One, comfort weeping woman. Two, punch cad.'

I don't feel up to laughing at either of these.

'Hey, sorry. It's hard to tell sometimes whether you're being Kit or Katie.' He gives me a quick hug. 'You mean Dickon brought Martin in? That alone's enough to lose him his job.' He looks round the chamber. 'He's gone. He'll know he's finished here. Finished anywhere.'

The paramedics in their green and silver jumpsuits are doing something with an oxygen cylinder. The chamber is filling with fire-fighters, milling around and looking faintly disappointed there's nothing left for them to do except set up some lights for the paramedics to work by, then escort the stretcher out. One is smaller and slighter than the others, a woman. She bends to snuff out the candles behind the altar, and the flickering light behind Mithras's crown disappears. When she straightens up she sees me watching, and gives me a little smile. I wonder if anyone ever tells her she's bad luck in a burning building. I lace my fingers in Gary's and give his hand a squeeze.

'I've got to go,' says Gary, squeezing fiercely back. 'Ted's right, we have to sort that ceiling before there's another fall. It's like a national emergency up top. They've already started evacuating the houses on the southern slope.'

And as he walks off towards the miners, I see that this

is the way it will always be, neither of us ever really saying it, neither of us comfortable with feelings. That's why we're drawn to each other. We sense each other's scars, but we know deep down there's not really anything we can do about them, except get on with things the way we always have. I won't tell Gary that Dickon was maybe going to kill me. Gary will never really explain to me why he and Tess fell apart. We're both soldiers, in our different ways: *invictus* and *invicta*.

One of the paramedics turns round for help and two of the fire-fighters lift the stretcher, handing it carefully to their colleagues on the other side of the pile of rubble. They pass through the beam of light from the loader, and I glimpse Martin's face, his skin deathly white against his dark beard, eyes still closed.

'How is he?' I ask the paramedic carrying the oxygen bottle. 'Will he be all right?'

'His pulse is thready, but he's holding his own. Big strong chap. Difficult to know what's going on with a head injury until we get him back, but I don't think it's too serious. Do you want to come with us?'

I glance over towards the corner, where Gary is deep in conversation with one of the fire-fighters and Ted. He turns and the light from the loader catches his jaw line, leaving his eyes in shadow. I look down at Martin on the stretcher: stone dust in his beard, hair wet and matted, eyes closed.

'Where are you taking him? The RUH?' He nods. 'His name's Martin Ekwall. He's forty-three. I'm the nearest thing he's got to next-of-kin.' I press my fingers lightly to Martin's forehead. 'Can I give you my number in case of — well, in case? Look after him. When he comes round, tell him I'll be at the hospital as soon as we've finished here.'

I watch them go, weaving a course round the blocks of stone Gary scattered with the loader, then I wipe a hand across my eyes. Mithras, god of the airy light, but also god of contracts and promises. No wonder soldiers liked him. It must have been useful to have a deity who could help you sort out where your duty lies.

But what about love? Always the complicating factor.

I join Gary and Ted to work out how to stop the ceiling collapsing further.

36

I let myself out of the tall house very early. A May morning, and the leaves on the horse-chestnuts by the river are bright green and juicy, white candles of flowers pushing up between them. The town is still sleeping, but the day shift starts at seven now the funding is through, and I want to be underground well before they arrive. The horizon is still golden and pearly: the sphere of Mithras, god of the airy light between earth and sky.

There are things that will always sleep between us, Gary and me. He doesn't get how I feel about my father. I think Martin understands, though. Yesterday he was showing me the rough cut of the *Time Team* they've made about the temple excavation, the scene where he's explaining the inscriptions on the altar stones, and suddenly says to Carenza Lewis, 'But that's the whole point of a god. Inscrutable, ineffable, arbitrary. Soldiers know that. Maybe you live, maybe you die. The question is not whether what he does is good or bad — the point is, he is your god, he is *invictus*. He just *is*.'

I drive up the hill out of the town, along the flat plateau of the Cotswold spur, down into the valley and over the bridge. Then I'm climbing up again to Green Down, taking the back road through the trees, the old Roman road, towards the barn conversions on Vinegar Lane with the Range Rovers and Jaguars outside, and the primary school Robert Klein designed. My foster-father.

I never saw my own father again, after they took me away in the big black car. I was in the children's home in Bristol for four months, and that was when I started to call myself Kit. The only way I knew how to survive there was to become another person, not the little girl in the headlines who found her mother's bones in the mines but someone hard and sharp with a tough skin and a short name. Mrs Klein asked for Katie when she came to visit me, and Philippa, the house parent, didn't know whom she meant.

That was the day Susie Klein told me she wanted to apply to foster me. Wouldn't that be good?

I remember staring at her to make sure she was serious. Her eyes met mine, and I knew she didn't see me but her own lost daughter, the one she had given up for adoption and could never find again. I didn't want to be a lost daughter, but there didn't seem much of a choice. The children's home terrified me. Girls climbed out of the windows at night to meet pimps, who drove them to the redlight district in St Paul's. I spent most of my time in my room, shaking.

'We'll leave Midcombe, and move to Dorset, Katie,' she said.

'*Kit.*'

'Sorry. I understand. It's a fresh start, for all of us. A new school for you. No one will know who you are.'

'Unless Trish tells them.'

'Trish will be at a different school. We're sending her away to board, like her brothers.'

So I said yes.

*   *   *

No need, this morning, to drive to the main site. I've got everything I need with me, and the key to the Stonefield gate. The car bounces along the alley behind the undertaker's, and I park next to the hearse. As I lace my boots, a late bat comes back from its early-morning sortie, a small black flick against the pale blue dome of the sky before it dips into the adit. I let myself in through the gate, padlocking it again behind me.

527

I hope Mrs Klein never regretted taking me in, but she probably did. She once suggested I called her Mum, as Trish and the boys did, but then she saw from my face that that was impossible. We compromised on Susie, but I always thought of her as Mrs Klein. However often she pleaded with me to face my demons, I couldn't and I didn't fit well into the family. Trish resented being sent to boarding-school and thought I had stolen her mother, the boys never understood why she felt obliged to give me a home, and Mr Klein was distant and polite, as if I was a dull house-guest who never got round to leaving. Pretty much what I felt I was, in fact.

Better that than the children's home, though.

When I went away to university on the south coast, and married Nick too quickly, Trish was in London, supposedly studying at UCL. She dropped out after she decided it was cooler to get fashionably wrecked with the New Romantics at the Blitz Club. Nick had been fascinated by her since she told him she'd had a bit part in a David Bowie video, and maybe she thought he had a certain glamour too. She and I kept up a pretence of friendship while her mother was still alive, but after Mrs Klein died — of the same breast cancer that had killed her mother — and left me money to buy the London house, Trish finally had a good reason to be angry with me. And I could never forgive her for telling Nick my secret at the funeral.

'Your father's not Robert? Your real dad's *in prison*?'

My face would have told him it was true.

'Jesus, Kit, we'd make a fortune if you'd let me ghost-write the story for you.'

★   ★   ★

The temperature underground in the quarries never varies, summer or winter. I don't bother with the main

528

lights; torchlight will be bright enough, and I've brought candles too. Occasionally the beam picks out a group of bats huddled in a crevice. Already some have gone to summer roosts in the woodland or in buildings, though plenty will stay in the workings right through the year now that Rupert has fitted the incubators.

It takes a while to follow the tunnels to the place I want to be. The underground roadway cuts through the hillside, under the primary school, past the passage where Gary made love to me. Further on is the new steel road that leads to where Martin has been excavating the Mithraeum, recording its secrets before it is filled with sand later this year. But I ignore that route, and continue south-east, as the tunnel bends in the direction of Crow Stone.

Here are the metal rails of the tramway. This time I am following them in the opposite direction; the years roll back. I haven't been into this part of the quarries since 1976. The miners reached it only last week. The metal roadway is built, and in an hour or so the day shift will be down to start filling the area.

Beyond the walkway, my torch shines on a heap of debris under a jagged ceiling, a roof collapse at least forty years old. I clamber out between the metal struts to stand in the void. It's not a very big one. The stone lay in shallow beds here and the pillars are heavily robbed, creased with fault-lines, creamy yellow in the beam of my torch. The floor seems dry; we haven't had any rain for a couple of weeks. There's something sweet and delicate overlying the usual limey smell, and the scent of a drawerful of scarves comes back to me, the scent of longing for something you can hardly remember.

I light one of the candles, and run a dribble of wax so I can fix it on a stone. The roof fall is bigger than I recall, and there are no clues to remind me of the exact spot. I pace slowly along it, trying to remember. Every few feet, I take another candle from my backpack, light it, and set it on one of the stones in the roof fall. Soon the void is full of golden, flickering light.

Someone else has been here before me. Set carefully between two bigger stones is a bunch of red roses and ferns. There's no card, but I'm certain who put them here. They're hardly wilted; he must have left them late yesterday, after the miners had gone. I pick them up, and the sweet scent pours from them: English roses, the first of the season, bless him.

I lay them back on the stones, and light another candle, the last in the backpack. In my pocket is my offering. My fingers slide over it for the last time, polished smooth on one side, rough on the other. Then I lay it next to the roses. The candle flames flicker and blur; golden streaks of light radiate from each one.

Love you, Mum.

Love you, Katie.

I, Kit Parry, this day fulfilled my vow to the unvanquished god . . .

I walk away, and duck back through the metal struts. The machines are coming to life; the miners have started their shift. I pass the first crew coming down the roadway.

'Morning, Mrs Parry.'

'Morning, Ted.'

'Lovely day up top.'

'Beautiful.'

I head back for the airy light.

Acknowledgements

Writers, like John Wood, play fast and loose with history. *Crow Stone* is a work of fiction, and therefore full of stuff I made up, but it also contains some tantalizing nuggets of almost-truth. I couldn't resist giving my story a realistic setting, but I have also moved a very long way beyond what is geographically and historically real. I have given Bath an eighth hill, and Green Down exists only in my imagination, as do the people I have described there.

But there are real-life underground quarries dating from the eighteenth century, or maybe even earlier, in Bath's Combe Down, and a real-life Stone Mines Reclamation Project. There is — or was — a void only a couple of metres under the Co-op in the village centre. Mysterious holes have appeared in people's gardens, and forgotten entrances to the underground workings have been found in cellars, and tucked away in the woods.

I am indebted to a number of people involved with the underground workings at Combe Down, and elsewhere in the area, for generously explaining the mechanics of mine stabilization to me. I must stress, however, that none of them appears as a character in this book; neither do any of the immensely able and efficient contractors and partners in the Combe Down Project bear any resemblance to the entirely fictional RockDek or Garamond and their employees. There are free miners from the Forest of Dean who work on the project, but Ted and his crew are pure invention. Among the many archaeologists I have known and talked to, none is in any way like the creepy and unprincipled Dickon. The team from Oxford Archaeology, who are

531

patiently and brilliantly recording the archaeology of the Combe Down workings, do not look, talk or behave like him. Nor are any mining engineers I have come across as chaotic or as paranoid as Kit — certainly not Carole Plummer, from Canada, who told me about her experiences as a woman engineer in what is still a male-dominated industry. The risks of the Combe Down Project are real, but it is infinitely better and more safely managed than its fictional counterpart at Green Down. While I was writing the novel, the project received government funding, and by now large areas of the mines have already been filled, making Combe Down a safer place.

Special mention should go to Mary Stacey, project leader for Bath and North East Somerset Council, who as well as explaining the background to the Combe Down Project, invited me to go walking in the woods on the hillside below Combe Down, to look for the quarry started by William Smith, the father of modern geology, and so introduced me to the Combe Down Heritage Society.

I used various helpful books on the history of Combe Down, which set my imagination working, as well as giving me an idea of what the underground quarries were like in their heyday. Peter Addison's *Around Combe Down* and Keith Dallimore's *Exploring Combe Down* guided my first steps through the area. Later, after I had met Dr Malcolm Aylett, I found his book on the Roman villa site useful, as well as Richard Irving's book on the Byfield mine, both published by the Combe Down Heritage Society. As a result, Green Down's mines share an almost identical historical background to those under Combe Down — with one important exception. There is not (as far as anyone knows) a Mithraic temple there. Martin is absolutely right to insist that no Mithraeum has ever been found in a non-garrison town in Britain, and it is generally accepted that the Romans took most of their building stone from surface quarries on Bathampton Down. It was Malcolm Aylett who first told me about the Naevius inscription on a coffin lid found near the villa, but it is not his fault that I used it to provide an entirely spurious justification for the Mithraic thread running through the novel.

I am also grateful to the Society for allowing me to join them on a trip to visit underground stone quarries near Corsham, led by the owner David Pollard, where I discovered that mobile phones can sometimes work underground, that it would indeed be very easy to get lost there, and that watching a man driving a loader to shift a very large block of stone is quite extraordinarily sexy. Meanwhile Bob Whittaker, who grew up in Combe Down and explored the stone mines as a boy, told me the story of the Camera Man, whom I transposed to Green Down and reinvented for the novel.

Staff at the Office of National Statistics were immensely helpful in remembering St Catherine's House, where the Register of Births, Marriages and Deaths was held in 1976.

For archaeological background, I have to thank in particular Nigel Clark and Carenza Lewis, two very good friends who bear no responsibility whatsoever for my wilder archaeological ideas. My TV boss and friend, David Parker at Available Light Productions, was responsible for encouraging me to discover there was a life to be lived outside broadcasting, which led to me studying for an MA in creative writing at Bath Spa University. There, Richard Kerridge, Richard Francis, Colin Edwards, Tessa Hadley, Mimi Thebo, Gerard Woodward and Mo Hayder all helped in various ways to make this book happen, and I met the workshop group who are my writing friends and support still — Jason Bennett, Sam Harvey, Karen Jarvis, Becky Lisle, Pam

Moolman and Anthea Nicholson. My friends Cresta Norris and Carolyn Brown also read the manuscript and made helpful comments, while I am grateful to Lesley Morgan for remaining my friend, even though I dumped an entire TV series in her lap when I decided to make writing my priority.

Thanks to my agent, Judith Murray at Greene and Heaton, for having the courage to take me on, and to Clare Smith and Annabel Wright at HarperPress, along with the rest of the marvellous team who helped design and publish this book.

Finally, a big thank-you to my mum, who 'bought the school uniform', funding me through more than a year of study and writing. Bless you, Mum — you always believed I could do it.

1	26	51	76	101	126	151	176	201	355
2	27	52	77	102	127	152	177	202	357
3	28	53	78	103	128	153	178	203	363
4	29	54	79	104	129	154	179	204	375
5	30	55	80	105	130	155	180	205	380
6	31	56	81	106	131	156	181	206	383
7	32	57	82	107	132	157	182	208	400
8	33	58	83	108	133	158	183	212	451
9	34	59	84	109	134	159	184	227	453
10	35	60	85	110	135	160	185	233	460
11	36	61	86	111	136	161	186	234	461
12	37	62	87	112	137	162	187	237	478
13	38	63	88	113	138	163	188	238	486
14	39	64	89	114	139	164	189	241	488
15	40	65	90	115	140	165	190	242	509
16	41	66	91	116	141	166	191	243	511
17	42	67	92	117	142	167	192	262	519
18	43	68	93	118	143	168	193	269	523
19	44	69	94	119	144	169	194	279	534
20	45	70	95	120	145	170	195	288	552
21		71	96	121	146	171	196	299	570
22		72	97	122	147	172	197	310	575
23			98	123	148	173	198	312	583
24			99	124	149	174	199	331	619
25			100	125	150	175	200	341	